DRUID BOND

PROF CROFT 7

BRAD MAGNARELLA

THE PROF CROFT SERIES

PREQUELS
Book of Souls
Siren Call

MAIN SERIES
Demon Moon
Blood Deal
Purge City
Death Mage
Black Luck
Power Game
Druid Bond
Night Rune
Shadow Duel
Shadow Deep
Godly Wars
Angel Doom

SPIN-OFFS
Croft & Tabby
Croft & Wesson

MORE COMING!

1

I knocked twice and hid my sword behind the left drape of my open coat. Above a television's murmur, heavy shoes paced toward the door. Seconds later, a shadow occluded the disc of light in the door's peephole.

"Who is it?" a voice barked.

I cleared my throat. "Pizza delivery."

I raised the large, grease-spotted box for easier viewing. A moment later, light returned to the peephole.

"Someone order a pizza?" the voice asked.

A muffle of negatives responded until one voice rose above the others: "Just take it."

Bolts thunked and the door opened until I was looking at a gaunt, whisker-faced kid in a black denim jacket and combat boots. The eyes that squinted back at me were raw. I tried not to react to the foul odor coming off him as I consulted the ticket still taped to the box.

"Let's see... That'll be twenty-four even."

"I have a coupon saying it's free." A switchblade popped from his fist.

"Whoa. Guess you do."

He grinned with crooked teeth as I held the box toward him, yellow flecks glinting from his eyes. That cemented it: I had my man. When he grabbed the weightless box I'd foraged from a Dumpster behind the building, his smile staggered.

"The fuck is this?"

My turn to grin. "Return to Hell day."

I drove my hidden sword through his gut and shouted, "*Disfare!*"

White light flashed from the blade's topmost sigil. The demon had time to release half a hoarse scream before the banishing enchantment blasted him from his host in a cloud of sulfuric smoke. At the same time, healing energy drew around the blade, and I slid it from the kid's stomach. I hip-checked him so he'd land in the hallway and willed a shield of crackling light around myself.

Inside the apartment the four remaining demons launched from couches and easy chairs. They had been watching *The Price is Right* on an old cathode ray TV, no doubt awaiting their master's next marching order.

Reaching into a coat pocket, I fisted a handful of vials and, shouting another invocation, slung them into the room. The vials exploded in pops, showering the hellion crew with holy water. Screams went up along with hissing bursts of steam. The demon closest to me reared back, fists grinding into his bleeding eyes. I drove my blade through him and performed my second banishment of the morning.

Something crashed over my head—the coffee table, judging by the raining glass—sending me into a stagger. I'd let a demon circle my blind side, dammit. Pieces of splintered frame crunched underfoot as I recovered my balance. Another demon palmed the television and hurled it toward me.

"*Respingere!*" I called, sending a bright pulse from my protective shield.

The pulse smashed into the TV in a geyser of sparks. The force also blew through the three remaining demons. Still weakened from the holy water, they rag-dolled over furniture and into walls. A heavy bookshelf toppled, burying a demon in magazines and an impressive collection of glass bongs.

Have to be careful. Don't want to cripple or kill the hosts before expelling the demons.

I grabbed the nearest two demons with shaped forces and pulled them onto my blade for banishments three and four. Prepossession, the gang of denim-clad teens had been using the apartment as a crash pad. The demons had claimed them wholesale, maybe to better disguise themselves. They had escaped magical detection, thanks to their passage through the Harkless Rift, but they still behaved like demons. Some demons were also known to have giant appetites. Disappearances around the building coupled with a high volume of jumbo pizza deliveries had led me to this unit.

I looked toward the fallen bookcase now and swore. The final demon wasn't there anymore.

"I blocked the doors and windows," I called, turning in a circle. "No way out. Might as well take your medicine like your friends."

I opened my wizard senses until the astral plane bloomed into full view. Faint void-like trails streaked the apartment, all filling in except for one. It trailed from the mess of the toppled bookcase, where rank bong water was spreading into a pool, to the back of the couch. Thin tendrils of steam rose past a set of drawn curtains above the couch: holy water wounds.

Using magic, I swung the couch out. The exposed demon tried to skitter for cover, but I hardened the air, pinning him to the threadbare carpet.

"Do you know who you're fucking with?" he spat toward the floor.

"No, tell me."

He rotated his head. Dank, dark hair dropped across a face highlighted by glowing yellow eyes. The eyes grew as they stared, pulsing brighter. Looked like the demon's master was coming through for a visit.

Good.

"Despus," he said in a voice that was suddenly deeper.

"Sorry, but is that supposed to mean something?"

He snorted. "You're in over your head, wizard."

"And yet you're the one making love to the floor."

I could feel hints of the demon master's power, but he was too large to breach the rift that my Order was defending and repairing. His presence, mediated by this minion, a lesser demon who had bum-rushed the rift with hundreds of others in Arnaud's wake, was just a sliver of the actual demon master.

"Release me," he said, "and I'll forget this happened."

Despus had been lucky to get five minions into the world, and now it looked like he was down to his final one. He knew that keeping him here was critical if he hoped to claim souls and maintain his place in the underworld hierarchy, never mind moving up. That gave me a powerful bargaining chip.

"I'm already on the shit list of a demon lord," I said, referring to Sathanas, whom I'd banished from St. Martin's Cathedral two years earlier. "So being on yours isn't exactly tremor inducing. You're going to have to do better than that."

Despus hissed and went into a fit of writhing against his containment. I crossed my arms and leaned against a wall. Within seconds, the demon came to a panting rest, sweat streaking the sides of his face.

"Release me, and I'll make it worth your while," he amended.

"Too vague."

He wriggled his fingers, releasing currents of infernal energy.

His transparent confinement rippled with the collision of magic, but I could barely feel it.

"You done?" I asked.

He swore and dropped his hand. "What is it you want?"

"Information."

"I'll tell you whatever I know *after* you release me."

"Before," I countered. "And I won't release you, but I'll agree to postpone your banishment for seven days, provided your information is useful." That would mean extending the host's servitude for another week, but I didn't feel too bad. According to the police, these guys had been far from Boy Scouts.

"No deal," Despus said.

I strolled toward him, looking up and down the length of my blade. "You'd rather I banish you now?"

I could feel the demon's glowing eyes on me, trying to determine just how badly I wanted that information. When I reached him, his eyes switched to the sword, the banishment rune now radiating holy light. I raised the blade overhead, tip centered on his back. When he flinched, I paused with the blade in thrusting position.

"Your terms are ... are acceptable," he grunted.

I lowered the blade as the energy of the demonic agreement bonded us.

"First question," I said. "Do you know where the demon Arnaud is?"

"No."

"Are you sure?"

"I don't know," he growled.

I believed him. Hundreds of lesser demons had come through the Harkless Rift back in October. My fellow magic-users had been hard at work tracking and banishing them. Claudius dispatched a sizable number at the stone quarry in New Jersey just days earlier, sending them to distant dimensions. Now only a few dozen demons remained. Given their heated competition for souls, demon masters were no doubt keeping the whereabouts of the survivors a closely guarded secret from one another. Even so, I was guessing the masters had intel on who their demon minions were competing against.

"But you know who he is," I said.

"I might," he replied.

"What do you know about him?"

"What's there to know?" he said, his voice sharp with condescension. "He's just another peon."

To a demon, anything beneath him in the hierarchy was a peon. "He's also managed to remain in the world," I pointed out. "Which is more than I can say for eighty percent of Team Despus." I looked over the sprawl of slumbering bodies. I righted one of the chairs and sat down, forearms propped on my knees. "What's his master's name?"

Despus glared at me from his prone position.

"The terms of our agreement give you a chance," I said. "A thin one granted, but anything's better than immediate banishment, right? That said, you're not getting out of this. I can tell you that right now."

I thought of the cell awaiting him at 1 Police Plaza. Warded by yours truly, it not only contained sufficient power to hold the demon for the next week, its dislocation sigils would sever him from the rest of demon-kind.

"Even so," I continued, "it doesn't mean you have to keep the other demons in the game. Tell me what you know, and we'll take out Arnaud and the others, make this round of Invasion Earth a wash. You can start fresh the next time."

Of course, there wasn't going to be a next time. The Order would make damn sure of that.

"Now I'll ask you again," I said, prodding his leg with my staff. "What's the name of Arnaud's master?"

When he drew his lips into a taut line, I thought we were done. "He's known as Malphas," he said.

Malphas, I repeated to myself. "That doesn't sound like his true demon name." Contrary to popular belief, having his true name wouldn't allow me to control him, but I could certainly use it to hunt him.

And Arnaud, by proxy.

"It's not," Despus spat back, "and I won't speak it."

More than defiance now, I heard fear. That suggested Malphas was higher than him in the hierarchy, possibly much higher. I considered threatening him with the sword again, but any penalty I could impose would pale in comparison to what this Malphas would do when he tracked the utterance of his true name back to Despus. Plus, he and I were still bonded by the original agreement, and he'd kept up his end so far. Failing to keep up mine could have any number of foul consequences, including tainted magic.

"All right, new subject," I said. "What do you know about the Strangers?"

He snorted. "They're off chasing creatures and half humans. They're not my concern."

"Does the same demon control all of them?"

"Yes."

That was important to know.

"Do you know that demon master's name?"

Despus seemed to weigh how much to reveal before giving a nod. Unlike with Malphas, he clearly thought the demon master in question was beneath him for going after merfolk, druids, and half-fae. "It's—"

He stopped suddenly, eyes gone wide.

"Hey," I said. "You all right?"

Gagging, he clutched his throat with one hand and stretched the other toward me like a man drowning. Before I could figure

out what in the hell was going on, much less what to do, the
yellow light shrank from his eyes and his host's body crumpled.
I peered around to make sure we were still alone. By the time my
gaze returned to the body, the host had stopped moving and
Despus was gone.

Something attacked him in the Below.

The host's face looked like a rubber Halloween mask
without a wearer, empty eyes sunk into his head. I dispersed his
confinement and checked the young man's pulse to make sure.
Yeah, dead. And there was no restoring him.

Behind me, the four hoodlums I'd released from demon
bondage started to moan and stir. At least *their* souls were still
intact. I peered around the room until my gaze landed on a
digital clock. I checked it against my watch. 10:59 a.m.

Why was that time important?

The answer arrived with a rude jolt. "Crap!"

I made for the door, bounding over two of the recovering
teens.

Surprise, surprise. I was late.

2

I arrived in the exam room, gasping like a blowfish. Vega was sitting on the end of a padded table in a plain hospital gown. Her sock-clad feet, which had been kicking idly above the floor, stopped. She cocked a stern eye at me in question.

"I am so sorry," I said, stuffing away the kerchief I'd used to mop my sweaty face. "Got tied up with a case, then had to run six blocks before I could flag down a cab." I leaned down and planted a kiss on her cheek. "Did I miss anything?"

In contrast to my harried, disheveled state, Vega appeared calm and composed, her midnight hair in a thick ponytail that showed the lovely nape of her neck. I decided to kiss her there too, lingering for a couple seconds.

"Only the urinalysis," she answered.

"Way to kill the moment," I joked. "And?"

She gave me a quick thumbs-up. Before I could respond, she cut her gaze meaningfully across the room. Partially blocked by the door I'd just thrown open sat a middle-aged woman with silver hair and a white lab coat. Oh, shit. The doctor stared back at me from a humorless face as I closed the door again.

"Dr. Greene's in the middle of our exam," Vega said.

"Oh, ah, please continue," I stammered, feeling like an idiot. I lowered myself onto the chair beside the exam table. The doctor cleared her throat and returned her attention to Vega.

"Breast tenderness or enlargement?" she asked, fingers poised above a computer tablet.

"Some tenderness," Vega replied.

"Nausea or vomiting."

"Not yet."

"Shortness of breath?"

"With exertion, a little."

"Increased urinary frequency?"

As I tried to keep up with the rapid volley of questions and answers, all thoughts of the demons I'd encountered only twenty minutes earlier were gone, replaced by the bass drum pounding inside my chest.

Holy shit, this is happening, it seemed to be saying. *This is really happening.*

I missed the next question and watched as Dr. Greene recorded Vega's response, which I'd also missed. As the doctor's silver hair glinted beneath the fluorescent lights, my mind clenched in suspicion.

Fae?

I wasn't picking up an aura, but that could be glamoured, especially if the doctor were an advanced caster. Before my over-protective thoughts could barrel out of control, though, I hit the brakes.

Lots of women color their hair silver.

"When was your last period?" Dr. Greene asked.

"Six weeks ago."

"Then we'll be looking at mid-July."

"Mid-July," I echoed. "That feels soon."

Vega shook her head. When I looked over at Dr. Greene, I caught the tip of her tongue slipping back into her mouth. *Wait, did she just lick her lips?* And just like that, my mind was thinking fae again, possibly even night hag.

I lifted my cane from beside the chair and set it on my right thigh. A reveal spell would tell me for sure, put my mind at ease. And if I had to hit her with something harder, I would.

Gathering power around my casting prism, I calibrated my aim.

"Croft," Vega said sharply. "Pay attention. She asked you a question."

I followed her gaze to find Dr. Greene staring at me. Pretending to get comfortable, I shifted in the chair and lowered the cane again. The gathered energy dispersed back into the room. "Sorry."

Dr. Greene regarded me coldly while Vega gave me an exasperated look.

"Any genetic issues in your family?" the doctor asked in a way that said she was repeating herself.

"Not that I know of. Well, nothing bad, anyway."

"It's a yes or no question."

I thought about my late parents—Marlow and Eve—both magic-users. Their powerful lineage ran through me, but I wasn't going to share that info with a doctor who may or may not have been human.

"No, then."

The doctor entered my answer and slipped her tablet into a coat pocket.

"All right," she said, seeming to thaw a little. "Are you two ready for your first look?"

"First look?" I stammered. "You mean at—"

"Yes," Dr. Greene said. "Your baby."

TEN MINUTES LATER, VEGA WAS RECLINED, HER FEET IN STIRRUPS. The doctor's hand with the gel-coated probe had gone under the draping, but we were all watching the monitor. For several moments it was a gray field, mysterious black shapes growing into view and shrinking away again.

My voice quavered in the silence. "Will we know if it's a boy or girl?"

"Not until the mid-pregnancy ultrasound," Vega answered for the doctor, who remained focused on her task.

"So, in the meantime what do we call the baby?" I whispered. "*It?*" That didn't seem right.

Vega smirked and gave me another of her patented head shakes. I slipped my hand into hers and squeezed, more to ground myself than anything. Though she had been through this before with Tony, her steadiness still amazed me. She'd known exactly what to do—scheduling the prenatal visit, scaling down to smaller, more frequent meals, drinking more water. She'd even started herself on a multivitamin.

Me? I'd been too tied up with work. Typical dad.

Back on the monitor, a black ovoid swelled into view.

"The uterus," Dr. Greene announced.

It looked empty. Cold sweat broke over my back as I searched the space for life. I snuck a peek at Vega, whose large, expectant eyes remained fixed on the monitor. When her lips turned up at the corners, I took another look. On the right side of the uterine space, a small blur was coming into focus.

"This is the yolk sac," Dr. Greene said, indicating a tiny donut. "And beneath that, your child."

Awe and fear pounded through me as I stared at the little miracle. It looked so small, so fragile.

"Just over a half centimeter," Dr. Greene said, as though to confirm my thought. "And that flutter in the center is the heart. A healthy heart."

Vega and I laughed at the same time. If the doctor licked her lips now, I didn't notice. I doubted I would have even cared. I was too riveted on the pea-sized critter on the monitor. *Our* pea-sized critter. When static washed over the image, I realized my wizard's aura was arcing all over the place. Centering myself, I drew my energy back to where it wouldn't interfere with the expensive electronics.

"Unbelievable," was all I could think to whisper.

Indeed, the moment felt more magical than anything I'd ever cast.

I looked over at Vega. Her moist eyes shifted from the monitor to mine, and she squeezed my slick hand.

"Congratulations, Papa," she said.

3

"What did you cast back there?" Vega asked me.

Folders shifted across my lap as she pulled the sedan from the hospital garage and veered into Manhattan's glinting midday traffic. I'd already started leafing through the dizzying amount of material the doctor had sent us home with —an owner's manual for the little miracle Vega was carrying.

So much to learn. And now of all times.

"Huh?" I asked, looking at the copy of the ultrasound image again. I could stare at that little sweet pea all day.

"When we were about to leave? Even if I hadn't heard you mutter in Italian, I felt the current of energy."

"Oh." I lowered the image and tapped everything back into a neat stack. "That was a reveal spell."

"A reveal spell? For what?"

"To make sure Dr. Greene is, you know ... human."

"She delivered Tony. I told you that."

"Yeah, I know. But I saw her lick her lips."

Vega squinted over at me. "What?"

"When she told us the due date," I added lamely.

"That's what people do when their lips are dry."

Or anticipating a fresh baby soul, I thought.

"In any case, she's human," I said. "So we can put that to bed."

"Thanks," Vega said thinly.

"How are you feeling?"

She took a deep breath and let it out. "Relieved after seeing that little beating heart. You?" When she looked over, she seemed to do so carefully.

It had only been four days since she'd told me about her pregnancy, right after I'd found Blade and her fellow hunters slaughtered in their East Village apartment. I suspected Arnaud, the vampire-turned-demon. The horrid scene coupled with Vega's reveal spurred me into action. After relocating Vega and Tony to an interfaith house in Brooklyn, I'd stocked up on spell implements and then worked furiously in my loft for the next forty-eight hours. My coat pockets now bulged with protections and stoppered potions. I also had a small unit of golems and ghosts monitoring the city. I even talked Tabitha into resuming her ledge patrols after having promised her the month off.

So the truth was, I'd had almost no time to consider the implications of Vega's pregnancy until today: what it meant for me, for us. When I looked down at the ultrasound image again, a staggering force moved through me.

"Croft?" Vega prompted.

"How do I feel? So in love with this thing that it scares the hell out of me."

"It's life changing," she agreed. We slowed toward a red light. "But are you good with this?"

"Of course I am."

She looked over at me. "You can be honest. I'd understand."

I caught a note of insecurity, which was unusual for her.

"How could I not be? It's you and me and..." I gestured at the image. "It."

"We didn't exactly plan this."

"Ricki." I took her hand. "I'm great with this."

She smiled tightly and moved her hand back to the wheel as she accelerated again.

Massive housing projects loomed to the east as she navigated Second Avenue. Being the day after Thanksgiving, we both had the day off from our respective jobs, and we were headed to the safe house to check on Tony. Afterwards, I had a meeting with the Upholders—my price for securing refuge for Vega and her son.

I studied the bonding sigil below my right thumb for a couple of blocks, a faint white pattern with both religious and druidic elements. A fair exchange, I decided. As we approached the Williamsburg Bridge, I voiced something I'd been considering.

"I think you should stay in the safe house until Arnaud's no longer a threat."

"I *am* staying there," she said.

"No, I mean twenty-four seven. Like Tony."

"Croft, I'm still active duty."

"But you're pregnant now."

"Yeah, for seven and a half more months. I can't take maternity leave yet."

I'd expected some resistance, but the strength of her pushback surprised me.

"I just don't like the idea of you out here." The passing buildings and side streets wavered slightly beyond the protective shield I had cast around the car. My gaze dropped to her stomach. "You, plural."

"That's why you gave me this," she sighed, drawing my grandfather's coin pendant from inside her blouse. "It packs the one-two punch of the Brasov Pact and the safe house, right? He can't touch us."

"Under normal circumstances."

"What's that supposed to mean?"

Inside Blade's apartment, the detectives had found remnants of gray salt, an element used to store magical items. It suggested that the vampire hunters might have found such an item in the course of their work. Vampires were renowned collectors of the enchanted, after all. But was it a protective item, one that neutralized spells? Ancient pacts, even? Was that what Arnaud had been after?

It seemed a long shot, but the paranoia was eating me from the inside.

"We still don't know why Arnaud went to the vampire hunters' apartment," I said at last.

"Well, I can't do my job on house arrest, and I've been assigned their case."

"We already know who the killer is."

"It's still a homicide investigation."

"Then let Hoffman work it," I said, referring to her partner.

She snorted. "As much as he's come around, Hoffman still doesn't know the supernatural from a salami sandwich. If he and the Sup Squad go it alone, they'll be tits deep in something they're unprepared for. Look, I've been with the NYPD for almost a decade. I have a responsibility to that family too."

I could see by the tension across her brow we weren't going to be settling anything between here and the safe house. Plus, the conversation was causing her stress, and that was a no-no according to Dr. Greene.

"Speaking of family," I said, changing the subject, "have you told your brothers?"

I'd met them only the week before. The oldest three had been cool with me, but that changed when Carlos, the youngest, convinced them I was a danger to Ricki and Tony. He'd convened a living room pow-wow where the Vega Brotherhood told me to stop seeing their sister.

Whoops, I thought as I looked at the ultrasound image.

"Let me worry about them," Vega replied.

"I'd like to be there when you tell them."

"They're *my* brothers."

"And you're *my*..." Girlfriend? That sounded too small for what we were taking on. Something else I wanted to discuss with her, but not here, not now. "Look, we're in this together. I want to be there when you make the announcement. I'm the papa bear, remember?"

She smirked. "I appreciate that, but there's no hurry."

"And when we get some time, I want us to talk. You and me."

Her expression flattened, and I felt her pull in slightly.

"Sure," she said.

THE SAFE HOUSE WAS LOCATED IN BROOKLYN'S COBBLE HILL neighborhood, about a ten-minute drive from Vega's apartment. The synagogue to which the safe house was attached belonged to New York's interfaith community, meaning it drew additional power from the beliefs of the city's major congregations and, by extension, congregations worldwide.

Translation: the protection was rock solid.

As we pulled in front of the granite building slotted in the middle of a block of brownstones, I could feel its thrumming energy. I got out and joined Vega, shrinking the shell of hardened air until it enclosed just the two of us.

We'd spoken little the rest of the ride. I didn't know why she'd shut down on the Williamsburg Bridge, and I hadn't pressed. With my critical lack of sleep, I couldn't trust what I might say. I doubted Vega had slept much the last several nights either.

At the edge of the sidewalk, I held the iron gate open for her. We ascended the stone steps to a set of stout wooden doors. Vega had already drawn her key, and she inserted it and pushed the door open. As I followed her through the thick curtain of energy, my bonding sigil glowed briefly. I was being admitted. Still, the lion's share of my wizarding power fell away, the equivalent of having my weapons checked at the door.

"You all right?" Vega asked, her brow creased in concern.

"Fine," I said, realizing I'd drawn a sharp breath through my teeth. "Crossing these thresholds is always a little jarring."

But it was a reassurance too. If the threshold could render me powerless, even with entry permission from the Interfaith Council, I could only imagine how the same energy would deal with a demon-vampire. Reduce it to a smoking pile, most likely. Which was exactly why I needed to convince Vega to stay here.

"No safer place in the city, though," I added in an offhanded way.

Vega shot me a dark look over her shoulder, telling me to drop it.

We took a staircase down to the safe house's basement level, where a collection of meeting rooms had been converted into small apartments—the only place they could fit us. We found Tony at a table in the common area, hunched over a workbook. Camilla, Vega's housekeeper and sitter, was there too, absorbed in her phone.

"Working hard, champ?" Vega asked her son.

Tony looked up. "Hey, Mom." When he saw I'd come too, his eyes brightened. "Mr. Croft!"

Ever since my role in the mayor's eradication program the year before, Tony regarded me as some kind of superhero.

"Hey, kiddo," I said as he jumped up and threw his arms around my waist. Chuckling, I tousled his curly hair.

"How's he doing?" Vega asked Camilla.

"Very good. He just finishing his last lesson. Very smart boy."

Vega had decided to keep her son here around the clock until the Arnaud threat was over, and that meant homeschooling. My grandfather's pendant, which Vega had given to him, went back to her; and my grandfather's ring, which I'd given to Vega, came back to me. I could feel both artifacts absorbing the power of the safe house now, lending us portable protection. In theory, anyway. The bloody scene at the vampire hunters' apartment hit me in flashes.

"Can I?" Tony asked. I looked down to find him reaching for my cane.

"Sure, go ahead." He wouldn't be able to release the sword, much less cast through it.

With a smile that revealed the gap where a baby tooth had been, Tony grabbed the cane and jabbed it around while making blasting sounds.

"Are you gonna hang out with us this afternoon?" he asked.

"I wish I could, buddy, but there's somewhere I need to be."

"Aw. It's so *boring* here."

"Yeah, sorry about that," I said, glancing around the windowless room.

Vega finished catching up with Camilla and watched her son in a way that was hard to interpret. Concern? Wistfulness? She hadn't told him he was going to be an older brother yet, and I wondered when she planned to drop the news.

"Mom, how much longer do we have to stay here?" he asked in the impatient voice of a seven-year-old.

"We've had this discussion. It's only temporary."

He stopped play-fighting and sagged over the cane. "Yeah, but for how long?"

"Tony, that's enough."

Hearing the fatigue in Vega's voice, I jumped in. "Hey, listen. When I finish my meeting, I'll pick up a pizza from Ratzo's and we'll all eat here. How does that sound?"

The words had barely left my mouth when I heard someone coming down the stairs. I turned to find Malachi rushing into the room, ponytail leaping over his narrow shoulders. He had been an acolyte at St. Martin's Cathedral when the demon lord Sathanas possessed the vicar. Not only had he shown me to the ossuary where the Big Battle would go down, he later saved my life by directing the police to the same location, where they found me unconscious and buried under a heap of bones.

Sometime later, Malachi began having visions of a demon apocalypse. The visions led him to the other members of the Upholders—a druid, a half-fae, and a mermaid—whose groups had been infiltrated by Strangers. Malachi's dreams had also led him to me, possibly because I'd put down the city's last major demon threat in Sathanas. Though, in truth, we still hadn't figured out the why.

"Croft," he panted.

"Hey, I was just about to head over to the townhouse."

His smallish eyes looked from me to Vega. "Detective," he said.

"Malachi," she answered, arching an eyebrow in question.

"What's up?" I asked him.

"We have a, um, situation."

"Situation?"

I extended a hand toward Tony, and he dutifully returned my cane.

"I'll tell you on the way to the townhouse," Malachi said.

I nodded and went over to Vega. "Sounds like I've gotta run."

"When you find out what's going on, let me know," she said, warning in her tone.

I drew her into a hug, her abdomen warm against my hips, and kissed the crown of her head. "I will. You going to be all right here?"

"Fine. Be careful."

"We're still doing Ratzo's tonight, right?" Tony asked.

Crap. When I glanced at Malachi, he shook his head and headed up the stairs.

"I'm really sorry, buddy," I told him, feeling like a jerk. "I'll owe you."

I was almost to the top of the stairs when I heard him grumble, "That's what Dad's always saying."

The words landed like a shot to the solar plexus.

His dad's still in their life?

4

"A merfolk pod is making its way toward the city," Malachi said as we settled into the backseat of a cab.

Still preoccupied with Tony's parting remark, it took me a moment to process Malachi's words. "The one Gorgantha belonged to?"

Malachi nodded, signaling for me to keep it down even though our driver spoke little English and appeared more interested in his digital meter. "They're likely searching for her and the others," Malachi whispered.

Gorgantha's merfolk pod had been living off the coast of Maine when a Stranger infiltrated the group and began claiming their souls for his demon master. He'd also transmogrified their cored-out bodies into monsters. Only she and about twenty others managed to escape. It sounded like the Stranger meant to fix that.

"When are they expected to reach the city?" I asked.

"Tonight."

Hence the *no time for pizza* look Malachi had given me inside the safe house. And with that, Tony's parting words came whipping back through my head.

That's what Dad's always saying.

Was this a recent development? The word *always* suggested history. So why hadn't Vega told me? Naturally, I'd been curious about Tony's father, but I figured he was Vega's business. Things were different now. She was carrying our child. If Tony's father was in the picture, I needed to know.

Realizing Malachi had just said something, I turned toward him. "Sorry, I missed that."

"I said this will be our first chance to strike back against the gathering forces of the apocalypse." A kind of messianic passion seemed to inflame his eyes. This was his life mission now: preventing his visions from manifesting.

I nodded, but between Vega and Tony, my thoughts were other places.

———

THE CAB DROPPED US OFF IN FRONT OF THE EAST SIDE TOWNHOUSE whose basement unit served as the Upholder's headquarters. As Malachi bolted the warded door behind us, Jordan Derrow looked up from a map spread over the table.

I raised a hand in greeting. "Jordan."

The druid was about my age, handsome with a stylish fade cut and thin beard that traced his angular jaw. Faint sigils adorned the brown skin at his temples. He nodded once and went back to consulting the map.

"Thanks for answering the call." He said it as if in afterthought, his tone suggesting he'd had his doubts that I would show. I wondered now if that's why Malachi had come for me instead of just activating the bonding sigil. Jordan hadn't been thrilled about me getting safe house spots for Vega and Tony before proving my commitment to the Upholders. But he had a lot on the line: a Stranger had not only infiltrated his druid circle, but his wife was among the possessed, present whereabouts unknown.

"I knew he'd come," Seay Sherard said, appearing from the kitchen.

The half-fae was fully glamoured, a sweep of preternaturally blond hair gracing the front of one shoulder like a Hollywood starlet's. It glittered as she strode toward me and air-kissed my cheeks. I reciprocated the best I could. Since meeting Seay, I'd learned she worked in the city's garment district for a top designer.

"Because if you didn't," she whispered, "we would have hunted you down and done all sorts of naughty things." Green light flashed from her wink, and her lips pinched into a lush smile that would have sent most men into a love-struck jig. It didn't mean anything, though. This was just her manipulative fae half coming out.

"Noted," I said neutrally.

"Ready to get some calluses on those soft professor hands?"

"Me?" I took hers and turned them over to reveal baby-pink palms.

She jerked them from my grasp. "Smartass."

And that was her scrappy human half.

"What's poppin', Everson?" Gorgantha called.

The massive, turquoise-colored mermaid was reclined in a claw-foot tub in the room's sunken corner, her fishtail riffling the water between eight webbed toes that hooked over the rim. She regarded me from dark orbs for eyes.

"Did Malachi give you the 4-1-1?" A fan of early hip-hop, Gorgantha had learned English from WBLS radio and block parties in the Bronx.

"The highlights, yeah," I said, removing my coat. "Your pod's coming down the coast."

"I dig a brawl as much as the next mer," she sighed, tucking a ragged length of hair behind a finlike ear. "But I'm sure as shit not looking forward to this one."

"Why doesn't everyone gather around," Malachi called from the table.

As Gorgantha stood from the sloshing tub and stretched a hand toward a cotton robe hanging from a wall peg, Jordan yielded his position in front of the map to Malachi. I joined Seay opposite them, draping my coat over a chair back. Now that I was here, I resolved to focus on the matter at hand rather than my own problems. After all, the Upholders had gotten sanctuary for the two people I loved most.

"Gorgantha's pod left Maine's waters two days ago," Malachi said. "They rounded Cape Cod yesterday. That puts them here." He pointed off the eastern end of Long Island.

"How do we know?" I asked.

"I saw it in a dream vision," he said.

"And it was that specific? Coordinates and everything?" I didn't mean to sound skeptical, but divinations were often symbolic, requiring skill and experience to interpret, and Malachi had only been at this for a year or so.

"It checked out," Gorgantha said, arriving at the opposite side of the table, water from her dank hair soaking into the robe. "When the ones of us who escaped made it down here, we set up watches along the coast. There's a narrow current closer to shore that moves against the Gulf Stream. A *gutter current*, we call it. Yesterday, the watch picked up the mers' scent in the gutter current."

"They'll reach Lower Bay tonight," Malachi continued, "presumably in search of Gorgantha and the other escapees."

"How did they know you were down here?"

Gorgantha shrugged. "Spies? One or two could've escaped our noses. That we're smelling them now tells us the whole pod's rolling out. Or most of it, anyway."

"The Stranger is no doubt being compelled by his master to harvest more souls," Malachi said, which reminded me of the morning's encounter with the demon pack and Despus. "But that gives us an advantage."

I raised an eyebrow. "In water?"

My skills had grown to the point where I could cast reasonably well in a driving rain, but a body of deep water—and salt water, no less—was another story. I imagined the same was true for Jordan.

"The plan is to draw them onto land." Gorgantha pointed out Lower Bay with a talon that looked like it was made of the same material as a fish fin. "Here's the reef of junked cars where we've been crouching. Over here is Staten Island. This green part? Great Kills Park." She indicated a two-mile stretch of coast along the island's southern shore. "That's the spot."

"Great Kills, huh?" I said, hoping that wasn't an omen.

"Gorgantha's group will leave a scent trail up into the park," Malachi explained. "We'll be waiting for them there. Jordan and Seay will entrap them with magic. Then you and I will move in and exorcise the possessed."

"How many?" I asked.

"If all of them roll up," Gorgantha said, "about fifty."

My eyes roamed the pencil markings on the map showing the plan. It looked too easy.

"You don't think they'll suspect a trap?" I asked. "Your whole group leaving the water like that?"

Gorgantha shook her head. "They'll think we came up to forage in the salt marshes. Crazy shellfish in there."

"Our main target is the Stranger," Jordan cut in.

"Yeah, *Finn*," Gorgantha said with no shortage of venom. "Talk about a janky-ass dude."

"We need to learn who he's working for," Jordan continued, "what the connection is to the Strangers who infiltrated my group and Seay's, and where they are." Though he managed to control his voice, I could see the cold rage in his eyes. I didn't doubt his commitment to his teammates, but he'd ultimately joined the Upholders to recover his wife.

"I actually have some info," I said.

The three listened intently as I shared what I'd learned from Despus and how he'd claimed that a single demon master controlled the three Strangers. "This Despus didn't seem to think much of the master," I said. "But before he could give me a name, something intervened. Tore him from our world with so much force that it killed the host." En route to Vega's prenatal appointment, I'd called in the death to Detective Hoffman on my flip phone. He was *not* happy about having to write up a supernatural case.

"That suggests two things," I continued. "One, that the demon master is more powerful than the other demons on the block believe, and two, that he or she wants to remain incognito. For lack of a name, I'm calling him Demon X."

Malachi nodded gravely. "The arrival of the Strangers is the first sign of a coming demon apocalypse. It stands to reason the master would be powerful."

I still didn't see Demon X's game plan, though. It was going to take a lot more than the possession of a few small groups to launch a full-scale apocalypse. But Malachi and I had been over this, and "*how* doesn't matter" was his answer to everything. To him, his visions were proof enough.

Jordan turned toward me. "Are you going to be able to make this Stranger talk?"

"I'll try."

His nostrils flared over his compressed lips. "We need better than that, Everson."

I felt my defensiveness kick in. "I'm not going to promise something I can't deliver. There's a good chance Demon X will just pull him back to the Below before we get a name or the whereabouts of the other Strangers."

"You can't disrupt that connection?" he challenged.

The answer was *not without making myself* really *vulnerable to possession*, but I just shook my head.

"Then what's the point?" Jordan muttered.

"Excuse me?" Gorgantha drew up her six-and-a-half foot frame in front of him. "How about getting my pod back?"

"All right, everyone," Malachi said, holding out his arms for peace.

"I meant interrogating the Stranger," Jordan growled. "Better just to decapitate and burn him."

Gorgantha glared at him another moment as if to make sure he wasn't dissing her pod before standing down. I turned to Seay, who had remained mostly silent. She was coiling and uncoiling a strand of blond hair around a finger. Though her face remained a picture of fae composure, the gesture suggested worry.

"Any updates on your Stranger?" I asked.

The one targeting the half-fae worked differently. Rather than infiltrating the group and turning its shared beliefs against them, this Stranger was possessing them one at a time. Possibly because the half-fae in the city were agnostic at best, many working in the fashion district. After the group had used their magic to reclaim several of the possessed, the Stranger changed tactics, disappearing his half-fae victims entirely.

Seay shook her head. "No more disappearances since Darian."

Darian, short for Phidarian, had been a half-fae who worked for the same fashion designer as Seay. He'd gone missing last week.

I glanced around the table before returning my attention to the map. Jordan had a point. To catch a Stranger only to banish him would be a wasted opportunity, especially if he could give up the location of the other Strangers or the identity of his master. With that level of info, we'd have a direction, a plan. Without it, we'd be pawing around like the blind. Plus, Malachi's visions bothered me.

"All right," I said, exhaling. "I'll prepare something to disrupt the connection between the Stranger and his master so we can get him talking." Jordan's eyes seemed to yield slightly before hardening again.

"Then let's go over the entire plan," he said. "This has to go flawlessly."

I nodded. The druid wasn't kidding.

5

Arnaud Thorne cocked his head as he sized up the young man sitting in the antique armchair opposite him. He had the build, yes, the almond-shaped eyes, the straight black hair. The cut wasn't right, but that could be remedied. An inch off the bangs, and the resemblance would be truly striking.

Still staring, Arnaud swirled his snifter of scotch, causing the ice to clink. The young man, Stefan, shifted in his chair as he peered around the lavish hotel suite overlooking Central Park, his discomfort competing with his evident wonderment. Arnaud took a long sip, relishing the cold burn over his tongue almost as much as the power he held over this young man in the ill-fitting suit.

So much like the old days.

"And where did you say you were from?" Arnaud asked.

Stefan's eyes snapped back to his. "Romania, originally. I came here as a boy. My parents wanted better opportunities for my sister and me."

"Hmm." Arnaud was hoping for Bulgaria, but the accent was close.

"I-I need this," he stammered. "I've been out of work for four years. I'll be the best assistant you've ever had. I'll run through walls for you."

Arnaud adjusted the yellow-tinted glasses that cloaked his demonic eyes and appraised the young man again. He had spotted him sitting on a park bench just across the street. Even from his penthouse vantage, Arnaud had been struck by the similarity. The *potential*. And so he'd gone down to have a chat. Like so many New Yorkers, Stefan had been out looking for work. But even though the economy was starting to crawl from the morass, there were still a hundred job-seekers for every new opening. Arnaud had only to dangle the prospect of work in front of Stefan to lead him to where he now sat.

Arnaud angled his head slightly. Yes, with a few modifications, he would be a close match to his faithful servant of so many centuries, the voice in his head taking form and structure once more. But would *close* be good enough? He pondered the question with his next sip, stroking the scepter that spanned his knees.

"Please," Stefan said. "I have a family. Two little girls."

Arnaud set his drink on the end table and stood. "Then fortune is smiling on you, my good friend."

Stefan blinked. "Do you mean—?"

"Congratulations. The position is yours."

The young man seized Arnaud's hand in both of his, not seeming to notice their iciness, more likely not caring.

"Oh, you won't regret this," he said.

"I hope you're right," Arnaud answered honestly.

"When can I start?"

Such ambition. Arnaud's smiling lips broke from his teeth, but Stefan seemed not to notice their sharpness. He was watching the demon-vampire's eyes, his own eyes bright with expectation. Arnaud could all but read his thoughts. The sooner Stefan started, the sooner he would be paid, and the sooner he could become the *man of the house* once more.

"How does today sound?" Arnaud asked.

As far as he was concerned, the sooner the young man started, the sooner he himself might have his old companion back.

"Yes, yes, whatever you need me to do. I'm ready."

"Well, first there is the matter of your *official* hiring."

"Sure, sure." Stefan hadn't stopped nodding.

And Arnaud had never released his hand. Drawing the young man closer, his eyes crossed toward the lovely pulsating groove in his neck. He could already taste the warm blood that would wash over the lingering bite of scotch.

And that's when Arnaud shrieked.

Stefan's eyes started wide and he jumped back.

The hooks tore through Arnaud's gut a second time, and he fell forward, nearly knocking down his new hire. On the floor, Arnaud curled into an agonizing ball, one hand clawing up tufts of rug. Stefan backed away with a meek sound, then turned and fled.

Arnaud's tinted glasses had come off, he realized, along with his wig of dark hair that hid his grotesque head. The sight had been too much for the young man who was to have become the next incarnation of his beloved Zarko. The penthouse door opened and slammed.

Damn you.

The psychic hooks that bonded him slackened enough for him to grasp his scepter and stagger to the bathroom. His master had no doubt waited until he'd been on the brink of consummation to summon him.

"Damn you," Arnaud dared to hiss this time.

He fell to his knees near the pool-sized jacuzzi and drew a talon across his wrist. Precious blood from his last meal two days earlier splattered over the tile floor. Arnaud smeared out the symbol for the Dread Council and fell to his forearms. With hatred filling the void left by the receding pain, he gargled Malphas's true name.

Infernal smoke gushed from the blood circle and took hovering form. For a long moment, his master only stared down from a pair of menacing red eyes. But if his aim was to intimidate, he only provoked irritation.

"What is it?" Arnaud demanded at last.

The force that wrenched him to the floor was the most savage one yet. Arnaud gasped through the pain.

"You dare use that tone with me?" Malphas said. "Have you forgotten who's in charge?"

"No, my master," Arnaud managed, remembering to whimper. "But what have I done that you would treat me so harshly?"

Arnaud knew that Malphas had timed his request for maximum inconvenience. Then he had hovered there, waiting for Arnaud to express his irritation so he could deal more punishment. The bond tightened as if Malphas were preparing to yank again, but he let out the tension with a dark chuckle.

"Considering it's me, many would deem my treatment of you *tender*."

"You understand my meaning," Arnaud groveled. "You can sense my thoughts."

"Yes, and they suggested you were growing too comfortable. A little reminding now and again doesn't hurt."

"Y-yes, my liege."

"And you *damned* me twice," Malphas added.

Rather than deny the charge, Arnaud kept his forehead to the ground, fully expecting more punishment.

But after a moment, Malphas grunted. "What are your updates? You may kneel."

Arnaud pushed himself from the bloodied tiles, his new silk

suit ruined, and pulled in his legs until he was perched on his bony knobs for knees. Malphas's smoky form loomed over him, filling much of the large bathroom, red eyes glaring down. Arnaud felt like a child—which was exactly what his master wanted, lest he forget his place.

"I have been watching the wizard," he reported.

Malphas scoffed. "Just watching? You have the means now to destroy him."

Arnaud pulled the scepter to his side. "Yes, but it's not just the power of the Brasov Pact he wields. He also carries the blessings of the Great Faiths. And the protection replenishes every time he visits one of their houses."

"Servants are claiming souls for my competition," Malphas said. "Perhaps I should be recruiting *them*." Something in his voice suggested this was more than idle threat.

"But how many souls?" Arnaud asked.

The disembodied pair of red eyes narrowed.

"What I'm saying," Arnaud added quickly, "is that they may be claiming souls, but in ones and twos, yes? When we take control of the city, the numbers will be in the hundreds and then *thousands*." He pushed a little vampiric persuasion into the words, a power that when used judiciously worked on his master. "With the wizard out of the picture, it will be a cinch. Why, look at what we've accomplished in just a few short days." He gestured around them. "The most expensive penthouse in the city's most expensive hotel. You should see the names on the waiting list, and yet I've leapt past them all. Do you think taking the reins of the city will be any more challenging for me?"

When Malphas fell into a brooding silence, Arnaud wondered if his boast had negated the persuasive power of his voice. He had also begun to straighten his body, he realized. He corrected this by hunching his upper back.

"Well, how much longer must I wait?" Malphas asked.

"The power protecting the wizard will flag after two days. With a third, I'll be able to overwhelm him. It's a matter of keeping him from the holy houses. Unless, of course..." He let the words linger and tease.

"Unless *what?*"

"Your greatness would deign to grant me more power."

"More power?" Malphas spat. "From my meager reserve?"

"It will not be meager for long," Arnaud reminded him, slipping more persuasion into the words. He had to be careful with just how hard he pushed, but he needed his master to accede, for he had plans of his own. Namely breaking his bonds to Malphas. He kept those plans hidden in the obscuring mists of his vampiric power.

"No," Malphas said. "I have another undertaking for you."

"Another? But—"

"Silence!"

Hastening to repair the snapping web of persuasion he'd spun around his master, Arnaud said, "But surely we should adhere to the plan. In just a few days—"

"I said *silence!*" Malphas thundered.

Arnaud cowered, fearing his master's anger now.

"You're too ambitious," Malphas said. "And I don't trust the ambitious. I want more eyes on you than just mine. I've made arrangements for you to join a unit."

"A unit?" Arnaud's teeth gnashed at the thought.

"It's a command position."

Arnaud raised his head slightly. "Yes?"

"You'll have lieutenants, a small army—one I'll expect you to *grow*. It will mean a power of sorts, though not the sort you were after." He went on to describe the position and who he would be commanding.

While Arnaud listened, he read between the lines. Though Malphas berated and demeaned him, his master also recognized his value. Not at first, no. Arnaud had emerged into the world a pathetic creature. He'd wriggled, crawled, and cowered in a hole, drawing meager strength from the foul blood of rodents and pigeons. Malphas had no doubt dismissed him, figuring he would expire sooner or later. But when Arnaud began to channel infernal energy and took his first human, Malphas took notice. He called Arnaud to a Dread Council, restored his leg—damaged by the bastard *Croft*—and granted him additional powers. Now, barely a week later, Arnaud had not only left his hole for this lavish penthouse, he possessed a valuable artifact, one he'd slain three skilled vampire hunters to claim.

Yes, Malphas understands my value, Arnaud thought. *But he also senses the danger.* Malphas could only yank the hooks that bound them so many times before that lost its edge. The solution was to surround his servant with forces Arnaud would command but that would also balance against him if needed.

"This will strengthen our position," Malphas finished.

"I understand. And the servant you promised me?" he asked meekly.

To preserve his own plans, Arnaud would need allies.

Malphas scoffed. "Do you mean that pathetic human you were lusting after? The one who fled at the first sign of trouble?"

Now Arnaud understood that his master had summoned him when he did, not to inconvenience him, but to deny him a loyalist. For Malphas's strategy to work, he needed Arnaud isolated.

Malphas grunted. "Please me in your new role, and we'll revisit the matter of a servant."

"Yes, master," Arnaud whispered.

"Now go. You have work to do."

The cloud dispersed, and Malphas's presence rushed from the bathroom. As Arnaud stood and dragged a foot through the blood symbol, a part of him wanted to be furious at the change in plans. But he'd been dealt setbacks before. He would determine how to turn this into an opportunity—not only to destroy the wizard Croft, but to sever his ties to Malphas. Clasping the scepter, he stalked from the bathroom.

"Come, Zarko," he called into the empty penthouse. "We have work to do."

Yes, master, his faithful servant answered.

6

W ith shivering hands, I cinched my coat against a bracing wind that carried the stink of rotten fish from Lower Bay. My feet, meanwhile, felt like mini infernos. It was the waders. The damn things didn't breathe. I curled my right foot, trying to scratch away a mad itch on the bottom of my big toe.

"You all right?" Malachi whispered.

I looked over to where his eyes hovered in the night. The rest of him was concealed by the stealth potion he'd taken a few minutes earlier. I could only see or hear him at all because the same magic cloaked me.

"Fine," I whispered back. "You?"

He gave me a ghostly thumbs-up.

I smiled even though I was ready to tear off the calf-length boot and dig my fingernails into the prickling flesh until it bled. But this was the last place to be caught without footwear. New York's tides had transformed the island marsh into a repository for washed-up drug needles, condoms, and other disease-ridden debris.

The timing would be bad too. We were at the ambush point on Staten Island. Gorgantha and her pod had already tracked across the marsh—*that* had been a sight—to deposit their scent before slipping downwind. Jordan waited on the other side of the marsh clearing, his druidic powers blending him into the ring of scrubby trees. Seay crouched opposite him, using a fae glamour to conceal herself. With no real abilities besides his exorcizing and dream-time divinations, Malachi remained at my side for protection.

"Shouldn't they be here by now?" he whispered.

A stack of dunes blocked our view of the shoreline and Lower Bay. I'd considered warding the beach to detect the creatures' arrival, but I didn't want the magic to tip them off to the ambush. The hands of my watch showed six past midnight. The creatures would latch onto their preys' scent soon enough.

"We're good," I told Malachi. "Just be ready."

When I caught the fear in his nod, I reminded myself he was still a boy, barely older than drinking age. He might have read and memorized everything in the Church archives on demons, but he'd never actually faced one. Neither had the other three. By default, that made me the authority.

Uncertainty nagged at me like the itch on my foot as I reviewed our plan. Had we overlooked anything? I responded by digging my toe hard against the bottom of the boot. *Take your own advice and get your head in the game.*

It took me a moment to realize that the marshland had fallen quiet, the full-throated chorus of frogs from just seconds before gone mute. I squinted toward Lower Bay. Though I couldn't see anything beyond the dunes, the rotten stench on the wind had turned fouler. I brought the bonding sigil on my hand to my lips.

"They're coming," I whispered.

The magic in the sigil broadcast the message to the others.

"I don't see anything," Jordan replied a moment later.

"Look again," Seay said.

Indeed, silhouettes had begun cresting the dunes in a low

creep. Even in the poor light, I could see the transformation from what the merfolk had been to the monsters they'd become. Ragged fins stood from their heads like mohawks and jutted from their thick shoulders. Purple eyes glowed beneath the sharp shelves of their brows while tendrils writhed around an underbite of jutting fangs.

Scary hardly began to describe them.

"Hold your positions until they're all here," I whispered.

The possessed merfolk appeared in twos and threes, tracking the scent of their kin. As they descended toward our clearing, I noted the lack of legs. Bladed tails that had turned serpentine shoved their upright bodies toward the salt marsh in squelching thrusts, hands wielding jagged spears.

Malachi clutched my arm as the first ones slid past where we were hunkered. Gorgantha had estimated fifty or so mercreatures, but after only a few groups appeared over the dune, they stopped coming. Had they sent a partial force, or were the others hanging back in the water?

"I only count thirteen," I whispered.

A moment later, Gorgantha answered, *"No more of 'em in Lower Bay."*

She and the rest of her merfolk had circled in behind to cut off their escape.

"Is Finn with them?"

"Has to be if they came for us."

Which told me she hadn't actually seen him. Shit, no going back now.

"Okay, wait on my word," I broadcast to the team, watching the monsters' progress. The final mer slithered past, feet from us. Malachi's grip on my arm tightened as the creature's glowing eyes roved toward us.

"Now!" I called.

Fae light burst from Seay's position in a beautiful flash that lit up the entire marsh. When the flash glimmered out, the closest mer creature to us was frozen, the purple of his eyes replaced by a full-spectrum shimmer. The others stood in similar statuesque poses, jaws gaping to reveal their lethal teeth.

"They're enchanted," Seay confirmed.

Jordan emerged from the trees and thrust the end of his quarterstaff into the marsh. Druidic power spread from the contact and went rippling out. When it reached the mercreatures, clutches of reedy grass thickened and began writhing up their tails. The dense growth soon cocooned the creatures' bodies to their necks.

"Banishment time," I said to Malachi.

We stood and splashed into the salt marsh. I wasn't planning to drive my sword into the thirteen creatures. That was for combat situations, and Malachi and I had worked out something more efficient, less violent.

Holy light broke over my blade as I aimed it at the closest mer and activated the banishment rune. With another Word, I sent the power into the bound creature. The light sputtered as it collided with its demonic energy, then sprang up again, joining the thirteen creatures in a web-like matrix.

"Ready?" I asked Malachi.

He reached a tentative hand forward. I took it and closed his fingers around the sword's hilt beneath my own grip. He drew a sharp breath as the light climbed his arm and enveloped the Latin Bible he held open at his chest. But he didn't falter like I thought he might. In a strong voice, he began to recite the exorcism. My body hummed as each Latin word sent more power down the blade.

Jordan and Seay watched from the edges of the clearing, the light glowing against their faces. One by one, the mercreatures' heads cocked back. The white light of the banishment began breaking through eyes, ears, mouths—not just purging the infernal energy from the hosts' bodies, but burning it away. With a final shouted phrase, Malachi completed the exorcism. I staggered as the light came roaring back into the sword.

Malachi unwrapped his hand from the hilt and stepped away. The power of the exorcism had exhausted our stealth potion, and I could see him plainly in the dim clearing. Points of light lingered in his eyes.

I scanned the mers' sagging heads. "Well done," I said.

"Why do they still look like monsters?" Jordan asked, stepping forward. "And where's this Finn?"

With a wave of his quarterstaff, the grass bindings fell from the mercreatures. Their bodies collapsed into the marsh with splashes. I waded over to the nearest one, knelt beside him, and touched my staff to his brow. A quantum of my magic pinged around the hollowness before fading out. I exhaled through my nose. I was going to need to be really damned careful how I worded this to Jordan.

"Listen," I said, rising as he squelched up beside me. "We banished the energy controlling them, but there was no soul to fill the void."

He looked from me to the mercreature. "What are you saying?"

"This one's dead. They all are."

"So, you killed them?"

"No," Malachi asserted, but his gaze wavered.

"Demon X had already put the souls to other purposes," I explained. "Used them up. The mercreatures were running on infernal crude. When we banished that energy, there was nothing left to power them." I'd known that was a possibility, but mission planning hadn't felt like the time to have that conversation.

"Then how were Seay and the half-fae able to recover some of their own?" Jordan challenged.

"They got to them early," I said. "And—"

"There's no way you can restore them?" His chest heaved. "Pull them back in?"

He was thinking of his wife.

"Listen to me, Jordan," I said softly. His dark eyes met mine in a way that said, *You better have some good answers.* "This doesn't mean all the Strangers' victims are beyond our help. The Strangers need agents up here. With the druids and half-fae, those agents are only as effective as their magic, right? Well, that magic doesn't work if the souls of the possessed are used up or ground down."

"Until you decide to tell us otherwise," Jordan said thinly.

I could see in his eyes that he knew I'd held back information.

Before I could respond, he turned to Seay, who was checking the other bodies. "Are any of them Finn?"

"No."

The answer came from Gorgantha, who was striding over the dunes, her tall, muscled form glowing faintly beneath the cloud-covered half-moon. When she arrived at our mercreature, she peered down at him somberly.

Malachi brought a hand to her shoulder. "I'm so sorry, Gorgantha."

"It's not your fault," she said. "They were ganked the second Finn got his hands on them. I felt it up in Maine. When they came back to the pod, there wasn't nothing left inside, even before they changed into these suckers."

She shoved the body with a webbed foot.

Jordan huffed. "And no sign of Finn in the bay?"

"Not where we were. I sent the rest of the pod back to the reef to check."

"Great," Jordan muttered. "So no leads, either."

How in the hell is this anyone's fault? I wanted to fire back. But he was just desperate to find and recover his wife. God knew, if I was in his position, Vega missing, I'd be half out of my mind. And with no merfolk recovered and no Stranger to put the screws to, the mission *had* been a disappointment.

I was about to express my own condolences to Gorgantha when her head cocked suddenly. The rest of us followed her gaze.

"It's the other mers," she said, concentrating into the pod bond that connected them. "They didn't find Finn, but they picked up a scent in the harbor. There are more mercreatures."

I pulled up a mental map of the park. The mercreatures had arrived from the south. Great Kill Harbor was only a short distance to our west, accessed from Lower Bay between a sandbar and greater Staten Island.

"They were flanking," I said in understanding. "Have the pod block off the harbor."

"They're coming this way?" Jordan asked, the air around his staff stirring with fresh magic.

"That was probably the plan before they realized they weren't just facing merfolk," I said. "They're in retreat."

Jordan got the message: it was now a race to the water. He bowed his head as druidic energy took hold around his body. In the next moment, a dark bird with a heavy bill and shaggy throat hackles flapped into the air. With a deep croak that sounded like a battle cry, Jordan broke toward the harbor in his raven form.

"Wait," I called, but he was already disappearing into the trees.

I swore as the rest of us splashed into a run behind him, light from my staff crackling into a shield.

7

We ran from marsh to woods before breaking out into a garbage-strewn field. And there they were: a mass of thirty-odd mercreatures racing toward the harbor's choppy waters. They'd been moving overland to cut off Gorgantha and her pod's escape before realizing it had been a trap. And now the damned things had a solid head start back to the water.

I'd managed to arrange our team into a formation behind a shield of light, me at point, Seay and Gorgantha flanking, and Malachi safely behind us. Jordan was somewhere ahead, but I couldn't make out his raven form against the night sky. Repeated attempts to communicate with him had gone unanswered.

What in the hell does he think he's going to accomplish on his own?

With my unwieldy boots kicking up clods of earth, I shouted in an attempt to slow the creatures. Several in the rear turned and began heaving spears. But the rest continued their slide toward the harbor. Sparks burst as the first coral projectiles shattered against our protection, their accuracy scary good.

"None of you hold back," Gorgantha panted as we closed the

distance. "They're not my crew anymore. I can't even tell who's who."

Seay took that as her cue, and a gold bolt shot past me. Her magic enveloped a mercreature in brilliant fae light, dropping it to the ground. Its body jerked under the lethal enchantment. She fired a second bolt, hitting another of the rear creatures. The mers ahead of them continued their race to the water.

"Try to keep your feet," I warned my teammates.

I'd been channeling ley energy into my mental prism, and now I released it with a shouted, *"Respingere!"*

The energy gathered briefly in my shield before pulsing away in a low and potent *whump*. The wave spanned the field and slammed into the rear merfolk, sending them tumbling. The pulse took down the next line too, but petered out before reaching those in the lead. I stumbled from the kickback and heard Malachi go down behind me. Probably just as well. Now that we were closing in, I wanted him well back.

As Seay continued to fire bolts, I eyed the thin strip of beach. *Need to build a seawall high enough and strong enough to hold them...*

I was gathering power for a massive invocation when the weedy beach grass began to twist and climb. Jordan had beat me to it, I realized. The grass snagged the first arriving creatures, twining around their tails and arms as it continued to grow. The creatures slashed back with taloned hands.

A moment later, I spotted our druid teammate. Still in raven form, he was ten feet above the creatures. Magic warped the air as he shifted back to human. He landed on knee and quarter-staff, his reconstituted cloak billowing out to the sides. Badass, sure, but he was also right in the mers' midst.

"What's he doing?" Gorgantha asked.

Being reckless as fuck, I thought in annoyance.

Jordan ducked beneath a swiping hand and brought up his

quarterstaff. It struck the mercreature's chin in a savage upper-cut. Druidic energy discharged, sending the creature flying back. More of them closed in, though, the monsters at least a foot taller than Jordan, not to mention twice as massive. Even with his grass animation as backup, the fool wasn't going to be able to take them all.

"I'm going in," I shouted.

"We'll be close behind," Gorgantha replied, no doubt recognizing the developing shit show for what it was.

I narrowed my wedge-shaped protection, aimed my sword behind me, and shouted, *"Forza dura!"* The force that rocketed down the blade sent me airborne, arcing toward the mass of merfolk. As I landed, my shielded form plowed into them, flattening some and battering others. I came to a skidding stop beside Jordan.

"How about some coordination next time?" I asked.

"I kept them from reaching the water, didn't I?"

Jordan struck another creature, brought his staff up, and drove it into the stomach of a third with a back thrust. I had to admit, he was handy with the thing. But that didn't change the fact he'd gone off half-cocked, literally dropping into the middle of danger and forcing the rest of us to do the same.

"That remains to be seen," I replied.

"Behind you," he said.

A merfolk's spear slashed my shielded body. Twisting, I countered with a sword plunge and banishment invocation. The mer slumped as it gave up its infernal essence in a burst of light and shadow. Planting a boot against the monster's hip, I withdrew the blade and shoved its gargantuan body away.

I hated dispatching them like this, but attempting to restore their souls would have required a trip to the Below—suicidal in itself—as well as magic far beyond my abilities. Even then, there were no guarantees.

"Nice one," Jordan said as I banished another mercreature.

Despite his earlier outrage over the dead merfolk, the druid wasn't holding back. Quarterstaff blows sent his attackers flying and stumbling into his animation. Upon cocooning them, the sharp grasses circled necks and squeezed until heads came off in gouts of glistening black blood.

"Not doing too badly yourself," I grunted.

Fae light burst over the beach as Seay targeted the mercreatures attempting to skirt Jordan's writhing wall. And now Gorgantha entered the fray, her punches landing like sledgehammer blows.

"Anyone seen Finn?" she called.

He was the only one of the possessed group of merfolk who hadn't taken on monstrous form according to Gorgantha, but I hadn't seen any normal mers besides her and her pod. I answered in the negative along with the others.

I dispatched another mercreature, then turned in time to see one rake Jordan's stomach, tearing away strips of cloak. Shouting in pain, Jordan took out the creature's tail with a staff sweep, then brought the staff's thick end down with both hands. The magic he'd gathered annihilated the creature's head.

But Jordan was hurt. He staggered back, a hand to his bleeding gut, and landed on the seat of his pants.

I rushed toward him, but he jabbed his staff toward the water. "Stop them!"

Injured, Jordan couldn't maintain his animation. The remaining mercreatures were already beyond the collapsing wall and diving into the harbor. Shaping energy as fast as I could speak, I attempted to box the creatures in the shallows. But the salt water kept the energy from bonding into anything solid. I swore as mercreatures broke through the fragile manifestation.

"Stay cool," Gorgantha said as she thudded past me. "We got 'em."

"Wait!" I shouted, but she was already submerging into the harbor beneath a foamy splash.

I cast a ball of light over the waters to see what was going on. Like many of the smaller harbors around the city, this one had been abandoned in the wake of the Crash. Skeletal docks jutted out a few feet before turning to naked pilings. Abandoned boats, smashed by successions of storms, fed great bobbing banks of detritus.

Just under the water's surface, I caught the torpedo-like motion of the mercreatures, their thick bodies pushing up humps of water as they sped away. Gorgantha was behind them, legs and tail kicking in unison, but I couldn't tell if she was gaining. Ahead, another swell was arriving to meet the creatures: Gorgantha's pod.

The opposing forces collided, and the waters churned with battle.

The itch on my toe started up again as I realized there was nothing I could do but watch.

Seay came up beside me, golden light licking around her hands. "I'd take a shot, but I don't know who's who."

"Gorgantha's pod has numbers," I said, trying to reassure both of us.

I turned to check on Jordan. He was still down, but he'd managed to open his pouch of healing herbs. Malachi was beside him, moving the rags of shirt away from the wound. Fortunately, druids were powerful healers. I'd offer my own help, of course, but I first had to know Gorgantha was all right.

In the harbor, the frothing water was darkening with what must have been blood. *Merfolk? Mercreature?* I began pacing the shore, the itch on my toe growing more and more maddening. Then, as quickly as it had begun, the churning settled.

"Gorgantha?" I called into our communication system.

No answer.

I hadn't known her or any of the Upholders long, but we were bonded. Not just by our sigils but by a common need to purge the demonic invasion from our communities, our lives. For them, it was the Strangers. For me, Arnaud. We couldn't fail on our first outing.

I watched for her to surface. I *needed* her to surface.

"Croft," a sputtering voice called.

I stepped from Seay and ran down to the water. Gorgantha's head had broken the surface, but closer to shore than I'd been expecting. She was swimming so slowly I figured she'd been injured. But then I realized she was dragging something behind her. Several merfolk swam up and helped her with the load.

"Is everyone all right?" I called.

"Those jokers put up a helluva fight," she said. "But yeah."

When she and the others emerged from the water, I could see their battle wounds. Raked and gouged flesh seeped thick, clear blood. I also saw that they were carrying another merfolk. He was smaller than them, leanly muscled. The orbs of his eyes stared skyward, while black blood oozed from an earhole.

Hurt teammate?

Gorgantha dropped the merfolk at my feet. "Meet Finn," she said.

I looked from the Stranger to the four merfolk arrayed behind Gorgantha. I was no expert in merfolk behavior, but their hulking body language told me they wanted to stomp Finn to jelly in the worst way.

"Would you guys back off?" Gorgantha snapped at them.

As they withdrew, I uttered, *"legare,"* channeling the energy into binding the Stranger's wrists and ankles. Seay walked up, fae enchantments radiating from her hands, ready to let loose. I took a moment to study the Stranger: the maverick cut of his face, the thick shoulder-length hair—a feature that probably looked even more impressive underwater. Demon X had fashioned Finn well.

But why merfolk?

"Where did you find him?" I asked.

"He was cowering behind a sunk boat like a li'l bitch," Gorgantha said. "Sent his goons up to grab us, so he could work his mojo in the water. Good thing I got to him when I did. My sisters were thrashing him good."

One of the merfolk who had been staring down at Finn stepped forward.

"Girl, back *off*," Gorgantha said. "We'll deal with him when we deal with him, but we need some info first."

Jordan limped up on his quarterstaff, Malachi beside him.

"Are you all right?" I asked the druid.

"So, this is the Stranger," he remarked, ignoring my question.

While he looked him over, I went back to considering why Demon X was targeting merfolk, half-fae, and druids. Why not humans, whose souls were more coveted in the Below? What was the payoff?

"You're not having second thoughts, are you?" Jordan asked.

I looked up, half surprised to see him directing the question at me.

"About blocking the connection to his master?" he added.

I didn't care for the challenge in his tone. The others were watching me too, Gorgantha and her pod, Seay. Malachi wore a troubled expression that seemed to pull his face from below. He, more than the others, knew how dangerous this would be. For several seconds I would be baring my soul to a powerful demon master. And that was several seconds too long.

When I spoke, I hoped no one else could hear the dryness in my mouth.

"Let's do this," I said.

8

G organtha had spotted a defunct yacht club from the harbor, and she led the way overland, the Stranger slung over her shoulder. The rest of us followed save Jordan, who was scouting the area ahead as a raven. Several species of baddie still inhabited the defunct parks, especially at night, and we didn't need anything jumping out at us.

"Are you sure about this?" Malachi asked between breaths.

We were having to hustle to keep up with Gorgantha. I ran with a stilted gait, one hand bunching up my coat in front in a futile effort to keep the potions in my pockets from knocking together.

"I have an obligation to the Upholders." I panted. "Have to at least try."

Malachi glanced over a shoulder. After wrapping Finn's mind in an enchantment, Seay had taken the anchor position, her eyes gleaming with fae light as she scanned the trees to either side. "Yeah, I know," he whispered. "It's just that if something were to happen, I'm not sure I could recover you from a demon master."

"Then I'll make sure you won't need to."

"Jordan has his reasons to push, but..." He looked up now to make sure the raven wasn't returning. "I'm afraid he pushes too hard sometimes, and in ways that could endanger the rest of us. Like now."

"I won't argue about the pushing too hard part, but he also has a point."

"What's that?"

"If we don't get a useful lead from Finn, we're screwed."

"There are my divinations," he offered.

"Granted, but you have no control over when they come, right? And we're pressed for time, not just for the sake of Jordan's wife and the rest of his druid circle..." I paused to catch my breath. "Or the half-fae. I mean, you saw what was left of the merfolk back there—almost nothing. All of that's important, but Demon X has a plan that involves these groups. One that's in motion, but we don't know jack about."

"To do with the demon apocalypse, maybe," Malachi said softly enough that he could have been talking to himself.

Beyond his dark eyes, I could all but see the visions he'd been having: wars, famine, pestilence, death. Though I remained skeptical that he possessed the ability to fully interpret the visions, I nodded to push my point.

"All the more reason to give this a go."

For several paces, Malachi didn't say anything. Once more, he struck me as young, and I felt a strange responsibility for him, as if he were my kid brother. When the first slivers of a cold rain began to fall, I invoked a shield to keep us dry.

"Is there someone I can contact if you need help?" he asked at last.

"Already covered," I replied, which was sort of true but mostly not.

Before making the trip to Staten Island, I'd called Claudius, my liaison to the Order. If he didn't hear from me again by six tomorrow morning, he was to alert the senior members of the Order. The only problem with the plan was that no one had heard from them in more than a week. They remained in the Harkless Rift, defending it from further demon incursions while repairing the rip.

For all intents and purposes, I was on my own up here. I hadn't even been able to contact my teacher, Gretchen—a fae-touched eccentric who wanted as little to do with this world, and me, it seemed, as possible.

"All right," Malachi said, "but going back to what I said earlier, don't be afraid to push back. We can't let him—" He flinched from a sudden batting of wings.

"Push what back?" Jordan asked, dropping beside us.

Before Malachi could answer, I said, "Just discussing some personal stuff."

"Shouldn't your head be in this?" He nodded at the Stranger slung over Gorgantha's shoulder.

"Jordan..." Malachi began.

"It's fine," I said. Though I was only going to be able to tolerate so much of the druid's brow-beating, this wasn't the time or place to have it out. Malachi must have decided the same, because he fell quiet again.

Jordan looked between us sternly. "I thought you'd want to know it's clear ahead."

Before we could respond, he picked up his pace to catch Gorgantha. Beyond the trees, the yacht club leaned into view. Even in its sorry state, it would give us shelter from the elements and a quiet spot for me to cast.

We entered the club through a missing door on the harbor side, where million-dollar boats had been blown helter-skelter or else rested in brown, half-drowned states. Passing through a trashed bar and dining room, we arrived in a large rotunda room at the club's center. Though the carpet was spongy, the floor was clear and the circle of windows high overhead intact. Rain smacked against the thick glass.

"This is good," I said.

Gorgantha stopped in the center of the room. "Want me to drop him here?"

"Hold on a sec," I said. "Just need to grab a couple things."

I made a sign in the air, and a platter-sized void opened from our dimension onto a parallel one. The cubbyhole was a place where I could store reference books and inert implements instead of having to port them across the city—one of a handful of useful tricks Gretchen had taught me. If only she were present more than absent.

My hand closed around a trio of folded polyethylene sheets. I removed them and a book on summoning in case I needed to consult it. I shook the largest of the sheets open in the center of the room to reveal a casting circle that I'd prepared that afternoon using copper filings and common glue. Jordan looked at the sheet askance. Druids carried an innate aversion for the unnatural, but the synthetic sheet's thinness and ability to cut and shape with scissors coupled with its durability were hard to top.

"In the middle," I told Gorgantha, sweeping its surface clean with a force invocation. "His head goes on this end."

She set Finn down on the sheet, straightening him until he was fully contained inside the circle. I shook open a second sheet, the circle that I would be sitting inside, and gave it a quick blast too. I'd learned the hard way that stray material could be hazardous. Stray people, too. The fewer inside the room during the casting, the better.

"Once this starts, I'm going to be vulnerable," I said. "The smallest interruption could land me God knows where, so I'm going to assign you each a sentry position to keep an eye on the building, make sure nothing gets in. Gorgantha, would you mind joining your pod in the harbor? Seay, I want you on indoor patrol. Make sure nothing's already here." Though they both nodded, I still wasn't entirely comfortable playing leader and giving orders. Especially as I turned to Jordan. "Can you watch from the air?"

"I'm staying here."

Irritation gripped my neck. "Why?"

"I want to make sure you ask the right questions."

"I know what questions to ask," I said, trying to keep a calm voice. "We went over this in planning."

He crossed his arms. "I said I'm staying."

"Jordan, this is important," Malachi put in softly.

"So why didn't Croft stick you on patrol?" Jordan asked him.

"Because he's staying here," I said. "I need his powers of exorcism."

I held Jordan's stern gaze until, in a burst of dusty magic, he took flight as a raven and disappeared from the rotunda room. Gorgantha and Seay exchanged glances before heading for the exits themselves.

"Good luck," Seay said, flashing a smile back over her shoulder.

"Just holla if you need us," Gorgantha added, tapping the bonding sigil on her hand.

"Thanks, guys."

When they left, Malachi blew out his breath. The tension in the team clearly predated my arrival, and it originated from Jordan. Probably for the delicate situation with Jordan's wife, no one wanted to stand up to him. I shook out the third synthetic sheet and set it about three feet behind my own.

"I'm going to have you back here," I said.

Malachi nodded and lowered himself until he was kneeling in the center of the protective circle, Latin Bible clamped in both hands.

I looked over all three circles now and their powerful sigils. Aiming my sword, I spoke softly. One by one, the circles lit up with power. As an added precaution, I drew a vial of slick wizard potion from a coat pocket. Suspended bits of crystals super-heated at my word, turning the potion from gray sludge into a steaming green liquid. I swallowed it in three gulps, then set the empty vial aside along with my folded coat. Cold air hit my sweat-damp shirt. I stepped inside my protective circle, where the entrapped air had already begun to warm.

"If you see me in any kind of distress," I said to Malachi, "start the exorcism."

He nodded uncertainly and held his Bible closer to him. "I'll do my best."

As I lowered myself, I could feel the potion taking effect: an oily film was beginning to slick my skin. Something similar was happening on a soul level. In the event of misadventure, it would make me that much harder to grab. Depending on the power of Demon X, that would either buy me seconds or frac-tions thereof.

"Ready?" I asked Malachi.

"Yes. Be careful, Everson."

As I closed my eyes, I saw Vega and our little sweet pea and experienced the stabbing sense that I was taking way too big a risk. But my magic was also talking, suggesting the risk carried a big payoff.

Pushing both thoughts aside, I began to incant.

––––––––––––

I OPENED MY EYES TO A WATERY BLACKNESS, MY BODY WEIGHTLESS, suspended. My first instinct was to stroke upward, but I didn't have to. I could breathe. Centering myself, I uttered, *"Iluminare."*

Light swelled from the end of what I'd thought was my cane,

but I was clutching an actual staff, long and knotted with a beautiful white stone at its end from which the light radiated. In my other hand, I gripped a silvery sword, its sequence of runes more ornate than the ones etched down the side of the blade from my father.

I'm in a parallel plane, I thought. *Somewhere between my realm and the demonic.*

And outside the bonds of the material, I was seeing everything in its truer form. I willed the crackling orb of light out further. As I did, something emerged from the darkness ahead of me. I kicked backwards before recognizing the large floating thing—more by its position than its appearance.

Finn.

The Stranger was lying on his back, arms across his chest, just as Gorgantha had arranged him. But he wasn't the handsome devil from the surface. No, down here he was one of the monsters he'd changed the merfolk into, only more gruesome. A jutting shelf of lower jaw dominated his face, its crowd of fangs jabbing toward his forehead. His body was a mosaic of ragged, battle-scarred scales. Back at his mouth, long catfish-like tendrils writhed from the motion of the water. Beneath a flutter of ragged hair, Finn's empty eyes stared upward, his mind still wrapped in the fae enchantment.

I ventured nearer and searched until I spotted what I was looking for. Starting at the back of Finn's neck, a thin cord twisted away into the inky blackness below: his connection to Demon X. The cord was translucent, and I could see thin currents of sulfur-yellow energy slipping back and forth inside.

Like an astronaut on a spacewalk, I had conjured a similar tether between myself and my protective circle. After testing it with a few gentle tugs, I maneuvered until I was beneath the Stranger. Severing Finn's cord was out. I didn't wield that kind of power. Few did. And any attempt to do so would only alert

Demon X. Instead, my plan was to send enough obscuring magic into the connection to scramble the signal. Then Finn and I would have our Q&A until the magic wore off.

Assuming this works...

Picking a spot on the cord, I aimed my sword at it. *"Oscurare,"* I whispered.

Magic trickled down the idealized blade and wrapped the demonic cord in a shadowy discharge. Through a kind of osmosis, the magic began to seep inside the cord. So far, so good. Though the slowness of the process was painful, I couldn't force it, couldn't risk broadcasting what I was doing.

Just a little at a time, I thought as I invoked again.

My magic, my unfiltered essence, was entering into direct contact with demon essence. Something powerful and watchful could take advantage of that. And down here, there would be little I could do to stop it.

As I counted down to the next dose, I caught my thoughts drifting back to Vega and our child. Who *did* I have a greater responsibility to? The Upholders, or my family? Could I even separate the two groups? After all, were I to ditch my work here, Vega and Tony would lose their places at the safe house.

And Arnaud's still out there...

The bloody image of Blade and the vampire hunters' apartment jagged through my thoughts.

Above me, Finn's body jerked.

My heart pounded as his arms came off his body and his tail flickered. A reflex? Inside his cord, the sulfur-yellow currents were damming up behind my obscuring magic, only slipping through in threads. Still, I was two doses from finishing the job. I whispered one of them quickly and waited.

Finn's next jerk was a thrash. A wall of water pushed against me, but it was arriving from below. I peered between my kicking feet. Something was surging up from the blackness. Something massive. I made out a pair of coal-like eyes. They radiated heat, hatred. And they were growing larger.

Demon X.

I rushed the final dose of obscuring magic into the cord and shouted, *"Ritirare!"*

The cord that anchored me to my protective circle tugged to bring me home. At the same moment, a hand closed around my sword wrist. Finn had turned over and seized me. A large grin showed beyond his writhing tendrils.

"Oh, do stay," he hissed through his mass of teeth. "We've been wanting *so* badly to meet you."

Below me, the approaching eyes grew to the size of footballs, their light illuminating the contours of a kraken-like face. I kicked frantically. A pair of massive jaws yawned wide. I struggled to bring my sword around, but the arm was still in Finn's grip. My gaze went to the cord trailing out behind his neck. The demonic flow was a gossamer thread now, filing through one cell at a time.

Work! I thought at my magic.

The flow stopped. Beneath me, Demon X stopped too. His furnace-like eyes searched the darkness. With the connection blocked, he could no longer see or sense us. His monstrous form circled the depths.

Finn's smile shrank. "Master?" he called.

I spoke a Word, and the sword's banishment rune glowed a brilliant white. Finn shied away, his grip faltering from my wrist. With the help of the slick wizard potion, I yanked my arm free. The cord to my protective circle did the rest, retracting me like a supernatural winch, drawing me back to Staten Island.

9

I jerked upright with a grunt, my face cold with sweat, heart slamming in my throat.

The rotunda room. I stared around. *I'm back in the rotunda room of the yacht club.*

I was sitting cross-legged in my protective circle, but the entire room seemed to be rocking up and down and side to side. Still gripping sword and staff, I pressed my fists to the floor to stop the motion. Malachi was standing behind me, reciting the first lines of the exorcism. He broke off.

"Everson?"

"I'm all right," I rasped. "I'm back."

I expected him to be leaning this way and that to keep his balance, but he wasn't. The motion was my own vestibular system working overtime to transit from a watery medium back to a solid one.

"You were struggling," he explained.

"Was I?" I grunted out a humorless laugh. "It was a close shave, but the Stranger's quarantined."

The room vacillated a final time and then steadied. I turned from Malachi's concerned eyes to Finn. His body remained in the glowing casting circle, wrists and ankles bound. Though he looked like a merman again, eyes staring upward, lips angled in a rakish grin, I couldn't help but see him as the horrid monster I'd just encountered.

"We don't have long," I said, imagining the sulfuric currents damming up around the blockage.

I incanted, igniting a pair of sigils on either side of Finn's head. I'd constructed the circle not only to contain the Stranger, but to get him talking. It meant a bigger energy cost, but resorting to threats like I had with Despus would have been too time consuming and with no guarantee of results. As I continued to incant, the light from the sigils spread over Finn's head, covering it in a caul that in magic circles was known as a mirage mask.

His body jerked.

"Finn, can you hear me?"

"Yes, master," he answered.

Good. The mirage mask was designed to convert sensory stimuli into the illusion that the wearer was engaging someone in authority. It sounded like Finn had gone straight to the top brass. Just as I'd hoped.

"Tell me my true name," I ordered.

"Y-you said never to speak it."

"I'm telling you to speak it now."

"You threatened me with eternal torture if—"

"*Speak it!*" I shouted.

Finn hesitated. "Is this a test, master?"

I could feel his resistance, dammit. If I pushed too hard, the illusion would come apart, mirage mask or not. That was part of why I'd wanted Jordan outside for this part. Subtlety wasn't his strength.

"Very good," I said, swearing inwardly. "You have passed."

The Stranger's body relaxed. "I am sorry the wizard escaped my hold."

"We needn't worry about him right now," I said. "What of the merfolk?"

"They laid a trap. A group was there, the wizard and some others. I couldn't pull our forces back in time. Many were slain. We will have to wait for another opportunity to seize them."

"I need an army," I said, testing my theory.

"Yes, but merfolk are scarce. We can search the waters further south?"

"What did I tell you?" I demanded, as though challenging his memory.

"T-to remain close to Manhattan."

And why would that be? I wondered.

I scoffed. "Do you remember the next step?"

"You've given no orders beyond claiming the merfolk."

"Then don't presume anything."

"No, master."

"And the others?"

"Others?"

"The ones like you."

"The Four? I'm never to speak of them either."

Four? There were four *Strangers?*

"I've lost contact with them," I said.

"All of them?" Doubt crept into Finn's voice.

Distracted by our limited time, I'd stupidly said the first thing to come into my head. Losing contact with minions was a sign of weakness, something a demon master would never confess, least of all to an underling. I could either back-scrabble or press on, and there wasn't time to back-scrabble.

"I'm taking you into my confidence, faithful servant."

"Yes, master." I could hear the hunger in his voice. Trust meant promotion.

"Someone is trying to frustrate our plans. I suspect magic."

"Perhaps the wizard?" he offered. "And there were others with him."

"Perhaps. Do you have a way of contacting the others in the Four?"

"I've not seen them since you separated us."

Damn.

"I did ask *Myss-u-traal-slaagth* where she was being sent," he babbled on. In his eagerness to please me, he'd slipped up and uttered a demonic name. I locked it away. "She wouldn't tell me, but she did say the question wasn't *where* she was being sent."

"What did she mean?"

"I-I don't know, master," he confessed.

"And what about the druids?" Jordan asked, striding into the room. "Who is with them?"

The son of a bitch had flown out only to slip back in. Who knew how long he'd been standing outside the rotunda room.

"Master?" Finn said.

I waved for Jordan to back off, but he continued forward.

"The druids," he repeated. "Where were they taken?"

"Who are you?" Finn demanded.

I sensed the illusion coming apart, and not because the magic that quarantined the Stranger was tapping out, but because of Jordan's bull-headed move. Power swirled around the end of his quarterstaff as he advanced. Malachi left his protective circle to head him off. I pushed more power into the mirage mask.

"Did you talk to the others of the Four?" I asked Finn.

He began to jerk, trying to escape his confinement. The jig was up.

"Listen to your master," I ordered in an attempt to bring him back.

He stopped and seethed, "You're not my master. You're that *wizard*."

I felt the pent-up demonic energy in the cord tremble and then break through my obscuring magic. Finn's back arced fiercely until only the top of his head and the ragged fins of his tail contacted the floor. Smoke began seeping from his body. Jordan and Malachi stepped back. Finn screamed as dark-yellow fire burst around him. As the flames washed over the hardened cylinder of air, I could feel their heat, their *anger*. When the flames vanished, all that remained of the Stranger was a scattering of gray ashes.

Demon X had reclaimed him.

With a series of words, I broke the circles. The smoke dispersed in a foul gust. I stood slowly and sheathed my sword back into my cane.

"So what did you learn?" Jordan asked me, standing too close.

I had expended a ton of energy and was physically, mentally, and magically spent. When I answered, it was more in weariness than the anger I felt. "Less than I would have if you hadn't barged in."

"I *barged in* because you were making a mess of the interview."

"Thank God you came then," I said, meeting his gaze. "Tell us, Jordan, what did you learn?"

His jaw line hardened. "You think this is a game?"

"Guys," Malachi said, trying to restore the peace.

"No, I don't think this is a fucking game," I said. "I risked my life to get him talking. As a minion, he has scant information— it's like looking for scraps of meat on a bone—but I was finding them. Then you came along and snapped the damn bone over your knee. And now look." I gestured at the ashes. "So, yeah, excuse me for being a smartass, but I'm not real happy with you right now."

When I turned away, Jordan grabbed my arm. "You're not happy with *me*?"

I could put up with a lot of things, but being handled wasn't one of them. I wheeled toward him. "No," I said. "And if I wasn't so sympathetic to your situation, I'd be playing tether ball with your raven form."

Jordan brought his quarterstaff into both hands. "I'm right here, buddy."

"Guys," Malachi tried again.

"You brought me in as an authority on demons, right?" I said.

"*He* did." Jordan cocked his head at Malachi. "And now I'm really starting to wonder."

I'd had my next response prepared, which was, *Then let me do my job*, but his retort effectively short-circuited it. When the sigil on my hand began to pulse, I realized Malachi had activated it to call the others. Jordan glanced at his too. A moment later, Seay raced into the room trailing fae light.

"Is everything all right?" she asked, peering from the circle with the Stranger's ashes to us.

"It's done," I said, taking a final look at Jordan. "I was able to score a little info."

"Oh, yeah?" she said.

"Let's give Gorgantha a chance to get here," Malachi said.

"She and her pod took off after another group of mercreatures," Seay said. "What happened to Finn?"

"Demon X recalled him," I said.

"So that's it? He's gone?"

Jordan grunted. "Until Croft decides to tell us different."

I ignored his dig and began cleaning and folding up the polyethylene sheets. After checking to ensure no magic lingered on them, I conjured my cubbyhole and stowed the sheets away along with the reference book I'd pulled.

"You said you scored some info?" Seay asked as I finished.

"Finn revealed the true name of one of the Strangers," I said. "I don't know which one—there were four according to Finn, but—"

"So what good is that?" Jordan interrupted.

I resolved to manage my temper by slipping into my professor's voice. "Knowing a demon's true name doesn't give one absolute power over it, as many stories would have you believe. Otherwise, demons would never share that info with their underlings. But the names carry enough power to act as focusing objects. Indeed, demons use them as an efficient way to locate one another for communications and councils."

"How does that help *us*?" he pressed.

"With the demon's true name, I can track it."

The hard muscles in Jordan's face let out as understanding sunk in. The Stranger in question could be the one who had infiltrated his druid circle and possessed his wife. He nodded in what seemed readiness.

"Then what are we waiting for?"

"It's going to take time," I cautioned. "But I'll get started on it right away."

10

I t was after two a.m. by the time I got back to my apartment. I shucked my coat, immediately losing twenty pounds, and tried to hang it gingerly on the rack. The potions clinked anyway. Tabitha, who was curled in her usual spot on the window-side divan, peered over and let out a monstrous yawn.

"How did it go?" she asked.

Ever since joining the team at Epic Con, she seemed more interested in what I was up to.

"Under the circumstances, okay. Might have a new lead. Thanks for asking. I was sure you were going to tell me how badly I reeked."

"I was getting to that."

I pulled off my mud-caked boots, scratched my big toe through the sock only to discover it didn't itch anymore, and padded to the kitchen. "I'm gonna make coffee. Can I heat you up some milk?"

"Coffee? At this hour?"

"I have some more work to do."

"Darling, you've been working for two days straight."

"Just need to check in on my golems, then figure out a hunting spell for a demon's name."

"And before you know it, the sun will be shining through the windows, and you'll be off on some other errand. I know I give you shit—and yes, you reek horribly—but I can also smell your exhaustion. You need your rest, darling."

I looked down at the jar of Colombian dark roast in my hand. The words on the label blurred in and out of focus, and for a second I could have sworn the woman bearing the basket of coffee beans winked at me.

Damn, Tabitha was right. But I'd made a promise to the Upholders.

And Arnaud is still out there, a voice nagged in my head. That got me thinking of Vega and Tony.

"Any calls?" I asked.

"No, but you did have a caller."

"A caller?"

"Someone came to the door shortly after you left."

That would have been after 11:00 p.m.

"Who?"

"How should I know? I never answer the door."

I double-checked my phone to make sure there were no missed calls or messages.

"But I was curious," Tabitha added in her teasing voice. "So I went out onto the ledge. See? I don't *always* need your prodding and guilt-tripping to get me to go out there. Anyway, I arrived outside in time to spot a delicious young man leaving the building and getting into a burgundy car."

The car's description set off a chain of associations. "Glasses?" I asked, closing the phone again. "Short hair? Dark complexion?"

"Why, yes. Who *was* that scrumptious morsel?"

"I'm pretty sure it was Vega's younger brother, Carlos."

"I thought the odor at the door was rather like hers," Tabitha mused. "But why come here?"

I was considering the same question. Had he learned about her pregnancy? Or was he following up on our meeting from the week before, the one where he and his brothers had told me to stop seeing their sister? Either way, it was one more hassle to deal with on time I couldn't afford. Tabitha watched me with an arched brow. I hadn't told her about the pregnancy yet and had no plans to open that can of worms.

"No idea," I said.

I brought a scoop of coffee to the maker and missed entirely. Coffee grounds spilled everywhere.

"Dammit," I grunted.

"Take it as a sign, darling. You're in no condition to cast."

Still swearing, I pulled the small broom and dustpan from the closet.

"Leave it," Tabitha said, thudding down from the divan and sauntering over. "I'll clean it up." She came around behind me and began butting me from the kitchen with her head. "Get some sleep."

I had it in mind to resist, but my sore, magic-spent body yielded to her blows.

"Why are you suddenly so interested in my well-being?" I demanded as I stumbled into the living room.

"What, I'm not allowed to care about you?"

"Since when?" I asked. "An hour ago?"

"You really are impossible sometimes."

This didn't sound like Tabitha at all. I stopped to face her.

"What's going on?" I asked.

She sighed and sat back. "It's this demon apocalypse talk."

"What about it?"

"If it does come to pass, they're not going to look kindly on a succubus who's been aiding and abetting a human for the last dozen years. I can only imagine the depravities I'd suffer under such a regime."

I looked from her forty pounds to the scatter of dirty plates and bowls around her divan.

"Yeah, I'm not sure your presence here quite reaches the level of 'aiding and abetting.'"

"Can't you be serious for once, darling. I'm scared."

"Look, I'm doing everything I can to make sure a demon apocalypse *doesn't* happen."

In fact, I needed to be casting on the demon's name like twenty minutes ago.

"*That's* what scares me."

"Gee, thanks." I headed for the ladder to my library/lab.

"Not the *you're doing everything you can* part," she said, trotting along beside me. "You've had some surprising successes, darling. Well, they've all been surprises as far as I'm concerned. But I've been around you when you're exhausted. Your magic's not as sharp. You overlook the obvious. And with you being the last line between me and what's coming..." She winced at the thought.

"It won't get to that point," I said.

The kinds of demons needed to trigger an apocalypse couldn't breach our world. In addition to whatever push they managed from the Below, they still needed a pull from above. A massive pull. And in the unlikely event people began worshiping a demon lord en masse, the Order would know well in advance. Once more, I questioned Malachi's vision, or the extent of it, anyway. I should never have mentioned it to Tabitha.

"Just a twenty minute rest," she was telling me. "I'll wake you up."

I stopped at the ladder and looked down to find her green eyes imploring me. She wasn't putting me on. She was actually scared.

"Are you feeling something?" I asked.

As a succubus, Tabitha sometimes reacted to infernal currents from the Below.

"Oh, the usual jostling for position," she said. "But underneath that, there's something else. I can't say what, but it's playing havoc with my hormones. I find I'm ravenous one moment and then want nothing more to do with food the next. When you mentioned milk earlier, I nearly vomited, darling."

I *had* been surprised when she snubbed the offer.

"And my existential dread tonight has been off the charts."

I peered up the ladder. The thought of climbing eight steps and then having to channel more energy made my vision blur again. If Thelonious hadn't suspended our agreement, I would have feared a visit from my incubus, but right now I was bothered by what Tabitha had said. Maybe there was more to Malachi's vision than I was giving him credit for. In which case, I couldn't afford to be foggy.

"Fine, I'll take a short rest."

"Praise God," Tabitha breathed. "Not literally," she added, peering around as if a demon might have overheard.

"Twenty minutes, no more."

I made a mental note to set my alarm anyway—Tabitha wasn't exactly reliable. But by the time I'd stretched out on my duvet, still dressed so as not to cue my brain that it was done for the night, I'd forgotten about the alarm. My head swam with a hyper kind of exhaustion that spoke to severe lack of sleep.

A moment later, I crossed the razor-thin veil into dreaming.

I WAS STANDING IN THE LIVING ROOM OF MY APARTMENT, WARM sunlight shining through the tall bay windows. A mug of fresh-brewed coffee steamed in my left hand. I took a sip, but only upon lowering it again did I notice the hefty little parcel in my other arm. A surprised laugh escaped me.

"Well, hello there," I said.

My daughter smiled up at me, her thick four-month-old legs kicking from a cloth diaper.

"What's got you so happy this morning?"

She gurgled, then squinted as I leaned in to touch my nose to hers. I inhaled her new-baby smell and blew a raspberry against her stomach. That got her squealing. I held my mug well out of range of her powerful legs.

"Do you want me to take kiddo or coffee?"

I turned to find Vega watching us with one of her forbearing smiles.

"You know the rules," she said, walking up. "You can't hold both if you're going to roughhouse."

"Hey, she's the one roughhousing."

"Is that true?" Vega asked her. "Are you being a little troublemaker?"

"Be honest," I whispered near our daughter's ear. "Your mom's a cop, and a darned good one."

She cooed in answer, which made Vega break into laughter. Tony, engrossed in a book he'd sprawled out with on the floor, looked up and smiled.

"Here." I transferred her to Vega. "She's especially warm and cuddly this morning."

As Vega hiked her up her side like a natural mother, the sunlight gleamed off her wedding band. I caught myself remembering how anxious I'd been that this wasn't going to work out somehow. And now look at us.

I took another sip of coffee and turned toward the kitchen. "Can I get you a cup?"

Vega paused in her play. "That's all right. I'll get mine in a few."

"How about your partner there?"

"She's plenty riled up, thanks."

I chuckled. "That's our little..." My voice trailed off. That's our little *who*? What in the hell had we named her?

I turned to ask Ricki—not sure how I was going to explain that I'd forgotten our daughter's name—and stopped like someone had swung a sledgehammer into my sternum. The apartment was trashed, the walls soaked in blood.

"Ricki?" I shouted. "Tony?"

I looked around wildly for my wife, daughter, and stepson. But I wasn't in my apartment anymore. I was in the East Village walk-up where the vampire hunters had been squatting, and it was the night I'd found them slaughtered. But was it *their* blood I was seeing or... The sting of bile climbed my throat at the horrible thought Arnaud had gotten my family.

"Ricki!" I called again, my voice verging on a scream.

Behind me, something gurgled. *Please, don't be...*

I turned around and found a woman pinned to a wall. Not Ricki, but Blade. Arnaud had skewered her body with her own katana swords, thrusting one through with such force that its tip had punched into the neighboring bathroom. I fixed my gaze on Blade's sagging head, her scythe of pink hair disheveled and blood-spattered. I didn't want to see the full horror of what Arnaud had done to her. Not again.

"Blade?" I asked, my voice scraping from my mouth.

This time her head shuddered. Her battered face came up.

Alive? How is she alive?

"Croft..." she rasped.

"Don't move. I'm going to get you down."

I forced myself to look at her savaged torso. There was no way she had survived this. Regardless, I couldn't just start pulling blades. I needed to sedate her. I pawed along my belt for my cane, but it wasn't there.

"He has ... the scepter."

I stopped pawing. "What scepter?"

"It negates ... wizard bonds."

I remembered the gray salt the police had found in the apartment and my theory that it had been used to store an enchanted object. A scepter that negated wizard bonds? Fear climbed my throat again.

"Is that what he came here for?" I asked.

Her head nodded before slumping again.

"Blade?" I reached for her shoulder, then stopped, afraid I might hurt her. In my peripheral vision, I could see the shadows of Bullet and Dr. Z. Arnaud had displayed their mutilated bodies for maximum horror.

"I'm coming," she gargled. "Coming to help."

"No, Blade. Just rest here. I'm going to get my cane."

I finally touched her shoulder. It was bony and cold. Her head shot up. I flinched back, only she wasn't Blade anymore. Her hair fluttered in white curtains that seemed to absorb the scant light in the apartment and then send it out again, making the place seem more radiant, less awful. The woman's face was aged, wise, and familiar. After a brief search, her eyes focused on mine.

"Arianna!" I cried out in surprise.

I took a quick glance around. The apartment was still there, but blurred. Objects had become moving shapes that appeared on the verge of coming apart. Even so, the red-brown tint of blood remained.

Dreaming, I understood in relief. *I'm dreaming.*

And Arianna had contacted me before in my dreams. The senior member of the Order nodded slowly. When she spoke, her words arrived as if traveling through a thick medium or from a great distance. I could barely hear them.

"Trapped..."

"Where are you?"

"Harkless Rift..." Her lips shaped the words more than spoke them. *"Trapped..."* she repeated.

"What's happened?"

She lifted a bloodied hand—her body remained Blade's, the skewering swords floating and indistinct—and touched a finger to the center of my brow. Elder magic pulsed through me, flooding my mind with images. And in an instant, I understood. Arianna and the other senior members of the Order remained on the fourth plane. They had succeeded in repelling the demons and closing most of the rupture that Arnaud and the demon horde had arrived through, but when several members attempted to return here to help me and the other magic-users, a powerful force prevented it.

This explained why, even with her vast power, Arianna was barely coming through now. It also explained why Claudius hadn't heard from her and the other senior members in more than a week.

Trapped...

The word, the feeling of it, seized my throat in a claustro-phobic grip. I backed from Arianna's touch. The apartment continued to bend and blur, as if sitting on top of a watery medium. I grasped Arianna's shoulders before she could come apart.

There was so much I wanted to ask her, about the Strangers and this Demon X and what his ultimate ambitions were, but freeing Arianna and the rest of the Order felt far more urgent.

"What can I do?" I pled. "How can I help you?"

"Find Arnaud," she said.

"Arnaud? And then what?"

When she opened her mouth to answer, a torrent of water broke through her.

"Arianna!" I called, but I was caught in the flash flood and tumbling head over heels.

The roiling waters pummeled me, carrying me far away. When they finally settled, I found myself floating in the same dark emptiness from earlier that night, the place where I'd performed my magic on Finn. Only now I was without my magical implements, and a dark fear gripped my insides.

"Ritirare," I said.

The Word had returned me to the casting circle the last time, to safety. But nothing winched me in now. Instead, a deep grumble shook the black waters below. I'd awakened Demon X. Grunting, I kicked and pulled, desperate to make my way to a surface I couldn't see and return to waking.

But Demon X was coming.

I didn't have to look to see his furnace-like eyes or mouth of soul-rending teeth. The water was pushing against me in a powerful wall, and I wasn't going to escape this time.

Jaws crashed over me, tearing through flesh, sinew, and bone. My remains swirled into a black abyss.

And then I was a spirit.

Four figures lay around me, one at each of the cardinal directions.

The Four? I thought, remembering what Finn had told me. I strained to look up, to see their faces, but I was pinned. We began to rotate like a giant mill stone. Powerful energy crackled through our formation.

Demonic energy.

Something terrible was about to happen, and I couldn't stop it.

Not by myself.

Arianna! I cried.

11

W*ake up...*
        I remained rotating in the abyss with the other four figures, dark energy gathering around us in stacks upon stacks of storm clouds. I strained to move, to scream, to stop the terrible thing that was happening.

Someone's laughter rumbled like thunder.

Everson, darling, wake up.

This time, the words were accompanied by a head shove.

My eyes opened, and I rocketed upright. Tabitha, who'd been beside me, jumped back, then scrabbled to keep from falling from the edge of the bed. I panted as I peered around, one hand to my chest. The abyss and energy were gone. I was back in my bedroom, bright light coming through the window.

My gaze shot to the clock on the nightstand.

"I'm sorry, darling," Tabitha said, clawing her way back beside me.

"N-nine-thirty?" I stammered. "It's already nine-frigging-thirty?"

My panic blew apart the already-receding dream like a fan through smoke.

"I overslept too, it seems," Tabitha said. "But it just shows how much we needed our rest."

My flip phone chimed out a faint ring. I thrashed off the bed and into the living room. At my hanging coat, I dug my hands into the potion-crammed pockets, spilling several vials, until I found the device.

Tabitha appeared from my bedroom. "You see? You're perkier than I've seen you in days."

Please don't be Jordan, I thought. He was going to want to know if I'd gotten any info on the Stranger's name when I hadn't even begun the damn spell. If I'd started it last night instead of falling into a deep sleep, it could have been working for the past six hours. I relaxed slightly when I saw that the caller was Vega.

I opened the phone. "Morning."

"How did it go last night with the Upholders?" she asked.

"Not bad for a first outing." As I gave Vega a brief rundown, Tabitha leapt back onto her divan and settled into a mound. Above her, light slanted through the bay window and glowed through her orange hair.

The angle of light resurrected last night's dream of Vega and our daughter. I remembered the way the light had gleamed from her wedding band and how contented I'd felt. But now a cold hand gripped my stomach. The dream had shifted, hadn't it? I nodded. To the blood-soaked horror of Blade's apartment.

He has the scepter, she'd said. *It negates wizard bonds.*

"Everson?" Vega said.

I jerked back to the present. "Sorry, spaced out."

"You were talking about doing some spell work?"

He has the scepter. "Where are you?" I asked abruptly.

"At the safe house, but I'm about to head over to the office."

"Stay there."

She sighed. "We've been over this."

"That hunch about Arnaud having an enchanted object? I

was right. It's a scepter, and it negates wizard bonds. That would include the Brasov Pact."

"Where is this coming from?"

"I had a visitor last night."

"Who?"

"Blade."

"The murder victim?"

"She came to me in a dream. That happens sometimes."

"How do you know it wasn't just a dream?"

The truth was, I didn't. But I'd had prophetic dreams in the past, especially after combining a high volume of casting with a lack of sleep. The first part of the dream—me, Vega, and our daughter in the apartment—felt like a warning now. Everything I stood to lose if I didn't take Blade's words seriously.

"It wasn't a dream," I said, more sternly than I meant to. "You need to..." I took a deep breath. "Look, just trust me on this."

"What about the power of the interfaith house?"

"The pendant you're wearing will absorb it, sure, but the second you leave the house, that power starts to deplete. There'll be a point where it won't repel Arnaud. And, frankly, I don't know what that point is, especially with Arnaud gaining strength. I'm not willing to take that risk with you and..."

For a second, my mind scrambled irrationally for our baby's name.

"It?" Vega finished for me.

"Yeah, but the baby's a *she*."

"Do you have intel I don't?"

"Just something else you need to trust me on."

"Okay..." Vega turned serious again. "I can work remotely this morning, but at some point I'm going to have to go in."

"I understand, just give me time. That's all I'm asking."

"What are you going to be doing?"

"Casting a spell to track a demon's name. After that, I want to see if anything's come back on Arnaud." When I said his name, it returned to me in an echo, but in someone else's voice. Another part of last night's dream?

"Do you mean your ghosts and ghouls?" Vega asked.

"Ghosts and *golems*, but yeah," I said, the recollected voice fading from my thoughts. "I'll try to stop in later." Remembering Carlos's visit last night, I said, "Hey, have you told anyone about our sweet pea?"

"Not yet."

"No one in your family?"

"*Not yet* covers them too."

So apparently Carlos had tried to visit me for other reasons.

"Have you decided when you're going to tell Tony?" I asked.

"I'm not sure I understand the urgency."

"Well, once he finds out, he's going to have questions."

"You mean about us?"

That damned pulling-in again.

"I think you and I should have that conversation first," I said. "Don't you?"

"I think we're dealing with enough right now. I'd rather wait."

"Does this have to do with Tony's dad?"

I hadn't meant to blurt it out, but there it was.

"What?"

"I heard what Tony said when I was leaving yesterday, about his dad breaking promises—present tense. I was under the impression he was no longer in your lives." Though I was trying to sound like a concerned boyfriend, the odd angle in my voice suggested something else.

"I said he was no longer in *my* life."

I didn't have a transcript of the conversation that had taken place more than a year ago, but I was pretty sure she'd said *our*.

Instead of forcing that argument, though, I said, "But if he's in Tony's life, he'd have to be in both of yours, right?"

When Vega answered, I could tell her patience was thinning. "He calls on the last Sunday of the month to talk to Tony. *Tony*," she repeated for emphasis. "Sometimes the call gets pushed to the next month. That's what Tony meant by what he said yesterday. I'm not hiding anything from you."

"I didn't say you were."

But there was still the part about him being a felon. She'd never mentioned that.

"Why just calls?" I asked, trying to sound casual. "Why doesn't he visit?"

"I'm done talking about him, Everson. You have a spell to cast, and I have work to do."

I swore at myself for pressing the issue and at such a terrible time. "I'll drop in later," I said.

"Okay."

"Love you."

"Love you too," she said, a little warmth returning to her voice.

I ended the call, then checked my voicemail. Three messages. The first two were from Jordan, brusque inquiries into my progress. The final message was from the youngest of Vega's brothers, Carlos.

"Everson," he said in a formal voice. *"I need to talk to you, preferably in person. Call me. My number is—"*

"Sure, buddy," I muttered, snapping the phone closed.

Vega was right. I had a spell to cast.

12

I pulled down a leather-bound book from my library and placed it on a wire stand in one of three casting circles I'd created, opening the book so exactly half of the pages rested on one side of the stand and half on the other. The book depicted the known planes of existence, its two-page center featuring the largest of the ink-drawn maps. Our Stranger could be hiding in just about any one of them after all.

Just hope we won't have to hunt the demon on foreign turf.

Hunting it on home turf was going to be challenging enough.

With a steadying breath, I lowered myself into a circle opposite the one that held the book. Between us, joined by casting lines, sat a third, much smaller circle. My magic hummed around the molecule-like arrangement, turning the circles and their various sigils from dull copper to the color of smoldering coals. Leaning toward the smallest circle, I uttered the guttural syllables that formed the Stranger's true name.

I felt the syllables hump along the casting lines and gather in the small center circle where they became tendrils of mist. *"Seguire,"* I whispered. Like an airplane toilet being flushed, the mist dropped from the circle with a sudden whoosh. The pages of the map book fluttered before settling back into place.

The hunt was on, but it would take time. Time I could use.

Sealing my circle off from the other two, I turned inward and focused on my four golems. Unlike with our Stranger, I had nothing with which to track Arnaud's current signature—no true name, no cellular material. Instead, the golems were operating off an image I'd instilled in their creation, a memory of my brief encounter with Arnaud in Container City the week before. I could only hope it was current enough.

I'd tagged the golems with names I could remember before setting them loose in the city. I found Golem 1, Archie, in the Hudson Heights neighborhood, near the northern end of Manhattan. Other than a few bullet holes, he seemed no worse for the wear. No matches to Arnaud's image, though.

"Keep at it," I told him, steering him south.

Next, I tuned in to Golem 2. "Well look at *you*, you little go-getter." Starting out in Battery Park, Veronica had already made her way up to the Lower East side, the flats I'd crammed her clay feet inside beating a fast rhythm along the sidewalks.

I left her to her search and aligned my mind with Betty, whom I'd put in charge of the west side. I found her pacing up Amsterdam Ave, the enchanted amulet that maintained her animation shifting beneath her blouse. A scan of Golem 3's memory revealed that she'd gotten into a couple of scrapes with cat-callers—her bruising fists had straightened them right out—but nothing matched to Arnaud.

Man. I'd known the golems were a long shot, but this sucked eggs. There was still my small network of ghost informants, but I couldn't consult them before nightfall. And given what I now knew about Arnaud's scepter, that felt like too long. Forcing my discouragement down, I tuned in to the final golem.

"C'mon, buddy," I whispered. "Tell me you've got something."

With more concentration than it had taken to access the others, I finally found Golem 4. He was sitting on a park bench, legs apart, arms stretched along the back, staring vacantly at a building across the busy street from Central Park. Judging from the bird droppings across his lap, he'd been there a while.

Oh, for the love of...

I tried to access his memory, but it was like wading through sludge. Had the energy in his amulet dropped out? No, I could still feel it pulsing away, feeding the animating magic. So, what in the hell was going on?

I spoke the words to reboot him.

"Vivere ... pulsare ... respirare ... levarsi!"

When he didn't stir, I shouted his name. "Jughead!"

A group of pigeons milling around his feet scattered, but the golem's gaze remained on the building across the street. The animated being was a composite of clay, black ash, grated mandrake root, and two splashes of my own blood. It was the blood ingredient that bonded us, and I concentrated into it now. If I wanted to get him moving and processing again, I'd have to go all the way in.

The floor beneath me lurched, and I started into a nauseating up-down, round-and-round motion. Seconds later, the journey was complete, and I was sitting on a park bench with bird shit across my thighs. I strained to move, but it was like being in a full-body cast. He *had* been sitting here a long time. Since last night, at least.

I finally managed to flex my shoulders and elbows, dry clay spilling from the joints. More clay broke from my knees as I stood. I was stooped over awkwardly, my back at a right angle to my hips. Pedestrians gave me a wide berth as I tottered toward a nearby trash can, braced my blocky hands against the rim, and forced myself up straight. A series of deep cracks sounded. Beneath my clothes, a small avalanche of dry clay cascaded down my back, forming a sizable load in the seat of my pants.

Oh, that's gonna look nice.

I shook as much of the debris from my pant legs as I could, then loosened up the rest of my rudimentary joints, finishing by grinding my neck back and forth. There. Jughead was free to continue his search.

I withdrew from him partway as a test, enough for his crude mentation to take hold. He plodded back to the bench and sat in the same position.

Dammit.

Even the most skilled magic-users ended up with duds in their golem batches—or so I'd read—and it looked like Jughead was mine. I was getting ready to recall the magic from him and have one of the other golems retrieve the amulet and kick his remains into the gutter when a realization struck me. The building he was staring at was the Ludwick, the premier hotel in the Upper East Side, if not the entire city.

A coincidence?

I took another wade through Jughead's memory, looking for —*there!*

The night before, he had seen someone leave the hotel. The diminutive figure was bundled in a trench coat, his head hidden by a fedora and scarf, but the way he moved—stooped and furtive—looked a lot like the creature I'd encountered in Container City. Jughead had sent me a signal as instructed, but it was during our pitched battle with the mercreatures. The signal hadn't penetrated my explosions of magic.

Jughead watched the figure climb into the backseat of a limo. The golem tried to pursue him in a taxi—I had given each golem several twenties and instructions on hailing and tipping—but the aging driver hadn't been game for a chase.

Having lost his target, Jughead dutifully took up a surveillance position on the park bench. He tried to signal me twice more, but that was after I'd returned home and fallen into a deep sleep.

Dud? Jughead was a damned prodigy.

I went back to the start of the memory. The figure stepping through the lights at the front of the hotel was a little taller than Arnaud had been, a little more upright, but that was to be expected. He was gaining strength.

Which means he's fed since your last encounter, a voice whispered in my head. *He's killed.*

I blocked out the macabre scene in Blade's apartment. Instead, I focused on the way the figure moved toward the idling vehicle. Everything was blurry in the golem's memory, but Jughead had discerned a quality in the figure's motion that suggested a match. I was inclined to agree. And what was he carrying in his left hand? A cane? No, too short.

It was a scepter.

"Stay there," I told Jughead. "I'm coming to you."

He had found Arnaud.

THE GOLEM WAS SITTING IN THE SAME SPOT WHEN I EMERGED FROM a cab twenty minutes later, his dull face aimed across the street. Pigeons scattered, several from his body, as I hustled up to the park bench.

"Has he returned?" I asked.

Jughead was bundled in Salvation Army attire, complete with a thick scarf and wool hat, so that only the gray skin around his sunken eyes showed. When he shook his head, I sized up the hotel's fortress-like facade. Arnaud had always appeared his most formidable when looking down on the city from his high redoubt, an expensive glass of scotch in hand. Something told me he hungered for that station again.

I searched the large windows on the penthouse level, half expecting to find a sallow face staring back at me. But I didn't. Neither did I experience the electric sensation of being watched by a vampire. That Jughead hadn't seen him return meant that Arnaud had either slipped in through another entrance or he was still away, maybe even rotating locations to keep people like me guessing.

Only one way to know whether he's in or out.

"Keep watch," I told Jughead. "Send a signal if he returns."

"Yes, master," he said in a deep, muffled voice through his scarf. I could have done without the "master" part, but the particular spell animating him was an old one, and it hadn't dated well.

With the first break in traffic, I dashed across the street and tuned into my ring. Beneath the power of the Brasov Pact, that of the interfaith community registered as a low hum. It had been almost twenty-four hours since my last visit to the safe house, and the ring was running at about three-quarters charge.

Enough for Arnaud?

With my dream about a scepter that negated bonds still haunting me, I had considered stopping over in Brooklyn on the way here to recharge the ring. But that was the problem. The safe house wasn't on the way here, and I didn't want to risk losing Arnaud's trail again. Plus, I wanted to keep this from Vega for now.

Though she maintained a good poker face, she was as afraid for me as I was for her. She would have insisted I have backup, preferably the supernatural variety, but who was there? The Order was in the Harkless Rift, the thought inducing a claustrophobic feeling for reasons that felt just out of reach. Gretchen was literally in faerie land. Mae and the goblin Bree-yark had volunteered their future help, but I had no plans to involve them against a being as powerful and sadistic as Arnaud. That left the Upholders, but I couldn't call them into this, not yet. The deal was Strangers first. Indeed, Jordan would have a shit fit if he knew I was chasing Arnaud and not hunched over the hunting spell back home.

That left my lookout man, Jughead.

A small force of armed guards manned the front of the hotel. They stood in pairs on either side of the doors in body armor, rifles aimed groundward. A fifth guard checked the credentials of those going in. It reminded me a lot of the scene at the old Financial District when the vampires ran the show.

Another reason to think Arnaud might be staying here.

I joined the back of the small line and scanned the guards in my wizard's senses to ensure they were fully human. When my turn came, I handed the guard my official NYPD ID and said, "I'm here on police business."

Two years ago I would have feared a rebuff, even rough treatment, but I was more powerful now. With my wizard's voice massaging his mind, the large guard nodded and returned my ID. I stepped between the two armed guards, entered the hotel's lobby, and headed to the reception desk. There, I repeated the same ceremony for an enthusiastic man in an expensive suit who introduced himself as Kyle.

"What sort of business?" he asked.

"There's a person of interest staying here, a man. Would have checked in within the last week. He goes by several names, so it's impossible to know which one he's registered under. He's about this tall." I held a hand to the top of my chest. "He walks quickly but a little stooped over. He left the hotel last night after midnight wearing a trench coat, scarf, and fedora hat. His voice might also stand out, sort of raspy."

Kyle had been frowning in concentration as I spoke, and

now he shook his head slowly. "No... I can't say any of our recent guests match that description. Do you know when he checked in?" He watched me expectantly, slender fingers poised over the keyboard of his sleek computer.

As doubt crept in, I consulted Jughead's memory again. The slinking figure, the fortress-like hotel, the armed guards, the short staff the figure had been carrying. I felt my magic nodding its head.

It was him. Had to be.

"Sir?" Kyle prompted.

"Are you sure none of your guests match the description?"

I pushed more power into the question until I felt it butt up against something: a fog of vampiric persuasion. My lips tightened into a bitter smile. As an additional layer of security, Arnaud had ordered the hotel staff to deny his presence.

Reacting to the collision of influences, the receptionist winced and brought his thumb and middle finger to his temples. Wizard and vampire juju didn't play well together.

"No, sir," he managed.

I probed deeper. He wasn't possessed, which was good, but it was going to be hard to purge him of Arnaud's influence without creating a scene. I slid my gaze to either side. The three other receptionists were occupied at the far end of the long marble desk. The rest of the lobby wasn't particularly active.

Fuck it, I thought.

Lifting my cane above desk level, I indicated the opal at its end. "See this stone?"

Kyle glanced at it. "Yes?"

"Take a closer look."

He leaned in stiffly. I had considered using my ring on him, but I didn't want to draw from the reserve of interfaith power. Instead, I whispered a Word. As the opal swelled with holy light,

I watched Kyle's face begin to wrinkle. Before he could draw back, I whispered, *"Liberare!"*

The sudden flash collided into the vampiric energy and knocked the man into a backward stumble. I blocked him with an invocation before he could crash into the mirror behind him. Rebounding forward, he steadied himself against the desk. A thin curtain of steam—the vampire essence—rose from Kyle's parted hair. The other receptionists looked over briefly before resuming their work.

"Are you all right?" I asked, lowering the cane again.

Kyle blinked several times. "Just got a little light-headed. I do apologize." He took another moment to gather himself, then straightened. "Now, how may I help you, sir?"

It was as if the last two minutes hadn't happened. I repeated my description of Arnaud. This time he nodded almost immediately.

"Yes. Mr. Grimes. He's staying on the penthouse level." He retrieved a keycard. "I can show you up if you'd like?"

13

K yle and I stepped from the elevator and into an ornate corridor with a Persian runner extending its length. Overhead, enormous chandeliers dripped with crystals. I hadn't wanted the receptionist to escort me up, but he'd insisted. I could tell the idea of being involved in a police investigation excited him.

"His are the two doors on the left," Kyle said importantly. "He asked that his room not be cleaned or serviced except at his request. He was very specific about that."

"I appreciate all your help. I can take it from here."

"Oh. Are you sure?"

"Yes," I said firmly.

Kyle dipped his head like a chastised puppy's, handed me the keycard, and retreated back into the elevator.

"Oh, and one more thing," I said, pushing power into the words. "Don't tell anyone I was here."

Two could play at Arnaud's game.

I waited for the elevator doors to wall Kyle off and the elevator to begin its smooth descent before invoking a shield around myself and starting down the corridor. As I opened my wizard's senses, energetic currents bloomed across the corridor. The demons' passage through the Harkless Rift may have hidden them from detection, but they still left fleeting void trails like the ones I'd picked up in the gang's apartment.

Nothing here, though.

I slowed as I approached the first door, then stopped. There was a symbol, hidden beneath the doorknob. Pulsing with demonic energy, it had been crafted to detect entry and alert the caster, not unlike a minor ward. After checking for other protections, I touched the tip of my blade to the bottom of the symbol and incanted. A tiny white flare breached it, and infernal energy drained out, rendering the protection inert.

Go carefully.

Sliding sword back into staff, I aligned my mind to the interfaith power in my ring. Not wanting to take any chances, I pulled a stealth potion from my pocket, activated it, and downed half of it. When I felt the potion taking effect, I inserted the keycard and turned the handle. The door released quietly from the frame. With a trembling fist, I aimed the ring through the opening and pushed the door wider.

Nothing rushed out at me.

I peeked into a lavish open floor plan. Heavy gold curtains covered tall windows that overlooked Central Park, casting the penthouse in a kind of twilight. A musky scent hung in the air, recalling Arnaud's former penthouse office. But beneath it lay a subtle stench of sulfur and decomposition. I listened until I could hear the soft swish of blood in my ears, but nothing was stirring in the penthouse.

I stepped inside and rested the door against the frame behind me. Though I could sense subtle energies warding the windows, there were none in the open space. Leading with my ring, I crept around the arrangement of dark leather furniture and antiques, avoiding the rugs in case they hid other symbols.

At an oak bar, I noted bottles of vintage scotch and a small collection of empty glasses. Condensation had puddled around one of them and then dried save for a thin ring of moisture. Otherwise, the room was immaculate. The bedroom suite as well, the giant bed not even appearing to have been slept in. I caught myself scanning the pillow for hairs, even though any Arnaud had shed would have sublimated by now.

From the bedroom, I entered a large bathroom. Since the scene at Blade's apartment, I'd become ultra-sensitive to the scent of blood, and it was here, hanging in the air. I scanned the sinks, counters, and jacuzzi tub. All clean. Not a single corpuscle. On a hunch, I opened my wizard's senses. On the floor near the jacuzzi, the image of a smeared symbol grew into view. Blood-rendered, then wiped away.

A pow-wow with Malphas? I wondered. *Is that why Arnaud left here last night?*

I produced my small notepad from my coat and sketched the symbol. When I finished, I swapped the pad for my handkerchief and a small vial that contained a bonding potion. Arnaud's demonic matter might have sublimated, but if he'd created the symbol with ingested blood, I could track that.

I wet the kerchief with activated potion, then wiped the tile floor where the symbol had been. Not only would the potion pick up everything it contacted, it would help isolate the elements for later casting. Upon finishing, I placed the kerchief in a Ziploc bag.

Back in the main room, I considered my next move. I wanted to continue searching, but that would only raise the risk of Arnaud knowing I'd been here. When my gaze fell to a large rug covering the center of the floor, a flashbulb went off. I rolled it back to expose a section of bare carpet and grinned.

Perfect spot for a demon trap.

SIGNING INTO THE AIR, I RETURNED MY BOOK ON CASTING CIRCLES to the cubbyhole and closed it again. On the floor, the ornate demon trap glowed with my infusion of power. It wasn't as strong as the containment cell I'd warded at 1 Police Plaza, but it would hold Arnaud long enough for me to put him down.

I watched the circle until it began to dim, then very carefully arranged the rug back over the trap.

With my stealth potion wearing off, it was time to go. But I felt good. For the first time since his return, I had an advantage over Arnaud. Unfortunately, I also had Upholder commitments. That was the deal. I would have to pull in the other three golems so they could watch the remaining sides of the building. Fix it so any alerts they sent would be sure to punch through whatever I happened to be casting.

As I left, I stopped at the door and listened into the corridor. Footsteps, approaching from the elevator. My breaths quickened as I retreated into the penthouse, rounded the demon trap, and slipped into the bathroom.

"Oscurare," I whispered, deepening the surrounding shadows.

The footsteps stopped at the door. Arnaud? I imagined him studying the sigil. He would sense the drained energy, but would he see the small blemish? A moment later, the door opened. The footsteps that entered sounded cautious. I set my jaw as visions of Blade's blood-soaked apartment flashed through my head.

No screwing around, I told myself. *If Arnaud doesn't walk into the demon trap, you have to put him there. The ring will do the rest.* I checked the interfaith charge. Still hovering around eighty percent. More than enough.

The progress of the footsteps continued, then stopped

suddenly. I fixed my slick grip on my sword and staff. The foot-steps resumed, but around the edge of the room now.

Damn, he senses something. Need to push the advantage while I have it.

I slipped from my concealment, a force invocation readied.

In the main room, a cloaked figure spun toward me.

"Vigore!" I shouted.

No sooner than the word had left my mouth, I could see it wasn't Arnaud. The druid's quarterstaff flashed as it spun around and absorbed the incoming attack. He was preparing to sling it back at me when he saw who'd thrown it. Frowning, Jordan lowered his staff and discharged the energy.

"Everson," he said.

"What in the hell are you doing here?" I hissed.

"You weren't answering your phone. I tracked your bonding sigil to see if you were in some kind of trouble."

I sighed. "I'm fine, but we need to leave. Now."

He peered around the penthouse. "Is this where the Stranger's name led you?"

"How did you even get into the hotel?"

He made a flapping motion with a hand: his raven form. "I asked you a question," he said.

"Let's discuss it outside." This wasn't a conversation I was looking forward to. "Stay there. I'll come to you."

He had stopped beside the bar, and the last thing I needed was for the demon trap to close around him. But something was off. One of the cabinet doors on the bar had come open. Through the narrow opening, I spotted a sigil. The dark marking was sizzling softly, like fat in a pan.

"Get down!" I shouted.

I hit Jordan with a force flash, knocking him to one side. A split second later the entire cabinet exploded, smashing bottles and glasses and sending comets of infernal energy storming around the penthouse. One comet glanced off my shield with a searing hiss. From his back, Jordan repelled another with his staff. But we didn't seem to be their intended targets. The comets disappeared into the bedrooms.

That couldn't be good.

"What's going on?" Jordan called.

"Someone planted a magic-detecting sigil in the cabinet." I'd been extra careful to hold my aura in tight while moving throughout the penthouse and building the demon trap. The invocation I'd slung at Jordan, and that he dispersed, must have triggered the damned thing.

Jordan climbed to his feet and peered around. "What happens next?"

As if in answer, shrieks sounded from the bedrooms. Infernal bags. The sigil had been the trigger, but the bags were the true bombs. Arnaud's security was more layered than I'd given him credit for.

"Get ready," I said. "We're about to have company."

I activated the banishment rune on my sword, casting the blade in holy light. The air swirled around Jordan's raised staff. The first imps to appear were nasty things the size of vultures. They flapped through the high-ceilinged penthouse, all ragged wings and skeletal frames. Fang-crammed beaks opened in piercing screams.

Wincing from the sound, I swung my sword. The blade's holy aura smashed through the company, sending several of the imps to the floor in parts. Those that made it past my attack, veered toward Jordan. He met them with deft staff strikes, expulsions of energy blowing them apart.

I cleaned up the ones that circled back. But the next wave of demonic creation was already swarming in: spiny devils.

"Why aren't we bailing?" Jordan shouted. "The way is clear."

"Because these things are designed to kill on sight. *We* can fight back. The hundred-odd people staying in the hotel can't." I grunted into a swing, my blade cleaving a devil's head. "Don't let any past you."

"Aye, aye, Captain," he growled, punching his staff into a devil's gut.

I drew in a sharp breath as talons raked down my shielded back. The pain that broke through me was psychic, the reaction of infernal energy to my magic. Wheeling, I severed the creature's knotted spine above the hip. The devil collapsed in two parts, still struggling as it broke into a foul gas.

There must have only been two infernal bags because the imps and devils were thinning out. What remained were easy pickings. Until a devil ducked past Jordan. The druid's quarterstaff came around, but too slowly. Before I could stop it with an invocation, the devil was darting out the door.

Shit. I took off after him, hacking an imp from my path.

"Finish the ones in here!" I called to Jordan.

By the time I emerged into the corridor, the devil was almost to the elevator in the right wall. I watched in horror as the door dinged open. Someone had come up. I was already thinking Arnaud when a human shriek sounded, followed by a stammer of words: "Oh my dear Lord what is that thing?"

The voice belonged to Kyle the receptionist. I began shaping energy, but the devil was already lunging into the elevator—and being met by a solid fist to the jaw. The devil staggered back into the corridor, its spiny mouth hanging to one side. Jughead lumbered from the elevator, hands balled into giant fists.

Hell, yes!

My favorite golem landed a haymaker to the devil's gut followed by a roundhouse to the side of its head. Another blow sent the creature staggering toward me. I wasted no time running my blade through its back and speaking the banishing word. The devil came apart in gobs of phlegm. I sheathed my blade as Jughead lumbered up.

"You don't know how happy I am to see you," I said.

The golem nodded and lowered his fists. "Thank you, master."

"H-he told me he was with you," Kyle called from the elevator. "So I brought him up." The doors closed on his final word, and he headed back down. I couldn't blame him.

Jordan emerged from the penthouse, his cloak billowing around his legs as he ran up. He looked from me to the golem and back.

"Who in the hell is this?"

"Be nice. His name's Jughead."

"Jughead," Jordan repeated, staring into the golem's sunken eyes.

"Did you finish them off?" I asked, cocking a head back toward the penthouse.

"Yeah," Jordan said distractedly. "I think so." He stopped trying to figure out Jughead long enough to glower at me. "Do you want to tell me what we just fought—hell, what we're even doing here?"

"Sure, right after I neutralize the infernal bags."

I returned to the penthouse in a mope. I'd set the perfect trap, only for this to happen. I stared around the trashed space. Even if I could somehow put everything back to the way it was, there was the tripped sigil. Arnaud would know I'd been here.

The advantage belonged to the demon-vampire again.

14

"So this was a personal project," Jordan concluded, his voice thick with anger.

"*While* my spell is hunting the Stranger's name," I said. "Believe it or not, I can do two things at the same time."

We were outside, standing beside Jughead's hotel-facing bench. After neutralizing the infernal bags, I took closer stock of the damage to the penthouse. The imps had torn open a couple couches and rendered long gouges in the wall. And that was to say nothing of the oak bar having been blown to shit. Still, I left the demon trap under the rug on the very slim chance now that Arnaud would wander into it.

I'd had to use my wizard's voice on Kyle the receptionist to explain away the spiny devil he'd seen. I also reinforced the suggestion that I had never been there. It was the best patch-up job I could do, but now I had a ticked-off druid to deal with. A shame I couldn't use my wizard's voice on *him*.

"That wasn't the agreement," he said.

"My priority remains to the Upholders."

"And yet I found you uptown, sneaking around someone's penthouse who's *not* a Stranger." He shook his head. "I told

Malachi this was going to happen. I said, 'We make an exception for him up front, and he's going to get it in his head he can call in exceptions whenever he damn well pleases.'"

"Well, you're wrong."

"This was about getting your woman and her kid safe-housed, wasn't it?" He edged closer as he spoke. "That's all you care about. You couldn't give two spits about the rest of us."

Jughead had been following our exchange from the bench. Now, seeing the challenge in Jordan's posture, the golem's instinct to protect his creator kicked in. He rose, shouldered his way between us, and pressed a blocky hand to the druid's chest. Jordan responded by raising his quarterstaff.

"You better tell him to step the hell back," he said.

"It's all right," I told Jughead. "We're just having a professional disagreement."

"Professional nothing. Did you or did you not ditch the hunting spell to pursue your own demon?"

"I didn't ditch anything," I said. "The hunting spell is still ... hunting."

"Well, maybe it would help if you put some more of your focus into it, instead of into clay brain over here."

Jughead, who'd begun to sit down, straightened again.

"Hey, you don't want to mess with this," Jordan warned.

I showed Jughead a hand, spoke a silent command, and waited until he was sitting before turning back to Jordan. "One, a golem doesn't take much energy to sustain. That's what his amulet is for." I made a special point of not mentioning the three other golems in my service. "And two, if I put any more energy into the hunting spell, our quarry is going to know we're targeting her."

Jordan glared back at me.

"Look, the spell is working. We just have to give it time." I made another point of not telling him I'd only started the spell that morning and not last night as promised. "As for Arnaud, I understand where you're coming from. Yeah, he's my problem. But if I can get a jump on him, take him out, it'll mean one less demon in our world, and one less threat to anyone I'm associated with. Including the Upholders."

"Why can't your Order deal with him?"

"Because they're in the Harkless Rift, making sure no more..." I broke off.

There had been more to last night's dream. I watched Blade's face turn into Arianna's. *Trapped*, she'd said. *In the Harkless Rift.* Then she'd touched my third eye. The same claustrophobia seized me as I watched members of the Order attempting to return only to be repelled by an unyielding force.

"What?" Jordan asked.

"They're trapped."

"Who, your Order?"

"Trapped in the Harkless Rift," I said, already pulling out my phone and dialing Claudius. As the line rang, I turned away from Jordan so I could shift the remaining golems. I wanted Archie and Betty joining Jughead on stakeout, while Veronica, the go-getter, would begin a search of the upscale hotels. If Arnaud was changing locations, I was betting the one constant would be luxury.

"Yes?" an elderly voice answered.

"Claudius, it's Everson."

"Everson..." He seemed to search his memory despite that we'd worked together in person just last week. "Ah, yes, Everson Croft. How can I help you?"

"Any word from the senior members of the Order?" I asked hopefully.

Maybe it all *had* been a dream, as Vega suggested.

"Not since, ah, let's see..."

"Last week?"

"That's right, last week."

My hope deflated. "Well, I have good reason to believe they're trapped in the Harkless Rift."

"Trapped? That's not good. Why did you say it was good?"

"I didn't. I said I had good—never mind. Is there anyone you can think of, anyone at all, who can make the journey to check on them?"

"To the fourth plane?" He made a puttering sound. "Sure, but they're already there."

"That doesn't help."

"No, I don't suppose it does."

"What about you?"

"Me?"

"You can open portals to other dimensions."

"I can?"

I sighed. "I was there, Claudius. At the rock quarry? You were conjuring portals left and right, sending demons to all kinds of places." I remembered the way he'd shuffled around in his tinted lenses and long black hair. He'd looked like a confused rock star from a bygone era, but he'd been effective. "With some time and focus, can you open one to the Harkless Rift? Give the Order a portal to return by?"

"I don't know..."

"I need you to try. If they're trapped, they're in danger. Plus, we need their help up here."

Jordan had been watching my side of the conversation, a steep frown set in his face, but now he nodded in agreement.

"Well ... all right," Claudius said, sounding distraught. "I'll see what I can do."

"Please do."

By the time I ended the call, Jordan was looking less upset and more thoughtful. "Will he be able to reach them?"

The honest answer was *probably not*. With Claudius's failing mind, the scales that kept measure of what he remembered versus what he'd forgotten were leaning more and more to the detrimental side. I wondered how much longer he'd be able to answer phones even. But if I shared that with Jordan, he would see the Order's dilemma as one more thing I would shirk my Upholder duties to address.

"Possibly," I replied. Before Jordan could press the question, I said, "Hey, I'm heading back to my apartment to check on the hunting spell. I'll be sure to give you a status update."

"You said that the last time. I'm going with you."

"That's really not necessary."

"With all due respect, Everson, I think it is."

"I work better alone."

"Not this time."

His tone and expression told me the matter wasn't up for debate.

Just what I need, I thought, raising my arm for a cab. *Birdman here breathing down my neck.*

"Fine," I said as a cabbie spotted me and pulled over, "as long as we go halfsies on the fare."

"I don't like riding in cars. I'll follow you."

Jordan turned, bounded up the stone wall into Central Park, and disappeared inside some burnt brush. A moment later, a raven rose into view, dusty magic scattering from its batting wings. The raven cawed once and circled overhead. I looked from Jordan's raven form to Jughead, whose sunken gaze had returned to the hotel.

"Keep doing what you're doing," I called to the golem and climbed into the cab.

As the driver started south toward the Village, my thoughts returned to the senior members of the Order. If Claudius failed, what other options were there? Could *I* do anything to help? As though in answer, another fragment of dream floated up from my subconscious.

Find Arnaud, Arianna's voice said.

I turned around and watched the Ludwick Hotel recede down the street. Find Arnaud and do what? As I racked my brain, another caw sounded. I looked out my window and found Jordan gliding above the pedestrians on the sidewalk. His brown eye shifted from me to our direction of travel.

Stay on task, he was telling me.

Swearing, I forced myself to straighten.

"AFTER YOU," I SAID, HOLDING THE APARTMENT DOOR OPEN FOR Jordan.

He was back in his human form, but instead of entering, he remained in front of the threshold. The sigils at his temples glowed white as he leaned forward to examine the wards. Did he think I was leading him into a trap?

After another moment, he muttered, "Not bad," and stepped inside.

As I closed and bolted the door, Jordan stopped a few paces beyond the coat rack and peered around the industrial loft space. His gaze finally settled on Tabitha. She was awake, surprisingly enough, and peering back at him with what seemed caution. I braced for one of her insults, but she remained quiet.

That had to have been a first.

"My cat," I said offhandedly. "The lab is over here."

Tabitha's green eyes tracked us as we made our way toward the ladder, her ears more flattened than normal. And was her hair puffing out? I turned up a hand to her in question. Her gaze broke from Jordan, and she jerked her head for me to come over. I shook my own head no, but she insisted.

"It's just up the ladder," I told Jordan. "I'll be there in a second. Oh, and watch the casting circles. They're still active. Actually, best you don't touch anything."

While Jordan scaled the ladder nimbly, I made my way over to Tabitha.

"What's the emergency?" I asked.

"Who *is* that?"

"His name's Jordan. He's a druid."

"Well, I don't like him."

"You don't even know him."

"I'm getting one of my feelings."

"Yeah, and last night you were mooning over Vega's brother, who I can tell you for a fact is a royal d—"

Then it clicked.

When Tabitha had been with me for about a year, I'd taken her on her first walk with a cat harness. In Washington Square Park, she drew the attention of a gang of ravens. No doubt sensing her succubus nature, they started harassing her. Dive-bombing before veering away at the last second, tugging her tail, cawing and cackling in her ears. By the time we made it back to the apartment, Tabitha was a spitting, quivering wreck. From that moment on, she feared and abhorred the creatures.

"He's a raven shifter," I said.

Tabitha looked at me, horrified. "You brought a *raven* into my home?"

"It's not your home, is it? It's our home. And Jordan won't bother you."

"How do you know? He's one of those filthy creatures."

"Would you keep it down?" I whispered, glancing toward the lab.

Her voice went from scandalized to pleading. "You of all people should know my feelings on the subject."

"Look, I'll see to it personally that he doesn't shift."

"Well, I still don't have to like him," she pouted.

"Fine, just … don't like him quietly. We're in the middle of something important."

And the sooner I could satisfy Jordan that I was doing the promised work, the sooner I could get back to hunting Arnaud.

I left Tabitha in her sulk and climbed the ladder to the lab. I hadn't restored the veil over my library, and I found Jordan scanning the collection of tomes. Druids like him mostly drew their power from innate energies in nature, so the concept of spell books was probably a little foreign to him.

He turned from the floor-to-ceiling bookshelf to the casting circles, his face largely unreadable. In the far circle, the pages of the book I'd set on the stand were flipping back and forth between maps.

"Your hunting spell?" he asked.

"Yeah. It's broadcasting the demon's true name like a radio signal in search of a receiver."

"And when it finds it…?"

"The book will show us the location."

"Any idea how long that will take?"

"Honestly, no. It's a thick book, as you can see."

I expected Jordan to keep prodding, but he only exhaled his impatience. He had probably come here expecting to find that I either hadn't started the spell or that I'd gone about it half-assed. Having established that I was on the ball, I expected him to leave. Instead, he pulled the chair from my desk, turned it around, and took a seat facing the casting circles, his quarterstaff clasped between his knees.

Oh, you've got to be kidding me.

"You know what they say about a watched pot never boiling?" I asked. "Same is true for spells. I can call you when I get a hit."

"I'd rather watch."

When I realized I was grinding my molars, I stopped. "So, what are the others up to?"

"Gorgantha and her pod are still tracking the mercreatures," he said. "Malachi is taking care of church business. And Seay?" He shrugged a shoulder. "Your guess is as good as mine. I've never understood the fae, and it's not like her being half-fae cuts that mystery in two."

Finally, something we agree on.

My thoughts went to Caroline Reid, my former Midtown College colleague and crush. A half-fae herself, she'd ceded to her queen mother, married a fae prince, and made a permanent move to the faerie realm in order to cure her human father of cancer. A part of me had admired that while another part felt spurned, especially when she sacrificed her feelings for me in exchange for being allowed to help me against the vampire Arnaud. But that was ancient history. I had Vega and Tony now, not to mention a child on the way.

If Arnaud doesn't get to them first, a sinister inner voice whispered.

I looked over at Jordan, who'd gone silent again. He showed no sign of getting up.

"You're more than welcome to stay here," I said. "But I have some things to do this morning."

Instead of answering, he stared past me, his torso straightening. I followed his gaze to the casting circles. The page-flipping had stopped on one of the maps, and a spot of red light, similar to the kind that appeared on my hologram of the city, glowed on the left page. Jordan came up beside me as a foghorn sounded in my head: the signal the spell was done.

I clapped Jordan's shoulder.

"We have a hit," I said.

15

A nxious to see where the Stranger had turned up, I lifted the book from the stand—and groaned.

"What?" Jordan asked.

I consulted the maps before and after, making sure I was reading the location right. "She's in another plane. And wait, it gets better. She's not just *not here*, but *not now*."

"What in the hell does that mean?"

"The demon we interrogated last night gave us more than the Stranger's name. He claimed that when he asked where she was being sent, she said the question wasn't *where*. Now it makes sense. She meant *when*. She's hiding in a time catch."

"Time catch?"

"Every so often, a piece of our timeline splits off and gets trapped in another plane, preserved there."

I watched Jordan's eyes as he struggled to make sense of what I was telling him.

"So the Stranger went back in time?" he asked. "That's where she's holding the possessed?"

"Yes and no. The time catches don't exist in our continuum. They're completely separate. They begin, end, then start over, ad nauseam, until they collapse. The people inside have no idea they're in a catch. They live their lives as they would have during the period in question. Sort of like ghosts but with substance."

"How does that work for outsiders?"

"Visitors can come and go, as long as they're out before the catch collapses."

"So we can travel there," he concluded.

"Theoretically, yes."

"What do you mean 'theoretically'?"

"It requires powerful magic."

"Isn't that why we brought you on?"

"I'm not sure even Malachi knows why he brought me on, but this is beyond my abilities."

"Then how are the demons managing it?"

"Through a portal of some kind, evidently."

If Jordan had been impressed with my magic earlier, his expression told me his opinion was souring.

"I'd consult the Order," I said, "but with the senior members trapped..."

Find Arnaud, I heard Arianna saying. I pretended to search for a book in my library, using the opportunity to check in with my golems. Jughead was still at his sentry, Archie and Betty converging. Veronica was casing an expensive hotel on Fifty-eighth Street. I shifted my concentration to the demon trap. It was still resting beneath the rug, unsprung. I snapped from my trancelike state and turned to find Jordan touching the bonding sigil on his right hand and speaking in a low voice.

"What are you doing?" I asked.

"Your head's not in this. I'm calling the other members of the Upholders."

"Look, everything's connecting up: Arnaud, the senior members of my Order, accessing the time catch." I fought to control my voice. "This is going to require elder-level magic. No elders, no access. Got it?"

"Then we need to consider other options," Jordan said, completing the call-out.

The sigil on my hand glowed white, and a moment later, I felt its psychic pull tugging me to the very spot where I was standing.

"Wait, you're calling them here?"

"Is that a problem?" he asked.

I peered over the railing. In the living space below, Tabitha was nodding emphatically.

"No, that's fine," I said. "I just assumed we'd be going to the townhouse."

Tabitha stared daggers at me before turning her head away in disgust.

"This will save time." Jordan stared at the map the spell had locked on. "Is there any way to know what era we're talking about?"

"Could be one of hundreds. The only way to know is to find the portal the demons are using and follow it."

"We need to get there, Everson."

"I agree."

And hopefully the others would see the sequence of operations as I did: Arnaud, then Order, then time catch.

———

THE FIRST KNOCK SOUNDED WITHIN FIFTEEN MINUTES. I OPENED the door to find Malachi, who had been downtown at St. Martin's Cathedral. Seay arrived a couple minutes later wearing a sleek white coat down to a fashionable pair of pumps. She threw me a hip bump as she stepped into the apartment.

"If I'd known you were throwing a party, I would have put on something more appropriate," she said. "Like a sheer top and mini."

"I like to keep these things business casual," I said. "Any word from Gorgantha?"

Malachi shook his head. "Presumably still tracking the mercreatures."

But no sooner than he'd said that, the door shook with more knocking. A look through the peephole showed our six-foot-six mermaid standing outside in a hooded robe. I unbolted the door and ushered her in.

"We weren't expecting you," I said.

"Trail went cold around Governor's Island. We circled but couldn't find jack."

I nodded, considering what that could mean. "Well, we're all here. Why don't we convene in the sitting area? I'll, ah, grab some snacks."

When Tabitha saw the motley crew coming toward her, Jordan leading the way, she made a sound of revulsion, thudded to the floor, and squeezed out the cat door onto the ledge.

Malachi, Seay, and Gorgantha sat three across on the couch, while Jordan took the loveseat. I set out some plates, glasses of water, two sleeves of saltine crackers, and a canister of squirt-on cheese that I'd found in the back of the pantry and hoped was still good. I then settled into my reading chair opposite Jordan.

On cold days like these, I usually had a fire going in the hearth, but I'd been too busy to maintain the fireplace this season. Probably just as well given Gorgantha's sensitivity to dryness. I watched her brush salt from a cracker into her water, stir it with a finger, and then dab the saline solution onto her temples.

"As Jordan told you," I began, "the spell located the Stranger. Only she's not in our world. She's in what's known as a time catch."

For the next twenty minutes, I explained the phenomenon and answered questions, most of them coming from Malachi and Gorgantha. Jordan remained silent, tracking the conversation with his serious eyes. When everyone was up to speed, he shifted forward on the loveseat.

"The question now," he said, inserting himself into the role of speaker, "is how to get there. Everson says it requires powerful magic, but he's hyper-focusing on the senior members of his Order."

I bristled at his word choice. "If I'm *hyper-focusing*, it's because they're the only allies we have that wield that kind of magic."

Jordan looked around our circle. "Does anyone have another idea?"

Seay, who was squirting a swirly design of cheese onto her cracker, said, "The fae?"

"What about them?" he asked.

"My mother's a fae princess. It's not as impressive as it sounds—there are literally thousands in Faerie. The queens have like twenty concubines apiece. Anyway, I spent time in my mom's court as a kid. The fae tolerate half-fae until we outgrow our cuteness, which is to say around eight or nine. Unless we're powerfully connected, and I wasn't, we're dumped back here with our human parent. Almost always the father, who has no earthly idea what to do with us. Mine gave up after a few years."

Jordan gave an impatient grunt and circled his hand.

"What I'm getting to is that back in the court days, I had a best friend who was true fae. She confided in me that she knew a time-walker. His job was to travel to these 'time bubbles,' she called them, and dig up dirt on rival fae. True fae live practically forever and have inserted themselves into just about every powerful human society, so if there's a period stuck in a bubble, you can bet you'll find fae. My friend was always telling me how dangerous the work was, because even time walkers can be killed there. And from the sounds of it, this one was shining his light into some pretty powerful beds. So, the fae have obviously figured out a way to access these places."

"Are you still in contact with this friend?" Jordan asked.

"I've seen her a few times since I was shown the door from Faerie, the last time about two years ago. I should be able to reach her."

"Excellent," Jordan said, giving me a look that said, *see?*

I shook my head. "All right, hold on a minute. I don't care how bosomy Seay and her friend are, the fae don't just help people. It's not in their nature. They'll want something in exchange, which I can guarantee you will be far more layered than it first appears, and to all of our detriments."

"Hey, you're talking about half my DNA," Seay said.

"Sorry, but it's true."

"And you know this how?" Jordan asked.

"Common knowledge in my line of work. Plus, I've experienced it firsthand."

"So you're making generalizations," he concluded.

"No, I'm making sense."

"Well, it couldn't hurt for Seay to ask her," Gorgantha said, her entire face glistening with salt water now. "Could it?"

"Yes, because the manipulation begins the instant the fae see that you want something," I said. "Before you know it, you're caught in their web. And even then, you don't really know it." When Seay crossed her arms, I said, "C'mon, I'm not lumping you in with the rest of faedom, but I'm also not saying anything you don't already know. You spent time in their court. You've seen the way they operate."

Seay lowered her gaze, teeth tugging on her bottom lip. "Brigid is ... different."

Great. She had a crush on her friend, which meant I was

wasting my breath trying to convince her of anything. I looked around at the others. "Helping is not in their nature," I repeated, in case they missed it the first time.

"Do you have an alternative?" Malachi asked.

"I do, but it's going to mean some intermediate steps." I scooted forward on my reading chair to make my pitch. "Last night, a senior member of my Order visited me. She said they were trapped in the rift where they've been for the past month, repairing the same tear that the demons entered through. When I asked how I could help, she said to find Arnaud. Wait, just hear me out," I said when Jordan began to grumble. "I already have a lead on Arnaud. If you let me pursue him, capture him, we'll get the senior members of the Order back. They'll hunt down the remaining Strangers and head off this demon apocalypse that Malachi is seeing. They're far better equipped to handle this than the five of us."

Malachi nodded in my peripheral vision, but Jordan only eyed me critically.

"How does capturing Arnaud lead to freeing your Order?" he asked.

It was the one question I'd hoped no one would put forward, because I had absolutely no idea.

"We'll find out when we have him," I said.

"So you don't know, in other words."

"I trust my Order."

"And Seay trusts her friend."

"Who happens to be fae," I said.

Though Jordan held my gaze, he spoke to the room now. "If I didn't know better, it sounds like Everson is looking for a way to pursue his own agenda under the guise of helping the rest of us."

"Well, that's bullshit," I said.

"Seay's plan, on the other hand," he continued, "gives us the most direct path to our target."

"Look, everyone," I said, trying to keep my voice even. I hadn't been this worked up in a long time. "Jordan's insinuations aside, there's no way Seay's plan is going to work. Not without ending up in a fae bargain that will take years to extricate ourselves from, and that's best case. My way means powerful aid and *no* bargain." By the time my gaze returned to Jordan's, my temples were pounding.

"Well, ah, why don't we put it to a vote?" Malachi offered.

Seay wasted no time piping up from her seat in the center of the couch. "I vote for my plan." She turned to Malachi.

"I'm going with Everson's," he said.

I was next on the rotation. "I'll second that. I think I've made my case."

"And I *know* Seay's made hers," Jordan said from the couch opposite me.

"All right, that's two for Seay's plan and two for Everson's," Malachi said.

We all turned to Gorgantha, who was sitting at the other end of the couch, applying salt water to her neck now. She lowered the hand, her orb-like eyes rotating from me to Seay and Jordan. At last, she sighed.

"Sorry, Everson, but I've known these players longer. I vote fae."

"Then that's that," Jordan said, clapping his hands once and lifting his quarterstaff from beside the loveseat.

Seay stood and straightened her coat. "I'll go find my manipulative friend now."

I returned her cutting look with a tight smile, but I could feel my cheeks reddening from the frustration of having been outvoted for an inferior plan. I needed some alone time to stew in my defeat and consider my next move.

"Tell us as soon as you know something," Jordan called to Seay, who was already heading for the door. "The rest of us should be ready to go on a moment's notice."

"I'm going to run back to the church and finish up a few things," Malachi said, casting me an apologetic look. Gorgantha said something about checking on her pod and followed him toward the door. The mermaid gave me a quick wave, but kept her eyes averted. She hadn't wanted to be the deciding vote, and I didn't hold it against her. Jordan watched them leave before facing me.

"I hope you don't take what happened here personally."

"You mean other than your attacks on my character?"

"There just isn't *time* to do it your way."

Beneath the insistence, I heard his pain. Every day his wife remained in the Stranger's clutches was another day her soul could be used up, another day he could lose her forever—if it hadn't already happened. The not knowing had to be killing him.

"Then let me pursue my plan as a backup in case Seay's doesn't fly."

"I'd rather you saved your power for the mission."

"I can do both."

"Look," he sighed. "I held off on doing this before because we didn't want the Upholders to feel like a tyranny, but I bonded the vote to our sigil."

"Meaning?"

"You won't be able to pursue Arnaud until we decide otherwise."

"So you're controlling me through the bond?" I asked, incredulous.

"I didn't want to, but..." He shrugged as though to say I'd left him no choice.

My voice turned so thick with resentment that it quavered. "Not cool, man. Not cool at all."

He turned toward the door. "I'll signal you as soon as we know something. Be rested and ready. We're going to need you."

I tried to access my golems, but the druidic power of the bonding barred it. Ditto when I attempted to attune my mind to the demon trap. The harder I pushed, the harder the bonding spell pushed back. Which meant I wouldn't be able to cast on the handkerchief with the blood particles either.

Oh, hell no.

But when I opened my eyes again, Jordan had already left. Behind me, I heard Tabitha squeezing and swearing her way back inside. "Are they finally gone?" she asked. "Most importantly, is *he* gone?"

"Yeah," I said, reaching for my coat and cane.

"Wait, where are you going? What about lunch?"

"There's something I've gotta do. I'll bring back take-out."

"Could you make it grilled tuna? It's all I've been thinking about since that fish woman got here." Tabitha sniffed around Gorgantha's spot on the couch, then began lapping up the remaining water in her glass.

"Sure..." I said.

As I looked around the scatter of plates and half-eaten crackers, my anger came crashing back. If the vote was for the fae, fine, but I still didn't have to trust Seay's contact. Fortunately, I had a contact of my own I trusted.

Sort of.

16

The sun was straight overhead, casting the streets south of Midtown in a bright wintry light when the cabbie dropped me in front of Gretchen's townhouse. I hadn't heard from Gretchen in weeks, and she wasn't answering her phone, but I'd surprised her at home before. One time she'd opened the door after a week's absence and acted like she'd never been away. Called me a weirdo for asking where she'd been.

Cinching my coat, I jogged up the stone steps and slammed the brass knocker several times. Then I waited anxiously. Gretchen wasn't fae herself, but she was a powerful caster who had spent so much time in Faerie, she'd retrofitted her entire magical repertoire to resemble theirs. Despite her many, *many* eccentricities, I much preferred the thought of Gretchen delivering us into the time catch than an actual fae. And she had aided me before, in her own strange way.

"Go away," a voice barked from the other side of the door.

"Gretchen?" I called. "Is that you? It's Ever—"

"For the last flaming time, she's not here!"

The multidimensional bands of protection that wrapped Gretchen's home were distorting the voice, but I recognized it, in part from the fact it was issuing from only four feet above the ground.

"Bree-yark?"

A pause. "Everson?"

A series of bolts clunked back and the door opened to reveal my stocky goblin friend. He was wearing a thermal top beneath denim overalls, sleeves rolled past his elbows to reveal the faded tattoos on his forearms.

"Holy thunder," he said, grinning up at me with his frightening set of sharp teeth. "Am I glad to see you."

"Hey, you too ... But what are you doing here?"

Bree-yark scratched his scarred brow with a pinky talon and averted his squash-colored eyes. "Yeah, yeah, I know. All that tough talk about cutting my strings with Gretchen, and here I am, playing house-sitter still. The thing is, she hasn't come back, and she's got some real temperamental houseplants back there." He jerked a thumb over his shoulder. "They'll curse you up and down, but they'll also shrivel to stalks if no one's around to water and feed them. I couldn't have that on my conscience."

I felt my own hope shriveling. "So, no word from Gretchen?"

"Not a frigging peep. And now I've got creditors calling and banging on the door day and night. Gretchen owes money all over the city—did you know that? My nerves are shot to hell, Everson. I'm on almost no sleep." He pulled a cigarette pack from a pocket. "Want one?" Leathery bags hung beneath the goblin's pinched eyes. When I shook my head, he drew one out and lit it with shaking fingers.

"When she left you in charge, she said she'd be back in a few days, right?" I asked.

Bree-yark blew a stream of smoke from the side of his mouth. "Yup. Same thing she says every time. Only for this goblin it's gonna be the last time. Soon as she gets back, I'm dropping the axe. Over and done with, sweetheart."

If I hadn't known my teacher, I would have been worried she was trapped like the Order. But Bree-yark was right. This was Gretchen being Gretchen. So what options did that leave me? I knew one other person in Faerie, but—

Bree-yark spiked his cigarette against the ground. "I don't frigging believe it."

I followed his squinted gaze to the street where a battered transport van had pulled up to the curb.

"Who's that?" I asked.

But the goblin was already storming past me. "She's not here!" he shouted. "Am I gonna have to pound that through your thick skull?"

The young man heaving himself out of the driver side had a boyish face and the beefy body of someone who'd played offensive line on his high-school football team. He stared back at Bree-yark with a pair of close-set blue eyes.

"Hey, I'm just doing my job, little fella."

His voice was pleasant, but he had no idea what sort of creature he was dealing with.

"Little fella?" Bree-yark picked up a rock from a bed of them and slung it at the young man's head. Anticipating the attack, I spoke a quick invocation. The rock rebounded from a wall of hardened air and clattered to the walkway. The young man, who had begun flipping through a messy bill pad, missed the whole show.

I hurried past Bree-yark. "What's this about?"

"My name's Otto, sir. Otto Vander Meer." *Dutch,* I thought automatically. "I deliver for my parents' store. The woman who lives here owes us..." He consulted the pad. "...twenty-eight hundred twenty in antique furniture. Either she settles up today, or I have to take them back. Poppa's orders."

He said it almost apologetically.

"She didn't make arrangements to pay you?" I asked.

"Nope, just the twenty percent down. She's missed the last six months."

Taking off with unpaid bills and leaving a goblin to deal with the fallout? That was bad even for Gretchen. Of course it was much more likely that the terms-of-payment details had flitted from her mind the second she'd left the antique shop. I glanced back at Bree-yark. He'd picked up another rock and was tossing it up and down in his hand. I gestured for him to cool it and turned back to Otto.

"Look, she's not here," I sighed. "But I'll make sure she settles up when she gets back. Can you give me a copy of the balance?" I nodded at the bill pad, where several pink carbon copies hung loose.

"Sorry, sir, but Poppa was clear as a bell: 'Come back with the money or the goods, or don't come back at all.'"

When he licked his lips worriedly, I peered back at the house. I had no idea what among Gretchen's hoardings belonged to the store, and with the townhouse warded six ways to Sunday, I couldn't let him search for the items himself, not without serious risk to his life and limbs. On the other hand, if he kept coming back, Bree-yark was going to end up cutting him. I considered using my wizard's voice to send him on his way, but he was too nice a kid, and I didn't want him to get bawled out, or worse, by his poppa. I dug out my wallet, not believing what I was about to do.

"Will you accept a check?" I grumbled.

Otto blinked in surprise. "Oh, absolutely, sir. Here's a pen."

I took a crumpled check from behind my nest of bills, flattened it against my wallet, and used Otto's pen to scrawl out the amount of Gretchen's impulse purchase plus interest. So not only had she been zero help, she was costing me almost three grand. I finished my signature with enough force to leave a tear. Otto took the check enthusiastically anyway.

"I'll get you a receipt, sir!"

While he climbed back into his truck, Bree-yark strolled up.

"You'll never see that money again, you know," he remarked, tossing his rock aside.

"Yeah, well, maybe I'll be able to leverage it for Gretchen's help in the future."

"Doubtful."

He was probably right, but I was too peeved to dwell on it further. "Hey, whatever happened that night you escorted Mae home?"

He appeared surprised by the question before smiling. "Oh, that was nice."

"You don't have to share the details," I said quickly. "I was just curious."

"No, nothing like that happened." He looked offended. "I was a gentleman. I walked her to her door, kissed her cheek, and then waited in the hallway while she went inside to find the pair of clippers she'd promised me. When she came back, she gave them to me like this." Bree-yark cupped the underside of my hand and pretend-placed a pair of guillotine clippers in my palm. When he withdrew his hand, he brushed my fingers with the backs of his trimmed talons, which sent the bad kind of shivers through me.

"Yeah, just like that," he said.

I grimaced more than smiled, while resisting the urge to scour my hand against my pants to kill the lingering sensation.

"She offered to let me keep the clippers, but I told her I'd bring them back. 'You know, when I pick you up for dinner.' That's what I told her. Oh, she liked that, Everson. We made plans for tonight. Six p.m. There's this great little oyster bar down on Delancey Street I want to take her to." He broke off suddenly.

"What?" I asked.

"That is, unless you need my help. I know you came looking for Gretchen, but when we last talked, I said you could count on me if you ever needed backup. Well, it's still on offer. Anytime, anyplace."

After being outvoted by the Upholders, having someone like Bree-yark staunchly in my corner, ready to drop everything at a moment's notice, almost had me tearing up. Though I didn't require his help as such, the fact he'd lived most of his hundred-plus years in Faerie got me thinking.

"You wouldn't happen to know any trustworthy fae?" I asked.

"Trustworthy fae? That's like asking if I know any nonvenomous basilisks."

I gave a dry laugh. "Yeah, that's what I thought."

"Why?" he asked. "What do you need one of them for?"

I gave him a brief rundown of the time catch and the challenges of entering.

"You might as well be speaking Satyr," he said. "But if you find a way to get there, let me know. I've got your back." He began throwing punches in the air, his short, corded arms popping out like pistons.

"Just enjoy your date with Mae. And tell her 'hi' for me."

At that moment, Otto climbed back out of the truck and handed me the receipt. I stuffed it away in a coat pocket, too sickened to look at the amount. Otto seized my right hand and gave it several hearty pumps. "I really appreciate you doing this, sir," he said. "Is there anything I can do for you?"

"Actually, which way are you headed?"

"I'm fixing to make a delivery uptown."

"Can you drop me off somewhere on the way?"

I could have caught a cab, but the thought of recovering a pinch of that money on saved fare eased the sting a little.

"Heck, I don't see why not," Otto said. "Hop in."

I climbed into the truck's cab and waved goodbye to Bree-yark through the window. He threw a couple final punches, then touched two fingers to his squat brow. As Otto swung the van around, the goblin disappeared from my view.

"Where do you wanna be dropped?" Otto asked.

My mouth was dry when I answered. Not from where I intended to go, but why.

"Midtown College."

17

O tto talked nonstop as the van shuddered up Park Avenue. There was a sincerity about him I liked, but though I made sounds of interest, I was only half listening. *Go to Midtown College, or go home?* A couple times I almost asked Otto to turn around, but that would mean doing nothing, and I was really bad at that.

On the other hand, going forward could mean opening a giant can of worms. It could even mean trouble. But more trouble than having Seay contact God knew who to get us into the time catch?

I seriously doubted it.

"...for being a warlock," Otto was saying. "Can you believe that?"

I squinted over at him. "What was that?"

"The original furniture store I was telling you about? I was saying that the man who owned it, which would've been my father's father's father's et cetera"—he circled his thick hand several times—"was accused of being a warlock."

"Why?"

"Oh, probably because he was taking up prime real estate—

the store was down on Duke Street. Plus he was Dutch, and New Amsterdam had long since become New York. Most British colonists didn't care, but some took issue, I guess. They tried to burn him out, but the fire didn't take. Probably 'cause the Dutch used ceramic tiles on their roofs instead of wood shingles." He grinned at the ingenuity.

"And they didn't try again?"

"Apparently not. And get this." He smacked my shoulder. "Afterwards, he made his sign twice as big." He moved his hand across the span of the windshield. "'Vander Meer's Furnishings.' Oh, man. I bet that got their long johns in a twist." Otto broke into a bout of full-bodied laughter that shook the van. "And we're still in business!"

Out of curiosity, I opened my wizard's senses. I didn't detect any magic in Otto's aura, but that didn't mean casters hadn't held spots on his family tree.

"A warlock, huh?" I said.

"Isn't that crazy? Oh hey, this is you."

I followed his nod to the approaching block of academic buildings. The warlock talk had been an interesting distraction, but now my heart was back to slugging over the thought of what I'd be doing.

"I can wait for you," he said, sidling the van up to the sidewalk.

"I appreciate the offer, but I don't know how long I'll be. Thanks for the lift."

We shook farewell, his thick, earnest hand swallowing mine. Midtown College was closed on Saturdays, which was good. Fewer people meant having to deploy less magic. I selected a key from my ring and unlocked the front door.

Inside, my footfalls echoed down the empty corridors as I took a right, then left. At the locked administrative office, I slid the bolt out with an invocation and stepped inside. The records rooms were in the back.

Summoning a ball of light, I sent it ahead to the room with the employee filing cabinets. The head of records, a stodgy old woman nearing ninety, had kept her system stubbornly low tech. I scanned the cabinets' neat hand-written labels until I reached the R's. With an uttered word, the stopper lock slid away, and I drew the door open. Caroline Reid's file was near the front. I pulled it out.

You don't have to do this, I reminded myself.

It's just a request for help, I shot back. *She can always say no.*

The problem was I had no way to contact Caroline. Following our last meeting well over a year ago, she had disappeared. But I was convinced she kept an address in the city. Just as I remained convinced that Caroline's mother had manipulated her into joining the fae for her political acumen.

Opening the file, I searched the page with her contact info. Though Caroline no longer taught at Midtown, she was technically on sabbatical, meaning that if anyone had updated info on her, it would be the college. Her number was the same, which I knew for a fact was out of service, but a line had been drawn through her old address. My heart sped up as my gaze dropped to the new one.

A P.O. box with an uptown zip code.

Balls. I'd been hoping for a physical address, but this was better than nothing.

I carried the file to the administrator's office and loaded a blank sheet of paper into her electronic typewriter. It ended up being one of the most challenging letters I'd ever written, but an hour and several balled-up drafts later, I was satisfied I'd made my case while keeping the right tone.

I reread what I'd written:

Dear Caroline,

Because of the serious nature of this letter, I'm going to get right to the point.

As you might be aware, a breach opened between the demonic realms and our world last month. Hundreds of demons entered, some servants to powerful masters. Among them were a group of Strangers, demons who infiltrate groups and undermine their collective beliefs, twisting them into devotion to their masters.

I'm collaborating with a team. One member, Malachi, is affiliated with St. Martin's Cathedral. The rest have seen their groups infiltrated by Strangers: a mermaid, a druid, and a half-fae. We have reason to believe a powerful demon is coordinating the Strangers. Further, Malachi sees the master's plans leading to a demon apocalypse. I don't need to tell you, Caroline, that this would be devastating for both of our races.

My team is doggedly tracking the Strangers, not only to eliminate them, but to determine the identity and ultimate ambitions of their master. We've had early success, but our present target is hiding in a time catch—a preserved bubble of time and space that we can't access without powerful magic.

I'm asking you, Caroline, as a fae in high position, to send someone to assist us. Not as part of an exchange or bargain, but in the mutual interest of our races. Perhaps, also, in memory of our close friendship.

I hope this letter finds you well.

Respectfully,

The formal tone was so at odds with our joking two-year relationship as colleagues that it was scary. But upon reclaiming her fae nature and marrying Angelus, Caroline had become a different being. Hell, I'd watched the transformation happen in real time. I had no choice now but to address my old friend as fae royalty.

I made a copy of the letter, signed the original, and folded it into thirds. After sliding it into an envelope and penning the address, doubts began sprouting up in my mind. How long would it sit in her P.O. box before she saw it? Would she *ever* see it? Deciding to hedge my bets, I signed the copy too and stuck it inside another envelope. On that one, I only wrote Caroline's name. It would be a hand delivery.

Really pushing the envelope, aren't you?

I frowned at my lame joke and stole from the office, making sure to leave everything exactly how I'd found it. Since helping Professor Snodgrass a month earlier, and ingratiating myself to his wife, my department chair had lowered the heat. But I didn't want to give him an excuse to crank it up again, because I was sure he'd take it.

I left the college the way I'd come in, locked the door, and nearly spun into someone. Grunting in surprise, I stumbled backwards. Wrapped in a scarf and camelhair coat, hands thrust into his pockets, Vega's brother had just arrived at the top of the steps. Above his gold-rimmed glasses, stern lines creased his forehead.

"Everson," Carlos said.

"Wh-what are you doing here?" I stammered, sliding my two envelopes into a coat pocket.

"Looking for you. I stopped by your apartment and left several messages on your phone."

"Yeah, I've been busy."

"We need to talk."

"Now's not a good time."

"It shouldn't take long," he said. "There's a café on the corner."

"If this is about your sister, we already had that conversation."

"And by all appearances, nothing's changed."

Oh, if you only knew. "Then that should tell you everything you need to know," I said, stepping past him.

I was halfway down the stairs when he said, "I believe I've met Arnaud Thorne."

I stopped.

18

As Carlos spoke at a corner table in the café, I hung onto his every word. He'd removed his scarf and gloves and opened the throat of his coat, but he kept both hands wrapped around his steaming coffee mug. His voice remained low. When he finished, he took his first sip. The mug trembled slightly.

"When was this?" I asked.

I ventured a sip of my own coffee, but it tasted acidic, probably from my nerves.

"Last Saturday, around one o'clock. The same day my brothers and I spoke to you."

"Right, the big meeting."

That was also the day I'd been in and out of Epic Con, hunting down the conjurer and ultimately his fire elemental. We tracked them to a rock quarry across the Hudson River, put down a conjured dragon, and rescued the efreet from a massive demon attack. When several of the demon hosts rose again as zombies, I suspected Arnaud's infernal hand and assumed he'd sensed the efreet's manifestation. But what if he tracked me down from info he'd extracted from Carlos?

"So you and Tony were leaving the house," I recapped. "A

man headed you off and then fell to the ground in agony." That might have been Arnaud reacting to my grandfather's pendant, which Vega had given to her son. "You said he was strange looking. How, exactly?"

"Short and thin. Very pale faced. He looked old, but he carried himself like someone younger. He was wearing a business suit and hat, both brown."

Sounded like the same suit a murder victim had donned before heading to work that morning. His corpse was later found bobbing in the East River near Roosevelt Park, naked, throat-bitten, and blood-drained.

"Eye color?"

"He was wearing sunglasses."

"Hair?"

Carlos shook his head again. "None showing below his hat. Or it was so fine, I didn't notice. When he fell, I saw something on the back of his neck, though. A symbol about the size of a quarter." He made a circle with his thumb and first finger.

"Like a tattoo?"

"More like a brand. I thought he'd been a POW or something."

A demon brand, most likely. Arnaud might not have even been aware it was there.

"Probably our man," I said. "And when Tony went back inside, Arnaud recovered and grabbed your wrist, and then you blacked out?"

"Not blacked out, *spaced* out." He said it as if losing consciousness was for lesser men. "I was standing when I came to, and he was waving at me from a cab. My head ached for the rest of that day and the next." He dropped his voice further as he leaned forward. "What in the hell did he do to me?"

"It sounds like he used ... powers of persuasion." I almost said *vampiric powers*, but caught myself. Thanks to his sister's assertions, Carlos accepted that strange things happened in the city, but I didn't think he was ready to accept he'd been in the grip of a vampire. I also didn't mention that he was lucky to be alive rather than dead or undead. "Most likely he was after information," I said.

"What information?"

"My whereabouts," I replied absently, still reviewing the account in my mind.

I wanted to drill down to a more detailed description of Arnaud. Carlos was the only one I knew who had seen him up close. But Carlos straightened back from me now as if establishing a more formal distance.

"You've just made my point."

I brought him back into full focus. "What's that?"

"You've just confirmed that the man I encountered was Arnaud Thorne. You also said that he came in search of you. Let me rephrase that, he came to *my family's house* in search of you. Think about that. A kidnapper and serial killer came to their house looking for you. Why do you think that was?"

It was a rhetorical question. He was circling back to my involvement with his sister.

"The house was protected," I said. "If you'd stayed inside like Ricki and I asked—"

"Oh, so we're all supposed to remain on permanent house arrest now?"

I looked down at my coffee and took several steadying breaths. I'd had a variation of this conversation with Ricki just this morning about the safe house. I had responded with concern and respect. Though it wasn't easy, I resolved to treat Carlos the same way. He was her brother, after all.

"I'm sorry that happened," I said. "Arnaud went to you for information. That was all."

"What's stopping him from coming back?" he challenged. "Or doing worse?"

"He won't."

"How do you know?"

"Because he wants to make this personal between me and him. You're too peripheral. So are your brothers' families." I had started out to reassure him, but the words emerged with increasing certainty, as if some spectral part of my mind was aligning with Arnaud's. "He wants to surprise me. Going after you guys wouldn't give him the same pleasure."

"Then what about Ricki?" he asked between clenched teeth. "Or Tony?"

"They're someplace Arnaud can't touch them. They're safe."

"Where?"

"In Brooklyn. I'd prefer not to get more specific."

"So you're managing my contacts with my own family now?"

I peeked around the café. It was about half full, and no one set off my baddie alarm, but Arnaud and his blood slaves could be anywhere. "If Ricki wants to give you more information, she will," I said.

He snorted dryly.

"What?"

"Ricki is playing off the same script as with Tony's father," he said. "Act one: get involved with a dangerous man. Act two: ignore our warnings, even as the dangers escalate. Act three: come to her senses before it's too late and send the man to prison." Carlos leaned forward. "Where he should have been all along."

"*She* sent him there?"

"We're still in act two, but Ricki will come around. She always does."

"What did she send him to prison for?" I pressed.

Carlos took another sip of coffee and regarded me coolly. "If Ricki wants to give you more information, she will."

Having taken my own words and smacked me with them, he stood to leave.

My cheeks burned with anger and futility. Before I could stop myself, I said, "She's pregnant, you know."

Boom.

Carlos turned slowly, scarf hanging from his hand. "What did you say?"

"Ricki's pregnant with our child." I cleared my throat. "I thought you and your brothers should know. I also want you to know that I'm fully committed to her. I wasn't going to quit our relationship at your say so, and there's no way in hell I'm leaving her now." Carlos's face paled as I spoke. "There are dangers," I continued, "but we'll manage them. I'm hunting Arnaud as we speak."

But was I? The meeting with the Upholders had sidelined those plans.

Carlos grunted and finished arranging his scarf with a sharp tug. "Like I said, same script."

19

S ome people had a talent for getting under my skin, and Carlos was one of them. Still, I couldn't believe I'd blurted out Vega's pregnancy, especially after she'd made it clear she wanted to share the news selectively and on her own schedule.

Vapor clouds blasted from my nostrils as I paced the sidewalk outside the café. It wasn't just that I was in deep trouble with Vega; I'd betrayed her trust. And it wasn't worth the counterpunch I'd dealt her brother.

Not even close.

I stopped and fished out my phone. I needed to get a jump on Carlos, make sure Vega heard it from me first. I wasn't even thinking damage-control—the situation was beyond that. How Vega chose to react, I deserved.

When I reached her voicemail, I left a "call me" message and clapped my phone closed. Besides getting under my skin, Carlos had also gotten into my head. If I'd been curious about Tony's father before, I was now borderline obsessed. To be honest, that was the other reason I'd wanted to talk to her.

Act three: come to her senses before it's too late and send the man to prison.

What in the hell could have happened that Vega would harbor a felon and then turn on him? I was returning the phone to my pocket, lost in the question, when I felt the envelopes with the letters to Caroline.

"Oh, yeah," I muttered.

I still had the damned fae thing to negotiate.

Stopping at the mailbox I'd been pacing around, I dropped in the envelope addressed to Caroline's P.O. box. Who knew if or when it would reach her, but that was why I'd prepared a second letter. I batted that envelope against my hand a few times in silent debate, then hailed a cab.

"East Seventieth and Fifth," I told the driver.

FOUND YOU.

I peered up the stone staircase that ended at an emerald-green door. The first time I'd come looking for the fae town-house, I had nearly missed it, a susurration of enchantments blending it into its immediate neighbors. But two years on, I was a more powerful magic-user, my senses better attuned to subtle energies.

I was a little smarter too. Pulling a stoppered potion from my pocket, I activated it with an incantation and drank it down. Moments later, a warm neutralizing field took hold around me. Drawing a breath, I climbed the steps and rapped on the door. The contact sent out faint tendrils of fae magic that explored my protection before falling away. Two years earlier, that bit of contact had knocked my magic offline for hours.

When no one answered, I knocked again and peered up the narrow edifice.

The townhouse was larger than it appeared from the outside. According to Caroline, it contained a strategic portal to the fae realm. Its sister portal was downtown, inside Federal Hall. Following Caroline's marriage to Angelus, her family controlled both portals, so I was betting she still came and went through them. Not that I expected her to be here. I just wanted the letter delivered to her in person.

But what if she is here?

The thought sent a clammy wave of uncertainty through me. I was debating whether to knock a third time when something zipped past my ear.

"What the—?"

I spun around only to be buzzed by something going past my other ear. The flying things left contrails of glittering light, one peach colored, the other meadow green. When high bubbly laughter reached my ears, I groaned inwardly. Relaxing the arm that had been preparing to draw my sword, I showed my hands.

"I'm Everson Croft," I said. "I come in friendship."

"We know you, Everson Croft," they said in unison so that it sounded like a sweet, taunting song.

They twirled around one another, creating a mesmerizing column of spilling lights. Sure enough, these were pixies, Faerie's most annoying creature. And, just my luck, they were somehow connected to the townhouse. But though irritating and silly, pixies could be flattered into lending aid. That would mean cranking up my charm. Pixies considered anything below a nine an insult, and my charm points were presently two.

Gathering myself, I bowed low and swept an arm out elegantly.

"I'm flattered to hear such," I said, rising again. "But I have not had the pleasure of meeting you. If you would cease your flight long enough that we might be introduced, I would be most pleased."

I struggled to fashion a fake smile around the fake phrasing.

The pixies giggled and circled my head several more times.

Though their laughter was light and infectious, I remained on guard. When they joined hands, a trail of pixie dust spilled over me. The magic might have been meant to dispel my powers or cast me into a sugar-plumb slumber, but like the fae magic over the door, it didn't penetrate my protection. I gave grudging credit to Gretchen for teaching me the potion.

At last, the pixies hovered a couple of feet from my face where I could see them.

I gasped and touched a hand to my chest. Except for their disparate colors, the one-foot beings were nearly identical: butterfly-like wings, cascading autumn hair, and cherub faces that appeared innocent, enchanting, and powerful at the same time. Gossamer garments fluttered in the wind from their wings.

My gasp had been a stretch but not much of one.

With appropriate reverence, I whispered, "Never have these eyes beheld such exquisiteness."

The pixies tittered some more and clasped one another's arms. It took me a moment to realize one was female and the other male. They appeared pleased with me, anyway. The meadow-green female returned a petite bow.

"I'm Pip," she said in a high voice.

"I'm Twerk," her peach-colored twin followed.

"And we bid you greetings, Everson Croft," they said together.

"You must be wondering what errand brings me here. I was—"

"Oh, we know your errand, Everson Croft."

I faltered. "You do?"

Pip hovered closer until I had to look at her cross-eyed. "Of course we do, silly poo." She touched a playful finger to my nose. Though my protection blunted her magic, I could sense the promise of flower-strewn meadows, moonlit feasts, and a wonderstruck bliss that only the luckiest knew in their childhood. A part of me was tempted to thin my protection, to allow a little more of the fae magic in.

"Got it!" a pixie voice cried.

I snapped back to attention. "Huh?"

Distracted by Pip, I hadn't noticed Twerk duck below my field of vision until he'd snatched Caroline's letter from my pocket. I swiped for it, but my hand broke through his peach-colored contrail. Twerk's sister joined him as they rose, twirling, beyond my reach and opened the letter. It took every ounce of self-control not to shout for them to give it back or to blast them with a force invocation.

Twerk secured the envelope while Pip drew out the letter.

I called up pleasantly, "The correspondence you hold is in fact my reason for coming, fair beings."

The envelope fell to my feet, and I stiffened as the pixies unfolded the letter, each one holding a side, heads joined in the middle. When I saw they had it upside down, I relaxed. Most pixies were illiterate. They giggled anyway as they pretended to read the type. Suppressing a sigh, I stooped for the empty envelope. The only thing to do now was wait until they lost interest, which probably wouldn't take long.

"Everson Croft has a troubled mind," the pixies sang. *"He needs her help, 'cause he's in a bind."*

I looked up sharply, but the letter remained upside down. Then it occurred to me that though the pixies couldn't read the words, they could still feel the emotions and memories I'd grappled with during the composition. They were siphoning them up like sugar water, and it was making them giddy.

"Croft loved her once, and she stomped his heart," they sang with even more glee. *"She wed her prince, and he fell apart."*

"I didn't fall apart," I muttered.

"Then lo she's back, like a wayward dove; Croft swept her to bed where they made sweet—"

"Hey!" I called.

My protest sent them into gales of laughter. They were referring to the night Caroline had come to my apartment unannounced. Her transformation underway, she was scared, confused, and in need of a friend from her old world. Someone who understood the woman she had been and the being she was becoming. That night had marked her crossover to her fae life. I'd felt it even as we were making—

I broke off the memory and glared at the pixies, all of my fake charm spent. "Getting a little invasive, aren't we?" I growled.

Eyes and cheeks glistening with tears, the pixies collected themselves long enough to continue their maddening song. *"Now Mister Croft has a brand new flame; so why does this note bear the old one's name?"*

I jumped for the letter, but the pixies darted higher, raining more dust and laughter down on me. That did it. I palmed the cold iron amulet in my pocket, ready to cast through it, when a distinguished voice spoke.

"That's quite enough you two."

The doorway was open now, a slight, silver-haired man in butler's attire standing inside it.

"Oh," I said in surprise, releasing my amulet again. "It's ... you." Though I'd encountered him twice before, I'd forgotten his name. Jasper? All I knew for sure was that, appearances aside, he was a powerful fae being.

"Return the letter to Mister Croft," he told the pixies calmly. "And tell him you're sorry."

The pixies' laughter thinned away, their winged bodies sagging as they descended. They held the letter toward me.

"Here, Everson Croft," Pip said in a sulky voice.

"We're sorry," her twin said. "We were only having fun."

"Sure," I said tightly. Accepting the upside-down letter, I refolded it quickly and replaced it in its envelope.

"Very good," the butler said. "Now back inside." He snapped his fingers.

Pip and Twerk took off like shots, their glittering contrails disappearing into the dimness beyond him. I managed to glimpse a parquet entrance hall, too big for the narrow townhouse, before the butler stepped forward and closed the door behind him.

For the first time, he leveled his gray eyes at me. "I apologize for the nuisance. Now, how can I be of assistance, Mr. Croft?" His voice betrayed no surprise. In fact, he sounded as if he'd been expecting me.

"Is Caroline in?"

"No, she is not."

"Well, I, ah, I have a message—a letter, actually—that I was hoping to give to her." When I caught myself glancing around and fidgeting like a school boy, I straightened and cleared my throat. "That is, I have an urgent communication." I held up the letter. "Is there someone I can entrust to deliver it to her?"

The butler's eyes didn't shift from mine. Though his face remained placid, I sensed dangerous undercurrents. My protective field must have looked as formidable to him as a layer of cellophane.

"I believe there was an understanding," he said at last.

"An understanding?" I lowered the letter again.

"Yes, involving you and Mrs. Caroline?"

I realized he was referring to the battle for downtown Manhattan when I was trapped in Arnaud's vault and Caroline had helped save my life. More accurately, the fae had *allowed her* to help save my life. In exchange, she had forfeited her remaining feelings for me. Typical fae bargain.

"Oh yeah, that."

"Very good." He nodded. "Was there anything else?"

"What do you mean? What does that have to do with my letter?"

"Mr. Croft," he said patiently. "There is nothing of Mrs. Caroline's that should concern you or vice versa. Your lives no longer overlap. Not in the slightest. Indeed, it would be most prudent for all concerned if we forgot this visit."

His dismissiveness made my face burn. "Well, listen here, *Jeeves*," I hissed.

"The name is Osgood." He adjusted his bow with a pair of white-gloved hands.

I faltered. "I thought it was Jasper."

"I go by many names, Mr. Croft."

"Well, anyway, I was making a joke. Listen, I'm out of Caroline's life and *vice versa*, so you can relax. This message deals with something much bigger."

"Be that as it may—"

"Is Caroline a prisoner?"

Osgood blinked once in what appeared mild surprise, but I couldn't tell whether it was from being interrupted or what I'd asked.

"I'm sorry?"

"It's a simple question. Is Caroline a prisoner?"

"No, Mr. Croft. She most certainly is not."

"Is she free to make her own decisions?"

"Naturally. She's quite influential, in fact."

"Then why is the butler playing gatekeeper?"

The edge of Osgood's mouth turned up in a way that suggested he knew that I knew he was much more than a butler. There was nothing dangerous in the look, only the mildest amusement. Which told me just how powerful he really was.

I held up the letter again. "It's important. All I'm asking is that it be delivered to her. She can decide what she wants to do with it."

Osgood opened the door behind him and stepped back over the threshold.

"Wait," I said, moving forward. I stopped, though, wary of the potent defensive energies covering the doorway.

"Good day, Mr. Croft."

"Please," I said.

The door swung slowly to, enshrouding Osgood's silver hair and knowing eyes in dimness, then clicked shut. Fae protections grew back around the frame, sealing it tightly. I swore and slapped the letter against the palm of my hand.

Only the letter was no longer there.

I looked from my empty hands to the steps, then to the closed door. I smiled. *That son of a gun.* There was no telling why Osgood had taken the letter, but he'd taken it. Whether he would give it to Caroline was another question.

"Thank you," I called anyway, and trotted down the steps.

I had done all I could on the fae front.

20

After trying Vega again, and getting her voicemail again, I took a cab to the safe house in Brooklyn. In the common room downstairs a woman from the synagogue was reading to a group of children in the far corner. Tony wasn't among them. I went to their small apartment and knocked. Camilla answered.

"Tony is doing his afternoon nap," she explained, stepping outside.

"And Ricki?"

"She went to work around lunchtime."

I wondered if Vega hadn't told me because she knew I would try to talk her out of it. In fairness, I hadn't told her about going to Arnaud's penthouse, and for the same reason. Fine, but why wasn't she answering my calls?

Either her brother reached her first, or she's wrapped up in something.

"Everything all right here?" I asked Camilla.

"Yes, Mr. Croft."

"Good, just be sure to stay inside."

She nodded as if she didn't need reminding, but I'd told her at least fifty times to call me Everson, and that hadn't taken. And after the story Carlos had shared about Arnaud...

Shit, I was being too hard on her. Tony had been abducted under her watch. Camilla understood the dangers better than anyone.

"Can I get you anything?" I asked her.

"No, Mr. Croft. We have everything we need."

"All right. Thanks for all your help, Camilla."

I worried about her coming and going, but I didn't think Arnaud would target her. Camilla provided him no advantages. If he turned her into a blood slave, or even charmed her with his vampiric powers, the safe house would bar her entrance. Plus, I was getting the same feeling as when I'd spoken to Carlos. Arnaud was gunning for me, not Camilla. She was too far from the bull's eye.

"Where are you going?" she asked.

"Oh, to the police station to check on Ricki."

Which was to say, to face the music.

I hesitated. Camilla had been Tony's sitter for years. Long enough to have known his father? When I started to open my mouth, she looked back at me expectantly. *No,* I decided, shutting it again. *Not this way.* I had already violated Vega's trust once today. If I started snooping around her past, where would it end?

"Thanks again," I told Camilla, and left.

I KNEW THE OFFICERS WHO MANNED THE SECURITY AROUND 1 Police Plaza well enough that they hardly glanced at my ID as they waved me through. I would need to talk to Vega about that. There were enough supernatural types who could impersonate me or her—mages, doppelgangers, dark fae, the list went on—

but right now I was too preoccupied with having to tell her I'd blabbed her pregnancy to Carlos.

I was actually palpitating as the elevator rose toward the eighth floor. She was *not* going to be happy. When I arrived, the elevator door opened to reveal Detective Hoffman stuffing his shirt tail into his polyester pants.

"Good timing," he said, hustling inside and placing a meaty hand against my chest. "We could use you."

"Wait, what's going on?"

"Vega's bringing someone into the Basement."

"The Basement?" I echoed as the elevator descended. The basement level held the two cells I'd reinforced with circle traps and powerful wards.

"Yeah. One of yours."

Vega went out and collared a supernatural? And without asking for my help?

"Vampire," Hoffman said, digging a finger into his wreath of brown curls. "Or so they say. She answered a ten-fifty-four over in the Bowery. Found the body. Also found a couple of vamps hiding nearby. Well, not *found* them. The vamps rushed her and the officers at the scene. But then the vamps freaked and tried to run." *Because of the stored power of the safe house in the coin pendant,* I thought.

"Vega shot one through the back," he finished.

When the elevator door opened at the basement level, I could already hear the commotion. Pulling sword from staff, I sprinted to the holding area. I found Vega standing apart from the four officers wrestling a wiry man toward an open cell. She stood in a wide-legged stance, service pistol aimed at the detainee.

The vampire's greasy hair thrashed as he jumped and kicked. Red-rimmed eyes seemed to shoot in every direction at once above a muzzled mouth. I noted the exit wound in the center of his shirt at chest level, steam drifting up. Fragments from the silver round must have only nicked his heart because even with his hands secured behind his back with reinforced cuffs, he was still putting up a good fight.

"Just get him inside," Vega snapped. "Don't worry about the door."

Hoffman arrived beside me, heaving for air, but I showed him a staying hand.

The officers shoved the vampire into the cell. All in a second, the vampire recovered and flung himself at the open doorway. The officers flinched back, but my ward met the vampire with a violent flash, and he staggered back. Screaming behind his muzzle, he threw himself at the doorway again. This time, the ward knocked him into the far wall and he fell on his ass. He peered around, smoke rising from his body. Rather than try for the door a third time, he eyed us with crazed hunger and pain.

Probably recently turned.

The largest of the officers stepped forward now and closed the heavy alloy door—steel, iron, copper, traces of silver—until the vampire could only be seen through a window above a feeding portal. I double-checked to ensure the protections were fully charged and functioning as they should.

They were.

"Good job," Vega said, holstering her pistol.

"I'll say," Hoffman grunted, prompting her to turn.

When our eyes met, I tried to read her face for signs of wrath, but she looked pleasantly surprised.

"I was coming down to help," Hoffman said. "But Mr. Chivalry here told me to back off."

"They had it under control," I said, still not believing they'd managed to collar a vampire.

Vega gave me one of her dry looks. "So we passed?"

She knew me too well. I had wanted to see if they could

handle the creature before intervening. I also wanted to make sure the cell was up to snuff. I wasn't always going to be around to help.

"With flying colors," I said. "And you're all right?" My gaze inadvertently dropped to her stomach.

"Fine. The boys did the heavy lifting. Something up?"

I thought about all that had happened since we'd last spoken. Arnaud's penthouse, the infernal skirmish inside, the time catch, the meeting with the Upholders, my visit to the fae townhouse to deliver Caroline's letter. But mostly I was thinking about my meeting with Carlos and my stupid blunder.

"Do you have time to talk?" I asked in a lowered voice.

"Sure, but let's take it upstairs. I've gotta start the paperwork on this guy."

Two of the officers who had helped wrestle the creature into confinement took seats at a desk facing the duplex of cells, their sidearms loaded with silver rounds. The vampire groaned behind his muzzle and eyed them through the window.

"Jesus," Hoffman muttered. "Sure that cell's gonna hold him?"

"Those are some of the most powerful protections I've ever built," I said. "He's not going anywhere."

Hoffman turned his skeptical face to Vega.

"It'll hold him," she said.

BACK UPSTAIRS, VEGA HAD ME CLOSE THE DOOR TO HER MODEST office as she sat behind her desk.

"I know, I know," she sighed before I'd even said anything. "You don't like me leaving the safe house in my condition, much less chasing vampires. On the first point, I warned you I was going in today. On the second, I got a call to a body. I didn't know the perps were going to be blood suckers."

"So, the protection held up?" I tapped my chest to indicate the coin pendant beneath her blouse.

"Yeah, it was pretty wild. They got within about a hundred feet, then hissed and recoiled like someone had bombed the street with tear gas. Took off in the other direction. I shot the one downstairs. Stunned him long enough for the officers to cuff and muzzle him. The other one got away."

"What did he look like?" I asked, my mind already going to Arnaud.

"*She,*" Vega corrected me. "About the other perp's age, but much faster. We couldn't get a clean shot."

I nodded as I took a seat in the folding chair facing her desk. "Probably the one who turned him. Some vamps prefer to work in pairs. She might have been training him to hunt. Is the Sup Squad looking for her?"

Short for Supernatural Squad, the tactical team operated in full body armor, complete with extra protection over vital arteries, and carried weapons loaded with enhanced rounds. The seeds of the Sup Squad were planted during the mayor's purge campaign, though back then they were called the Hundred. In the year that followed, the unit had slimmed down to twelve with Vega and I providing occasional training. Their equipment and armor came from Centurion United, the big defense company.

When Vega nodded, I said, "Have them destroy the other perp, if possible. That will restore our boy downstairs. I can testify that he wasn't responsible for his actions."

Vega called the squad commander and relayed the info.

"Thanks," she said to me as she ended the call. "So what have you been up to?"

My heart rate bumped to a faster tempo. I would tell her

about my conversation with Carlos—I had to—but I decided to get the other things out of the way first. I might not get a chance later.

"I have a location on Arnaud."

Vega looked up, her eyes saucer round.

"Or a former location," I amended. "But I don't want a police response."

The old Vega would have argued. This Vega understood the danger, even to the Sup Squad.

"The Ludwick Hotel," I said. "I have some golems surveilling the location and another checking out other hotels in the area." I didn't mention that I couldn't currently access said golems thanks to the damned druid bond. "Just promise me you'll stay away from the hotel—the entire Upper East side, for that matter."

"All right, but not even a cordon?"

"No," I said firmly. "He already knows I was there—I sort of stumbled over a tripwire. If he finds my golems, he can do whatever he wants to them, but I don't want him taking out his anger on the NYPD. I set a trap in case he returns to the room. Otherwise, I'll have to hunt him the old-fashioned way." That was, once the business with the Strangers had wrapped up.

Vega nodded, agreeing to stay away.

Next, I filled her in on the Stranger and the challenge of the time catch.

When I finished, she stared at me. "So you're planning to go back in time, battle a demon, and hope you make it back here before that world, what, implodes? And you're worried about me driving to the office?"

"Hey, I'm not the one carrying our little passenger." I patted my belly.

She cocked her head impatiently. "Croft, you know what I'm saying. That sounds super risky, even for you."

"Well, we're working on getting some help."

"From the Order?"

"Actually, the Order is stuck in another plane." I dragged a hand through my hair. "Yeah, it's been that kind of day. Claudius is working on it." The fact was, *I* should have been working on it, hunting down Arnaud instead of following a Stranger into a frigging time catch. Vega was right: risky as hell.

"Who does that leave?" she asked.

"The, um…" I coughed into a fist. "The fae."

"I thought you said you couldn't trust them."

"You can't, but I'm working through some more reliable channels."

"And which would those be?"

I'd been hoping to avoid the topic of Caroline, not because Vega knew about our history—she didn't. In fact, I doubted she would have even cared. All of that had happened long before we'd paired up. It was more that I was struggling with why approaching Caroline now was making me so damned anxious. I didn't have romantic feelings for her. Vega had total claim to those. So, what was it?

Vega watched me, the question she'd just asked lingering in her eyes. She could read me well enough that if I brought up Caroline, she would know something was bothering me. Something I couldn't put into words yet.

"Seay and I have fae contacts," I said at last. "*Tenuous* contacts. We'll see if anything comes of them." All absolutely true. And it was very possible nothing would come of them, making the whole thing moot.

"Just look before you jump," she said.

"Believe me, I will."

Vega began to access the reporting system on her computer.

"There's something else I wanted to tell you," I said through a dry mouth. "I talked to Carlos today."

"Oh, yeah?" she said absently. "He called me earlier. Looks like he left a message."

"Arnaud paid him a visit last week."

Vega looked over sharply. *"What?"*

I described the encounter, watching her face harden at how close the demon-vampire had come to her son again. There was no telling what might have happened if she hadn't given him my grandfather's coin pendant that day. A mother's intuition, indeed. And then there was the safety of the rest of her family. I gave her the same assurances I'd given Carlos—that Arnaud had gone to their house for information and then left once he'd obtained it, that I didn't see him bothering them again.

"How confident are you in that?" she asked.

"I admit, it's more a gut assessment than anything, but pretty confident."

"Even after what happened to Blade and the vampire hunters?"

I suppressed the bloody image of the apartment before it could take lurid form. "If Arnaud had wanted to do something to your brother, there was nothing stopping him," I said. "It was just the two of them and an empty street."

Vega sighed, sat back in her chair, and rubbed her temples.

"Carlos was more worried about you and Tony than anything," I said.

"Well, that's never going to change."

"I told him you were pregnant."

There. It was out.

Vega lowered her hands from her head.

"I wasn't planning to," I added quickly. "He thought everyone would be safer if I stopped seeing you, and I was making the point that, well, that was sort of impossible now. It just came out. It was bone-headed and—"

"It's all right."

My lips stuttered to a stop. Not the response I'd been expecting.

Vega gave a tired wave. "Seriously, it's fine."

"No, it's not. You said you would tell your family when *you* were ready."

"Well, maybe that was how Carlos needed to hear it. There's being concerned and then there's being controlling. He's been doing too much of the second lately." It sounded like he and his brothers had had a version of the Talk with Ricki too. "I'm a grown woman, and he's not my father."

Though Carlos had taken a hard line against me, I didn't want to see a wedge driven between him and his sister over it. "At the end of the day, he's just looking out for you and Tony," I sighed.

Vega dropped her gaze to the pen she'd begun rolling back and forth on the desk. She appeared to be weighing something. After a moment, she said, "It all goes back to some things that happened a few years ago."

I leaned forward. Was I finally going to get the story on Tony's father?

Just then, my right hand began to throb. I looked down to find the sigil below my thumb pulsing away.

"Need to be somewhere?" Vega asked.

"The Upholders are calling me to meet." *Dammit.*

"Do you think the fae contact came through?"

"No telling," I said, standing. "I'll let you know if I'm off anywhere."

"You better." She set her pen to one side.

I leaned over the desk and kissed her. We lingered there for a few seconds, longer than either of us meant to, it seemed, savoring our little refuge before the other parts of our lives intruded again.

When we separated, Vega stroked my cheek.

"I appreciate everything you've done for us," she said, refer-ring to her and Tony. "Let me worry about the rest of my family." Her dark eyes shone into mine. "We'll talk more when you get back."

"Sounds good."

I kissed her again and she gave my cheek a final pat.

Not wanting to, I yielded to the bond's pull and left her office.

The rest of the Upholders were waiting at the townhouse when I passed through the potent wards and locked the door behind me.

"What's up?" I called toward the table where they were gathered.

"Seay has an update," Malachi said as I walked up, the sigil on my hand fading until it was faint lines in my skin again. When I took the spot beside Malachi, I noted how our arrangement mirrored our earlier vote: Malachi and me on one side, Jordan and Seay on the other, and Gorgantha at the end of the table, but on their corner.

Fresh bitterness broke through me as I muttered, "All right, let's hear it."

"Sure thing, Mr. Enthusiasm." Seay threw me a frown. "I contacted my friend, and she found someone in Faerie willing to get us into the time catch, *like I said she would*." The emphasis was directed at me.

"Who?" I asked.

"A fae lord. Well, a former fae lord."

"Former?" I said. "He was excommunicated?"

"More like booted from the kingdom under threat of death."

"So, excommunicated," I said. "I'm not even going to ask for what. Why would he help us?"

"Because my friend brings him delicacies from the kingdom from time to time. She felt he was dealt a shit hand."

"And he wants nothing in exchange?" I asked skeptically. "That doesn't sound like the fae."

"Well, he wants to meet us for starters. His name's Crusspatch. He has a place in the Fae Wilds."

"The Fae Wilds?" I was already shaking my head. "Forget it."

Jordan, who had been watching our exchange with a stern face, spoke up. "Why dismiss it out of hand?"

"I think the name does a pretty good job of explaining itself."

"Have you ever been there?" he challenged.

"No. I have too much at stake in something called *my life*."

"So you don't know anything about it," he said with finality.

"Look, I know books aren't your thing, but there are plenty of written accounts. The Fae Wilds are where the worst creatures of Faerie live and play: goblins, trolls, night hags. Assuming we get through the Wilds in one piece, we'd still have a disenfranchised fae lord to deal with, and on his home turf. I wouldn't be surprised if living out in the wilds has made this *Crusspatch* screwy. There's no telling what he'll want."

"She did call him eccentric," Seay said. "But in a fun way."

"Yeah, all the more reason to advise against that option," I said. "Hard."

"Let me guess," Jordan said. "You're going to suggest we hunt Arnaud Thorne instead."

I wasn't about to mention Caroline or my visit to the fae townhouse. It was a long shot, one. And two, I didn't want to postpone action that could lead to freeing the Order, which would in turn lead to hunting down and eliminating the Strangers.

"It's our best course of action," I said. "Once I distill the blood I collected at Arnaud's penthouse, we'll have a target. We'll be able to hunt him." My heart was already galloping at the thought.

"How long will the distilling take?" Gorgantha asked.

"Conservatively? Twenty-four hours."

Jordan grumbled his disapproval. "So a full day."

"In light of the new developments," Malachi spoke up, "I suggest we put it to another vote."

"We already voted," Jordan said. "The decision is bonded."

"Hence the word *another*," I said. "If the fae lord were willing to come here, that would be one thing. But journeying through the Fae Wilds is madness. You guys have to trust me on this."

"Everyone for Everson's plan?" Malachi asked, preempting further debate.

His and my hands went up immediately, while the other three kept theirs down.

Here we go again, I thought.

"Seay's plan?" Malachi said.

While Jordan and Seay raised their hands, Gorgantha massaged the sigil on her webbing, eyes downcast.

"Gorgantha," Jordan prompted. "You can't abstain."

Her orbs looked as heavy as stones as she raised them toward him. "Look, guys. You know I've got your backs through thick and thin, but the Fae Wilds? That doesn't sound like the kind of hood you want to get caught asking directions. I'm afraid I'm gonna have to side with Everson on this one."

I pumped a mental fist. *Thank God for mer reason.*

"Then it's decided," Malachi said. "Let's bond the new vote to the sigil so Everson can get started on the distillation."

But Jordan was staring past me, his pupils dilating. Seay followed his gaze and started back, fae light breaking around her. Gorgantha shot up from her bar stool, hulking arms bowed out to the sides.

"Intruder!" Jordan shouted.

I spun, sword and staff drawn. The figure was standing beside the door, his aura seeming to pull the shadows into a shroud around his slender form. There was no telling how long he'd been there, much less how he'd gotten past the wards, which showed no sign of breaching. The figure wore a hat with a brim and indented crown.

And was that a scepter in his hand?

Seay's bolt flashed past me. The enchantment exploded where the intruder had been standing, but he wasn't there anymore. Jordan shouted, sending a jet of druidic energy from his staff. The reveal spell broke throughout the basement space, but highlighted no one.

I aimed my ring back and forth.

"Spread out," I whispered, still sensing a presence. "Malachi, hang back."

He did as I said, while the rest of us moved from the table. If this *was* Arnaud, he was making a ballsy move. He might have had an enchanted instrument that negated the Brasov Pact, but my ring, recently topped off at the safe house, was singing with interfaith power. At my word, the collective belief of billions would incinerate the son of a bitch. There would be nothing left to send to the pits.

"Where'd that joker go?" Gorgantha muttered.

"Lower your weapons, please," a voice from behind us spoke.

Malachi cried out in alarm. The rest of us spun as Malachi scrambled from the rematerialized figure.

"Liberare!" I shouted, thrusting my grandfather's ring forward. Holy light gathered around my fist and released with a low boom that I felt down to the struts of my soul. The shaft of light enveloped the shadowy form, and dimmed.

What the...?

"Your weapons," the intruder repeated in a refined voice.

The handful of vine seeds Jordan flung at him were already sprouting by the time they landed. The druid's magic sent the growths writhing up the figure, binding his legs and arms. Before I could stop her, Gorgantha lunged past me and swung a fist at his head. Though the intruder didn't move, she missed high. Frustrated, Gorgantha grunted into her next two punches but they both sailed wide.

In the next moment she was sitting on the floor, as if placed there by a force. Seay's fae glow flickered down to nothing. Jordan thrust his staff toward the figure repeatedly, but no forces emerged. When I rattled off a series of invocations, it was as if the mental prism I used to channel energy had vanished.

In desperation, Malachi heaved his Bible. It nailed the wall five feet to the intruder's right and fell harmlessly to the floor.

"Are you finished?" he asked.

The vines wrapping him didn't wither; they simply thinned to nothing. When he stepped forward, the shadow slipped from him. A distinguished-looking man with gray eyes peered back at us.

"Osgood?" I stammered.

The fae butler gave a small bow. "At your service." He wasn't dressed in his formal attire. Instead, he wore brown khakis and a denim shirt, the sleeves rolled neatly up his forearms. What I'd mistaken for a scepter was a slender field telescope. Vintage hiking boots and a felt hat with a leather band completed the expeditioner look.

"Why didn't you just announce yourself?" I asked.

"I wanted to make sure I'd come to the right address."

The fae couldn't lie, so on some level he was telling the truth. But his faint smile told me he'd enjoyed the sparring session.

Jordan stepped forward, hands still clamped around his quarterstaff.

"Who is this?" he demanded.

Before I could answer, Seay said, "He's fae."

"The one your friend contacted?" Jordan asked.

"No," I replied with a sinking feeling. "The one I contacted."

The others turned toward me.

"Caroline received your message," Osgood told me. "Per her directive, I'm to deliver you and your crew into the time catch."

"So you withheld this information?" Jordan asked me, nostrils still flaring.

We were back at the table, but no one was sitting. I'd brought the team up to speed on my activities that morning, including my letter to Caroline. Needless to say, tempers had spiked, especially Jordan's and Seay's.

"The possibility seemed remote," I said. "I didn't even think my letter would reach her."

I glanced over at Osgood, who was strolling the apartment, hands clasped behind his back as though to give us space. He'd hung his coat upon entering, apparently, and now the field telescope jutted from a pocket. He hadn't described his exchange with Caroline, and he didn't appear prepared to now.

Had the letter spoken to her reason? Her emotions?

Seay faced me, hands on her hips. "And yet you sat there acting like my fae plan was the stupidest thing you'd ever heard."

"Hey, I didn't even like *my* fae plan," I shot back. "I was exploring the least bad options."

"Which you withheld so you could circle the discussion back to Arnaud," Jordan said.

I caught my fists clenching. "Regardless of what you two *think* happened, I put forward what I still consider our best option."

"Well, that's tough," Seay said, "because we're still bonded by the old vote, the one about using the *fae* to access the time catch."

"That's right," Jordan said. He didn't wait for Malachi or me to respond before turning to Osgood. "So, what's the plan?"

Osgood nodded as if coming out of a pleasant reverie and walked over to us. "The best time to cross over will be twilight. I've identified a location that offers the least bumpy ride. An old fort on Governor's Island."

"Where the mercreatures ducked out," Gorgantha said.

Though still simmering over the accusations against me, I nodded, not doubting there was a connection. Was Demon X using the time catch as a kind of cubby hole to move his Strangers and their hosts in and out?

"Your magical implements should make the journey fine," Osgood continued, looking from Jordan's quarterstaff to my walking cane. "However, I would keep them to a minimum. Perhaps two items apiece. I would also strongly discourage you from carrying anything volatile. This includes combustibles, electronics, most potions. If they were to discharge in transit, the consequences would be ... well, tragic. The lighter you travel, the better. No more than five mundane items and something for carrying them, so choose wisely."

"I have an interplanar space I use for storage," I said. "Will I be able to access it from the time catch?"

Osgood confirmed what I'd already guessed with a head shake.

"Can I assume by your threads that you're coming with?" Seay asked.

She appeared to have taken an interest in Osgood, despite

that he would have been centuries her senior. He gave a soft laugh that sounded more amused than condescending. "I'm afraid I have other duties that I must be getting back to, Miss Sherard. I'll escort you as far as the island and ensure your entry into the time catch."

"And what do we have to give you in exchange?" Malachi asked.

Osgood showed his empty hands. "Not a thing. I'm simply following orders."

"We were under the impression it worked differently," Jordan said to Osgood while shooting me a sidelong look.

"It does," I said.

Only the bargain hadn't been struck between Osgood and us, but between Caroline and the fae. Once more, I wondered what had compelled her to grant my request, no doubt at a cost. I caught Osgood watching me with his knowing eyes.

"Do you happen to know where this time catch is set?" I asked.

"Why, yes," he replied, surprising me. "New York City, circa 1776."

I paused. "During the American Revolution?"

"That's correct, Mr. Croft."

22

With only a few hours until twilight, I picked up the tuna steaks I'd promised Tabitha, stopped at a used bookstore, and returned to my apartment. While Tabitha ate, I launched into final preparations. Twelve years earlier, I'd thought packing for a trip to a lost monastery in Romania was a challenge.

Try a trip to eighteenth-century New York, kid.

Head buzzing, I grabbed an old backpack from my closet and signed my cubby hole open. From the void, I pulled out my go-to casting book and dropped it inside the pack. I then added a book on New York history that I'd bought at the bookstore, mainly for its 1776 survey maps of the city.

That's two.

Osgood told us not to worry about era-appropriate attire or money. He would take care of those. I decided to use my three remaining slots on spell implements. In the upstairs lab, I dug through my plastic bins. My pre-made potions were a no go, unfortunately, the suspended gems inside too unstable. Instead, I packed a vial of copper filings and two of my rarer ingredients, both inert: chameleon scales and slug essence. I would have to trust that the remaining ingredients for the potions I had in mind would be available in 1776 New York.

Now for the two magical items.

My cane sword was a given. Osgood had already assured me the two parts could count as one—he would bond them for the journey. But now came the tough choice: Grandpa's ring, my mother's emo ball, or Gretchen's cold iron amulet. They all had their utility against beings we might encounter.

I consulted my magic. Sometimes it gave me answers, but now it only shifted around, seeming to indicate none of them. The ring made the most sense, I decided. It would protect against vampires and, assuming the interfaith charge held, demons. And since we were going there to take on the second...

I checked to ensure the ring was secure at the base of my finger.

"Tabitha," I said, climbing down the ladder with my loaded pack, "I'm leaving you in charge."

She looked up from her plate and licked her grease-wet lips. "For how long?"

"If all goes well, I should be back later tonight."

"So soon?"

"We could be days, even weeks, in the time catch, but little time will pass here."

"I won't pretend to understand that, darling, so I'll just say good luck."

I couldn't resist a little teasing. "Sure you don't want to come along?"

"You said you're leaving from an island?" She scrunched up her face. "You know my feelings about water."

"Well, you wouldn't be swimming there. Vega's arranged for a police boat to take us over."

"Be that as it may, the answer remains no." When she caught my smirk, she said, "Make that, hell no."

"Suit yourself." I checked to ensure I had everything I intended to bring, then paused, a hand on the doorknob. "Hey, how are you feeling?"

She looked back at me blankly.

"About the demon apocalypse stuff?" I prompted.

"Oh, much better, darling. Almost back to normal."

"Great to hear."

With Tabitha acting as a canary in the demonic coalmine, her response suggested we might already have disrupted Demon X's plans by capturing Finn and purging half his pod. Now it was a matter of finishing the job. Then I could get back to pursuing Arnaud, hopefully as soon as tomorrow.

I gave Tabitha a final wave, locked up, then called Vega to tell her the Upholders and I would be heading to the dock soon.

THE SUN WAS JUST SETTING AS THE POLICE BOAT CLEARED THE southern tip of Manhattan and sped toward Governor's Island. Malachi, Seay, and I sat in the back with the packs. Jordan flew off the boat's port side in his raven form, while Gorgantha was in the bay, she and her pod acting as underwater escorts. Vega had offered to send the Sup Squad along, but I told her we had enough firepower for the short crossing.

And then there was Osgood.

The mysterious fae being stood at the head of the boat, peering at the approaching island through his field telescope. The tails of his long brown coat flapped behind him, enhancing his whole adventurer look.

"Can you trust him?" Vega had asked on the phone.

"Yeah," I'd replied after a moment.

"Okay, then why the hesitation?"

Because the question wasn't whether I trusted Osgood, but Caroline. "Because fae are fae," I answered instead. "But I think they realize this is in their interest too. The demon master *is* targeting half-fae."

"Well, listen to your gut," she said. "If it's telling you something's off, don't ignore it."

"I won't. I'll see you later tonight."

"I'll be waiting, babe."

The police boat slowed into a back churn of water as we approached the old dock. Up ahead, dense growth glowed in the twilight. Like with most of New York's parks, the funding for Governor's Island had been eliminated post-Crash and only recently restored. A long way from rehabbed, the island remained closed to visitors for the foreseeable future.

As the boat throttled to a stop, the three of us in back stood and gathered the bags. Jordan flew ahead to scout our end of the island. I thanked the two officers as we disembarked and joined Osgood on the dock.

Moments later, the boat was backing out and speeding toward the New York City skyline. Only eight hundred yards from southern Manhattan, and I felt like we were standing on the edge of a wilderness. As my gaze ranged past the distant figure of Lady Liberty, Gorgantha's head broke from the water below.

"Bay's clear," she announced, pulling herself onto the dock.

In a burst of druidic magic, Jordan dropped beside us in his human form. "The way to Fort Jay looks good."

I'd carried his leather pack from the boat and now handed it to him. He took it with a nod and slung the single strap across his torso. With the voting behind us, he seemed to be softening his stance toward me.

Yeah, 'cause he got what he wanted, I thought, not without bitterness.

Osgood led the way along an old road, the asphalt ravaged by roots. A former boathouse stood in ruins to our left. Beyond a failing retaining wall, we entered a band of woods. "The fort is just ahead." Though Osgood spoke with his usual decorum, I sensed he was enjoying the outing.

We were well into the trees when a series of hog-like snorts sounded. Osgood held up a hand. The rest of us stopped and peered past him. It took me a moment to spot the two hulking figures hunched over the ground, no doubt foraging for animal carcasses.

I turned toward Jordan. "Hey, I think you missed something."

"What are they?" Seay whispered, fae light glowing around her hands.

Jordan shot me a scowl. "Ghouls."

"Ugh," Gorgantha muttered. "Hate those things."

Though Mayor Lowder's eradication program had rid the city of most of the foul creatures, survivors turned up from time to time, usually in remote places like this one. And by the direction of the wind, they were going to know they had company in about three, two...

One of the ghouls threw his body upright with a sudden moan and thrust his lump of nose into the air. The other stared our way with dumb eyes. Judging by their large but not quite massive builds, these were juveniles. They were still going to be a pain in the ass to put down. And here I'd been hoping to save my magic for the time catch. I'd already drawn my sword when they let out a pair of yowls.

Osgood cleared his throat. "Would you like to handle them, or should I?"

The creatures broke into a charge, trees crashing around them.

I opened a hand toward the ghouls. "By all means."

"Very good, sir."

Osgood turned and faced the onrushing ghouls. They were easily twice his size. Within moments, they were breaking through the final trees, one of them lashing a clawed hand at Osgood's head. I was opening my mouth to cast when a soft light pulsed, and both creatures disintegrated without a sound. Osgood looked at the spot where their dust was floating to a rest, then peered over a shoulder.

"Shall we continue?"

I couldn't help but smirk. He was definitely enjoying this.

He led us along the broken swath left by the ghouls, and we soon emerged from the trees. An outer wall rose before us. We passed through an arched tunnel to access the fort's central quadrangle. Crumbling buildings stood on all sides. The energy was different here, and my wizard's senses showed why. The fort's star-shaped design was focusing the ley lines into the middle of the quadrangle.

Osgood stopped where two intersecting walkways formed a cross. As we gathered in front of him, I peered around, wary of the dimming fort and what could be lurking inside.

"You will be entering a city under British rule," Osgood said. "Further, you will be entering during a time of war against the Americans. When you arrive, take the most direct route to the water and procure a rowboat."

"Under the nose of British soldiers?" Malachi asked.

"I will address that," he said. "But your time will be limited. Row straight to the mainland. You can find lodgings in one of several inns along Nassau Street. If your allegiance is questioned, I advise you to answer *loyalist* to the King's soldiers and the wealthy and *patriot* to the common man in the tavern. It should avoid complications. In general, though, it will be best to avoid people altogether."

I wondered how much of this info was coming from Caroline, whose areas of expertise at Midtown College included urban history and affairs, and how much from Osgood's quiet knowledge of All Things.

"Also, your magic will create larger ripples in that place. If you wish to go quietly, forego its use."

Great.

"Can you tell us anything about the Stranger we're hunting?" I asked.

"I'm sorry, I cannot."

"Can't or won't?" Jordan pressed.

Osgood's faint smile suggested that while the fae had green-lighted his involvement with our mission, they had him on a short leash. "I trust your collective skills and intelligence will be up to the task," he said. "What I *can* do is send this along with you." From his coat, he retrieved a small leather pouch, which he offered to me. A layer of silvery magic, the color of starlight, moved around it.

"What's inside?" I asked as I accepted the supple pouch. Seay leaned toward it, her perplexed look telling me she had no clue either.

"Assistance, should you require it," Osgood said. "But please, only open it as a last measure."

Apparently it wasn't too volatile to make the journey, whatever it was. I stored the pouch in my pack. Per Osgood's instructions, I was carrying nothing in my coat pockets, and the coat now felt strangely light.

"The best way to return will be from this location," Osgood said, tapping his foot twice. "Note it when you arrive."

"Will we need to signal you?" I asked.

"That will not be necessary," he replied without elaborating.

Gorgantha made a doubtful face. "And if for some reason we *can't* get back to this spot?"

"The British troops," Malachi put in, clearly bothered by the idea of their presence.

"Yes, a backup plan would be wise," Osgood agreed. "Is there a location in the here and now you can suggest as a focus? It must hold a high concentration of energy."

"How about the townhouse?" Jordan asked.

"The energy is too diffuse, I'm afraid."

"Too diffuse?" Malachi echoed.

"As are your safe houses," Osgood added, preempting him.

I cleared my throat. "There's a cell in 1 Police Plaza that—"

"Yes, that will do," Osgood decided before I could explain further. I was already connected to the empty cell through my own magic, but now I felt a new bonding take hold. Subtler, yet stronger. One I sensed would maintain its connection across time and space. And Osgood had done nothing more than make eye contact with me.

"That will not be the safest method of return," he said, "especially for all five of you, so you must not rely on it. Make every effort to come here, preferably after dark." He peered up at the sky, whose deep gray color now mirrored his eyes. "Quickly now, gather into a circle around me and join hands."

We did as he said, my mind scrambling for final questions but not coming up with any. I consulted my gut, as Vega had urged me. The entire thing felt surreal but not off. We could trust Osgood.

I had ended up between Gorgantha and Seay. The mermaid swallowed my left hand in her webbed grip while the half-fae slid her slender hand inside my right. She gave it a playful squeeze, which I found reassuring.

"Close your eyes," Osgood said.

I did so without hesitation. *This is it.*

"Open them," the fae being commanded.

When I did, my breath caught in my chest and I stared around.

"What in the...?" Gorgantha muttered.

"Holy shit," Seay breathed.

We had arrived, and we were right in the middle of a group of—

"*Soldiers,*" Malachi gasped.

23

W e dropped each other's hands and moved into defensive postures. I pulled my sword at the same time Jordan's quarterstaff appeared from his cloak. Faint light glowed around Seay's fists.

But as I recovered from my initial shock, I noticed our attire had changed. My trench coat had turned into a long greatcoat. Underneath, I was wearing what looked like a linen shirt and waistcoat. My pants, meanwhile, had become form-fitting breeches tucked inside a pair of leather boots. Similar clothing showed below Jordan's cloak. Seay's hair fell in golden ringlets over the shoulders of a dark green gown, a frilly stomacher accenting the swell of a bodice. Malachi, meanwhile, wore a priest's robe.

But Gorgantha took the prize. Her massive mer form hulked inside a red satin dress, thick petticoats concealing her tail. A mass of dark plaited hair hid the fin running down the back of her neck while her face was glamoured into that of a woman's with bulbous eyes. It wasn't a flattering look, but it worked.

I also noticed that although there were red-coated British troops everywhere, they weren't paying us the least attention.

And not because we blended in—none of us were in military uniform. It had to be something else. When a pair of soldiers bearing infantry guns approached, Jordan drew his staff back.

"Wait," I whispered. "I don't think they can see us."

We watched them cautiously, Jordan's staff remaining in striking position. But the soldiers were walking casually, chatting to one another about what sounded like a cricket game. When they reached us, they veered around and continued on their way, bayonet scabbards slapping their thighs.

"Must be Osgood's doing," I said. "A blending enchantment, most likely."

"That's right!" Malachi blurted out. "He said he'd take care of the issue of the British troops, but that we'd only have so much time."

"Meaning it's not going to last," Seay remarked, the light that enveloped her hands fading.

"His instructions were to take the most direct route to the water." I looked around to get my bearings, but the fortress we'd entered was no longer here. In its place were earthen ramparts topped with soldiers and cannons. The precursor to Fort Jay, I guessed. Lantern light shone here and there in the growing dusk. Not wanting to be caught on the island when the enchantment wore off, I was about to suggest we just pick a direction and go when I remembered that we had a mermaid on the team.

"Can you lead us to the water?" I asked Gorgantha.

She was inspecting her satin dress and rustling petticoats. "What *is* this mess?"

"Let's worry about our costumes when we're somewhere safe," Jordan said.

"He's right," I said. "We need to get to the water."

With a grunt, Gorgantha released the dress and raised her head. "This way," she said.

As we made our way through the earthworks, I noticed our

packs had become era-appropriate linen and leather rucksacks and purses. But I was much more fascinated by our surroundings, namely the soldiers in their formal military uniforms and powdered wigs. I tuned into bits of passing conversation.

"...that miserable lot..."

"...give General Howe credit..."

"...only roused my taste for American women..."

A faint explosion of laughter, probably from a barracks, burst up and settled down again. It was like walking through a hobbyists' reenactment or a public television documentary, too real to seem entirely real.

We cleared the earthworks and crowds of soldiers and crossed a trench on a plank bridge. From there we got our first look at where the salt-water estuary that was the East River met Upper Bay. Massive warships occupied the bay like sentries, their towering sail-furled masts silhouetted against the darkening sky. Beyond them, points of light glimmered along what must have been the southern end of Manhattan, the tallest buildings no more than three or four stories.

Wow, I kept repeating to myself.

But with the clock ticking down on Osgood's enchantment, now wasn't the time to gawk. I focused on the stone seawall below, scanning its length until I spotted a dock where several small boats rocked.

"There," I said, pointing them out.

We hurried down a path and then onto a wooden pier. Choosing a boat, I waved for the others to board. When they were all on, I began uncoiling the thick rope that secured the boat to a piling.

"Hey!" a voice called. "What d'ye think yer doin'?"

I looked over as a heavyset man in a British uniform emerged from a small building and lumbered toward us. Given its darkness, I'd thought the building empty. Regardless, he shouldn't have been able to see us. I peered over at my four teammates, who were settling into the boat. Was the enchantment wearing off?

"I asked ye a question," the man said.

"Um, we're taking a boat out?" I answered.

"And where d'ye think yer taking 'er?" His voice was thick with challenge as he arrived in front of me.

"The mainland."

He squinted at me from a jowly face sheened in oil and sweat, then at my teammates. I picked up a sour odor of booze and observed the effect in his bloodshot eyes. Was drunkenness allowing him to see through Osgood's enchantment? His right hand closed around the hilt of a sword sheathed at his belt.

"We're going to the mainland," I repeated, this time risking the use of my wizard's voice.

His eyes shot back to mine, a burbly growl sounding deep in his barrel chest. Damn. If I had to drop this man with an invocation, what kind of ripples would that send out? Even beating him with my cane could have consequences, such as earning us a place on His Majesty's most wanted list.

"God save the King," I said, channeling power into the words. I held the man's gaze. After another moment, he burped loudly and wiped his mouth with the back of the hand that had been clenching the sword hilt.

"Well, go careful," he said. "Rumors of sharpshooters in Brooklyn."

My shoulders let out a little. "Thanks for the warning."

"Rebel dogs," he scowled. "Imagine them an' that coward Washington tryin' t' run the colonies."

"I'd rather not." When I faked a shudder, the man gave an appreciative snort.

"I'll signal yer passing," he said and hustled back up to his building.

I finished uncoiling the rope and tossed it aboard before climbing in myself. Gorgantha already had the oars in hand, and she began rowing us out into the East River. I looked up the broad waterway, struck not only by the absence of the iconic Brooklyn and Manhattan bridges, but by the undeveloped shorelines that stretched away into darkness. When I peered back, the man was covering and uncovering a lantern through a window, which explained why he kept his building unlit. A moment later, the closest warship signaled back.

"'God save the King?'" Seay asked.

"I heard it in a movie. Hey, it worked."

She made a skeptical face. "Nice hat."

I'd barely been aware I was wearing one. I removed it now and took it in my hands. A black revolutionary-era three-cornered hat. I ran a hand over my pulled-back hair to where it had been gathered into a ponytail and secured by a ribbon. It appeared Osgood's magic had actually altered our clothes and hair. Other details had been glamoured so we'd better blend in. Gorgantha's mermaid features, for example.

But our encounter with the British soldier was worrying.

I replaced my hat and addressed the team. "Listen up, everyone. It looks like the blending enchantment is wearing off, so we need to keep our heads down and speak as little as possible until we're safely lodged."

"No argument here," Malachi muttered, his gaze transfixed on the massive warships.

We crossed the river in good time, thanks to Gorgantha's powerful strokes, and drifted toward a waterfront of docks and warehouses on the eastern side of Manhattan's southern tip. Though the air smelled like fall, it was cool instead of cold, and humid. I directed Gorgantha past some merchant ships to where several smaller boats were tied up. A few figures moved around the wharfs, their shouts crude-sounding, but it looked like the day's cargo work was done. We disembarked quickly and quietly.

"Where are we?" Jordan whispered as I led the team across a rutted dirt road and away from the waterfront.

I brought my pack around—linen now with a buckled flap—and pulled out the book I'd bought at the store. I opened it to one of the 1776 survey maps I'd earmarked.

"Let's see." On the map, I ran a finger along the shoreline. "We docked here, so we must be close to..." I peered around. "Yes!" We had accessed another dirt road that ran into the city, but it wasn't just any road. "Ladies and gentlemen," I said, pointing to a sign on the cornice of a building. "I present Wall Street."

"Unbelievable," Malachi said, staring down its length of modest brick buildings. Far ahead, street lamps glowed, and the occasional horse-drawn cart clattered past an intersection. Because of his work with St. Martin's Cathedral, which stood near the Broadway end of Wall Street, Malachi knew this section of modern New York well.

"This isn't a tour," Jordan said.

Seay was giving me an unimpressed look too. They had come to hunt a Stranger and recover their loved ones, not marvel over how the city had looked two hundred fifty years ago. For her part, Gorgantha continued to grumble over her dress.

"Wall Street will lead us to Nassau," I said, trying to recover a tone of authority. "Seay, walk up here with me. Malachi in the middle. Jordan and Gorgantha in the rear. We need to look like we've walked this street a hundred times before."

As I started down Wall Street, Seay slipped her hands around my arm and drew herself against me.

"What are you doing?" I whispered.

She flashed a flirtatious smile, light sparkling in her eyes. "Just playing the part."

I sighed but let her stay there, in part because her perfumed hair was helping cover the stink of raw sewage that seemed to come from everywhere. I marked the intersections: Burnett, then Queen. What must have been a meat market by day appeared on our right, a corner plot of hard-packed dirt, wooden stalls stained with blood.

Down the next long block, a door opened, and light and laughter spilled onto the street along with a pair of men. As they passed us, the obviously drunken duo leered at Seay with bleary eyes and missing teeth and slurred unintelligibly. They'd emerged from a tavern named McGowan's. Beyond a steamed-up window, I could make out the impressions of patrons, but the large space wasn't very crowded.

"Are you trippin'?" Gorgantha hissed behind me.

I turned to find Jordan pulling open the door to the tavern.

"Hey!" I called. "Stick to the plan!"

"We need info," he called back, and went inside.

I was pissed enough to say the hell with him and continue to Nassau Street, but we couldn't separate so soon after arriving. Swearing, I nodded at the others and led the way into the tavern after him.

24

The faces that turned from their tankards looked like the men who had just stumbled out: bearded, dirty, and either drunk or well on their way. Dockworkers and mariners connected to the waterfront, I guessed. Their conversations fell to murmurs as they eyed us. And we did *not* fit in here.

Jordan was already halfway across the plank floor, cutting past tables like he owned the damned place. His destination was a stout woman behind the bar wearing a plain blouse and apron. The thick forearms folded below her chest were the color of bricks. She shifted her hard eyes from Jordan to us.

Wonderful.

I had half a mind to drag the druid back into the street by his cloak, but I didn't want to draw any more attention than we already had. As if a group that included a minister and a six-and-a-half-foot woman *could* draw more attention. Seay, who must have read the situation, waved us over to a large table in the corner where the light from the candles placed around the tavern didn't fully reach. With the humid heat of bodies warming the place, a large stone hearth beside the table remained dark.

Seay and I ended up on the side of the table facing the bar. "It's not a bad idea," she remarked.

I stared at her, incredulous. "Not a bad idea? We had one immediate goal: find lodgings. And now look at us."

"So?"

"So? What are we doing here?"

"And how do you sit in this wack thing?" Gorgantha asked, trying to shift the bulk of the petticoats out from under her. When her tail popped out, I peered around anxiously to make sure no one else had seen.

"Look, hon." Seay rested a hand on my forearm. "I did some bartending back in high school. Glamoured ID," she explained. "Well, I glamoured pretty much everything. Made a killing in tips. Anyway, we had a few regulars who knew what happened in the neighborhood, down to which rat crossed MacDougal Street at 2:22 a.m. the Monday before. Trust me. If anything strange is happening in 1776 New York City, chances are good someone has told Miss Personality over there."

At the bar, Jordan was leaned forward, one elbow resting on the polished wood. The woman's expression remained hard and unyielding. I'd tagged her as a barmaid, but now I was thinking tavern keeper.

"You mean like ganky types coming and going?" Gorgantha asked when she'd finally gotten herself settled.

"Exactly," Seay said.

Jordan turned and gestured toward our group.

"I have a bad feeling about this," Malachi muttered.

"Yeah, you and me both," I said.

After a moment, the tavern keeper gave a curt nod and shouted something behind her. Jordan pulled a pouch from a pocket. I had one too, I realized, in the front pocket of my breeches, heavy with coins. I checked my other pockets. In the opposite one, I found a bronze watch whose filigreed hands indicated 7:10 p.m. Nested in the breast pocket of my coat were a wooden pipe and a tin packed with tobacco leaf. Osgood hadn't skimped on the details.

I returned everything as Jordan set a pair of coins on the bar. He said something else to the tavern keeper, set down one more coin, and walked toward our table.

"We're not staying," I said.

"Relax." He sat on Seay's other side. "I just ordered our dinner. We have to eat sometime, don't we?"

"What was the final coin for?" I demanded.

His eyes shifted to the bar, where the tavern keeper was filling a cluster of tankards from a tapped cask. "We'll know soon enough."

"Look," I said in a lowered voice. "In case you haven't noticed, we're not from around here. You waltz into a place like this asking questions and showing your bulky coin purse, the only thing you're going to get is a knife in the back." A few of the patrons were still peering at us over hunched shoulders and from behind tankards. "Now I say we stand up, walk out, and get back to our plan. No needless interactions, remember?"

"Too late," Gorgantha said.

The tavern keeper had rounded the bar and was coming toward us with five sloshing tankards in her fists. "Here ye go," she said in an Irish accent, setting them around. "The stew'll be out shortly." The place reeked of smoke and body odor, but at the mention of stew, I picked up an undercurrent of cooked fish that wasn't unpleasant.

"Thank you," Jordan said, looking at the tavern keeper meaningfully.

She seemed to hesitate as she glanced around the tavern. "My cook might have something t' tell ye," she said in a lowered voice. She returned to the bar and disappeared into what must have been the kitchen.

Jordan sat back. "You were saying, Croft?"

"Yeah, I'll congratulate you when we actually have some useful info," I replied thinly. "In the meantime, I'm not trusting anything that woman poured."

Jordan raised his tankard to his mouth and left it there a moment, eyes shifting. At last he swallowed and lowered the tankard. "It's clean," he declared. I was about to ask how he knew, but druids had uncanny senses, and that included detecting poisons.

I took a swallow of my own ale, for no other reason than to calm my nerves. The drink was hard and flat and landed in my empty stomach like a stone. The alcohol found my bloodstream almost immediately. I was contemplating another swallow when a lanky man appeared from the back of the tavern. He was young with a narrow face, long hair, and honest eyes. He arrived with a platter of steaming bowls and stooped over to set it on the end of our table.

Up close, I sensed his nervousness.

"I understan' yer asking after strange doin's," he said in a lowered voice, tossing loose strands of hair from his eyes. "Well, there's been strange doin's aplenty lately." He set the first bowl in front of Gorgantha, obviously going about it slowly to buy himself time. "My father was a Patriot soldier, captured in the Battle fer Long Island. Fer months we didn't know if he was prisoner or dead." He set another bowl in front of Malachi. "But then he turned up sudden a couple weeks back. No shoes on his feet. Shirt and pants covered in..." He glanced at Seay. "Pardon me for saying so, but shit and piss. And smellin' like the grave. Best we could tell, the British Army had held him prisoner but then turned him out fer some reason." He lowered his voice further. "But it's not him."

"What do you mean?" Jordan asked, taking his bowl.

"He stares at my ma and me like he dunno who we are.

Wanders about the city at all hours. It's like there's nothin' inside him."

A zombie?

"How does he seem physically?" I asked. "Any injuries or wounds? Gangrene?"

"No, sir," the boy answered. "We cleaned him up, and those he had are healed. It's his mind that's gone."

"War can do that to people," I said, not sure if they had a word for PTSD in the late eighteenth century.

But as the boy set a bowl down in front of Seay, he shook his head.

"It's not jus' him. There are more in his state turnin' up around the city."

"Are any of them wearing cloaks?" Jordan asked, holding up the hem of his. "Something like this?" He was asking if any possessed druids were among them, but the boy frowned in thought before shaking his head.

"Any women?" Seay asked.

"No, ma'am," the boy answered.

"How about dark-skinned folks?" Jordan pressed.

"I've seen a few freemen in that condition, but they're all Patriot soldiers. Most of 'em white. Must've given a loyalty oath or something to get turned out, 'cause the Brits don't bother 'em now. Either that or their minds are too broke for the Crown to care. And I've seen some of 'em with weapons."

I was wondering if the soldiers' brains had been chemically altered somehow so they'd no longer pose a threat, but I couldn't remember reading anything like that in the history books. No, this felt like an evil force at work. But was it some unspoken facet of history, or was it special to the time catch?

"Do the returned soldiers associate with one another?" I asked. "Meet up anywhere?"

"Aye. A few come in here sometimes." The final bowl he set

on the table was mine, steam from the fish stew rising past my face. "They'll order drinks and food, but 'sides that, they don't talk. Jus' sit there watching. Usually gather right here, in fact." He nodded at our table.

Vampire spawn? I wondered now. *Demon possessed?*

"Have you noticed an increase in murders or disappearances in the city?" I asked.

The boy straightened from his stoop and reclaimed his platter. "Lots of Patriots left when the British Army came, but murders? No more than usual, I reckon. Fewer people about after dark, though, I can tell ye that. A month ago, we'd've been wall to wall, so loud ye couldn't hear yourself think. Now?" He indicated the sparse crowd. "All these returned soldiers wandering about have gotten folks spooked. It's ... it's not right."

I nodded gravely. Something was happening, and I was betting it was connected to Demon X's involvement with the time catch.

"Can we meet your father?" I asked.

"Meet him?" The boy's Adam's apple jumped sharply when he swallowed. "What fer?"

"I might be able to help."

The tension in his face let out. "The doctor's already been 'round to see him. Said nothin' can be done."

Jordan had gone quiet after learning the boy hadn't seen anyone resembling the others from his circle. Now he held out a coin. "Thanks for your time." With a nod, the boy pocketed the coin and left with the platter.

"That could have been a lead," I said.

"To what?" Jordan asked, taking a bite of stew.

"To how Demon X is using the time catch, which could lead us to the Strangers."

Jordan muttered, "If there's two dozen steps involved, it must be a Croft plan."

"That's a lot better than going off half-baked," I countered.

"Let's just finish our meals and leave before it's full dark," Malachi said. "Sounds like we have more to worry about than British soldiers. When we get to our lodgings, we'll hold a team meeting."

We ate quickly, Gorgantha finishing her stew in two bowl-tilts to the mouth. She was crunching on a fishtail when her protuberant eyes froze over the bowl's rim. I followed their aim. I hadn't heard them enter in the din of surrounding conversation. Neither had my teammates, judging by their reactions.

Three disheveled men stood halfway between the door and our table. The hollowness of their staring eyes marked them as the former soldiers the cook had described. The tavern fell silent. I looked over at the bar. The tavern keeper was watching the men cross-armed while the cook peered out from the kitchen. When I made eye contact with him, he gave a furtive nod—*that's them*—and retreated back behind a curtain of steam.

The former soldiers resumed their walk toward us. One had what looked like an old flintlock pistol in a holster at his belt while the other two bore sheathed knives.

"How 'bout this table here," the tavern keeper called. She had come around the bar and was pulling the chairs from another table. "I'll have yer drinks poured by the time ye get settled."

The man with the pistol, burly with a floppy felt hat and thick ginger beard, looked over at her then back at us. The other two men, one with ratty brown hair and the other with a gaunt, pock-scarred face, never stopped eyeing our table.

"Oy, over here," the tavern keeper said sharply.

After another moment, they complied. As she returned to the casks, the three men lowered themselves but continued to watch us. Whether it was because we were sitting at their table or they saw something in us, I didn't know.

"Is anyone else feeling weirded out?" Seay asked.

"As in creep detector off the charts?" Gorgantha asked, setting her bowl back down. "Hell to the yes."

Malachi was already standing. "Uh, maybe we should—"

"Hold on," I said.

I opened my wizard's senses and watched the tavern become a mosaic of astral patterns. In the time catch, a thin, honey-colored energy layered everything—a consequence, maybe, of having been pinched off from the time continuum. I focused on the three men. Dead space, like I'd observed around the mercreatures. Something had stolen their souls, or rather the time catch equivalent.

Though I remembered Osgood's warning, I pushed a little more energy into my vision. I was looking for an indication of *what* had stolen their souls. But while the patterns in the tavern grew more vibrant, the men remained dark voids. Only now glowing points were taking hold in the big one's staring eyes.

Shit.

I shut down my wizard's senses and blinked to speed the tavern's return to focus. The man's eyes weren't glowing anymore, but I knew what I'd seen. Standing, I turned toward my teammates.

"Let's go, but keep your faces averted," I said. "Don't let them get a good look at you."

As we moved toward the door, I could feel the soulless men tracking us. I kept my head turned, listening for the cock of a hammer or the scrape of chair legs over the wood floor. When we made it outside, I closed the door. Beyond the foggy glass, I could see the men's figures. They hadn't moved. I led the way west on Wall Street at a fast walk.

"No more stops," I said.

Seay took my arm again. "What did you see?"

"They're possessed. Something siphoned out their souls and

are using them as watchmen. We must have been interesting enough to send up a signal, because I caught someone or something coming in for a closer look."

"Demon?" Malachi asked.

"Or a powerful mage," I said. "But yeah, probably demon."

I peeked back, relieved to see no one emerging from the tavern. Instead of continuing straight to Nassau Street as originally planned, I turned right on William Street and then took a quick left onto King. Except for the occasional rattle of a horse-drawn carriage in the distance, the streets were quiet.

Just let us get to an inn without drawing any more attention.

The intersection with Nassau street was just ahead, but I stopped suddenly. Several figures had stepped into the street, blocking our way.

"Got a gang back of us too," Gorgantha said. "And they're packin' heat."

I peered back.

Crap.

25

"**K**eep walking," I said in a lowered voice. "Are they following?"

"Yeah," Jordan said. "Four of them."

"All right, you and Gorgantha slow down. Let them get within arm's length." With Osgood's warning about magic ringing in my head, I wanted to take their firearms out of the equation, force them to use their blades. "Malachi, come up here between Seay and me. We're going to try to file past the ones ahead."

"And if they attack?" Jordan asked.

"Then we fight back—but without magic."

"With all due respect, Prof," he said. "I think the jig is up."

"I'm not so sure. I think whoever's controlling the men wants a closer look at us."

I heard Gorgantha popping her thick knuckles. "Not a problem for me."

"Jordan?" I said.

"Yeah. I can handle them with my quarterstaff."

As his and Gorgantha's footfalls slowed and fell back, I peeked over a shoulder. The soulless men behind them continued forward, closing the distance. None had aimed their guns yet. Neither had the three men ahead, though the long-barreled muskets they braced across their chests were presumably loaded and ready to fire.

When we'd closed to within ten feet, I nodded at the men and made a move to sidle past them. They shifted over, blocking our path again. Like the men in the tavern, they wore tattered homespun coats and stained trousers. Their felt hats featured large brims that hid their faces from the glow of a nearby oil lamp.

"May I help you?" I asked, trying to sound pleasant.

"Where ye going?" the closest man asked in a hollow voice.

"We're returning from dinner."

"Where ye staying?" the one behind him asked.

"Oh, Uptown," I said.

When the men looked at one another, it dawned on me that there was no such thing as "uptown" in 1776 New York. It would all be farmland, country estates, and woods. There was probably a name for that part of the island, but it sure as hell wasn't "uptown."

"Yes, the, ah, Upton Inn," I amended. "Lovely place. I highly recommend it."

The faceless gang stared at me until I thought I could feel the glowing eyes I'd glimpsed in the tavern, only now peering from the sockets of the man in front of me. I tightened my magic, needing to convince the possessing force that we were mundane. Jordan and Gorgantha arrived behind us, the four men close at their backs.

"Well, if that's all," I said, "we bid you men a fond good night."

When I put a hand on the closest man to guide him aside, he batted it off with his rifle.

"Show us the Upton Inn," he said.

"Oh, screw this," Seay muttered.

Something flashed in my peripheral vision, and in the next moment the man was gagging on a dagger. Seay ripped the weapon from his throat, releasing a spray of blood. The weapon, which I hadn't even known she was carrying, gleamed in a way suggesting it had been forged in Faerie. Seay glanced over and gave me a semi-apologetic look before driving her blade into the next man's chest.

I got my sword up in time to catch a knife slash from the third man in front of us. On instinct, ley energy coursed through my mental prism. But though I could have *really* used a shield at that moment, I stopped short of speaking one into being.

"Whoa!" I cried, jumping back as the man slashed at me twice more.

On his third wild swing, his hat fell away, revealing disheveled gray hair and a snarling mouth of mossy teeth. I blocked his next slash with my staff and brought my blade down on his neck. The metal crunched through muscle and bone, sending the man into a sideways jig. His blade thudded to the road as his unmoored head bobbled around a blood-slick neck. Lunging forward, I finished the job with a final chopping blow.

Behind me, Jordan's quarterstaff was in action, sweeping legs and pounding heads, while Gorgantha dealt damage with her fists. I caught her pummeling one of the soulless men with a right hand that sent him into the side of a building.

I looked around to make sure Malachi was safely out of harm's way and found him backed into a doorway down the block. One of the men was advancing on him, tossing a blade between his hands.

"Hey!" I called, trying to draw his attention to me. But as I ran toward them, the soldier continued his advance. Malachi dug at the neck of his priestly robes for his cross pendant. When he couldn't find it, he switched to his pockets. The man caught the blade in his left hand and drew it back to strike. Malachi's hand emerged with his Latin Bible, and he thrust it out. The man hesitated, and I decapitated him from behind.

By the time I turned, the rest of the men were down.

"Everyone all right?" I asked.

"Peachy," Seay said, returning her blade to a thigh sheath.

"Didn't realize you were carrying," I said.

"Have to toughen up my hands somehow," she replied with a wry smile.

Jordan and Gorgantha grunted that they were fine, the mermaid rubbing her right fist.

I looked around the scattered bodies, considering how we'd just committed the most unpatriotic act ever. Soldiers of the frigging American Revolution. I had to remind myself that someone had already claimed their essence, turning them into soulless vessels. Meat bags, essentially. That alone marked the possessing force as malevolent.

Malachi shuffled up beside me. "I think he caught me earlier," he said, almost apologetically. When he held up an arm, blood dripped from a flap of slashed fabric.

"How bad?" I asked, gripping Malachi's shoulder to steady him.

Whether from fear or trauma, color was already leaching from his face. "I ... I don't know."

"Here," Jordan said, coming up and moving Malachi's hand over the wound. "Clamp down as hard as you can. That'll slow the blood loss. Once we get to the inn, I'll take a look. I brought my kit."

"We're not going to an inn," I said.

Jordan's brow creased. "That's all you've been talking about since we got here."

"Change of plans. The destination now is St. Martin's."

"St. Martin's?" Jordan repeated. "Isn't that going to mean interacting?"

"Yeah, well, we no longer have the luxury of discretion. We need better protection than an inn can afford."

I wanted to be pissed at Jordan for our tavern stop, but with so many soulless men out and about, they would have spotted us eventually. At least our stop had provided us a little advanced warning, courtesy of the young cook. Jordan appeared ready to say more when a musket cracked, and a ball whistled past.

"Let's go," I called, waving the team left onto Nassau. "The church is that way."

The musket cracked again, but it was coming from the other end of King Street and early firearms were notoriously inaccurate. At that thought, my hat flipped from my head. *Son of a bitch just shot it off.*

Before he could reload, I scooped up the tricorn and raced until I'd caught up to the others. As we passed what must have been the original City Hall building, I called, "Right!"

Ahead, the way was clear to St. Martin's, whose first incarnation had been more church than cathedral. Only it wasn't there. I passed my teammates and stuttered to a stop at the edge of Broadway's wide expanse. Elegant homes and businesses lined our side of the dirt road, but opposite stood the husks of burned buildings—where anything stood at all. The destruction extended for blocks.

"The Great Fire of New York," Malachi said.

I could have smacked myself in the forehead. "Of course," I muttered.

"What's going on?" Seay asked, taking in the damage with a cocked eyebrow.

"There was a huge fire in September 1776," I said. "No one knows what started it, but the fire burned everything west of Broadway."

While I spoke, I stared at what must have been the church-yard. A large pile of charred debris stood at one end, as if efforts were being made to clear it. A massive fount of ley energy gushed up from the ground. The second incarnation of St. Martin's wouldn't be built until well after the war. Lacking a channeling structure, the ley energy was dispersing in all directions, much of it into the night sky.

"Where did the parishioners go during this period?" I asked Malachi.

He blinked as if struggling to think, and I wondered how much had to do with blood loss. I looked down at the hand clamping his forearm but couldn't tell whether the blood I was seeing was fresh or from earlier.

"Saint Mark's Chapel," he said at last. "It's a few blocks up Broadway."

"We'll head there, then," I said. "But we need to stay off the road."

I checked both ways before leading our team across Broadway, away from the street lamps and into the charred landscape. When we were fully cloaked in darkness, I peered back. No one had emerged onto the main thoroughfare yet. Off toward the Hudson River, I could see large groupings of tents that must have been serving as barracks for British soldiers. Thankfully, none were patrolling this way. We moved through the ruins as fast as we reasonably could, Jordan assisting Malachi.

After a couple blocks, I spotted a tall spire. Soon, the rest of the chapel took form beyond a line of trees. The handsome little chapel appeared to be the only structure in the fire zone that hadn't been incinerated.

We entered the manicured grounds through a side gate and accessed a columned portico in front. Gorgantha pounded the wooden door with a fist, the sound shuddering throughout the sanctuary. We waited anxiously, all of us glancing back at Broadway. A moment later the door opened. An elderly face illuminated in candlelight peered out. Hard, dark eyes stared over a hooked nose and pinched lips.

"Are you the rector here?" Malachi asked.

The man regarded us with naked suspicion. "Aye."

"We've come for sanctuary," I said. "Brother Malachi here has been attacked."

Jordan held up Malachi's arm. The rector's gaze narrowed in on the bloodied tatters and then made another pass over the rest of us. He'd never emerged fully from the doorway, and I could just make out a black robe with a white cravat at his throat. Protective currents coursed around his head. The chapel was sitting on a fount too, though not one as powerful as St. Martin's. Even so, I would never get inside without an invitation, and the same was probably true of Seay and Jordan.

"Who are you?" he asked.

"Travelers from elsewhere," I answered, peering over a shoulder. Still no one on Broadway, but for how much longer?

"Please," Malachi said.

The rector, who had trained his eyes on the street as well, snapped them back to Malachi. "Can you recite the catechism on God the Father?"

Malachi did so quickly, his voice weak and quavering.

Far down Broadway, men began to appear from side streets. The damned wandering soldiers. They hadn't spotted us, but that wouldn't last. When Malachi finished the final question and answer, the rector shifted his pinched lips around as if in deliberation.

C'mon, c'mon, c'mon, I thought.

At last, he gave the barest nod.

"You may enter." Then after another moment: "All of you."

We wasted no time filing inside after Malachi, the protective energy of the threshold crashing through me like falling water, negating most of my magic. Though my incubus had weakened our bond as part of a recent agreement, I could feel his remaining hooks digging deeper into my soul.

The rector watched me with critical eyes as I passed.

I took a final glance back at Broadway to find several of the men moving our way—but still in search mode, it appeared.

When we were all inside, the rector closed and locked the door. I exhaled. We were at the rear of the chapel's nave. In the wavering light of the rector's candle, I observed a back row of boxed pews as well as a pair of columns that rose into the darkness of a high ceiling. The energy inside the chapel felt soothing, benevolent. Though we were at the rector's mercy, I trusted him.

"Thank you," I said.

He nodded. With a softly spoken "this way," he led us down an aisle that ran alongside the nave. He continued past the altar and into a back room, where he went around lighting several candles with his own. They illuminated what looked like a dormitory consisting of two beds, two wooden desks, and a basic armoire.

"I'll return with water and some linen," he said.

Jordan already had Malachi sitting on the edge of a bed and was peeling back his sleeve.

"Damn," Gorgantha muttered as the wound came into view. The slash was ugly and deep.

The rector returned with a basin, and together, he and Jordan cleaned the wound until the basin water turned almost as dark as Malachi's robe. I noticed Jordan hadn't taken out his druid kit, which was smart. Many religious officials in the present day considered any and all magic the work of Satan, and I knew that went triple for the colonial era. With Jordan holding Malachi's arm, the rector poured what smelled like drinking alcohol over the cleaned wound, then wrapped it tightly with strips of linen.

"There," he said, tying off the final strip. "We'll check it again in the morning. Make certain there's no infection. I have a pallet I can bring in for a third bed. I'll prepare the room next door for the women. You may stay two nights. No more. The vicar and curate return from Boston on the tenth," he explained.

"We're friends of the Church," Malachi assured him.

The rector looked at each of us in turn, his gaze lingering on mine. Deep inside, I felt Thelonious stir. *The rector's a shadow exorcist,* I realized in alarm. *He can see the demonic essence I'm harboring.* I expected fear and hatred to take hold in the man's eyes. Instead, they softened with what seemed empathy.

He returned his attention to Malachi. "I understand, but others won't."

"Can you tell us what's happening out there?" I asked him.

"I believe the less said, the better." He backed toward the doorway.

"Wait." Jordan stood from the bed. "We've come to the city to recover people. Loved ones stolen from us. We believe there might be a connection to the returned soldiers." He glanced over at me as though to concede what I'd said earlier. "The same soldiers who injured Brother Malachi here."

The rector paused in the doorway.

"What you know could save lives," Jordan finished.

"Someone paid the British to have the soldiers turned out," he said.

"Who?" I asked.

"I don't know. I received the information from a minister at Middle Dutch Church. When the British occupied the city, the only religious houses allowed to remain in service were those loyal to the Church of England. Indeed, I'm required to ask the allegiance of anyone who seeks sanctuary here." He dipped his eyes and added under his breath, "As if there's a higher allegiance than to the Creator. The remaining churches were seized and turned into officers' quarters or soldiers' barracks. Middle Dutch became a prison for American soldiers."

"But they were released?" I asked.

"Not from there, the overflow north of here on Broadway," he said. "A converted sugar house. And very suddenly. According to the minister at Middle Dutch, someone paid an enormous sum for their freedom."

"They sprung the ones they're still fighting?" Gorgantha asked. "That's straight up stup—I mean, that doesn't make sense."

"No it doesn't," the rector agreed. "Nor does what those soldiers have become."

As a shadow exorcist, he would have discerned their soulless natures.

"Have you noticed anything else amiss in the city besides the freed soldiers?" I asked.

"There's plenty amiss and always has been," he said with a weary breath. He was likely referring to the darker of New York's supernatural inhabitants. "But perhaps more worrying than that, or even the soldiers, is that the Church is considering selling the site where St. Martin's stood before the fire."

"What?" I exclaimed.

Had this happened in our actual history with the Church ultimately deciding not to sell the land and its powerful fount of ley energy? Or was someone from the outside messing with the time catch?

"The buyer in this case is not a secret," the rector said. "He's an aggressive financier."

"His name?" I asked with growing dread.

"Mr. Thorne."

26

"Arnaud Thorne is here?" Jordan asked. "*Your* Arnaud Thorne?"

The rector had finished setting up our rooms, brought us basins and towels for washing, as well as two bottles of wine and some hard bread, and bid us good night. The five of us reconvened in what was in effect the men's dormitory.

"Yes and no," I replied, pacing. "Arnaud came to the New World sometime following the war against the Inquisition in Eastern Europe. He ended up here, in Manhattan, where he began building his empire."

"But when you asked, the rector said the pimp's first name was Renault," Gorgantha pointed out.

"He changed his name every few decades claiming to be a son or nephew so as not to draw attention to his undead nature. Much more easily done before the digital age," I added. "So yes, Arnaud Thorne is here, but it's the eighteenth-century version, not the twenty-first."

"Do we need to worry about him?" Malachi asked.

"He'll have no idea who I am, much less the rest of you. As for the proposed purchase of the church site, he could just be after the real estate. He's ambitious, always has been. I wouldn't be surprised if he's making similar inquiries into the other properties in the fire zone. He might also see that particular property as insurance. You know, keeping the church from shaping the ley energy into a force destructive to his kind."

"So to be clear, you're not going after him," Jordan said abruptly.

"There'd be no point," Seay answered before I could. She was the only one to have partaken in the wine, and she cupped a goblet of red in her lap. "The time catch is a bubble. Killing someone here would have no effect on our time stream. Arnaud would carry on in the present as if nothing had happened."

I nodded. "What she said. And if you're still worried about my commitment—"

"I'm not," Jordan cut in. "So let's talk about what we came to the time catch for. You tracked a name here. We need you to track it again."

"It's not going to be that easy."

"Why not?"

"I won't be able to cast inside the chapel, one. The threshold stripped my powers. Beyond that, it takes my magic time to adapt to a new location. We're technically in the same place, but the organization of energy here is different. I need to get a solid handle on the pattern before attempting something as delicate as tracking a demon's name." When Jordan pressed his lips together, I said, "I get it, we're in a hurry. Normally, I'd wait forty-eight hours, but I'm going to attempt the spell in twenty-four."

"And what are the rest of us supposed to do?" he asked.

"For now, everyone is safest inside the chapel," I said. "No evil can enter, and that includes the former soldiers and whoever's possessing them."

"I can't do that," he said.

"Do what?"

"Wait here."

When he strode toward the door, I grasped his arm. "Where are you going?"

I expected him to shake me off, but he stopped and turned. "A druid circle is stronger than its members. When the Stranger infiltrated ours, it damaged that whole, weakened it. My abilities aren't what they were. And they're even more out of sorts after the jump here, sort of like yours. I'm having a hard time telling natural from unnatural. But there's a druid circle about forty miles north of the city."

"How do you know?" I asked, releasing his arm.

"During the Revolutionary War, the British announced that slaves who fled to their side would be freed following military service. A forebear of mine, Lee Derrow, took the chance. Left his master in Virginia and joined up with the Redcoats. Served bravely and ended up in a fort on the Hudson. When the tide shifted toward the Americans, the Brits released him. Rather than risk capture, he made for Canada. He didn't know the land up here, though. The Raven Circle found him in the woods, starved and half dead. They healed him and initiated him into their druidhood. It was the circle I was born into."

I saw where this was going. "So you're thinking of...?"

"It would only take me a couple hours to fly there. Once I'm connected to the circle, I'll be able to locate the Stranger."

"And the druids will let you in?" I asked.

He tapped the symbols on his temple. "I have the mark."

"Let him do it," Seay said, knowing the Stranger in question could just as easily be the one holding the half-fae as the druids.

Still, Jordan's plan was dicey. Forty miles. Communicating through the bonding sigil over that distance would require powerful magic I couldn't afford to cast. We would never know if something happened to him. But his fellow druids were missing, including his wife. Hell, if it were Vega, I'd fly four thousand miles to get her back.

"I'll walk you out," I said, picking up a candle.

We returned through the nave, this time along the center aisle. I unlocked the main door and peered out. The front of the chapel was clear. So was Broadway for as far as I could see. The soldiers must have given up their search and resumed patrolling. I backed from the power of the threshold.

"You're good," I said.

"I'll be back by noon tomorrow."

"If you get into trouble, call us," I said, referring to our bond. I preferred to deal with the consequences of the ripple effect than leave Jordan to fend for himself. He started to edge past me, then stopped.

"Delphine is close," he said with trembling lips. "I can feel her."

"We'll find her," I assured him.

With a determined nod, he crossed the threshold and ducked around the edge of the chapel into darkness. I remained in the doorway, sword in hand, listening for signs of trouble. A minute later, Jordan flapped past the front of the church in his raven form, tilted a wing, then climbed into a night sky of pale clouds.

RECTOR HARLAND RETURNED THE FOLLOWING MORNING TO CHECK on Malachi's arm. The gash was ugly, but there were no signs of infection. Seay and Gorgantha entered the room as he was wrapping the wound with fresh linen.

"Where's the other one in your party?" the rector asked.

"Jordan left on an errand," I said. He hadn't signaled us during the night, which seemed like a good sign—unless of course he'd been taken out before he could activate it. But I needed to stay optimistic.

"And what will the rest of you be doing today?" he asked.

"We were about to discuss that," I said, which was true.

The rector straightened from Malachi's side and looked us over. "If you wish to go out now, it should be safe. There are fewer rebel soldiers about during the day, and their vision doesn't seem as keen. Still, I would advise that you not go out as a group. That's what they'll likely be looking for. No more than two of you together." He reached into a pocket in his robe and drew out a pair of iron keys. "These will get you back inside the chapel if I'm not here. Just be certain to lock the door when you leave. I'm sorry I can't give you sanctuary beyond tomorrow morning."

"We understand, Father," I said, accepting the keys.

"There's more wine in the kitchen, and I've set out bread and cheese."

We all thanked him.

When he left, I turned toward the others. Seay and Gorgantha were wearing the same dresses from the night before. If we wanted changes of clothes, we were going to have to purchase them in the city, but that was low on my list of priorities. "I think we should venture out," I said. "I need to study the ley energy. Plus, there are some ingredients I want to gather for a stealth potion."

"I could be looking for Darian and the others," Seay said. She turned to Gorgantha. "Wanna come with?"

"Sure, but I'll need to take a dip at some point."

As I handed Seay a key, Malachi looked up at me. "I can go with you."

"I'd rather you stay here and heal. You lost a lot of blood last night."

He set his jaw. "I came along to help, not be a convalescent."

"Hey," Gorgantha said, "you got us in the chapel here, didn't you?"

"She's right." I lowered my voice. "And you can actually be of help here by picking the rector's brain. I get the feeling he knows more than he's doling out. He might be more comfortable just talking to you."

Malachi seemed to consider that before nodding importantly.

"Let's all plan to meet back here around noon," I said.

THE WIDE LANE OF BROADWAY WAS BUSTLING WITH HORSE-DRAWN carriages and all class of people, from uniformed soldiers, to laborers in dusty shirts, to stately women in colorful dresses, to street urchins scampering the rutted road on bare feet. I could see only one of the soulless soldiers, and the rector was right. The man in grimy clothes stared around blankly, at one point seeming to look right at me, before wandering off in another direction.

I headed north past a triangular park that would one day contain City Hall. After several blocks the street traffic thinned and the structures separated until I was coming up on a plain brick building—the sugar house the rector had mentioned. Several British Redcoats stood guard at the entrance.

Must not have released all the prisoners.

I continued past the prison to avoid suspicion, surprised when Broadway ended a few blocks later. Hilly farmland with clusters of trees stretched beyond. I considered how my future apartment in the West Village would be about a mile north, Midtown's iconic skyscrapers, like the Chrysler and Empire State buildings, rising beyond. But now it was all pleasant countryside and bird song. When I passed the sugar house on my return, the British guards were opening the front doors. Two of them bowed as a young woman exited.

What do we have here?

Though the woman wore a plain dress and bonnet, something in her bearing marked her as upper class. She started south at an efficient clip, a large basket hanging from one arm. My destination was south anyway—the prison had been a side trip taken out of curiosity—and now my gut was telling me to follow her. I remained on my side of the street, slowing until I was about a half block behind her.

As Broadway began to bustle again, I closed the distance to a quarter block. We passed St. Mark's Chapel and approached the ruined grounds of St. Martin's. Several blocks ahead I could make out the walls of a military fort. The woman turned left onto King Street and then right onto Broad Street. With fewer people, I hung back again, pretending to become interested in the passing homes, many of them mansions.

A scream made me snap my head back around. The woman was being pulled into an alley by two men. As my legs kicked into a run, I reminded myself that this was a time catch, that I shouldn't get involved.

She doesn't know it's a time catch, I shot back.

27

I arrived at the mouth of the alley to find the two men dragging the woman by the arms toward a third man whom I recognized from the tavern the night before—the burly, ginger-bearded soldier. The other two were his ratty cohorts.

"What do you think you're doing?" the woman demanded, sounding more furious than afraid. Her bonnet had gone askew, and she was kicking her legs. "Unhand me!"

Her midsection wasn't tightly strung in what seemed the common fashion, and I saw why. A swell showed above her waistline. She was pregnant. In an explosion of rage, I yanked my cane into sword and staff.

"You heard the lady!" I shouted.

The soulless men stopped and looked up, the pocked-face one bracing a dirty dagger between his teeth. Beyond them, Ginger Beard pulled a pistol and leveled it at my chest. He wouldn't miss from this range.

I uttered a Word, and the air sparkled before hardening around the bore of his weapon. An instant later, the pistol fired in a cracking gout of flame and smoke, and the muzzle blew off.

Ginger Beard staggered back. His compatriots dropped the woman and eyed me, daggers now in hand.

"Get out of here!" I shouted, slashing the air between us with my sword.

The soldiers peered back at the big man. He was staring at what remained of his weapon with dead eyes, coils of smoke rising from his tangled beard. My breaths cycled harshly. I'd already cast a minor invocation, which had been risky enough. I didn't want to have to go bigger.

At last, Ginger Beard dropped his weapon's wooden stock and lumbered away. The other two backed from me, then turned and shambled after him. I waited until they'd rounded a bend in the street before sheathing my sword and exhaling. The woman was sitting up, one hand holding her stomach.

I rushed to her side. "Are you all right?"

She turned toward me, eyes bright with shock. She was younger than she'd appeared from a distance, no more than twenty, twenty-one. A length of brunette hair had fallen across her soft face, and I had to stop myself from brushing it aside. But for the period dress, she could have been one of my students at Midtown College. At last she nodded, tucking the strand behind an ear herself.

"Yes, thank you," she said in an English accent.

"You're not hurt?"

"No." She accepted my hands and I helped her to her feet. She straightened her dress and fixed the basket still hanging from her arm. As she adjusted her bonnet, she peered at where the men had disappeared.

"Brutes," she muttered.

"Is there somewhere I can walk you?" I asked.

"It's kind of you to offer, but I'm just down the street."

"I don't mind. I'm heading that way myself."

She hesitated, then nodded. "I would appreciate that."

As we returned to Broad Street, she peered back as if to ensure the men weren't returning. I did the same, but the lane they had dragged her into was empty save for the length of gun barrel.

"Has that happened before?" I asked. "With them?"

"You mean the Patriot soldiers?" She shook her head. "But it was only a matter of time. I believe in treating the enemy with compassion, Mister...?"

"Hanson," I said, coming up with the name on the spot. "Thomas Hanson."

"Pleased to meet you, Mr. Hanson." She peered at me through her slender lashes. "Especially under the circumstances. I'm Elizabeth Burgess."

When she offered a bent hand, I panicked. What was the protocol? Was I supposed to kiss it? I accepted her hand and bowed my head slightly. "A pleasure, Mrs. Burgess." If I'd committed a faux pas, she didn't let on.

"Yes," she said, bringing her hand back to her stomach, "I believe in treating the soldiers with compassion. But to turn them out in their state? I can't fathom what General Howe was thinking."

My gut was still telling me there was a connection between the Stranger's presence and the soulless soldiers. I couldn't imagine that the soldiers had been allowed to roam the streets in our history, attacking Loyalists. Especially pregnant ones.

"There's a rumor that someone paid for their release," I said.

"Paid General Howe?" I picked up a note of offense. "That doesn't sound like him."

"A case of prison overcrowding then?" I suggested.

"Hardly. I was just in one this morning delivering apples and some of my husband's shirts." She held up her basket. "Conditions may change as the war continues, but for now, there's plenty of room in the prisons."

That explained what she'd been doing at the sugar house that morning, but her husband's shirts?

I must have looked at her oddly, because she said, "Rest assured, Mr. Hanson, I remain a devout Loyalist. My husband is a British captain." She sighed. "I suppose I see my donations as a form of sacrament. If my husband were ever captured, I want to believe someone on the Patriot side would show him the same compassion. Plus, the state of the prisoners..." She clucked once. "They just look so pathetic, hardly a flicker in their eyes." Her face hardened. "That doesn't mean they should be turned out, though."

Someone must be possessing their souls while they're in captivity.

"Have you seen anyone else in there on your visits?" I asked. "I mean, besides the guards."

Her eyes cut to one side as she considered the question. "I did see Mister Harland from St. Mark's Chapel there recently. Ministering to them, no doubt. Other than him? I can't say that I have."

Rector Harland?

"Here we are," Elizabeth said. I followed her gaze to a two-story Georgian colonial with a flagstone drive. "Can I invite you inside for tea? It's the least I can offer." She gave a demure smile, her hand absently caressing her swollen stomach.

"I appreciate the offer, but I must be going."

"Well then, thank you, Mr. Hanson." She stepped back and curtsied.

"Be careful on the streets. Better you not go out alone."

I felt a strange responsibility for the young woman, even though she would only exist as long as the time catch did. The *actual* her had already lived and died.

"No," she agreed. "I'll have one of our servants escort me from now on. I'll also be writing General Howe," she added sternly.

I couldn't blame her, though I doubted it would do any good. Whoever or whatever had arranged for the prisoners' release was also possessing them. But to what end? My magic was telling me I needed to find out. I tipped my tricorn hat to Mrs. Burgess, not knowing if that was proper either.

"Good day," I said.

I CONTINUED DOWN BROAD STREET UNTIL I REACHED DUKE. Following a left, I began scanning storefronts until I spotted what I was looking for: the sign Otto had described to me from the driver's seat of his cargo truck. And there it was, the largest one on the street: VANDER MEER'S FURNISHINGS.

That part of the story had been accurate, anyway.

Finding the front door ajar, I pushed it open and stepped into what must have been the eighteenth-century equivalent of a showroom. The space was crowded with tables, chairs, cabinets, armoires, you name it—all finely crafted. A scent of stained wood dominated. To one side, a fire crackled in a cast-iron stove. I opened my wizard's senses slightly. If Vander Meer was casting magic in here, it wasn't obvious.

Voices sounded from the back of the store.

"Hello?" I called, craning my neck down a narrow hallway.

"Yes, yes, be there directly," a man called back. In a lowered voice, he spoke instructions about the length of something, probably to an assistant. A moment later, a heavyset man in a leather apron and striped trousers bustled out. He was clean-shaven, tufts of blond hair flipping up above his large ears.

"Can I help ye?" he asked.

Struck by his resemblance to Otto several generations later, I stared for a moment. He had the same boyish face and close-set baby blue eyes. He was even sporting a similar smile as he watched me expectantly.

"Mr. Vander Meer?" I asked finally.

"Yessir, that's me."

"I'm, ah, hoping you can help me."

"If you don't see what you need in stock, I can make it. I do fast work, and you'll not find better quality in all New England."

"It's not furniture I'm looking for, actually," I said. "Do you know where I might acquire some pale root or dinji oil?" They were specialized ingredients that would complete my stealth and slick wizard potions. Ingredients you couldn't just purchase at any marketplace in eighteenth-century New York.

"And what would you be needing those for?"

Though the man's face remained pleasant, I caught a glint of suspicion in his eyes. Nothing notable in his aura, though, which bothered me. Then again, if he were an advanced magic-user, he could be hiding that.

"I'm trying to track someone," I said. "Someone who shouldn't be here."

If he were a fellow magic-user, he would know what I was talking about. But Mr. Vander Meer shook his head.

"I'm afraid I'm not following ye."

I was on the verge of apologizing and leaving—I'd come into the wrong shop—but my magic seemed to be nudging me from behind, telling me to keep going. And I *was* trying to learn to listen. I steeled my nerves.

"Spell work," I said in a lowered voice.

I watched for his eyes to alight with understanding. Instead, they darkened as if by sudden storm clouds, and his face balled up.

"This shit again?" he shouted. He searched around, his hair flopping wildly, before stooping down. When he stood again, he was wielding a thick table leg. "Ye wanna see magic, huh? How 'bout I disappear this up yer backside?"

"No, no," I said, backing away, hands held out. "You don't understand."

"I'll not be driven from my own store, d'ye hear me? I'll never leave!"

"We're on the same side," I cried as he rushed forward.

But he was beyond listening. I collided into the closed door of the shop. When he drew back the table leg, I fumbled for the knob. Managing to get it open, I fell backwards, the table leg whooshing inches from my face. I landed hard in the street. Expecting the portly Dutchman to press the assault, I was already shoving myself away on hands and feet. At that moment a lean man appeared from the back of the store. He restrained Mr. Vander Meer's arms, pulled him back inside, and drew the door closed.

I gained my feet, dusted my hands off on my breeches, and retrieved my hat, which had fallen to the road. A few passersby had stopped to watch, but now that the show was over, they continued walking.

"Holy *hell*," I breathed.

Ever since learning the time catch was in old New York, I suspected that my meeting with Otto had been no accident, that I was *meant* to hear about his furniture-making forebear. My magic gave me those little gifts sometimes. So up until a minute ago, I'd been counting on not only acquiring the needed spell ingredients, but understanding what was happening here. As a magical resident, Vander Meer would have had insights.

But he wasn't a magical resident. And with the visit a colossal bust, the only thing to do now was walk the streets in search of an herbal shop or its equivalent. The one positive was that it would give my system time to adapt to the patterns of ley energy.

But man, what a frigging misread.

As I walked off my shame, I wondered how my teammates were faring. I also thought about Jordan. I checked my pocket watch. It was a little past eleven, meaning he still had an hour to get back.

Still no signals from the bonding sigil, which I chose to view as a good thing.

I'd set off in an aimless direction and now found myself in an alleyway near the southern end of Manhattan. Beyond a narrow lane lined with barrels, crates, garbage piles, and stacked wood, I could see the fort I'd glimpsed from the north, only now I was facing its eastern side. The surrounding buildings looked like homes and offices, not shops. I needed to get back to a commercial district, one that dealt in food and, hopefully, herbs. I was trying to orient myself when a voice sounded behind me.

"Well, hello there," it purred, disturbingly close.

I knew the voice. The texture made my back break out in gooseflesh.

It belonged to Arnaud Thorne.

28

The vampire wore a thick powdered wig beneath a tricorn hat lined with gold trim. His dark, regal cape was open in front, revealing a colonial-style three-piece suit, the blood-red coat matching his knee-length breeches. White stockings and a pair of black shoes with gold buckles completed his wardrobe.

He looked princely, powerful. And it was definitely Arnaud. Like the predator he was, he'd used preternatural stealth and speed to steal up from behind without me hearing.

Control yourself, I thought now. *No surprise. No fear.*

Arnaud watched closely, searching for a chink in my calm facade. His vampiric eyes were red-rimmed, probably from a recent meal. The rest of his face had been heavily powdered as if to conceal his waxy flesh. Though only half the age of the vampire I would come to know in the present era, he was no less dangerous. His lips broke into a sharp grin, as if picking up the final thought.

I cleared my throat. "May I help you?"

"I don't believe we've seen you before," he said. "Have we, Zarko?"

The man standing behind him and to one side wore a

tailored blue suit over a silk shirt, a frilly cravat tied around his throat. I immediately recognized his bowl cut and almond-shaped eyes. This was Arnaud's faithful servant of centuries.

"No, master," Zarko replied in a chilly Eastern European accent.

"No, I didn't think so," Arnaud agreed.

He began to circle me in a way that was creepily reminiscent of our first encounter in his office almost three years before. An ornamental walking cane appeared from Arnaud's cape, and he tapped it against the dirt lane. I'd placed Grandpa's ring in my pocket before setting out. Now I slipped a hand beside it and fingered the humming band.

"May I ask your name?"

"It's Thomas Hanson."

"And your provenance, Mr. *Hanson*?"

He was behind me now, his voice low and leering.

"I grew up here," I said, affecting slight impatience.

Arnaud clucked his tongue. "I'm afraid that's quite impossible."

"How is that impossible? I should know where I grew up."

The vampire swept in front of me, his cold eyes peering into mine. If he was searching for a lie, he wouldn't find it. Technically, I *had* grown up in the city, only it had been the late twentieth-century version.

I squeezed the ring, wondering if I was going to have to deploy the power of the Brasov Pact.

Arnaud stepped back suddenly, his expression bright. "Then I do apologize." He remained at the edge of my personal space, not quite outside it. One of the subtle ways vampires controlled their prey. "It's just that I don't forget a face, and I believed I'd encountered all who call New York home." He smiled seductively—careful, I noticed, to keep his teeth concealed. "You would certainly have stood out in my mind."

I understood now that Arnaud's finding me was no coincidence. He had blood slaves combing the streets in search of fresh additions to his growing legion. One of them must have alerted him to my presence.

"That's all very well," I said, "but I have to be going."

He slid in front of me. "But you haven't asked who *I* am. Or perhaps you already know?"

"Everyone has heard of you, Mr. Thorne."

"Is that so?" He sounded pleased. "Then perhaps you've also heard that I'm always on the watch for enterprising young men. Men like yourself, Mr. Hanson."

I caught my head nodding before realizing he was using his vampiric voice, the words massaging deep into my limbic centers. Screwing my thoughts to a point, I checked our surroundings in my peripheral vision. Except for the three of us, the narrow lane was empty. Just the way Arnaud wanted it. I could repel him—I wasn't worried about that. But the amount of magic required, even through the Brasov Pact, would be the equivalent of a Fourth of July spectacular.

No way that would go unnoticed.

"I'm not interested," I said, taking a deliberate step past him.

I'd risked the use of my wizard's voice, but it didn't do any good. Arnaud seized my arm and pulled me sharply around. If I'd needed any reminding of the vampire's strength, there it was. "You *are* interested," he said in a rasp barely above a whisper. "And you're going to come with us."

In his fever-bright eyes, I saw bloodlust, power hunger, and a virile hatred for humans—all the qualities that made him what he was. I tried to draw back, but he maintained his death grip on my arm. Red lights jagged through my head in time to my racing pulse as Arnaud struggled to bend my mind to his will.

"Come," he seethed. "I'm right over here."

He gestured with his cane to a dark building with a

crenelated tower that rose two stories above the neighboring rooftops. As I followed his gaze, I used the opportunity to angle my pocketed fist so the ring was aimed at his heart. I would gain nothing by destroying this version of Arnaud, but what was the alternative? If I escaped him through magic, he would hunt me, creating major problems for our mission. On the other hand, the ring's booming release of energy would alert Demon X, eliminating our element of surprise. The demon could shift his Stranger and the possessed victims before we located them.

Arnaud squeezed my arm until I felt the bone yielding. In my head, I had already shaped the Word that would unleash the power of the Brasov Pact, but on the brink of releasing it, I hesitated. There had to be another way.

"Release him!" someone shouted.

I turned to find a tall man in a gray work shirt and trousers running toward us. Dammit. Time catch or not, I didn't want to put an innocent in harm's way, and this guy had no idea what he was stepping into.

"Stay back," I called.

But the man arrived in front of us, chest heaving. He stared at Arnaud with icy blue eyes.

"Release him," he repeated in a thick, no-nonsense accent that might have been Dutch.

Arnaud's lips leaned into one of his dangerously charming smiles, not relaxing his grip one degree. "I'm afraid you've misread the situation, *friend*. This gentleman and I have just met, and he's agreed to come to my office so we might meet in less *intrusive* environs. Isn't that right, Mr. Hanson?"

"Yes," I said, willing the man to leave.

But he crossed his arms as if to say he'd read the situation perfectly. Expecting Arnaud or Zarko to fly at him, I readied the Word in my mind. My ring resonated like a struck tuning fork in a way I'd never quite felt before. Arnaud's smile shrank inside his hardening face. Then, with a scowl, he released my throbbing arm. I backed away, still angling my pocketed fist at his chest, but Arnaud appeared too fixated on the man to notice. The man's returning stare was fearless.

"I preferred it when we left the other to his own affairs," Arnaud said.

When the man remained silent, Arnaud turned to me and forced a final smile. "Perhaps we'll run into one another again, Mr. Hanson," he said in a slippery voice. "Yes, I think I'd like that very much."

Don't be so sure, I thought.

With a sweep of his cape, Arnaud turned and paced in the direction of the fort, cane tapping beside him. "Come, Zarko," he called. His servant grinned at me over a shoulder as he caught up to his master.

The blue-eyed man stared after them. I drew my hand from my pocket, leaving the ring.

"Do you know them?" I asked, trying to make sense of what had just happened.

"You were asking after some ingredients earlier," he said. "There is an apothecary on Fieldmarket Street. You will find them there." When he brushed absently at the sawdust clinging to his sleeve, it clicked.

"You work for Mr. Vander Meer," I said.

I hadn't gotten a good look at him earlier, but this was the same man who had been in the back of the store and emerged when Mr. Vander Meer came at me with the table leg. He'd apparently overheard my question.

"Aye," he said, and started to leave.

I almost let him. I'd already engaged three soulless soldiers, two humans, and one vampire that morning. But then I realized something else about this man. There *was* a magic-user in that furniture shop, but it wasn't Mr. Vander Meer. It was Mr. Blue Eyes.

I opened up my wizard's senses a crack. I wasn't surprised to see a magical hue in his aura, but I was surprised at its thinness. Where was the power that had protected the store from would-be arsonists, not to mention compelled a vampire like Arnaud to back down?

"Hold on a second," I called.

Blue Eyes faced me again, but his gaze was firm, unfriendly.

"I was wondering if I could, ah, ask you a few questions," I said.

"There's no time," he replied, striding away again. "I must return to work."

I caught up to him at a jog. "The ingredients I want are for potions," I said in a lowered voice, "but I think you know that." He gave no indication either way. "There's something demonic here." I was having trouble keeping pace with his long strides. "Something that might be connected to the Patriot soldiers who were recently released. The ones without souls. Do you know anything about this?"

"How could I? I am just a furniture maker."

Yeah, and I was Thomas Hanson. I knew people had been burned and hanged in the colonies for witchcraft, but was the man's fear of persecution so great that he would keep his identity a secret from someone who just admitted to being a fellow practitioner? Who told him a demonic threat was looming?

As the furniture shop came into view, Blue Eyes turned on me suddenly.

"You must leave now or Mr. Vander Meer will attack you again. He is convinced there is a conspiracy to take over his shop, and he is not wrong." I wondered now if Arnaud had been the one to accuse the store owner of being a warlock.

"I just need help," I said, not knowing how else to appeal to him.

I could see by the slight glazing of his eyes that he had opened his own wizard's senses. His brow creased in what seemed bafflement. After another moment, his gaze dropped to my cane, then flicked to the pocket where I'd stashed the ring. It was still vibrating in that high frequency. By the time his eyes returned to mine, his face was composed.

"Do not come to Vander Meer's again." I started to renew my appeal, but he held up a hand. He wasn't done. "I am staying in a farmhouse two miles up Bowery Lane. You can find it by the rooster in the road. I will be there tonight. Come quietly." And with that, he strode back toward the furniture store.

"Thank you, Mr....?"

"Croft," he said over a shoulder. "Asmus Croft."

The name bowled through my head, blowing my thoughts in every direction. I could only stare dumbly as my grandfather opened the door to Vander Meer's, issued a final look of warning, and disappeared inside. As he pulled the door to, I caught the silvery glint of an ingot on his right ring finger.

When the door closed, the ring in my pocket stopped vibrating.

29

I returned to the chapel with a sack of spell items and an alchemy kit. I found Malachi at a desk in our dorm room, poring over his Latin Bible.

"Are the others back yet?" I asked.

He started as if he'd been deeply absorbed. "Oh!" he said, pausing to catch his breath. "Sorry, this place has just been so empty. No, Seay and Gorgantha are still out. I haven't heard from Jordan, either."

I checked my bonding sigil. There had been no alerts all morning.

Malachi closed his Bible and rotated on his seat, injured arm propped over the backrest. A spot of blood showed through the bandage, but the bandage was much cleaner than it had been that morning before the rector changed it.

"How did it go out there?" he asked. "Anything happen?"

I blew out a laugh as I placed the sack and kit on the neighboring desk. "Yeah, a few things."

I told him about my observation of the sugar-house-turned-prison, my encounter with the soulless soldiers, and my conver-

sation with Mrs. Burgess. I also shared the details of my interesting trip to Vander Meer's furniture store. His eyes went wide
as I described my encounter with Arnaud and wider still when I
got to the part about the blue-eyed man who turned out to be
my grandfather.

"H-how is that even possible?" Malachi stammered.

"Magic-users live a long time," I said. "Especially the
powerful ones. From what I'd pieced together, I'd always
thought my grandfather was in Europe around this time, that he
hadn't come to Manhattan until the eighteen hundreds." I shook
my head, still dumb with disbelief. "I'd thought wrong."

"What were the chances of running into him?" Malachi
mused.

"Probably a lot higher than it would seem at first blush." I
told him how I believed my magic had arranged my meeting
with Vander Meer's descendent the day before, so I'd have the
info about his store when I arrived here.

"And you went to the store under the impression Vander
Meer was a magic-user?"

"Yeah, turned out it was his assistant, my grandfather. He
must have overheard me asking about the spell ingredients and
gotten curious. After settling Vander Meer down, he went out
and found me in a standoff with Arnaud." I snorted. "No wonder
Arnaud backed down. Not only had he seen my grandfather's
magic up close during their campaign in Eastern Europe,
Arnaud knows he wields the power of the Brasov Pact. My
grandfather was one of the magic-users who forged the original
enchantment."

I eyed my ring. That explained the resonance I'd felt earlier.
It had been responding to the ring on Grandpa's finger. The two
rings were twins, after all, separated only by different time
structures.

"Did he know who you were?" Malachi asked.

"He had to have seen the familial patterns in my aura. Beyond that?" I shrugged.

"But ... if he knew you were family, why did you have to chase him down?"

I'd thought about that on my walk back; given Grandpa's history it made sense. "Because he's lying low."

"Lying low?"

"While studying the ancient history of our Order, he began to suspect that some of the later accounts were lies. There had been a rebellion centuries before. The youngest member of the First Order, one of the nine original saints, discovered a shaft to an ancient being called the Whisperer. He drew power from that connection and tried to overthrow his brothers and sisters. According to the history, Lich's rebellion was put down and the portal to the Whisperer sealed. But my grandfather began to suspect the rebellion *had* succeeded and that this Lich was still alive, that he was harvesting the souls of powerful magic-users for a portal that would deliver the Whisperer into our world."

Malachi watched me, his face rapt. As often happened when I lectured, I had slipped into my story-telling voice. The result was that he was now seeing and experiencing bits of what I was describing.

"My grandfather used the war against the Inquisition to meet with other magic-users, including the man who would eventually marry his daughter and become my father. They started a resistance group to defeat Lich. To succeed, though, would require time and resources. That meant faked deaths, alternate realms, the hoarding of enchanted items, basically a lot of sneaking around. After the war, my grandfather claimed he'd lost most of his power from a head wound and was granted a dismissal from 'the Order.'" I air-quoted the words. "This freed him up to become a full-time leader of the resistance."

Malachi blinked. "And I'm assuming they succeeded?"

I caught myself studying the scar on my first finger, the one Grandpa had inflicted with his cane sword. For a long time I thought it had been punishment for sneaking into his locked study when I was a kid. In fact, he had drawn my blood in order to bond me to the powerful blade that would one day destroy Lich. From that memory, I saw my father plunging into the portal to the Whisperer, shouting the Word of Creation that collapsed that channel once and for all. And sacrificing his life in the process.

I curled my finger and looked up. "They did," I said. "But this alternate version of my grandfather doesn't know that. He's still in covert mode, pretending his magic is broken. He might have been planning to keep tabs on me from afar, see if I was trustworthy enough to bring into his confidence, but I forced his hand. He's invited me to his farmhouse tonight."

"For what?"

"Probably to start my recruitment into the Order in Exile."

The idea of being recruited by my grandfather sent a wave of unreality through me. My father, Marlow, would be in the Refuge at that moment. I laughed at the improbability of it all, even as I tried not to well up. The only one missing was my mother, whose last name I had been given to protect the Order in Exile, but who wouldn't be born for a couple hundred years.

"You're not thinking of going, are you?" I emerged from the thought to find Malachi watching me with a small frown set in his forehead. "I mean, aren't you planning to cast the tracking spell tonight?"

"Yeah." I wiped a sleeve across my eyes. "That's why I picked up the spell ingredients."

It came out more defensively than I'd meant it to—probably because Malachi had a point. I was getting too caught up in the sentimentality of having encountered the time catch version of my grandfather. Maybe even more so for knowing I had a baby on the way but no living family to share her with.

"Plus, are you sure you can trust him?"

I looked over sharply. "What do you mean?"

"We're not the only visitors in the time catch. We don't know who else is in here. You said yourself that you didn't think your grandfather would be here for, what, another fifty, hundred years? What if—?"

"Someone's pretending to be him?" I finished.

"Well..." He scratched the dusty stubble on his chin. "Have you considered that?"

"Listen, it's him."

"When I was an acolyte at St. Martin's, I thought Father Victor was himself too." He paused for a beat. "So did you."

He was referring to the vicar who had been possessed by the demon lord Sathanas.

"That was a long time ago," I said, still trying to tamp down my defensiveness. "I can see things now I couldn't then. My grandfather's aura checked out." But did it? I had only gotten a glimpse. "Plus, he was wearing the same ring. I felt a resonance. And his eyes..." I was about to describe how, with a little gray, they were dead ringers for the stern set I remembered from boyhood. But it sounded lame in my head. Instead, I started organizing the ingredients I'd purchased.

"I'm just looking out for you," Malachi said after a moment. "For everyone."

"I know. A lot happened, and I'm still in processing mode. You're right to counsel caution."

But even as I reassured Malachi, I still believed that my magic had led me to the blue-eyed man for a reason, that he was my grandfather. "How was your morning?" I asked. "Were you able to talk to Rector Harland."

"I tried, but he was heading out. He did tell me about a grotto behind the church. He said its protections weren't as *complete* as those of the chapel. I'm not sure what he meant—or why he even brought it up in the first place. Seemed sort of random."

"He might have been tipping us off about a safe place to cast. I'll check it out."

I stopped as I remembered what Mrs. Burgess, the pregnant woman, had told me earlier.

"Hey, would it be normal for someone like Rector Harland to visit rebel prisoners?"

"Well, you heard him last night," Malachi said. "He feels that allegiance to the Creator supersedes wartime loyalties. Why?"

"Mrs. Burgess, the woman who was bringing food and clothing to the prison, said the rebel soldiers were mindless before they were turned out, which means someone or something is claiming their souls on the inside. The only other person she's seen on her visits, besides soldiers, is the rector."

"I'm not getting a demonic vibe from him," Malachi said. "But I guess I have to take my own advice and not assume anything."

Harland wouldn't have been able to enter the chapel if he were a demon or possessed. That didn't necessarily rule out dark magic, though. But I wasn't getting that kind of vibe either. "Any recent visions?" I asked.

Malachi started to shake his head, then stopped. "After the rector left, I took a short nap. And I had this, I don't know, *experience* I guess you could say. I was on my back, and there were four other beings around me—"

"And you were rotating while a dark energy was gathering."

Malachi stared at me, his mouth still open. "H-how did you know?" he stammered.

"Because night before last, I had the same dream." It had come on the heels of my dream of Arianna telling me she was trapped in the Harkless Rift and that to help her and the others I needed to find Arnaud.

"It felt awful," Malachi said, his eyes haunted by the memory. "Like something was about to happen, and I couldn't stop it."

"Did you get a look at the other four?" I asked.

"No."

At that moment, a key sounded in the chapel's front doors. I looked out to find Seay and Gorgantha returning from their outing. Seay had changed into breeches, a dark blouse, and a form-fitting coat that she wore well and must have bought while out. Gorgantha was still in her dress, the satin now dusty and stained with what looked like grease. She was carrying a basket in one arm and eating a chicken leg. As they crossed the nave, Gorgantha polished it off, bone and all, and wiped her hand on the side of her dress. When they entered our dorm room, she set the basket down on a desk.

"We got lunch if anyone's hungry," she said.

I wasn't at the moment, but Malachi picked out a drumstick.

"How did it go?" I asked.

"Interestingly," Seay said, plopping down on a bed.

Gorgantha, who was still crunching on bits of bone, sat on the other bed and began untying one of her shin-length boots. She grunted with relief when it came off and began picking at the laces on the other.

"We covered a lot of the city," Seay explained.

"Sure did," Gorgantha said through her final chews. "From this big lake up north, all the way down to a hospital at the southern end. I am flat assed-out." She pried off her other boot and splayed her large feet. Even glamoured and stocking-covered, they looked monstrous, especially beside Seay's petite shoes.

"There are some strange energy patterns out there," Seay said.

"How so?" I asked, pulling the chair from the desk and straddling it in reverse.

"The best way I can describe it is like someone shifting mirrors around. It's hard to tell what's what. I would need a week to figure it all out."

"So someone's manipulating the energy here," I said.

"It's definitely not a random pattern," she agreed.

That probably explained why the pattern felt so much different from its present-day equivalent. I had begun to adapt to it, regardless. I would be able to cast the hunting spell that evening. And if I'd correctly guessed why the rector had told Malachi about the grotto, I could cast without drawing attention.

"That's not all," Gorgantha said. "We've got mercreatures in the East River."

"You saw them?" I asked.

"Smelled them. My skin started drying out late morning, and I had to take a dip. We found an old pier near some farmland. I shucked these wack threads and got into the water under the pier where no one would see. Out in mid river, the smell hit me. At least a dozen of them, maybe a half mile upriver."

"The ones that fled you the other night?" I asked.

"Probably, though they all smell like death to me."

"Is Jordan still away on his mission?" Seay asked.

"Yeah, and it's getting close to noon," I replied, checking my watch.

"How about you?" Gorgantha asked. "What'd you do this morning?"

I gave a brief account of what had happened on my outing. When I got to the part about the blue-eyed man, Malachi shifted uncomfortably. Not wanting to rehash the debate over who he was, I left out the "my grandfather" bit. Seay remarked that she and Gorgantha had seen several of the soulless soldiers from a distance, but they showed no interest in my teammates. Like the one I'd spotted, they seemed to be wandering aimlessly.

"Good thing too," Gorgantha muttered. "'Cause I about dislocated a knuckle on one of their skulls last night."

"All right, let's go over what we know," I said, standing and pacing to one end of the room. "The demon master controlling the four Strangers sent at least one of them here, possibly with the possessed victims."

"So there's a chance they're *all* here?" Seay asked.

"The presence of mercreatures would seem to strengthen that argument." I turned on a heel. "But why the time catch? Maybe as a place to hide them, to hold them in suspension until Demon X has his cards arranged."

"How do the soldiers figure in?" Gorgantha asked.

"Assuming Demon X stowed his Strangers here," I said, "chances are good they're the ones responsible for the state of the soldiers. Claiming their souls to build up their master's power, then inducing the British Army to release them so they can use them as sentries and spies throughout the city."

"How, though?" Malachi asked, setting down his half-eaten drumstick.

"Based on what Mrs. Burgess told me," I said, "they would have to have access to the prison."

"No, I get that part," he said. "We're in a time catch, right? The ones who actually lived during this period have already died and moved on. So how would the ones here have souls to be claimed?"

"Like everything here, their souls will be more like echoes than the actual articles," I said, wondering now if that was what

Malachi had been searching for in his Bible when I'd returned. "But even soul echoes hold power."

Malachi nodded slowly, as if trying to assimilate the concept into his existing beliefs.

"We drew the soldiers' attention in the tavern last night," I said. "And later in the street. But I think the combo of Osgood's glamours and us hiding our magic made whoever's running the show decide we weren't a threat. We didn't create enough ripples. Otherwise, there would have been some sort of coordinated response." I hoped the same still held following my run-in with the three soldiers that morning.

"So we have a demon master stashing his Strangers and their vics here," Gorgantha said. "Ganking soldiers and turnin' them into creeps. But then also playing with the energy here, like Seay saw?"

I snapped my fingers and pointed at her. "Bingo. Which leads me to think Demon X is doing a lot more than just hiding his cards in the time catch. I think he's stacking the deck, planning a big move."

"Like what?" Malachi asked.

"The answer's probably in the energy configuration, but like Seay said, that would take time to map out. The blue-eyed man might be able to help—as a resident magic-user, he knows the energy better than anyone." I glanced over at Malachi. "But I think the best course right now is to go ahead with the hunting spell. Whatever Demon X is planning, he's doing it all through his proxies."

"The Strangers," Malachi said.

"That's right. And I'm betting that taking out the Strangers will collapse his plans." Hell, we wouldn't even have to know what his plans were.

"Agreed," Malachi said, pushing the word out like a block to keep me from changing my mind and talking about visiting my grandfather again.

Gorgantha nodded. "Sounds dope to me too."

"When will the hunting spell be ready?" Seay asked.

"If all goes well, by early evening. So we're going to need to be ready to move. The longer we stay in the time catch, the greater the chances of being detected. Lord knows, we've had some close calls already."

"Plus, we lose our sanctuary in the morning," Malachi pointed out.

Seay opened her mouth as if she were going to say something else, but her lips trembled and then her whole expression crumbled. She buried her face in her hands, her slender shoulders hitching with powerful sobs.

I sat beside her on the bed. "Hey, what's wrong?" I asked, rubbing her back.

Gorgantha came to her other side and wrapped a giant arm around her. "We gotcha, hon. What's up?"

Seay cried harder, as if whatever she'd been damming up was overwhelming the gates. I met the mermaid's gaze over Seay's bowed head and made a questioning face—they'd spent the morning together—but Gorgantha only shrugged. Malachi watched from the desk, seemingly uncertain whether to rise or stay where he was.

When Seay finally peered up, she was no longer glamoured. Sniffling, she brushed a swath of plain hair from her brow. Tears streaked her freckled face. She accepted my handkerchief with a burbled "thanks" and cleaned up. When she finished, she stared at the floor between her shoes and released a weary sigh.

"What is it?" Gorgantha asked with surprising gentleness.

"Listening to everyone talking just now..." She paused to sniffle. "It's just ... it's the first time I've felt like I'm going to get my friends back."

Given that ninety percent of what came out of Seay was either sharp or sarcastic, her show of vulnerability touched me. But it was clear now that she'd been leaning heavily on her fae half all this time to keep from having to confront her human fear and pain. I kissed the side of her head firmly.

"We're going to do everything we can," I said.

"You better, jerkoff."

30

The grotto behind the chapel was set back in a copse of trees that had been blackened by fire. I sensed what the rector had meant as I approached it. A small fount of ley energy was coursing up through the fire-damaged brick structure, but it lacked the strength and focus to wrap the grotto in a protective field.

But will it conceal magic from the outside?

At the opening, I stepped through the weak fount. My powers remained intact. Crunching down a short, leaf-strewn tunnel, I arrived in a domed room that resembled a cave. With a softly spoken word, I sent up a ball of light and studied the hovering creation through my wizard's senses. The flow of ley energy swept up the light's magical discharge, effectively hiding it, before dispersing it into the sky.

The rector's tip had been a good one. I would be able to cast safely in here.

As I arranged my ingredients and implements across a stone altar, I thought about Seay's teary episode just now. Since joining the Upholders and becoming the de facto authority, I'd been doubting my ability to lead them. Jordan had obviously felt the same way in that regard, but I'd also picked up skeptical looks from Seay, even Gorgantha. They had a right to them. I wasn't leading a cat, a goblin, and Mae Johnson through a sci-fi and fantasy convention. The Upholders were more powerful, the stakes more personal. So Seay's vote of confidence was a welcome shot in the arm. And that confidence went both ways.

"While I'm working on the spell," I'd told her, "I want you to mission-plan different scenarios. The hunting spell could lead to a house, a wharf, a wilderness. And where there's a demon, you can bet there'll be possessed hosts or minions."

"What about our powers?" she asked.

"We keep them on the down low until we've located our Stranger," I said. "But once we open up, we fucking open up."

Seay had smiled at that, the sparkle returning to her eyes.

When I finished arranging everything on the stone altar, I started on the potions. The alchemy set I'd found in the market included a mortar and pestle, as well as tubes and beakers of various sizes and stands to hold them. The whole set had only cost me a pound. I ground different combinations of ingredients in turn, added absinthe, and poured the mixtures into beakers. The plan was to prepare several stealth potions—you could never have enough—a couple slick wizards, and a neutralizer.

With the potions cooking over candles, I began clearing the grotto floor for my casting circles. From a few hundred yards to the west came the brusque calls of British soldiers drilling. A good reminder that once this operation kicked off and we started opening up, as I'd put it, all hell could break loose.

I checked my pocket watch, then the bonding sigil.

Where was Jordan?

By the time night fell, I had an active hunting spell and a group of teammates ready to roll, but still no druid. I called the rest of the team to the grotto.

"Should we look for him?" Malachi asked, his face solemn in the light of my hovering ball. The same light crackled above my work of the last hours: stoppered potions on the altar, smoking casting circles on the floor.

"I tried to call him through our bond, but no response," I said. "That could have more to do with me, though. I haven't been here long enough to assimilate the greater networks of ley energy, and if he's out of my range..."

Seay eyed the casting circle where my cane jiggled with the Stranger's name, ready to hunt. "I believe Jordan would want us to go ahead," she said.

"I think so too," I said with a sigh. "Does anyone disagree?"

When Gorgantha and Malachi shook their heads, I grasped my primed cane. "All right, Seay and I are going to recon. You two stay here until we get back." I turned to Seay. "You ready?"

Though she'd restored her glamour, she looked more human to me now.

"Hell, yeah," she said.

With night fallen, the length of Broadway running past St. Marks Chapel had largely emptied. A few solitary carriages sped past, the horses' hooves kicking up divots of road. After ensuring there were no soulless soldiers in sight, Seay and I stole from the shadows of the chapel yard down to the edge of the street.

She took my arm as she had the night before, only now it felt less flirty, more sincere. I'd draped my greatcoat over my shoulders in order to conceal my cane against my thigh, and I was struggling now to restrain its tugs.

The spell's strength suggested our Stranger was close.

My cane guided me along the same route I'd taken when I'd set out that morning, and we were soon passing the park that would one day house City Hall. Just a couple out for an evening stroll. After several blocks my cane began to pivot toward a familiar building on the opposite side of the street.

The sugar house turned prison.

"See those Redcoats?" I whispered. Seay glanced over. "Our target is inside."

Though we were still more than a block from the prison, the British guards had already noticed us. I slowed to a stop, pretended to point out something to Seay farther down the street, then checked my watch and turned us around.

"Oy, there!" one of the soldiers called.

"Keep walking," I whispered.

"Oy!" he repeated.

A scuff of running boots sounded. As they drew closer, I gathered energy around my casting prism. I felt Seay's hands warm with fae magic. I released a harsh breath. Were we going to have to blow our damned cover on a soldier? In another few moments, he was in front of us, a bayoneted musket in hand.

"Didn' ye hear me?" he panted.

"My apologies," I said. "I thought you were calling someone else."

He peered around the empty street, the confused face beneath his powdered hair and tricorn hat soft with youth. I glanced over a shoulder to find the other soldiers watching us and tightened my grip on my cane.

"Someone else?" the boy soldier repeated. "There's no one else out tonight 'cept for those addled rebels." He redirected himself to us. "Listen, the other soldiers an' me was just wondering if you had some tobacco ye might spare."

Seay's hands cooled around my arm, and I released my gathering energy. Though I could feel the bulge of the tobacco tin in my coat's breast pocket, I patted around my other pockets in a pretend search. The soldier's eyes followed my hand expectantly.

"How are the prisoners tonight?" I asked, nodding toward the sugar house.

"Mostly quiet," he said distractedly. "Not the rioting we 'ad last month."

"How many are inside?"

"Only twenty or so now, but ye can bet they'll be set out sooner than later." He didn't sound happy about that.

I reached into my breast pocket and drew out the tin. "Here," I said. "You fellows enjoy."

When the soldier felt its packed weight, he nodded appreciatively. "Many thanks, good sir. God save the King."

"God save the King," I echoed, sliding Seay a look that said, *See?*

She rabbit-punched me in the side, almost causing me to lose my grip on the jerking cane. Before the boy soldier could hustle back with his prize, I said, "Tell me, is anyone visiting the prisoners tonight?"

"Just the rector from St Mark's, but he's always about."

Seay's grip tightened around my arm.

"I see," I said. "Well, good night then."

"Night!" he called, already hurrying off.

TWENTY MINUTES LATER, I WAS WALKING TOWARD THE SAME SPOT, only now wearing a black priest's robe, white cravat, and powdered wig, all procured from Rector Harland's room. My pockets bulged with stoppered potions as well as the mysterious pouch Osgood had given me. Malachi paced beside me, each step a tense hop.

"I still can't believe it," he whispered. "Harland?"

I was still puzzling over it myself. Why would a demon give us food, shelter, protection, and tips on where to safely cast? Hell, why would a demon be inhabiting a chapel in the first place? And how?

"It doesn't make a lot of sense," I agreed. "But we have to go where the magic takes us."

Up the block, I could see smoke drifting from the front of the prison, where the four guards were enjoying Thomas Hanson's tobacco. Malachi and I crossed Broadway at an angle. As we passed under an oil lamp on the far side, one of the guards set his pipe down. The others followed suit and stepped forward, bayoneted muskets in hand.

"Who's there?" the lead one called in a husky voice.

"Visiting priests," I called back, pushing power into my wizard's voice.

Malachi and I arrived in front of two of the soldiers. The other two, which included the boy I'd talked with earlier, moved out to the sides, muskets in firing positions. I was concerned the boy would recognize me in spite of the dimness and my change of attire, but he wasn't eyeing me any more than he was Malachi.

"I'm Father Dean," I said. "And this is Father Sam. We come from Boston and are here by order of the Church to join Father Harland at St. Mark's Chapel. We were told we could find him here?"

The two soldiers in front of us were older, and they looked between us skeptically. Priestly attire or not, they weren't taking any chances. No doubt because someone had told them not to trust anyone.

At last the husky-voiced soldier grunted. "Do you have Church papers?"

"Of course." I reached into a pocket in my robe and with-drew a folded parcel.

The soldier handed his musket to the soldier beside him. He frowned as he unfolded the parcel and tipped it so the lantern light at the front of the sugar house would catch it. I followed his gaze to the official-looking document complete with signature and ecclesiastic stamp. Seay had glamoured it well.

The soldier studied it for a long minute before refolding it. As he handed it back to me, he looked over at the boy. I tensed, ready to invoke a shield.

"Go tell Harland these two're here," he grunted.

"Wait," I said quickly, pushing power into the word. "We'd prefer to surprise him."

The boy stopped and turned toward Husky Voice, who remained staring at me, blades of suspicion in his eyes. This was someone under strict orders not to let anyone unknown in. Maybe even orders from the general himself.

I caught a nervous glance from Malachi.

"Harland loves surprises," I said, chancing even more power.

At last something yielded in Husky Voice's eyes, and he nodded. "Let 'em inside."

He and the other older soldier moved aside while the boys returned to the doors, unlocking and opening them. I thanked them as we stepped into the prison's murky interior.

The appalling odor I'd been getting drafts of outside hit me like a truck: a toxic brew of urine, excrement, and misery. I fought the urge to bring a forearm to my nose and breathe through the robe's fabric and instead took thin breaths.

Single candles burned where soldiers were posted, four around the periphery of the open space that had once stored sugar and molasses. Dark brick walls climbed into darkness. In another moment, the prisoners began to take shape, shackled men strewn over scatterings of hay. Some groaned or garbled, but they all looked half dead. A few lay so still, I wondered if they'd completed the transition to full dead.

I wasn't expecting the Four Seasons, I thought, *but holy hell.*

The doors behind us slammed closed, sending my heart into my throat. Malachi flinched as the bolts clunked home. I re-centered myself. My cane, which I'd affixed with a belt to the side of my leg, tugged toward the back of the building, where light barely reached. If the rector was there, though, I couldn't see him.

But the ol' magic's insisting...

And I was learning to trust my magic.

I got Malachi's attention and jerked my head toward the back of the prison. He nodded quickly, pupils huge. With shaky hands, he drew his Bible from his robe. The guards watched us with what seemed haunted eyes as we stole past them.

Malachi let out a breathless gasp. A stick-like arm had shot out and seized his robe. I stepped in and shoved it away with a foot. Like a grotesque animal, the arm retreated back under the hay to join the rest of the shackled prisoner.

I gave Malachi's shoulder a reassuring squeeze, but I was starting to lose it a little myself. Though nothing had changed since we entered, I had the claustrophobic sense everything was closing in.

"Stay here," I whispered to Malachi.

I caught the click of a dry swallow as he nodded.

I stepped beyond the light from the final candle, pausing to draw my cane and separate it into sword and staff. The guards didn't react, suggesting they couldn't see me now. As my eyes adjusted to the darkness, I made out a deeper darkness ahead in the shape of an alcove. My staff jerked toward it with such force, it almost shot from my hand.

Little by little, the rector took shape, his bowed back to me. He appeared to be kneeling over something. When my cane tugged again, I released the hunting spell. As the magic dissipated, the rector's body shook with what sounded like soft laughter.

"So you've found me," he said in a high, chilly voice that sounded nothing like him. "Everson Croft."

I froze. How did he know my real name?

His stooped body began to straighten. "New York's resident *wizard*."

And how did he know *that*?

With nothing to hide now, I whispered a series of invocations. The first one gathered the darkness into a wall to obscure me from the guards. The next one drew light from the end of my staff and shaped it into a shield that conformed to my body. With the final invocation, the banishment rune on my blade pulsed to life.

The radiant light gave me a better look into the recess where the rector had come to a full stand, his back still to me.

"Your arrival here surprised us at first," he said. "But that surprise didn't last."

"We appreciated your hospitality, *Father*," I growled. "Or should I speak your true name?"

"My name wasn't made for mortal lips. Why not 'Mistral' for short? And that wasn't me hosting you, but our poor friend here."

I'd been inching forward, but now I stopped. The rector's head had begun to swivel. I saw immediately that there was something very wrong. Where his eyes should have been were bloody sockets.

Gouged out.

"Oh, if you could see your face, wizard," the voice laughed.

But the rector's mouth wasn't moving. As if the infernal strings of magic suspending him had been suddenly severed, his body collapsed to the ground. I recoiled when his head rolled toward me. Above his decapitated body, a pair of violet eyes blazed, and a figure stepped from the deeper darkness.

"This is our domain, wizard."

The figure resolved into the outline of a woman, a riot of impossibly long hair thrashing in every direction. When she thrust her arms forward, a tangled mass of energy stormed from her fingers.

"And you're *not* welcome."

31

I n the violet light of Mistral's attack, I got a full look at the demoness. She was wearing an airy midriff blouse and gypsy-like skirt. A headdress with a black gem at its center sent midnight hair down the sides of her curvy body in wild, thrashing lockets. Intricate, linear tattoos glinted across her exposed skin. The same tattoos accented her glowing eyes and rapacious smile of razor-sharp teeth.

Feeding energy from the banishment rune into my shield, I cried, *"Respingere!"*

White light pulsed out and blew through Mistral's attack. The tendrils of infernal energy she'd sent from her fingers fell writhing to the floor. The demoness stumbled back with a grunt. Before she could recover, I thrust my sword and shouted, *"Vigore!"* Rune-enhanced energy emerged in a gusher of holy light.

But Mistral had spoken a demonic word, and a twisting mass of infernal energy gathered in front of her. The collision of magic sent out a shockwave through the sugar house that had me bracing against my shield, boots skidding over the floor.

Mistral laughed. "If you were expecting another Finn, you're going to be severely disappointed." She was referring to the

Stranger who had infiltrated the merfolk. "And you couldn't even *destroy* him," she taunted. "He was recalled."

That explained why there were still mercreatures about.

"And what can I expect from the other two?" I asked.

"Oh, I'll see to it that you never need worry about them," she replied, confirming there *were* two more Strangers. But I wasn't going to get their names through this kind of back and forth. I needed to put her demonic ass in a casting circle.

A sudden infernal attack writhed from her fingers. I strengthened my shield, but this one shot past me and into the wall of shadow I'd invoked to hide our light show from the soldiers. Before I could reinforce the darkness, her infernal energy tore through it. The demoness and I now stood out like beacons. The soldiers jerked back, muskets raised, while the prisoners moaned and rattled their chains.

"Hold fire!" I shouted to the soldiers in my wizard's voice.

The last thing I needed was a hail of musket balls. The soldiers hesitated.

"Shoot him!" Mistral shrieked.

The balls wouldn't get through my shield. Her aim was to sow confusion, making it difficult for me to focus on her. Seeing the fear in the soldiers' eyes, I pushed more power into my wizard's voice.

"Begone!" I shouted, the word thrumming with force.

The four soldiers dashed for the door at the same time, one of them dropping his musket.

Malachi remained standing in the center of the room. Holding up his cross pendant with one hand, he began speaking the Latin exorcism. But a tendril of Mistral's magic slapped the Bible from his grasp while another lashed across his face, causing him to cry out. He staggered back, a hand to his jaw.

Mistral shook with malicious laughter.

I'd been gathering energy, and now I released it with a shouted *"Vigore!"*

Radiating with banishment energy, my sword shot from my hand. The blade skewered Mistral's midriff. She fell to her knees and doubled over, the ends of her hair clawing the floor like hands. I was tempted to shout the Word that would send the full banishment into her and reduce her to ashes, but I held back.

We needed info.

Mistral wailed a string of obscenities at me, but it wasn't anything I hadn't been called before.

Encasing her in an orb of light, I drew a sleeping potion from my robe. Before I could activate it, her hair flew up and began lashing the inside of her confinement. I'd been stung by a jellyfish on Long Island once, the contact leaving blistering welts. The pain that seared through me now was similar, but deeper.

I bit back a scream as the manifestation failed in a cascade of sparks.

Mistral thrust a hand out, sending another wave of infernal energy my way. I recovered in time to reinforce my own shield, but the mass of tendrils stormed past again. Speaking quickly, I shaped protection for Malachi, who had recovered his Bible, but she wasn't targeting him either. Snaps of metal rang out. In rustles of hay, the prisoners began lurching to their feet. She'd just freed them.

"Malachi!" I shouted.

He nodded quickly and made for the door. Mistral rose, a hand grasping the hilt still buried in her gut. She struggled to pull it free, but the blade was lodged, the banishment power bonded to her infernal energy. Black fluid oozed around her fist.

"That's not going anywhere," I said.

"Your soul will pay for this," she seethed.

Yeah, see you in dreamland.

But as I spoke the words to activate the sleeping potion, her eyes flicked past me. Inside her snarling face, a small smile quirked her lips. I glanced back. The prisoners were up and lumbering toward me. I'd handled the soldiers in the street, and these weren't armed. But I wasn't looking at American rebels, I realized. An infernal veiling was dissolving from their soiled, shambling bodies to reveal slender, robed beings with glowing eyes.

The young woman in the lead raised an arm. A dark gold bolt shot from her hand and nailed my protection, causing it to waver. Having a demon-controlled sentry was only one reason Demon X had released the rebel soldiers. The other was to make room for his Stranger's victims, effectively hiding them in plain sight.

These were Seay's friends, the half-fae.

With the sweep of my staff, I sent a force wave toward them. Their inherent fae-ness neutralized the weight of the attack, but it was enough to send them staggering back several paces. Enough to buy me time.

I hurled the glass tube of sleeping potion at the floor in front of Mistral. It shattered, sending up a plume of pink mist. I then grabbed a neutralizing potion from another pocket, activated it, and without waiting for it to cool, drank it down. The still-charging potion burned my mouth and throat as it slid down.

Two more fae bolts hit me, dissolving what remained of my shield.

The neutralizing potion required another few moments to take effect, moments I would need to buy. I wheeled, staff raised to repel another attack. The closest half-fae aimed his hand at me, but before a gold shaft could break from his palm, he staggered as if something had clobbered the side of his head. Something had: Gorgantha's fist. Glamoured, she was barely a ghost in the dimness.

"Go gentler!" Seay called from the doorway.

"Hey, *you* try pulling your punches when your teammate's about to get wasted," Gorgantha shouted back.

Seay shrugged as if to say the mermaid had a point before unleashing a series of shimmering bolts.

"Sorry, guys," she said as more half-fae went sprawling.

With Seay and Gorgantha handling the possessed, I turned back to Mistral. The sleeping potion had enveloped her, but beyond the pink mist I could see that she'd used her hair to wrap her face in a protective cocoon, blocking out the magic.

Her hair opened suddenly, batting the mist in all directions.

"Protezione!" I shouted, manifesting another orb, this one around her head. Before she could rake it apart like she'd done the last one, I began closing it like a fist. She claimed to be a step above Finn, but I doubted she'd be able to withstand the kind of pressure I could bring to bear on her head.

Screaming through bared teeth, she clamped the outside of the orb with her hands.

I responded with more power. Black ichor burst from one of her ears, then the other.

I could feel my neutralizing potion kicking in, meaning I didn't have to worry about half-fae attacks. And from the sounds of it, my backup force was handling them fine. I cast a weak shield around myself anyway. But something broke through it and wrapped my torso in what felt like razor wire.

The hell?

Mistral's hair. She'd sent a thick lock in on my blind side. It seemed to grow as it wrapped my body in stinging tendrils. I struggled to focus through the searing pain, to increase the pressure around her head. But she backed around a corner and into a corridor, her hair lifting me and carrying me after her.

She's separating me from my teammates, I realized.

Bruising pain shot through my shoulder as she slammed me into a brick wall. I dug a hand into a pocket and seized Grandpa's ring. Holy energy from St. Mark's Chapel sang inside it. I thrust a finger through the band and pulled my hand from my pocket.

A healthy blast should take the starch out of her.

"Liberare!" I shouted.

The ring's power released with a satisfying *whoomph*. For a moment, I was worried I'd summoned too much. I wanted Mistral incapacitated, not annihilated. But though she winced, the power that broke around her had little effect. And I was going into the wall again. I tucked my chin. The collision bruised my upper back and shot electrical pain down my spine. I congratulated myself for sparing my skull, but when she brought me upright, I saw that the orb around her head had come apart.

I incanted to restore it, but my casting prism had shattered as well.

She grinned at me through a set of bloody teeth, then dropped her gaze to my ring.

"The holy power here doesn't pack nearly the same punch as in your world. And your friend has been helping to build our immunities." She glanced past me to indicate the body of Rector Harland. "Unwittingly, of course. He thought he was ministering to soldiers, the poor man. In fact, he was empowering demons. A little exposure here, a little there... After a time, we became *inoculated*."

That explained why Demon X had allowed the rector to come here. Harland was a shadow exorcist. He'd recognized the possessed states of the soldiers and half-fae, but though he'd tried, restoring souls was beyond him. His attempts had effectively immunized the Strangers, making the ring worthless here. Blocking out the sharp, stinging pain that enveloped me, I started into a centering mantra.

"It has truly been a pleasure, Everson Croft," she said. "But you're too little, too late."

A tendril broke from the mass around my body. Knowing where it was going, I thrust up a hand before it encircled my neck. The tendril seared my palm and drove my knuckles against the cartilage of my throat. I gagged. Out of good options, I dropped my watery gaze to where my sword still speared her midriff. Her own gaze must have followed, because her hair tightened in desperation.

Too little, too late, indeed.

"*Liberare!*" I shouted.

Gathered power shot through my restored mental prism and out the banishment rune. A star of white light took hold in Mistral's center, then blew out in all directions along with her final screams. Her mass of hair dissolved from my body, and I fell to the stone floor at the same time as the impaling sword. In the light of the blade's dimming rune, nothing remained of the demoness.

I recalled my sword with a force invocation, then took a moment to catch my breath.

Infernal burns lingered over my body where her hair had seized me, but it could have been much worse. Spending as much time as I had in St. Mark's had infused my body with holy power. The demoness might have become immune to that power, but it had blunted me from the full extent of her infernal wrath.

Pushing myself to my feet, I took a final look around the empty corridor and swore at myself. I'd banished Mistral, but without eliciting a name or any information. And there were two more Strangers.

I was returning to the main room when I nearly ran into Gorgantha.

"Was just coming to see what was up," she said. "All the half-fae went down a couple seconds ago."

"Yeah, I took the Stranger out."

She frowned. "You sound disappointed."

"I didn't get a name. Are Seay's friends all right?"

"She's checking them out."

Gorgantha stooped and thumbed away the blood from a cut above my right eye I hadn't realized I'd suffered. Back in the main room, the twenty or so half-fae were indeed down. Seay was kneeling beside a young man. Fae light glowed from the palm of the hand she was touching to his forehead. I wanted to ask how they were doing, but the lines across Seay's brow told me she was deep in her work.

"C'mon, Darian," I heard her whisper. "Wake up."

I glanced over at Gorgantha who was watching the soul-healing intensely. I couldn't read her expression, but something told me she was thinking of the lost members of her pod. "Hey," I said. "I never told you how sorry I was that we weren't able to..." Gorgantha let out a sound of surprise, causing me to trail off.

The half-fae Seay was tending to shifted on the floor, then raised his head. He looked from Seay to his surroundings and murmured, "What is this foul place?"

Seay slipped her arms around his back and pulled him gently against her. "I'll explain later, dumbass." Fae light glowed warmly with their contact. "Right now I need you to help me with the others."

Without warning, Gorgantha seized me under the arms and hoisted me into the air. When she caught me, she brought me into a fierce hug. She didn't say anything, and she didn't have to. Her joy that Seay had recovered her friends despite, or maybe because of, the loss of her own pod touched me. Half laughing, half choking, I clapped her thick back.

When she set me back on the ground, tears glimmered in her large eyes. I smiled up at her, almost forgetting my disappointment at failing to get anything actionable from Mistral.

But now that I thought about it, maybe I had gotten something.

32

Fresh air broke against my face as I pushed open the door of the prison and stepped outside. The British soldiers had drawn back to Broadway, but their numbers had grown. All watched me over aimed muskets.

"Don't shoot!" Malachi called. "He's one of ours."

He hustled to meet me as I walked toward the road. I was still wearing the priest's robe, but I'd lost the wig, and my cravat had come undone.

"I told them about the demon," he whispered. "I told them you were exorcising it."

"And they accepted that?" I asked, peering past him. I couldn't see the soldiers' faces in the darkness, but they were murmuring among themselves while keeping a safe distance from the building.

"It's 1776," he replied, which was true enough. "So what happened in there?"

"The Stranger wasn't Rector Harland. She and the others were using him to immunize themselves against the holy power in the time catch. I banished her, but not before she killed him. She was holding the half-fae captive inside, veiling them so they'd look like prisoners. Seay is helping to restore them." She and Darian had been working on two of the other half-fae when I left. "Once they're all up, we need to clear out."

"The British commander is demanding an account," Malachi said.

At the front of the troops, a tall soldier with gold epaulettes on the shoulders of his red coat stood stiffly. When he saw us looking over at him, he marched toward us, two more soldiers flanking him.

"Wonderful," I muttered.

"I am Captain Saxby," he said when he arrived. He had a serious-as-cancer face, coal black eyebrows standing in sharp contrast to the white wig under his hat. "What happened here tonight? Where is Mister Harland?"

"He was killed, sir," I said.

"Killed?"

"Yes, by a demon I've just exorcized."

He watched me for a moment. "You are visiting from Boston, you say?"

"That's correct, sir."

Though I was using my wizard's voice, I had expended so much energy in banishing Mistral that I couldn't gauge how effective it was. Judging by his next question, not very.

"May I see your papers?"

I drew the parchment from my robe again. As he unfolded it, I glanced around. More soldiers were trotting in from the tent camps west of Broadway. There had to be at least sixty amassed in the road now, all armed. Even with my depleted power, I was confident we could handle them, but I wasn't ready to declare war on England. Not with thousands of troops in the city and two more Strangers to track down.

"What's this?" he demanded.

I looked back to find the captain holding up the parchment,

his dark brows crushing together. Crap. With Seay using her magic to restore her friends, she was no longer glamouring the parchment. It was blank now.

I patted the pockets of my robe. "I must have, ah, dropped it inside."

He narrowed his eyes at me. "You're not a minister, are you?" Before I could answer, he turned to the troops. "Detain these men!" he ordered. "And search the prison for collaborators!"

A group of Redcoats hustled forward, separated Malachi and me, and surrounded us with aimed muskets.

"They're coming," I whispered into the bonding sigil to warn Seay and Gorgantha.

"Take his cane!" the captain barked.

I reflexively redoubled my grip on my weapon. When one of the soldiers seized the other end, I considered invoking a shield and blowing everyone back. It wouldn't have been hard, but there were my teammates to consider, not to mention the half-fae, most of whom were probably in no shape to fight.

As my hold on the cane began to slip, I spotted the boy soldier I'd spoken to earlier. He was part of the group encircling me. Still under the influence of my wizard's voice, he looked between me and my opponent with uncertainty. In a moment of magical insight, I twisted my cane free and held it toward the boy. He hesitated a moment before taking it. I wondered myself what I'd just done.

Off to the left, a line of soldiers was filing into the prison. The soldier I'd just deprived of the cane grumbled and patted me down roughly. Though he encountered the pouch Osgood had given me, he didn't stop to remove it. I suspected some sort of protective fae enchantment. He did, however, find and seize my remaining potions. He opened one, sniffed it, and scrunched up his red face.

"Looks like 'e's got poisons here, Captain!" Then to me,

"Maybe I should save the Crown the rope and force one down yer bloody throat."

Unfortunately, none of the potions would have done my team much good: a few stealth potions and a single slick wizard. When murmurs broke through the ranks, I looked over to find a soldier emerging from the prison carrying the rector's headless body. Though I knew the actual rector had probably lived to old age, seeing this echo of him reduced to a mutilated corpse kicked me in the gut.

"The rest of the prison's empty!" a soldier behind him shouted.

"What of the prisoners?" Captain Saxby called.

"Gone, sir!" the soldier answered.

I relaxed slightly. Seay, Gorgantha, and the others had gotten out in time, probably by virtue of a glamour. I looked over and found Malachi peering back at me, his eyes asking what the plan was. The captain shouldered his way through the pointed bayonets encircling me. He looked at the stoppered potions in the soldier's hand before glaring back at me. "What sort of devilry have you done this night?"

"None, sir," I replied. "May we go now?"

He leaned down. "A wiseass, eh? You'll burn for this."

A musket cracked in the distance, and then several more. I craned my neck but couldn't see anything past the mass of men.

"Rebels!" one of them cried.

The captain looked over. "Fighting formation!" he called.

The Redcoats shifted and began aiming their muskets down Broadway. Past their bowed heads, I could now see the distant figures of disheveled men entering from side streets. Some had taken positions at building corners and begun firing. Demon X must have ordered them after us for wasting one of his Strangers. Musket balls whizzed past. A Redcoat to my right cried out. Soon, cracks began sounding from our end.

"Guard them!" the captain called over his shoulder, referring to Malachi and me, then hurried away. But eager for action, several of the soldiers had already abandoned the rings around us and now only a handful remained, including the boy who was still holding my cane. Unfortunately, the soldier who had threatened to make me gag on my own potions was still here as well. He leered up at me.

"Oh, we'll guard 'em all right," he said, drawing a short sword from his belt. "What a shame this one tried to run."

"Any time!" I called out.

A glimmering bolt enveloped the sword-wielding soldier and dropped him like a bag of dirt. The bolt had been transparent, barely visible—like the glamoured half-fae who had shot it. The remaining guards looked around in confusion. One by one, they began dropping too. I knelt to recover my potions, but all the vials had shattered except for a stealth potion. I pocketed it, then remembering the boy soldier, stepped beside him.

"Not this one!" I shouted. "He's coming with us."

The rest of the soldiers were too engaged with the rebels to notice what was happening behind them. Barely anything could be heard above the shooting anyway. As gunsmoke covered us in a light fog, Seay and the half-fae remained busy dispensing bolts.

When the final soldier in Malachi's ring collapsed, he stepped over the man's enchanted body and faded from view. I felt myself being glamoured too. The sensation was pleasant, like slipping into a warm bath on a cold day. Most importantly, it would cover our escape. I gripped the upper arm of the boy soldier.

"Him too," I called.

"Wh-whut's goin' on?" he asked as he began to fade.

"We're taking a little trip," I said, reclaiming my cane from him.

Still under the influence of my wizard's voice, he nodded. As the glamour finished cloaking me, the rest of our group came into clearer view. Most of the half-fae were moving under their own power, though Seay was supporting Darian around the waist and Gorgantha bore two over her shoulders. I led them up Broadway at a fast walk, away from the action. By the time the city turned to countryside, the shooting had faded.

"Thanks for the assist," I told Seay.

"I could have taken care of the soldiers sooner, but I've never gotten to see you squirm."

"Satisfied?"

She grinned. "Totally."

I gave her a deadpan look before turning serious. "How is everyone?"

Seay appraised her friends. Though some had taken on mild glamours to enhance their appearances, they all looked around with gaunt faces and shocked eyes. "They'll be all right," she said. "But they need somewhere to recover." Her gaze hesitated on the boy soldier. "What's with baby Redcoat?"

He had stopped beside me at stiff attention, but his face couldn't have looked more perplexed.

"I wasn't able to interrogate Mistral like I did Finn," I explained, "but I realized something back there. Demon X had his Strangers possess the soldiers for soul fuel and to act as spies, right? That much we'd guessed. But he also stashed your friends in an emptied prison."

"And if he did that with the half-fae," Seay said, catching on, "he probably did the same with the possessed druids."

Gorgantha nodded. "Just a matter of learning where else soldiers were released."

We all turned to the boy soldier now. "What's your name?" I asked him.

"D-Daniel," he replied.

"You weren't happy about the American soldiers being turned out from the sugar house, were you?"

Defiance grew in his young eyes. "No, sir. And ye saw what 'appened just now. Damned rebels have reorganized right 'ere in the city. They won' be happy till all of our heads are lookin' back at 'em from pikes."

"Where else were they released?" I asked.

"Up in Wallabout Bay, from that old warship. You can tell those from their smell. They really stink."

Under different circumstances I might have chuckled, but I was pulling up my mental map. I knew Wallabout Bay. It was an inlet between the modern-day Brooklyn and Manhattan bridges on the Long Island side.

"That's right up the river from where you took your swim," I told Gorgantha.

"And where I smelled mercreatures," she agreed darkly. "They're probably guarding that ship."

I nodded. It sounded like we'd found the possessed druids, which meant the Stranger responsible for them wouldn't be far.

"Anywhere else?" I asked Daniel.

He stared back at me, incredulous. "That's not enough for ye? How many more 're ye wantin' turned out?"

With his anger burning through the remaining effects of my wizard's voice, I dosed him one final time. "Return to your company," I ordered, power thrumming through the words. "You never met us."

Daniel's face flattened immediately, and he nodded. "Yes, sir."

He gave me a crisp salute before taking off south at a run, his five-foot musket bouncing awkwardly against his right shoulder.

"All right," I said, turning back to the team. "We have our intel, but we need somewhere for Seay's friends to recover and for the rest of us to assemble a plan. I also want to attempt to reach Jordan again."

"I suppose the chapel is out," Malachi said.

"Even if there wasn't a major battle happening right in front of it, I'm not sure how much protection it affords us anymore," I agreed. Whether the immunity Mistral spoke of would allow the remaining Strangers or possessed soldiers to penetrate a holy sanctuary, I didn't know and wasn't up for testing.

"Where does that leave?" Gorgantha asked.

I didn't even have to think about it. "My grandfather's farm."

A small wrinkle formed between Seay's glamoured eyebrows. "Your whose what?"

"Malachi will explain. It's a good hike northeast of here."

33

I led the team across pastureland and around a sizable lake that would be drained, filled in, and paved over long before our time. A cool wind rippled its surface and sent clouds scudding past a quarter moon. The stars were out in brilliant force. In the silvery glow of the night sky, our glamoured bodies looked like specters.

We accessed Bowery Lane and continued north on the dirt road, through what would become Chinatown and Little Italy, the domains of mob bosses like Bashi and Mr. Moretti. In 1776, though, we were in the countryside, where common farmers ruled. Instead of fish sauce and garlic, the smells of barn animals and plowed earth dominated. Candlelight glowed in the windows of distant houses. Though the crackling of musket fire continued, it remained in the city, which was falling farther and farther behind us.

Malachi hustled to catch up to me.

"How's everyone doing?" I asked. The pace I'd set was fast, and we'd spread out into a line, Seay watching the rear.

"Fine." Malachi fell silent.

"Something on your mind?"

"Look, I didn't want to bring it up in front of everyone," he whispered, "but are you sure about this?"

"Going to my grandfather's?"

"That's the thing. We still don't know—"

"C'mon, Malachi," I said with a flash of irritation. "We've been over this."

"There are two more Strangers out there," he argued. "One possessed the druids, but we have no idea who the other one is. I overheard what Mistral said back there. She and the other demons knew we were here. So why didn't they come after us? Why didn't they lay siege to the chapel? Maybe they set a trap instead."

I drew a calming breath before responding. "One of the senior members of my Order, Arianna, told me that our magic is always talking to us and that it's our job to listen. Even when the message seems to defy logic. That's what separates the competent magic-users from the masters. And you're right—bumping into my grandfather does seem a little too convenient. If I overthought it, I'd probably have the same doubts as you. But my magic led me to him for a reason, and until it tells me otherwise, I'm listening."

I braced for another round of debate, but Malachi nodded. "Sounds a little like my visions. I don't always understand them, but I have faith that I need to act on them. Assembling our group, for instance. Reaching out to you." He went silent for several paces. "I just hope we're not too late."

He was thinking of the demon apocalypse.

"Not gonna happen," I said. "We're the Upholders, dammit."

When I nudged him with my elbow, he allowed a small smile.

"Now keep your eyes peeled for a rooster," I said.

"A rooster?"

"That's how we're supposed to find his farmhouse. By 'the rooster in the road.'"

"An actual rooster?"

"You can never tell with wizards."

I pulled ahead of Malachi and scanned the road, hoping to hell my magic was right about this.

————

THE ROOSTER IN THE ROAD TURNED OUT TO BE A STAKED PIECE OF metal forged into the shape of a chicken with a pronounced comb and sickle feathers. It stood at an intersection with a dirt track that cut through a grove of trees. I opened my wizard's senses. A warding spell glimmered into view around the rooster's head. But the spell was basic, meant only to send an alert that someone was coming.

"This is it," I said as Seay and Gorgantha joined us. Darian, whom Seay had been supporting, was walking under his own power now. Gorgantha was still carrying two of them, one apiece cradled in each of her bulging arms. The remaining half-fae continued to move silently, their faces shell shocked.

Seay peered down the dirt drive. "You sure he's home?"

At the end of the drive stood the silhouette of a two-story farmhouse. No lights flickered in the windows, and no smoke issued from the brick chimney. A strange silence wrapped the entire property.

"No offense," Gorgantha said, "but your grandpa's place looks creepy as fuck."

"Probably a minor veiling," I said.

I stepped closer to the rooster. Not wanting to just trip the ward, I aligned my mind to it and sent out four gentle pulses: a mage's knock. A moment later, deep barks erupted from the farmhouse. A pair of large dogs bounded from the shadows.

"Oh, hell no," Gorgantha said, backing up.

They were mastiffs. The same breed the Order in Exile had used in the Refuge as an outer ring of security.

"They're just going to check us out," I assured her.

"You don't understand, Everson. I don't *do* dogs."

The pair of mastiffs slowed to a trot at the end of the drive. Their barks descended to rumbling growls as they padded around us on their giant paws. When they circled Gorgantha, she squeezed her eyes closed.

We were no longer glamoured, but I doubted that would have fooled the mastiffs. Hot breaths snuffed my crotch and then my cane. The one sniffing Malachi's neck was almost as big as him. For their part, the half-fae appeared unconcerned. Seay even held a hand out for one of the dogs to inspect.

At last the mastiffs let out low grunting barks and took off back down the driveway. After several paces, they stopped and turned, eyes bright, tongues lolling. A look that said, *Aren't you coming?*

I waved to the others. "We've been cleared."

We followed the dogs through the grove. The approaching farmhouse was slightly weathered. A few outbuildings stood in back beside an overgrown pasture. The place was unremarkable —which was the point. Through a combo of basic magic and neglect, Grandpa had designed a sanctuary for himself that was sufficiently guarded but wouldn't raise eyebrows, especially if Lich decided to drop in.

When we arrived at the farmhouse, one of the mastiffs faced the front door and let out a sharp bark. A moment later, a candle flickered to life in a front window, suffusing the porch in an enchanting glow. The door opened, and a tall figure emerged wearing trousers and a work shirt. Smoke rose from a pipe cupped in his right hand. Though I couldn't see his stern blue eyes, I felt them.

"Yes?" he asked.

I stepped forward. "I met you earlier today, Mr. Croft. You invited me here."

"You have brought friends." It wasn't a question but an observation. In his German accent, it came out hard, almost accusatory. Malachi shuffled over until he was standing behind me.

"Some are recovering from possession," I said. "We need your help."

He took a puff from his pipe. For a moment I thought he was going to send us away. We were a group of over twenty, several of us humming with magic. And here he was, posing as a man who'd lost his connection to that world.

"Come inside, then," he said.

I waved the others forward before he could change his mind, and they filed into the house. Malachi stayed close to my side, I noticed.

Asmus turned as I passed him. Though our rings hummed with the same resonance as earlier, his eyes never left mine. In them, I saw the man I'd grown up under. My memory placed gaunt lines over his lean face and thinned and silvered his fair hair. But though that man had been emotionally distant, my heart ached with the memory of him. He would ultimately sacrifice his life in order to protect the Order in Exile, to protect me. But right now his gaze lacked even the barest recognition, and that shook me.

Is Malachi right to be worried? I thought.

A curtain of defensive energy rippled through me as Asmus closed the door behind us. Like the ward in the rooster, his defenses were modest. But he was a grand mage who wielded powers far beyond mine.

Everyone gathered in a main room where a fire now crackled in a large cast-iron stove. Gorgantha set her two half-fae on a thick bearskin rug, and Seay and others went back to work on them. I didn't realize the dogs had come in too until they trotted past and took sentry positions near the doorways of the crowded room. Though Gorgantha eyed them warily, she appeared less bothered by their presence.

"There is a water pump in the kitchen and salted meats in the pantry," Asmus announced.

Gorgantha perked up at the mention of meats.

"A word, please," Asmus spoke in my ear.

"Yes, of course."

I followed him through another curtain of defensive energy and into a back room. Though I'd never seen the room, it spoke to some part of my memory. A lone candle flickered on a wooden desk. To the right, bookshelves had been built into the wall, the shelves holding classical works of literature. I didn't have to access my wizard's senses to know they were in fact magical tomes and grimoires. My eyes fell to a black steamer trunk, one I would see more than two hundred years later.

This was Grandpa's study.

When the door clicked closed, I turned and was seized by a dizzying wave of déjà vu. A long blade glinted in the candlelight, and it was aimed at me. Asmus's looming stance, the way he glared, sent me back to the night I'd turned thirteen. Though this wasn't the same sword—he wouldn't find the Banebrand until years later—a ghost pain flashed through my first finger. I pulled the hand to my chest.

"Who are you?" he asked.

He angled the blade up under my chin. Power vibrated the air around the tip.

"My name is Everson Croft," I replied, showing my hands, "and I'm your grandson. I know that doesn't make much sense, but hear me out. We're in a time catch. This time, this place—it's an echo. It's not the real thing. A demon master is using it as some sort of staging area. We came here from the twenty-first century to track his minions and recover the possessed, the ones in the other room."

His firm eyes betrayed nothing. I tried to put myself in his place, in his head:

A young man turns up whose energy shows familial patterns. He seems to know I'm a magic-user. He asks for my help. And then he tells me he's from the future and I'm his grandfather. An elaborate ploy to expose my deception and reveal my true power? Or is he actually who he claims to be?

The skin around his eyes creased slightly as if he were weighing the very questions. I caught his lips move, and in the next moment energy surged around me. Before I could react, it slammed me into the wall opposite the bookshelves. I tried to talk, but I was being pinned by the strongest force invocation I'd ever felt.

With the flick of his fingers, another force jerked my cane from my hands. He was no longer holding his sword, though where he'd put it, I hadn't the slightest. He caught my cane deftly. After studying its length, he gripped the wood in the middle and pulled the handle. My father's blade slid free.

As Asmus looked over the sword and staff, I could only imagine what was going through his head. Marlow's energy in the steel and silver. His own embedded in the ironwood. His gaze now jumped from rune to rune. My magic had only developed to the point where I could cast through the first two: banishment and elemental fire, but the second remained hard for me to control. I was ignorant as to what the other runes even did. But as I watched each symbol glow briefly, I understood that Asmus had the power to access all of them.

He switched his gaze to the staff, bringing the opal nearer his eye. At last he returned the sword into the cane. The locking enchantment that sealed the two would have been familiar to him as well. He had fashioned it.

"Where did you get these?" he asked.

His force released my mouth so I could speak. "The staff came from you, though it used to hold another blade. The sword was a gift from Marlow."

"Marlow," he repeated.

"Your ring also passed to me, the one that holds the power of the Brasov Pact. Your coin pendant too, though I've given that to someone for protection." When I thought of Vega and our child, an upsurge of love hit me.

"How do you know Marlow?" he asked.

"He was my father. He married your ... your daughter."

A daughter who would one day fall to Lich, the man he was hiding from.

"I was born in the Refuge," I said before he could ask about her. "Delivered by Arianna. I was given the Croft surname to protect Marlow."

I was dropping some serious names in the Order-in-Exile community. It would either convince Asmus I was telling the truth or further stoke his suspicions. Still holding my cane, he began to pace a slow circle around the room, something I did when I needed to think. But he was doing more than thinking. I felt energy running along the wooden planks and floorboards, gathering into a low, thrumming note.

Okay, this can't be good.

"I-I'm telling the truth," I stammered. "Ask me anything, and I'll answer it."

"That is the problem, isn't it?" he muttered, locking my jaw with another uttered word.

I struggled with what he meant, but the answer came quickly. *Whisperer magic. Bending minds, shaping thoughts, making one see what isn't there, believe what isn't real. The magic Lich wields.*

Dammit, I should have thought about that before coming out here. Asmus was questioning whether he'd fallen under the influence of Whisperer magic, which meant nothing I said would convince him of who I was. Not info about him or Marlow or the Refuge or that entire history. He would think Lich had infiltrated his thoughts and warped them into this walking, talking illusion standing before him.

The building note of energy inside the room began to rattle the window. Asmus stopped in the center of the room, his eyes locked on mine. He was pushing power into the room's wards with the idea it would overwhelm that malevolent magic, purge it from his house, his head. And when it succeeded, I would disappear.

A book tumbled from the shelf behind him, and then an entire row of them. Outside the room, the mastiffs launched into a torrent of barking. The door shuddered as the dogs collided into it and began raking it with their paws.

Asmus never looked away from me. I made a determined point of holding his gaze. My magic was depleted in here, useless, but I needed him to see I was flesh and blood and soul, somehow. That I was real.

The note grew to a high, penetrating ringing in my ears, one that threatened to burst my casting prism, if not my head. His own body began to vibrate with the power, mouth drawing into a taut line, hair falling across his brow. Even someone as potent as Asmus had to be approaching his limits.

How much harder is he going to push?

The answer came a moment later when the note vanished, and the room fell still. The pain left my head. Outside the door, the mastiffs snuffed along the frame, then padded away. Asmus wiped his hair back into place.

The force pinning me to the wall dissipated, and I lurched forward. Asmus caught me with a strong hand and steadied me. I glimpsed a moment of deliberation in his gaze before he returned my cane to me.

"I believe you," he said.

34

Ten minutes later, Gorgantha, Malachi, Seay, and I were sitting around a wooden table in Asmus's kitchen, porcelain cups steaming with English tea. My grandfather finished pouring his own cup and took a seat at the head of the table.

"What do you need?" he asked.

"First, thanks for the refuge," I said. "I know this is risky for you, but I couldn't think of anywhere else to go."

"And my friends are recovering," Seay said, referring to the half-fae in the next room.

Malachi and Gorgantha murmured their own thanks. With his stern bearing and unflinching gaze, Asmus Croft was an intimidating presence. He gave a small nod in response. Never one for small talk, he was waiting for us to get to the point.

"So, I mentioned the Strangers," I said. "There was one in the sugar house on Broadway, holding Seay's friends. We believe there's another one on the prison ship in Wallabout Bay. That's the other spot where possessed soldiers were turned out in large numbers. We think the ship now holds possessed druids." I tried not to think about Jordan, who was ten hours late at this point. "What can you tell us about it?"

Asmus rotated his cup on his saucer for a moment. "You've likely observed more in your short time here than I have. My focus has been elsewhere." He gave me a knowing look. "But, yes, I have seen the soldiers without souls, and I believe it is as you say. If you intend to reach the ship, you will need boats."

"And spell power," I said.

"I can arrange for boats," he said as if drawing a line.

Naturally, I was hoping to recruit him to our cause, but I understood his position. The test back in his study hadn't been foolproof. If he'd been under the influence of Whisperer magic, he would have believed he was increasing the power of his wards when, in fact, he wouldn't have been doing jack squat.

He had to know this too, but he was choosing to believe me anyway. Maybe because if he *had* been under the influence of Whisperer magic, the mind-bending power would have concocted a more plausible story, and mine was so damned *im*plausible. His grandson visiting from two hundred fifty years in the future?

Still, he was taking a risk. And he wasn't ready to up that risk by casting powerful magic outside his sanctum. Unless, of course, I could convince him he was inside a time catch. That wasn't going to be an easy pitch, telling someone they weren't really themselves. In any case, I sensed now wasn't the time.

Malachi cleared his throat. "Something else we learned, Mr. Croft, is that there were three Strangers operating here. Your grandson—that is, Everson, banished the first. We believe the second is in the ship. That leaves one more, but we have no leads. Would you happen to know anything about that?"

I had to hand it to Malachi for coming around on the question of whether Asmus was who he claimed to be. Our encounter in the study had resolved my own lingering uncertainty. If anything, I was having trouble tamping down my emotions. The love I felt for this man and all he had done was immense. I watched him now for his response.

"I've sensed no demons," he said simply.

"They passed through a rift to arrive here," I said. "One that cloaked their infernal signatures, making them hard to sense. We tracked down the one at the sugar house by hunting her name. Deduction led us to the second."

"Have you consulted your magic?" he asked.

"I did, and it led me to Vander Meer's. To you."

His eyes seemed to twinkle over the rim of his cup as he took another sip. I expected him to say more, but upon lowering the cup, he simply laced his long fingers together and looked around the table.

"What about the energy?" Gorgantha ventured.

When she glanced over at me, I took the speaking baton. "That's right. The ley lines are different here than in our time—we have a denser city with a lot more people and structures. But Seay thinks they're being shifted."

My grandfather nodded. "Yes, I have seen this too."

"Do you know who's doing it?" I asked. "Or why?"

I was beginning to think the final Stranger had been tasked with reorganizing the lines as part of Demon X's plan. A plan I hoped we were thwarting by taking down Strangers and recovering the possessed.

"The pattern is interesting," Asmus remarked.

He stood and left the room without saying anything, only to return a minute later with an ink well, quill, and piece of parchment. Using bold lines, he began to draw out what I recognized as the southern end of Manhattan.

"You have four ley lines coming in here," he said.

"And here is...?" I asked.

"St. Martin's Church. Or where it sat before the fire."

Where there just happens to be a giant, untapped fount of ley energy, I thought.

"Didn't the rector say Mr. Thorne had been trying to purchase that property?" Malachi asked.

"Yeah, the vampire Arnaud tried for centuries to buy it," I said. "Up until his demise. Fortunately, the faith instilled in the site prevented it."

Asmus nodded. "Mr. Thorne's money buys much in this city, but not everything."

I knew from Arnaud that he and my grandfather, after being allies of convenience in Europe, had largely avoided one another in New York. Grandpa had allowed the vampire Arnaud to build his financial empire while he himself carefully cultivated a resistance of magic-users and hunted the weapon that would one day destroy Lich and repel the Whisperer. That was the greater menace in his mind. It probably also explained why he was paying so little attention to the shift in ley lines now.

He completed his drawing and pushed the piece of parchment toward me. Something about the cross-like pattern of lines looked familiar. Then it hit me. I turned the paper toward Malachi so he could see. As he tilted his head, I watched his face blanch.

"My vision," he said.

"What are you guys seeing?" Seay asked.

Gorgantha looked between us in confusion.

"Malachi and I had a similar dream recently," I said. "We were in a cross-like arrangement with four others and rotating. Somehow that motion was generating an immense, malevolent energy."

"Demonic energy," Malachi put in.

"This pattern," I said, tapping the paper, "reminded us both of that dream."

"What does it mean?" Seay asked, looking from us to my grandfather.

"It sounds as if someone intends to perform powerful spell work," he said.

Gorgantha's face furrowed. "Do we need to be worried?"

"Only if it comes to pass," my grandfather replied. "But you are in the presence of one who heeds his magic." Though he didn't look at me, I understood why his eyes had twinkled earlier. He was proud.

A lump formed in my throat. Growing up, I had always thought Grandpa tolerated me more than anything. My grandmother was the affectionate one. I could only remember one instance where he'd demonstrated an interest in me, and that was the night he'd asked about my intent to study mythology in college. It was the first time I'd felt a real connection to him. It was also the night he'd given me his coin pendant, producing it through sleight of hand. I understood his distance in hindsight, of course. He'd been busy trying to save his family and the world. Still, to receive that yearned-for approval now...

"What about Jordan?" Malachi asked.

I sipped my tea, the leaf strong and bitter, and tried to swallow away the lump in my throat. "Yes," I managed. "One of our teammates, a druid, left last night to join up with a druid circle in the woods about forty miles north of here. He was supposed to be back at noon today, but he hasn't returned."

"The Raven Circle," Asmus said soberly.

"You know them?" Seay asked.

"They arrived in the city with the early settlers," he said. "When a member was seen feeding her baby blood from a raven's skull, a mob gathered. The group fled into the wilderness before they could be lynched. They carried a sacred tree with them and became a closed community. Very wary of outsiders."

"That doesn't sound good," Gorgantha muttered.

No, it didn't. And now we had a choice to make.

"It's been twenty-four hours since Jordan left," I said to the team. "Do we go in search of him? Or do we make a move on the prison ship?"

"Prison ship," Seay said. "We reached my friends in time, but if the demons suspect we're onto them, they could decide to move the druids. Or claim their souls permanently ... like they did to the merfolk." She said the last part haltingly and rested a consoling hand on the back of Gorgantha's.

"I agree," Gorgantha whispered.

Malachi nodded even as he frowned. "More than anything, Jordan wants his wife rescued. I vote ship too."

"It's ship for me as well," I said.

"Then you will travel due east," my grandfather said, "over pasture, stream, and salt meadow until you reach the East River. There, you will be opposite Wallabout Bay. I will ride ahead and arrange for boats."

"Can your friends travel?" I asked Seay.

"They'll have to. Our portal back to the present is on the Brooklyn side of the river."

"Good point." I turned to Asmus. "So we'll be a party of twenty-four."

"Five boats will be waiting." He scooted back his chair and stood. "You may stay and plan, though I advise you to move this night. The air is damp. The river will provide a good mist for cover." With that, he strode from the kitchen.

I took the quill and ink well and expanded his drawing until I had produced the Manhattan and Brooklyn shorelines, Wallabout Bay, and the approximate locations of the farmhouse and the prison ship. I estimated the distance to the shore to be a little over a half mile and that across the river another quarter.

"I know your friends are still recovering," I said to Seay, "but will they—"

"Oh, they'll want a piece of the action," she cut in. "They are *not* happy about the whole getting demon-possessed."

"Good," I said. "Because I have a feeling we're going to need all the firepower we can gather."

I pushed the parchment over to her and Gorgantha's side of the table and set the quill and ink beside it.

"The ship will have a deck and a large hull," I said. "The druids should be below. Assume British soldiers, mercreatures, possessed druids, a powerful demon, and come up with an approach and attack plan."

"Gee, that's all?" Seay said.

"We'll review it when I get back."

"Where you off to?" Gorgantha asked.

"To try to convince my grandfather of something."

I FOUND HIM LEADING A HORSE FROM A STABLE BY THE REINS, THE large chestnut creature already saddled.

"Wait," I called, running toward them through the tall grass.

My grandfather stopped, but rather than turn, he began adjusting the harness.

"I was, ah, hoping to talk to you," I said.

"Are you referring to me or my horse?"

My panting breaths caught on a sudden laugh. I'd almost forgotten his droll sense of humor which peeked out from time to time, always when least expected. He had a mischievous side, something I only recognized after his death. Though his tall back remained to me, I imagined his thin smile.

"Does she talk?" I asked, arriving behind him.

"This one? No."

"I only ask because I have a cat that does. Unfortunately."

"That must get interesting."

"Oh, don't get me started."

He chuckled as he finished adjusting the harness, then his voice turned serious. "I know why you've come. It is about the time catch."

"It sounds farfetched, I know, but if you'd just consider the possibility."

He exhaled through his nose as he faced me. "Whether it is true or not, Everson, I cannot allow myself to doubt this." He motioned around the farmland, then patted the horse's solid flank. "I cannot begin to second-guess what I am doing. If you know Marlow, as you seem to, then you understand our situation."

"Would it help if I told you—"

"No," he cut in, his gaze suddenly fierce. "I want no information about what happens."

I was only going to say that everything turned out okay. But I understood his reaction. If he accepted this was a time catch, then he would also have to accept that nothing he did here would make any difference. And if he accepted that, and this *wasn't* a time catch, everything could be jeopardized.

Still, I wanted him on our team.

"Isn't there a way to test this reality?" I asked.

He smiled, though whether at my earnestness or naïveté I couldn't say. "Anything I cast would only reinforce the reality of here. This version of Asmus Croft and this version of reality are inseparable. The only true test would be for me to view this place from the outside. But if it is as you say, I cannot leave without being obliterated. Though a positive result in theory, it would be very negative for me."

I couldn't help but smile at his quip, but my mouth quickly straightened.

"We could really use your help," I said, deciding to just drive to the point.

He looked at me for a long moment. Behind him, the horse nickered and began cropping grass. Crickets chirped in the blue pasture. My grandfather stepped forward and gripped my shoulders. "You are a powerful magic-user. More powerful, I believe, than you realize." He slapped my back, then turned, thrust a boot into a stirrup, and hoisted himself onto the saddle. "I will ready the boats."

He drew the horse's head around with the reins.

Sensing I wouldn't see him again, I blurted, "You're a great man."

He stopped. "It was good to meet you, Everson."

My vision blurred, but I pulled myself together. There was something I'd regretted not telling him before his death that I wanted to tell him now. It would sound awkward as hell, but I didn't care.

"I love you, Grandpa."

Though his expression didn't change, his eyes seemed to soften. With a nod, he turned and spurred his horse into a gallop.

35

An hour later, I was leading the team on a cross-country march toward the East River. Malachi hustled at my side, struggling to keep his priest's robes from snagging on brambles. Gorgantha, still in a frilly dress, lumbered behind us, while Seay and her twenty friends took up the rear, most of them recovered from their possession. To avoid any run-ins with werewolves or undesirables from the Fae Wilds, such as goblins or trolls, I okayed Seay to conceal us in a light glamour.

As we crested a small rise, the East River appeared below shrouded in mist, the cover Grandpa had promised. I considered how, in the modern era, we would have been standing in the Lower East Side housing projects, not far from Container City. Now there were only salt meadows and shore—and five rowboats in a line.

I pumped a fist. Grandpa had come through.

To the southeast, points of light flickered in and out of the river mist like will-o'-the-wisps. Lanterns, likely. Disembodied voices sounded, more echoes than words. I hunkered low and signaled for the others to do the same.

"Is that the prison ship?" Malachi whispered.

"Has to be," I said, wiping my brow with a sleeve. The air was damp, and I'd worked up a healthy sweat on our march. Anxiety was doing its part, but we had a good plan in place. Now it was a matter of execution.

I turned to the team. "Our boats are ready to launch," I whispered. "Everyone should know their assignment, but if you have questions, ask. Sounds carry, so keep your voices to this level from here on out."

I started leading the way down to the shore when the crackling of musket fire sounded. Balls hissed past. I threw myself flat, and peered into the mist, but the musket fire wasn't coming from the direction of the ship. It was coming from behind us.

As I crawled back toward the rise, several of the half-fae poked their heads up and swiveled them back and forth like periscopes. Having spent most of their lives in fashion, this was their first action.

"Stay down," I whispered as I moved past them.

I ended up between Seay and Gorgantha, Malachi off to our right. Through the grass, I could make out bursts of fire and smoke. The air glimmered, then hardened around us as I invoked a protective shield.

"It's the soulless soldiers," Seay said.

"Aw, man," Gorgantha complained. "These jokers again?"

"A good-sized group too," I said. "I'd guess forty to fifty."

Must have picked up Seay's glamour, I thought. *But that's on me.*

And now our element of surprise was blown. Already I could hear shouts coming from the prison ship.

"What should we do?" Malachi asked nervously.

As I considered our options, cracks sounded from the ship. The British guards must have interpreted the musket fire as an attack. If we pushed ahead with our plan, we'd be in the middle of their crossfire while attempting to row the river. And if the assault became heavy, I would have to maintain a protection around all twenty-four of us, power I'd hoped to save for whatever we'd be encountering on the ship. On the other hand, engaging the soldiers would give the ship time to move the druids. But engagement was the only way I could fathom to stop the shooting. My magic seemed to agree.

"Listen, guys," I said. "We're going to have to take them out."

But before I could say more, the grass swarmed up and swallowed the advancing soldiers. Their firing broke off as moans echoed over the meadow. Gruesome sounds followed, suggesting breaking bones and severing appendages.

"Jordan's back," Seay whispered excitedly.

I looked down to find the sigil on my hand glowing. He'd located us through the bond. Though I'd had my differences with the druid, joy broke through me.

"About damned time," Gorgantha muttered, but I could hear her relief too.

With the shooting from the fields stopped, the firing from the ship tapered off as well. Moments later, wings batted the air overhead. I opened the shield to let Jordan in. He shifted from raven to human in a dusty burst of magic and settled in the grass beside us, one hand gripping his quarterstaff.

"Starting without me?" he asked.

Smiling, I punched his shoulder. "What in the hell happened to you?"

"I found the circle, but convincing them who I was took longer than planned. Had to pass a series of tests. Those druids of old are damned thorough. Same with their locating spell. The thing took six hours."

"And it led you to the ship?" I asked.

"Sure did," he said, peering into the mist. "You too, I see."

"The locating spell actually led us to a prison in the city," Malachi said.

"The demons had swapped out the soldiers for Seay's

friends," I explained, cocking my head at the group of half-fae, who still looked largely bewildered. "When we learned the prison ship was the other place the Brits had turned out soldiers, we figured this was where they would be holding the druids."

"Well, you figured right," he said approvingly, but his gaze hadn't left the half-fae. "And they're ... themselves?"

"They're fine," Seay assured him. "Fae magic restored them."

"You took out those soldiers all by your lonesome?" Gorgantha asked.

"Not quite."

Jordan was about to say more when magic broke around us, and two more ravens took human form. The man and woman were wearing cloaks like Jordan, except theirs were black. With their fair skin and reddish-blond hair, they could have been twins. I pegged them as Irish, where much of druid-kind originated.

"They're of the Raven Circle," Jordan said proudly. "They're going to help us."

"Excellent," I said, knowing we could use all the support we could get.

The druids introduced themselves in thick accents, the woman as Failend and the man as Lorcan. Both wielded sturdy quarterstaffs.

"So what's the plan?" Jordan asked.

The druids listened intently as I gave them a condensed version of our approach and attack strategy.

I braced for pushback, but Jordan surprised me by nodding. "Sounds good. The druids and I can fly ahead and check out the deck and surroundings. We'll cover your approach, take out any threats. We need to get moving, though. Coming in, we saw a company of soulless soldiers about a mile south."

"Everyone ready?" I asked the team.

Jordan had started to turn away, but he stopped and said, "I won't miss anything this time," referring to the ghouls that had escaped his notice on Governor's Island, the ones I'd given him crap about.

Even though he was smirking, I clasped his hand. "No worries, man. I'm just glad you're here."

He pulled me into a hug and clapped my back twice with his staff hand. "Me too. Let's do this."

We separated, and he and the druids jogged off a short distance before taking flight as ravens. I led the team down the hill. As we squelched into the mud flats, the druids disappeared inside the mist. The rest of us boarded the rowboats and shoved out into the East River. Malachi and I were in one boat, Seay and Gorgantha in two of the others. The twenty half-fae filled the remaining spots. I shaped energy until our boats were shielded and bonded, careful to keep the manifestations above the salt water.

From a seat at the rear of my boat, I angled my sword toward the river and incanted. The emerging force sputtered upon hitting the choppy waters, but the thrust was enough to propel us forward. I sustained the incantation, upping the force slightly. Fortunately, the wind wasn't an impediment. We slid through the mist like a ghost crew, much more quickly than if we'd tried to row.

So far, so good.

We were halfway across the river when Gorgantha swore. "We've got mercreatures."

I stood and squinted around the mist-covered waters. "Where? How many?"

Without warning, the far right boat canted nose down as the back leapt in a burst of planks. Three of Seay's friends went overboard. Water splashed over my bonding invocation, dissolving it. Our boats began to drift off in different directions.

Before I could pull them together and restore the protection, the boat to my left capsized, spilling everyone, including Seay. Fae light flashed underwater, showing the silhouettes of several circling mercreatures. In contrast, the flailing half-fae looked puny.

"The hell with this," Gorgantha said.

She ripped her dress down the middle, tore off her boots, and dove into the river A moment later, the water began to roil. I shouted as our own boat was knocked into a spin. Shit was getting out of hand, fast.

"Malachi," I called.

He crawled and joined me in the back, recoiling as a webbed hand with monstrous talons gripped the side of the boat. I hit it with two hard chops of my blade, drawing blood. The hand disappeared back into the water.

"We're going to do what we did at Staten Island," I shouted above the commotion. "Group exorcism."

"Here?" he asked, fumbling open his Latin Bible.

I activated the banishment rune on my sword and plunged it into the water. Malachi gripped the hilt and began reciting the Latin verses. My invocations didn't move well in water, much less salt, but I only needed to channel energy as far as the rune. My father's enchantment, bolstered by Malachi's exorcism, would do the rest. That was the theory, anyway. The boat Gorgantha had been inside capsized now, leaving only ours and one other upright.

"Faster," I urged.

The sword shook as Malachi upped the cadence of the exorcism. The banishment rune pulsed with greater and greater energy. With Malachi's final line, a powerful light detonated from the blade.

Then everything fell silent, our boat bobbing in a slow circle as the waters settled again. Half-fae began to surface, most of them sputtering and coughing up water. I spotted a head of drenched blond hair.

"Seay!" I called.

She wiped the hair from her face. "Help me get them back in the boats."

"Are there any more mercreatures?" I asked.

"No. They went down like stones."

From beside me, Malachi grunted out a disbelieving laugh. "It actually worked."

"Good job, man," I said, tousling his hair.

The first boat to have been attacked was damaged beyond repair and half-sunk, so we crammed the half-fae into the other four. Seay and her friends had been able to stave off the mercreatures with enchantments. As a result, their wounds were few and minor. Gorgantha surfaced as we fished out the final half-fae.

"That's all of them," she confirmed.

Cracks sounded from the ship. Musket balls smacked the boats bow and splashed around Gorgantha's head.

"About a dozen guards on deck," Jordan said through our bond. *"We'll take them."*

"Thanks," I replied. "We're on our way."

Damn, it was good having air support. I shielded the boats and locked them into formation again. With balls sparking off our protection, I turned to Gorgantha.

"Mind playing motor?"

With a nod, she ducked underwater and surfaced behind my boat. Webbed hands pressed to the rear, she thrust with her legs and tail and off we went.

Before long, the prison ship grew through the mist. A onetime warship, the masts, sails, and rigging had been taken down, but the monolith that remained was colossal, and we were coming on it fast. I craned my neck back. Several thick ropes dangled past sealed gunports. From the high deck, shouts sounded and musket fire flashed, but the balls were no longer pinging off my protection. The druids had arrived and were engaging them.

"Take up the oars," I whispered to Darian, who was in the boat beside mine. "We split here."

I recalled my power and signaled to Gorgantha. She nodded and began pushing the boat that held Seay while pulling a second boat of half-fae around to the far side of the ship.

I aimed our own boat toward a platform that had been built for loading and unloading prisoners and cargo. About a half dozen tied-off boats bobbed around it now. When we knocked up against the platform, a half-fae leapt out and secured our boat. The rest of us joined her and helped the other boat, which had ended up with the most half-fae, to dock. Darian had taken charge of that crew, and I spoke with him now.

"Think you can have these other six boats untied and ready for evacuation?" I asked.

"Hey, I'll do anything that will get me closer to losing this dreadful thing," he said of his linen gown.

I gave him a thumbs-up. From the platform, a ramp climbed steeply to the deck. Above, I picked up detonations of druid magic and the sounds of bodies thumping.

"Follow me, but stay back," I whispered to Malachi and the half-fae from our boat.

As I hurried up the ramp, I could hear planks snapping on the opposite side of the ship. Gorgantha and Seay were in place and doing their part.

I arrived on the edge of the deck just as Jordan drove his staff into the chest of the final guard. A burst of magic knocked the musket from his hands and the man from his feet. He nailed the side of a cabin and landed in a sprawl. I scanned the red-coated guards scattered across the deck, all of them out cold.

The druids hadn't held back.

"There's a hatch over here," Jordan said when he spotted me. He was already running toward it, the two druids following him. I waved for Malachi and the other half-fae to come on deck. I joined Jordan as he inserted the end of his quarterstaff into a padlock and blew it apart. He was reaching for a rusted ring to draw the hatch open when Gorgantha spoke through the bond.

"We've breached the hull," she said. *"We're inside."*

"And?" Jordan asked anxiously.

"It's empty," Seay said.

36

I cast a ball of light ahead as Jordan and I descended a ladder into the ship's hull. A foul stench rose past us, and I pressed the sleeve of my priest's robe to my nose to keep from gagging. The sugar house had been bad, but the ship's hull was worse. It was the lack of ventilation. There was so little oxygen that I was having to push more power into my light ball to keep it from sputtering out.

Rats scattered as Jordan jumped the final few feet into the hull. I released the ladder and, cane drawn into sword and staff, followed him.

"Down here," Seay called.

Jordan and I made our way toward a glowing orb of fae light. We passed filth buckets and opened shackles. Dirt had been spread over the floor, as if we were walking through some kind of animal enclosure. Jordan prodded the occasional straw pile but only succeeded in producing more rats.

He shouted his wife's name: "Delphine!"

The rocking ship clicked and creaked in answer. When we reached the others, I observed the hole they'd ripped through the ship's side. Damp, salty air pushed past me. Beyond the opening, several of the half-fae manned rowboats in the fog, ready to start evacuating the druids—who weren't inside.

"Druid magic led us here, dammit," Jordan said. "And there was nothing leaving when we flew in. There's no way they got them out of here that fast." He cupped his hands to the sides of his mouth and shouted his wife's name into the cavernous hull. The anguished strain in his voice was hard to bear.

"We've already searched—" Seay started to say.

"Then we search again," Jordan cut in. "And we keep searching till we find them."

I nodded and addressed the others. "We're dealing with a demon, remember. They're masters of deception. We'll do another sweep. Gorgantha, why don't you check the river. See if there's any sign of them out there."

"You got it." With three running steps, she dove through the opening and into the water.

Using the bond, I called Malachi, who had remained on deck, and asked him to send down the druids and any spare half-fae to help. When they arrived, we dispersed throughout the hull, each of us attuned to our own preternatural frequencies. I opened my wizard's senses to the ship's astral patterns.

Remembering the cloaking effect of the Harkless Rift, I focused past the brightest patterns in search of voids. There were a few small ones around the shackles, the surrounding energy slowly reclaiming those empty spaces. Jordan was right. The druid prisoners had been here too recently to have been moved. I scanned the hull until my gaze locked on a massive void near the ship's front.

I approached cautiously, shifting my vision back to normal. I was facing a wall. But the fact I was at the nose of the ship meant there had to be a good chunk of space beyond. I called Jordan and Seay through the bond.

"Might have something," I whispered.

As I waited for them to arrive, I studied the plank wall more closely. Sweeping away a layer of dirt from the bottom exposed a groove in the floor. This thing wasn't a wall; it was a door.

"What do you have?" Jordan asked when he arrived. Seay was behind him, along with the two druids and several half-fae.

"There's a space back here," I said.

"Yeah, full of dirt," Jordan said. "I sensed it earlier. Same stuff they spread over the floor. There's a loading hatch on the deck. If the druids were in there, I would have felt them..." His words trailed off, but I knew what he was thinking. That would only be true if the druids were still alive.

"Open it," he said suddenly.

With his quarterstaff in attack position, Jordan backed off a pair of steps. The other two druids spread to either side, while orbs of light glimmered to life around Seay's and the other half-faes' hands.

Aiming my sword at where the door met the side of the ship, I shouted, *"Vigore!"*

The force hooked the sliding door and slung it open. In the space beyond stood a mountain of earth, small avalanches of dirt rolling down its side from the disturbance. Above its peak, lantern light from the deck outlined the hatch Jordan had described. He shouldered past me now and began digging into the pile with his hands.

"Careful, man," I said. "We don't know what's in there."

But Jordan wasn't listening. He was clearing the dirt around something.

A bare foot.

Holy hell. Checking to ensure Seay and company were covering us, I knelt beside him, set my sword and staff to one side, and plunged my hands into the earth. I was soon holding the other leg, the skin blessedly warm. Whoever this was, they were alive.

"Pull!" Jordan shouted.

He had the other leg by the ankle. I choked down until I was gripping an ankle too, and we leaned back with our collective strength. The body emerged by degrees. The cloak-wrapped thighs told us this was a druid.

"Don't let up," Jordan urged.

I paused to adjust my grip, and that's when a force pulled back. Surprised, I lost my hold. The legs disappeared into the mound. Jordan, who hadn't released his side, fell forward, arms plunging into the earth. In the next moment, he was buried to his shoulders.

"Let go!" I shouted.

"Can't..." he said through gritted teeth.

And not because he didn't want to. The earth was seizing his arms like a mass of muscles. I scooped up my sword and activated the banishment rune. My first impulse was to drive the blade into the mound, but I didn't want to skewer a druid. Instead, I aimed the blade at the heap and shouted, *"Vigore!"*

A bright-white force emerged and nailed the mound. The earth shuddered with a rumble that rocked the entire ship. Freed, Jordan fell onto his back. Reclaiming his staff, he sprang up, a look of *wtf?* on his face.

The mound was changing, morphing into the likeness of an earth elemental from the waist up. But the void told me it was demonic: our Stranger. The druids were buried underneath its body, its energy concealing them.

Chunks of dirt tumbled from the Stranger's head as a crevice-like mouth appeared below swirling voids for eyes, a single dark flame set inside each one. He rose up, a torso with two thick arms and a large head.

"Who the hell are you?" Jordan asked.

"Call me Loam," the Stranger said in a deep masculine voice. "Destroy me, and you destroy them."

"Yeah, that's not how it works," I said loud enough for everyone to hear, especially Jordan. I wasn't going to let the Stranger bluff his way into a stalemate. "More like, destroy you and you'll have no more claim over them."

With a shouted Word, I let my sword fly. I was going to run this joker through and banish him back to hell, like I'd done with the other Stranger. But Loam swung a fist around and batted my sword into a wall. His other fist reached toward the rafters with the clear intent of bringing it down on my head. No time to dive out of the way, I chanted to reinforce my shield, bracing for a trip through the ship's floor.

But a bolt of fae light broke against Loam's face, and then another. Seay and the half-fae were opening up on him. Loam's fist missed me wide, the landing force sending the ship into a violent fit of rocking.

With an angry grunt, Loam thrust his other arm forward. I leapt to the side as chunks of earth blew from his hand. One piece knocked Seay to the floor, while more pelted the half-fae, prompting them to duck or scurry for cover. Energy crackled from the end of my staff as I invoked a shield over Seay and her friends. The remaining earth assault met the wall of hardened air and broke apart.

With another shout, I returned my batted-off sword to my free hand. In the meantime, Jordan and the other two druids had come together, the ends of their quarterstaffs touching in a tripartite formation aimed at Loam.

"*In the name of the Raven Circle,*" they shouted in unison, "*we condemn thee as unnatural!*"

The energy in the hull seemed to gather toward their joined staffs before detonating as a current of dark, druidic energy. Loam, who was gathering himself to launch another attack, took the magic bolt directly in the chest. A deep crater appeared there, driving straight through the demon's middle and out the other side. With a wounded yowl, the Stranger lost all form and collapsed back into a heap. The druidic energy snapped over him for several more moments before petering out.

Except for the constant creaking and slapping of waves on wood, the hull fell silent.

The druids stepped apart, their staffs still braced for casting. I'd read of powerful druidic magic banishing demons, but had they succeeded? I opened my wizard's senses to a large void. Energy seemed to be gathering along its edges, perhaps preparing to seep inside, but we would need more time to tell.

Jordan stepped forward. "We need to dig them out."

"Wait," I said.

Before he could begin, I leveled my blade at the mound. Starting at the top, I called one force invocation after another, removing a layer of earth at a time. When my next invocation blasted a woman into view, I stopped.

She was lying supine in a bed of earth, legs straight, arms at her sides. The hood of the long cloak she wore was bunched behind her neck to reveal a soft sleeping face nested in an afro. Even half buried, she was beautiful.

"Delphine!" Jordan cried, going to his wife.

He pressed his hands to her cheeks, then sat her up. Dirt fell from her sagging body.

"C'mon, baby," he whispered in her ear. "I need you to hold yourself up, need you to open your eyes." It was the most tenderness I'd ever seen from him, and it made my eyes moisten. Seay and the half-fae walked up—they appeared all right—and together with the druids, we watched to see what would happen.

"C'mon, baby," he repeated.

Dirt spilled from her eyelids as they began to move. "Jordan?" she rasped.

He stroked her back. "That's right, Delphine. I'm here. I've got you."

Her body stiffened now as one hand braced against the ground and the other held Jordan around the neck.

"Where are we?" she asked.

"That doesn't matter right now. I'm going to get you home." He spoke calmly, but when he turned to address us, tears streaked his face. "While I heal her, can you work on recovering the others?"

"Yeah, of course," Seay said.

Jordan looked at me, awaiting a response. "Everson?"

"That's not your wife," I said.

"The hell are you talking about?"

"Loam is a shifter," I said. "That's why no one in your druid circle ever saw him. He posed as earth, trees, other druids. He used disguises to get to your members, possess them. Your attack here weakened him, but didn't destroy him. Now he's taken the form of your wife. He wants you to think you need to heal her so he can use the connection to siphon off your essence, just like he did the others."

"What's that man saying?" Delphine murmured.

"Shh. Nothing, baby." He glared at me over her shoulder. "Get out of here, Croft."

"Think about it, Jordan," I said. "What were the odds of finding her first?"

"I said get out."

With a whispered Word, I activated the banishment rune. As it pulsed to life, Jordan moved Delphine to his other side. Everyone else looked between us. Cloaked by his passage through the Harkless Rift, Loam would show no demonic energy, only a void. The problem was someone recently possessed, such as Delphine, would exhibit a similar void. There was no good way to discern demon from victim here. Except that I was tuned into my magic, and it was telling me in no uncertain terms, *demon*.

"Jordan," I began.

A series of far-off thuds sounded followed by the violent splintering of wood on deck. A scream tore down into the hull.

I activated the bonding sigil. "Malachi, what's happening?"

"Cannons firing from downriver," he responded in a weak, wincing voice. *"Something caught me in the leg. I'm down."*

Shit. Jaw tensing in concentration, I grew my shield around the entire ship, careful to keep it above the water.

"I'll check on him and get all of our boats to the far side of the ship," Seay said.

Her sparkling green gaze lingered on mine. Beneath the glamour, I saw her trust. She believed what I was telling Jordan and was counting on me to get it done down here. Breaking eye contact, she jerked her head for her friends to follow and ran for the ladder just as another series of thuds sounded.

I grunted as my shield absorbed two cannonballs and what felt like grapeshot.

"Those are British warships firing on us," I said to Jordan. Through some infernal connection to Loam, the final Stranger must have learned that the ship had been taken over and contacted the British fleet. "Your wife is probably underneath all of that dirt, but the thing you're holding isn't her. If you don't listen to me, we're going to lose you, her, and the rest of your circle."

"Does someone want to hurt me?" the Stranger-as-Delphine asked.

"No, baby," Jordan said, still keeping his body between us. "Nobody's going to hurt you."

The next series of booms was the heaviest of the three. In my effort to maintain the large shield against more cannonballs and shot, I contracted every muscle until they trembled and then cramped. When the assault ended, I relaxed just enough to recover my strength, I had to, but another attack followed on its heels.

This time I was too late pushing power into the protection.

The wall behind me exploded as a ball ripped through the hull. Planks flew everywhere. I ducked, arms wrapping my head, while Jordan covered what he thought was his wife. When I peeked out, I couldn't see the two druids. They had either flown up onto the deck or been buried in debris. The ball left a ragged hole in two walls. The one nearer me stood a few feet above floor level, but the ship was rocking so badly now that with every violent dip, a fresh wave of salt water gushed in.

I refashioned the shield, already knowing that the assaults would only grow heavier.

Seay's voice sounded through the bond. *"Malachi and a couple of my friends were hit with what looks like shrapnel. Our enchantments are helping with the pain, and the druids are up here trying to heal them, but the British warships are getting closer. I can see their gunfire through the mist."*

"Can you enchant them?" I asked.

"Not from here. There are too many soldiers."

"What about the druids? Can they do anything?"

"The injuries up here are bad, Everson."

Shit.

With the next concussion of shots, I pushed every ounce of energy I could gather into the shield. Half a dozen balls must have hit this time, and I felt every blow to the deep matrices of my bones. The protection held, but my legs didn't. I collapsed into a layer of foul water that had reached the height of my ankles. My power fizzled. I wasn't going to be able to repel the next round.

I dug a hand into a pocket until my fingers closed around supple leather. If there was a time to open the pouch-of-last-resort Osgood had given me, it was now.

I drew it out and removed the binding string. The pouch fell open. I'd had a couple guesses as to what it might contain, but I'd been way off.

In a burst of light and giggles, two contrails rose in a twirling column of peach and meadow green. In my exhausted state, I wasn't sure whether to laugh or cry. Osgood had given me Pip and Twerk.

The two pixies circled the hull, then swooped down until they were hovering a foot in front of my face.

"Look!" Pip said in her tinny voice. "It's Everson Croft!"

"But what's he doing in toilet water?" Twerk asked in perfect innocence.

That struck his sister as funny, and they both fell into a fit of gut-busting laughter.

"Guys," I panted, water dripping from my sopping robe as I pushed myself upright. "Listen to me..."

"Everson Croft doesn't look too fit," they sang. *"And now he smells like a pile of—"*

"Guys!" I shouted. "I need your help."

I expected more song and laughter, but the pixies stopped suddenly and snapped to attention.

"We are here to carry out one duty of your choosing," they said in unison.

That's why Osgood had warned us to only use the pouch as needed—because we'd only get a single shot. I looked over at Jordan, who was helping the Delphine lookalike to higher ground on the mound. He hadn't attempted any healing magic yet, but it was only a matter of time. All the while, I was bracing for the next bombardment from the British ships. Demon-banishing wasn't in the pixies' purview, but they could fly fast as hell and cast powerful enchantments.

"There's a fleet of ships coming up the river," I said quickly, "and they're shooting at us."

"Shooting at Everson Croft?" Pip asked.

"That's right. I need you to put them to sleep."

Twerk's face lit up. "Ooh, that will be fun."

"Can we play with their dreams?" Pip asked.

"You can play with them all you want, but it has to be now."

"We are honored to serve Everson Croft," they said and bowed deeply.

And then they were shooting through the ragged hole in the ship's hull, glittering contrails fading behind them. I climbed onto an island of torn planks to get out of the salt water and focused on gathering my sputtering energy. I wouldn't be able to deflect another bombardment, but I had enough for a banishment.

"Jordan!" I called.

He had set down his "wife" and was kneeling over her, one hand covering her eyes, the other holding his staff above her. Dammit, he was preparing to perform a healing. I leapt from plank to plank on the drowning ship until I was on the mound. Sword in hand, I climbed toward them.

"Back off, Croft," Jordan warned.

"Don't do it, man," I said. "It's what the Stranger wants."

"You don't know what you're talking about. You never did."

Great, we were back to this.

"Then let's see how she reacts to the glow of banishment," I said, pushing more power into the rune. As white light grew over the mound, Delphine's mouth drew into a tight grimace. But Jordan apparently missed it.

"Get back!" he shouted.

Energy detonated from his staff, and dirt burst up beside me.

"That was a warning," he said, still glaring at me. "The next time I won't miss."

When I looked down at Delphine, her grimace broke into a smile.

"Jordan—"

"Back," he repeated, his hand still covering her eyes.

But he was doing something with his own eyes, cutting them toward the right. Now he gave me a small nod. When I followed his gaze, I saw what he'd done. At some point he'd spilled a handful of vine seeds over the dirt.

A life force he could animate.

"If you don't want this to end very badly for you," he said, affecting a seething voice, "you're going to go up on deck with the others. Now." But I only half heard him. I was rehearsing the steps in my head.

Backing away, I said, "Damn you, Jordan."

When I was in front of the seeds, I nodded my head. He returned a final nod, shifted into his raven form, and lifted away. The Stranger-as-Delphine swiped at him but only caught a falling tail feather.

"*Vigore!*" I shouted.

The shaped force seized Loam. Caught by surprise, he couldn't have realized what was happening until he was being slammed onto the seeds. The seeds exploded into green shoots, then thick woody tendrils that wrapped Loam's arms and legs, binding them. I sensed powerful magic in the animation, magic that was frustrating Loam's ability to shift into another form. As the Stranger squirmed and hissed, Jordan opened his animation so that I had a clean shot at the demon's gut.

I drew back the glowing blade, channeling more and more power into the banishment rune. The Stranger stopped writhing suddenly. Still in Delphine's form, he screamed, "Jordan! Don't let him kill me!"

"Do it," Jordan said calmly.

My blade crunched through Loam's stomach.

"*Liberare!*" I shouted.

Holy light exploded from the blade and into the demon. The

Stranger-as-Delphine released a piercing scream. He began to shift then, back into an earth being, then into a tree, then various men and women I assumed were members of Jordan's circle, then into a horrifying amalgam of all of them.

With the blade's final pulse, Loam blew into dust.

I stood there panting in the dim hull, sword still thrust forward, the vine animation falling to pieces around it. A chorus of muffled cries brought me back. They seemed to be coming from chambers under the mound. As I staggered back, a hand clasped my shoulder and steadied me.

"Let's rescue the druids and get them on the boats," Jordan said.

I patted his hand and nodded.

The others came down and helped us excavate the buried. The druids were all there, chambered deep in the earth. Some were awake, others unconscious, but with the possessing force destroyed, they were themselves again. We passed them in a line from the sinking ship, the cold water almost waist deep now, to the boats being manned by the half-fae and Gorgantha. Malachi and the fae who had been injured by cannon shot were already on board our small fleet, bodies veiled in healing energy.

Jordan and I emerged from the ship last, his wife between us. She was among those sleeping, but she was aglow with fae magic to help restore her soul. Once we got her and the others to land, the druids would complete the healing.

Jordan climbed aboard a boat, and I handed her up to him. As he lifted her onto one of the bench seats, two of the half-fae wrapped her in a thick blanket, part of a store of supplies they'd found in the deck cabins.

"How did you know?" I asked Jordan.

"That the Stranger wasn't her?" He seized my arm and helped me aboard. "I've been with Delphine for twelve years. There's not an inch of this lovely woman I don't know. The

Stranger's resemblance to her was uncanny but imperfect. And what you said made sense. The final proof was in the way she reacted to that light of yours. She's never made a face like that."

So he *had* caught that.

Jordan wrapped his arms around her to keep her warm.

As I took the seat next to him, he smiled. "We did all right back there, Croft."

"We did," I agreed. "Your seed toss was brilliant."

"Not bad, huh?"

The half-fae manning the oars began rowing. We rounded the leaning prison ship and went with the flow of the river toward the silent warships. Having completed their mission, Pip and Twerk had probably returned to Osgood. I couldn't help but smile at the image of all those British Redcoats slumped out in faerie slumbers. As strange as it sounded, I hoped to see the two pixies again.

"I owe you an apology," Jordan said, breaking up my thought.

"For what?"

"Oh, come off it, man. I doubted you. Doubted you hard. But you did everything you said you would. Seay has her group back. I have mine." He nuzzled against his wife's wrapped body. In the soft glow of fae light, she looked like she was having a very pleasant, very restful sleep. "You're solid, Croft."

"I probably wasn't always so understanding with you," I said. "I'm just glad I could help."

"The second we get back, I'll release you from the bond. You'll be free to hunt Arnaud. And if you need me, I'm there. I can't speak for the rest of the Upholders, but I'm sure they feel the same way."

I nodded my thanks, but something was bothering me. We were acting like our mission here was ending, but there was still another Stranger. One who was manipulating the ley lines and

God knew what else. And Demon X clearly knew we were here now. He'd sic'd his soldiers on us twice.

So why hadn't the final Stranger tried to stop us?

"Any idea where Arnaud might be?" Jordan asked.

"I have something I can use to hunt him," I said, thinking of the cloth with the bonding potion and blood corpuscles. Fortunately, little time had passed back home. The blood would still be in him and...

Wait a minute.

I reviewed everything we'd learned during our time here and considered how Demon X had used both sides—the American soldiers as possessed sentries and spies and the British Redcoats as unwitting guards. Pulling that off would have required someone with intimate knowledge of the period. Someone moneyed and adept at manipulation. Someone like...

"He's here," I said.

Jordan's brow creased. *"What?"*

My magic gave a pair of hard nods.

"Arnaud's in the time catch," I said. "He's the final Stranger."

37

F ollowing the gun battle on the East River, Governor's Island was a hornet's nest. Redcoats ran along the earthen ramparts and manned cannons, while others scuttled around the western docks. Several rowboats were already making their way upriver, no doubt to see why the warships had gone silent. Under the cover of glamours, our fleet rowed around to the backside of the island where we found a small inlet.

We pulled in and helped the recovering druids to a patch of woods beyond. The trees would help their healing. I called the Upholders together around Malachi, who lay on a bed of leaves. He'd suffered a savage leg injury during the first bombardment, but druid magic was already at work on him, repairing torn tissue and fractured bone.

"Do you remember the departure point?" I asked everyone.

"Center of those earthworks," Seay said, nodding past the ring of half-fae who were maintaining our glamour.

"That's right. Osgood will know you've arrived, and he'll transport you back."

"What's all this 'you' stuff?" Gorgantha asked me. "Aren't you coming?"

I'd thought about my revelation on our trip downriver. "I'm pretty sure the fourth Stranger is Arnaud Thorne," I said, "and he's here, posing as himself from a couple centuries ago. Which means Demon X is his master, Malphas. He must have acquired the other Strangers from a weaker demon and brought the whole show here."

"Why?" Jordan asked.

"The demon apocalypse," Malachi answered from the ground.

I nodded in agreement. "I think Malphas is manipulating the energy here in an attempt to build a channel to his corner of the demonic realm."

"And from here it's just a short hop to our world," Seay said in understanding.

Malachi pressed himself up to an elbow. "And if he gets through, other major demons will follow."

"That would take a lot of energy, wouldn't it?" Jordan asked skeptically.

"He must have a plan," I said. "The fact Malphas let us take out the two Strangers and recover the possessed suggests they might have already served their purposes. Arnaud may be the only one he needs here now, and it has to do with the manipulation of ley lines. They're probably happy to see us go. If I grab Arnaud, I'll not only mess up whatever Malphas is doing, but help free my Order from the rift. Arnaud is key somehow." Eliminating him as a threat would also free Vega and Tony from their de facto imprisonment.

"Then I'm going with you," Jordan said.

"Me too," Gorgantha said.

"And me," Seay chimed in.

"I'd go if I could," Malachi said from the ground, "but..." He gestured to his wrapped leg.

I waved my hands. "I appreciate that guys, I do. But my

magic is telling me this needs to be a solo mission. Plus, you have to make sure everyone gets home. That's *your* mission right now. And you should get moving soon. You can't maintain this glamour forever."

"What about you?" Gorgantha asked.

"I have my own ride back, remember?"

I checked to ensure my bond to the warded cell at 1 Police Plaza was still intact. Thanks to Osgood's magic, it felt as solid as ever.

"Do you even know where to find Arnaud?" Jordan asked.

I remembered the tall, dark building with a crenelated tower I'd seen that morning.

"Yeah," I said. "He has a small fortress in the city."

To preclude any further debate, I stepped up and hugged Gorgantha. Her return hug was surprisingly tender. In contrast, Seay squeezed me hard enough to pop a couple of my vertebrae back in place. "I'll never be able to thank you enough for helping find my friends," she whispered.

"You're not home yet," I reminded her.

Jordan's hug was solid and wordless. He finished by clapping my shoulder.

I knelt beside Malachi. "Are you going to be all right?" I asked him.

He nodded, but his eyes looked troubled. "Are you?"

"Hey, my magic hasn't let me down yet."

As true as that was, I'd lied a moment ago about this needing to be a solo mission. My magic hadn't said that. But I had already exposed three people who trusted me to the demon-vampire, and the result had been a blood-drenched apartment. I wasn't going to expose four more. Plus, I was confident I could handle Arnaud.

"At least let me send Lorcan and Failend along," Jordan said, referring to his new druid friends. "Make sure you get across the river all right."

I thought about it, then nodded. "Thank you."

My four teammates watched as I drew out my final potion, activated it, and drank it down. It would kick in by the time I shoved out into the river. And now my magic *was* talking, telling me shoving-off time was a minute ago.

"See you in two hundred fifty years," I said.

With a final wave to my teammates, I turned and made my way down to the boats. Behind me, Jordan uttered a series of druidic words. The sigil on my hand glowed briefly before dimming. I felt something unlock in my mind. He had just released me from the bond, freeing me to hunt Arnaud Thorne.

"Go safe," he called.

ON THE FAR SIDE OF THE EAST RIVER, I DOCKED THE ROWBOAT and climbed onto the pier. With my stealth potion hiding me from everyone except those preternaturally attuned to my presence, I raised a hand to my raven escorts. The druids circled around, released soft caws, then flapped back toward Governor's Island.

I slipped from the wharves and wound my way through the dark, misty streets. An occasional soulless soldier wandered by, vacant eyes staring past me. I was still in the priest's robe, which felt fitting considering who I was about to confront. The pockets might have been empty, but I had what I needed for Arnaud.

With every silent step, I felt calmer, more confident. I couldn't explain it other than that I was taking the initiative, not Arnaud. That had been my biggest fear: the demon-vampire catching me or my loved ones by surprise.

I passed Vander Meer's furniture shop, the windows dark,

and aimed for the side street where I'd encountered Arnaud earlier. Had he known who I was then? Recalling the way his voice had dripped with familiarity, I nodded. And it was probably no accident he found me right after my meeting with Elizabeth Burgess. He was the one I'd caught peering from the soldiers' eyes. He'd had them attack her in order to see whether it was actually me. My display of magic would have confirmed the suspicion.

But then why had Arnaud played games instead of pouncing?

I put aside the questions and called up his building in my mind. I could expect sigils on the doors, concentric rings of slaves. I was confident I could get past them all, though. I would find Arnaud in a sanctum on the top floor.

And then it will just be a matter of—

I had been turning the corner into the alleyway, and now I suddenly pulled up.

I wasn't going to need to do any of those things. The son of a bitch was right here.

Halfway down the alleyway, the demon-vampire was circling someone who could barely hold himself upright. "Yes, you're lost, you poor, poor soul," he was saying in his soft, seductive voice. "You need guidance. Allow me to provide it."

The recipient of his words was a young man whom Arnaud must have caught walking home from a tavern. He clearly intended to claim his soul and add him to his growing army in the time catch. The man swooned, but Arnaud seemed to catch him with eyes that glowed blood red in the night.

"Allow me to deliver you unto the light," Arnaud purred.

The man slurred out a laugh as he leaned his head back and tugged away the stained cravat that covered his neck.

"Very good," Arnaud whispered, fangs glinting from his mouth. He was behaving more vampiric than demonic; regardless, I couldn't stand here and watch him prey on another victim, time catch or not.

"Vigore!" I shouted.

The force from my blade lifted Arnaud from the street and slammed him through a stack of crates into a brick wall. Wood planks and mortar dust burst around him. As Arnaud fell to the ground, his would-be victim snapped to and stared around.

"Get the hell out of here!" I shouted in my wizard's voice.

Because of my stealth potion, the directive emerged faintly, but the man caught enough of it to stagger into a run in my direction. Arnaud sprang up and raced after him. His tricorn hat had fallen off, and his cape was in disarray, but his eyes burned with hunger. With another shouted Word, I willed a wall of light into being and brought it into him. The opposing forces met in a blinding collision. Arnaud flew from his feet once more. This time, he landed in the street on fingertips and toes.

"Who's there?" he demanded, his inflamed eyes scouring the alleyway.

I enclosed him in an orb and stalked forward. The channeled energy had burned through much of my stealth potion, and now I appeared as a ghostly apparition. His gaze locked on mine. The priest's robes seemed to confuse him for a moment, but as I formed a shield around myself for protection, Arnaud rose and straightened his cape.

"Mr. Hanson," he said, affecting a genteel smile. "I thought I smelled wizard blood earlier. But why the hostility? Have I done something to offend you?"

"Cut the crap," I said. "We both know who we are."

His head tilted. "Are you saying you're not Mr. Hanson?"

"Malphas sent you here to claim souls and arrange the conditions for his arrival through some sort of channel. You're the one who paid to have the rebel soldiers turned out. You're also the one trying to buy the St. Martin's property, but for Malphas this time. Well guess what? It's not gonna happen."

I strode toward him, confident I had my demon, but there was one way to be absolutely sure—the demon brand Carlos had seen on his neck.

Arnaud began inspecting the orb that contained him. "I *have* been making investments as you suggest, yes," he said distractedly. "But I'm afraid I've never heard of this Malphas."

"Oh, really."

"Mr. Hanson, I know all of the moneyed principals on this side of the Atlantic and most on the other, and no, I've never heard the name." He smiled sweetly. "Now, I see that your powers are considerable. We *could* engage in a messy struggle, yes, but I assure you that it wouldn't end there. You have a family, I presume? Loved ones?" He tsked twice. "I'm a reasonable man, but I'm known to get a bit zealous when it comes to exacting retribution. A character blemish, I suppose. But what a pity it would be to involve other, *innocent,* parties. I'm sure we can come to more amicable terms?"

"So how did it feel taking out your 1776 version?" I growled. "Did you get off on butchering yourself?"

"Now you've really lost me, Mr. Hanson."

I had no idea why he was keeping up the ruse, but I was done talking. I pushed energy into his confinement and slammed him face-down on the street. Arnaud shouted in surprise. With a fingerlike force, I jerked down his collars and inspected the back of his neck. The pale skin was waxy smooth. No demon brand.

Impossible.

I spoke the Word for *reveal*, but there was no concealing magic either.

"I promise you, Mr. Hanson," Arnaud seethed from the street. "You are making a *fatal* error."

Grandpa's ring was pulsing away now, keen to unload the power of the Brasov Pact. But if this was the demon-vampire Arnaud, why wasn't that power being negated? Where was his scepter?

"Why have you been making those investments?" I demanded.

"Because it's what I do. I have wise counsel, and I follow it."

"Whose?" I asked.

Sensing I wanted something, Arnaud began to chuckle. I upped the pressure that pinned him.

"Whose?" I repeated.

"My servant's," he managed.

Servant's?

The blast of infernal energy that broke through my shield sent me in a staggering dance across the alleyway. I landed against a wall. My protection had absorbed much of the attack, but that protection was now gone.

"He was referring to me, Mr. Croft," an accented voice said.

I looked over to find the silhouette of a tall figure strolling down the alleyway, smoke drifting from his hands. And I knew him. He had grinned at me that morning following my encounter with Arnaud.

Now I understood why.

I ducked behind a stack of split wood and began incanting to restore my prism.

"You were quite right," he said. "I couldn't countenance the prospect of disposing of this version of myself, so I assumed the guise of my faithful servant. And I didn't have to harm a hair on dear Zarko's head. I simply ordered him to the basement, and he was quite happy to go. I am still his master, after all."

His footsteps continued toward me in a soft, steady cadence. Meanwhile, the vampire Arnaud had recovered. From behind my woodpile, I heard him growl with the indignity of having been man-handled.

"Stay where you are, master," Arnaud-as-Zarko told him. "I'll handle this little nuisance."

I tried to focus on my prism, but my mind was scrambling for a plan. Arnaud had caught me by surprise—not only by assuming Zarko's form instead of his own, but in the strength of his attack. Whatever the reason for shifting the ley energy, he was accessing a concentrated form somehow, increasing his power severalfold.

"Have you nothing to say?" Arnaud-as-Zarko asked.

Regardless, my plan hadn't changed. I just needed to get a hand on him.

"I'm disappointed," he continued in a taunting voice. "I was certain you'd have so much to tell me. So much to get off your chest. That little exhibit I arranged at your friends' apartment, for example?"

The image of the bloody carnage at the vampire hunters' ripped through my mind, and for a moment everything went wavy and gray.

He laughed. "Yes, I thought that might elicit a reaction."

I squeezed my sword and staff until the world steadied again.

"What are you doing here?" I growled.

"Oh, you deduced much of it, Mr. Croft, and I'm impressed. As for the details? Loose lips sink ships, as they say, and we can't have that. But since the question's been broached, what are *you* doing here?"

"Helping rid the world of your filth."

"Oh, come now, Mr. Croft. You've been in this business too long to be that naïve. We are as essential to this world as the shadow is to light. The balance may shift, but it can never be all one or the other, now can it? But I understand your willful ignorance. You wish a safer world for your lovely detective friend and her son."

He wanted me to react again, but I blocked him out. I had managed to restore my casting prism, and now I was struggling to pull energy around it. It shouldn't have been this hard, though. He stepped nearer.

"And do I understand you're to be a father?"

His words speared my chest. I'd come to terms with the fact that he knew about Vega and Tony, that he might target them to get to me, but this revelation that he knew about our daughter felt like the sick twist of a blade.

"Oh yes," he said. "I caught that little flutter of a heartbeat while following Ms. Vega the other day. Such a *precious* sound."

Time to fucking end this.

With a pair of shouted Words, I stood and thrust my sword toward him. The banishment rune glowed white, feeding the force that shot from the blade. A white light gathered around Arnaud-as-Zarko, seizing him like a fist. He grimaced, but before I could pull him to me, he threw his arms out to the sides. Black infernal energy billowed from his body dissolving my invocation.

Twisting his face in concentration, he shot an arm toward me.

I invoked layers of shielding between us, grunting as the infernal attack shattered each one in turn. And then it was plowing into me, demonic energy lancing my skin with a thousand red-hot blades. The pain was excruciating. And that was despite having blunted the brunt of the damned attack.

I hit the street in a series of backward rolls before flopping to a rest.

Spotting my sword on the street several yards back, its blade still glowing white, I extended a smoking arm and spoke a Word.

But the force meant to return the sword to me only gripped the hilt weakly.

Arnaud brought his foot down on the blade, and the force fizzled out. He grinned at me.

Through the fog of pain, I grinned back. He might as well have stepped on a land mine.

I focused on the banishment rune, shouted, *"Liberare,"* and squinted from the anticipated nova.

But it never came.

"You don't get it, my poor boy," He stooped and picked up my sword. He was wearing the regal blue suit I'd seen him-as-Zarko wearing earlier in the day, the tails of his coat extending all the way to his white-stockinged calves. "You may be powerful in your world, but here in mine, and particularly in my presence, you are a puny bug. *I* control the forces here. I can grant them," he said with a little lift in his voice. Suddenly ley energy was crashing around my prism like released dam waters, too ferocious to channel. "Or deny them." He dropped his voice, and the energy I'd been trying to gather for another trip through the banishment rune disappeared. I was left grasping at air.

With only my staff and ring now, I crawled behind a pair of oak barrels and invoked a shield. It crackled weakly around me.

Arnaud-as-Zarko laughed heartily. "Now that really is quite pathetic."

I heard the discharge of infernal energy before I felt it. My shield dispersed as if it had been held together by masking tape, and I was suddenly writhing on the ground, the molten blades I'd felt before now plunging into the marrow of my soul. I screamed for what seemed minutes, though only seconds passed.

When the energy broke off, I lay there semi-conscious and panting.

"You had to have considered the things I would do if you

were ever at my mercy," Arnaud-as-Zarko said. "I've considered them as well. Perhaps more than is healthy, but after what you did to me..." For the first time, I caught the rage that must have been boiling beneath his breezy exterior this whole time.

I *had* considered what he might do. Possibly keep me in his service for a time as a twisted joke. But ultimately, he would torture me in ways I didn't want to think about before staking my flayed soul in the pits for lesser devils to savage for an eternity, or what would feel like one. I had pissed him off that much.

"Oh, I'll spare you the details, Mr. Croft. Except to say this. With centuries as my teacher, I've learned to become patient. Mortals?" He scoffed. "How long do you think it will take before Ms. Vega tires of her confinement in that little holy house? At first she may venture out for a few hours. When nothing happens, an hour more, then two. And then one day, I'll have her. And on that day, I'll be wearing your soul like a bib so you can witness everything that happens as it happens. The vampire hunters' apartment will seem like a pleasant stroll through a rose garden in contrast. Do you follow me, Mr. Croft?"

I didn't answer. I was thinking about my ride home, but I wasn't going to take it without Arnaud.

I glanced over at where the vampire Arnaud stood, his gaze cutting from me to whom he believed was his servant. I could see the entrancement in his eyes. He would only do what Arnaud-as-Zarko told him, and right now that was to remain silent and out of the way. But his presence sparked an idea.

"Everyone will remark on how tragic it was," the demon-vampire continued. "The senselessness of it. Two lives lost: mother and unborn baby. And all because of their unfortunate association with you."

Gathering my strength, my will, I thrust myself to my feet and aimed my ring.

"*Balaur!*" I shouted.

The power of the Brasov Pact didn't require ley energy. The power was stored inside the ring. I only needed to set spark to grain, and the enchantment would do the rest. The ring contracted, then released a deluge of super-focused magic into Arnaud-as-Zarko. I was gambling that with his ability to control the ley energy here, he was no longer depending on his enchanted item for protection.

The energy broke to either side of him, shattering windows up and down the alleyway, but left him unscathed. Grinning at me as he had that morning, he pulled something from his back pocket. The object was slender and gold, a black gem seated at the ornate end.

Shit. I'd bet wrong.

He gave the bond-negating scepter a little waggle. "Anything else you'd like to throw at me?" he asked. "Perhaps that rotten cabbage over there?" His eyes glowed a sulfuric yellow through the night.

I backed away on unsteady legs. I was scared, yeah. But I was also pissed. I'd listened to my magic, and look where it had gotten me. What in the hell could it have been thinking? But there it was, nodding its head again.

In frustration, I turned and aimed my fist at the vampire Arnaud. Without the scepter for protection, he screamed as the full force of the Brasov Pact ignited his body and plowed him into the wall.

Arnaud-as-Zarko reacted quickly, enveloping the vampire in a cocoon of infernal energy. The blackness drew the flames into itself and dissipated in a cloud of smoke. The demon-vampire wheeled back toward me, but I'd already made my move. I was behind his scorched and stunned counterpart, one arm around his throat, the fist with Grandpa's ring pressed to his right temple.

"Lose the scepter," I snarled. "Or your 1776 version isn't going to have a head."

He tossed my sword aside and showed his hands in a gesture of mock surrender. "Oh, we wouldn't want that." The scepter was no longer in his other hand, but he hadn't dropped it. It was still on him somewhere.

I pressed the ring's ingot with the rearing dragon into the vampire's waxy flesh. "I'm serious."

"Well, that's the difference between us, isn't it? I may have my peculiar sentimentalities, but I don't allow them to become weaknesses."

I was slow to catch the swirl of infernal energy, but it wasn't directed at me. The vampire in my grasp choked and began to shrivel. I shoved him away as his body broke into foul smoke, then yellow flames. I glanced up, sure the real Arnaud was coming at me, but he hadn't moved. He was simply watching, head tilted slightly, as if the dissolution of his historic self were vaguely interesting. On the street, the vampire Arnaud's eyes seemed to plead up at me as the surrounding skin melted into a spreading pool.

Now the real Arnaud broke into a smile that showed his demonic teeth.

"You humans, on the other hand," he continued, "become absolutely crippled by them."

Bleeding and exhausted, I was ready to take my ticket home, to give Arnaud his damned victory, when another voice spoke.

"I respectfully disagree."

Arnaud wheeled, but too slowly. A column of magic broke into him, knocking him to the ground. He rose, batting out licks of blue fire that had broken out over his body, only to be nailed again. This time the scepter flew from his coat and went clattering into a pile of garbage. My grandfather stepped from the shadows at the end of the alleyway, the same blue fire whispering around his hands.

"Our sentimental bonds make us stronger," he said. "Not weaker."

I choked on a noise of surprise. Asmus Croft had said to hell with Lich, to hell with his cover. He'd chosen to believe me again. My final words at the farm must have left an impression. Now, though, I was speechless.

Arnaud groaned from his back, but he was making a weak sign in the air, shifting the ley energy. I watched in horror as the blue fire around my grandfather's hands dimmed.

But Arnaud had fucked up. The shifted energy now poured through me.

My sword rattled on the street before leaping into my outstretched hand. My next Word was directed at Arnaud. This time, the rune-enhanced force I'd attempted earlier grabbed him and slung him toward me like a doll.

Fortified, I set my legs apart and caught him.

Focusing into my channel home, I shouted, *"Retirare!"*

Light crackled around us. The alleyway in 1776 New York disappeared. For a moment, all I could see was an afterimage of my grandfather's silhouette, one hand raised.

And then that too was gone.

38

The next moments were like riding in the back of a Winnebago hurtling straight down a rugged, roadless mountainside, sideswiping an old growth tree or thirty, plummeting off the occasional cliff, and all at speeds exceeding hundreds of miles an hour. No wonder Osgood had said this wouldn't be the safest method of return.

Throughout the violent trip, I focused on one thing: keeping my hold on Arnaud. He struggled, but stunned from Grandpa's attack, his efforts were weak. And he had none of his cultivated energy to channel here.

We landed hard on concrete, and I lost my grip. Beneath a glaring white light, we bounced apart, and I landed against a metal wall.

Holy crap, I thought through my receding vertigo. *We made it.*

Arnaud had come to a moaning rest opposite me. Gone was his Zarko disguise from the time catch. Here, he was a bald, naked demon, the back of his neck branded. And we were in the other cell I'd warded at 1 Police Plaza.

I struggled to my socked feet and recovered my sword and

staff. In only boxers and a white T-shirt, I backed from Arnaud and toward the open door. He went from curled up in a moaning heap one moment to launching himself at me the next, teeth and talons bared. But I had my ring trained on him.

"*Balaur,*" I spoke.

The power I'd called forth was weak, but Arnaud was scepterless. The Brasov Pact slammed against him in a burst of ghostly flames and drove him into the far wall. The counterforce pushed me the rest of the way through the cell door, where I fell ass down. I could hear the officers at the desk scrambling to their feet behind me.

"Where the hell did *they* come from?" one shouted.

"Hey, is that Everson?" another asked.

"Stay back," I called to them.

Arnaud recovered and sprang at me. For the briefest moment, a fingernail scratched at my doubt, and I wondered if my wards were up to the task of containing him. He slammed into the field of energy that coursed over the doorway and recoiled with a scream. Flames broke briefly down his arm, bubbling the skin.

The wards were fine.

I pushed myself to my feet and stepped forward until I was staring down at Arnaud, the powerful containing magic oscillating the air between us. He had evolved since our encounter at Container City. He stood taller, more upright. The veins that once mapped his body had faded. His head had even begun to sprout a fine layer of hair. Indeed, he looked almost like the Arnaud of old, almost human.

But he was neither, and I could never forget that.

He glared back at me from a pair of malevolent yellow eyes.

"Got you, you demonic son of a bitch," I said, and slammed the cell door.

AN HOUR LATER, I WAS TIPTOEING INTO THE SAFE HOUSE IN Brooklyn. It was late—more time had passed here than I'd thought—and the basement level was dark. I found our unit, slid my key into the lock, and stepped inside.

The converted room was small, not much larger than the cell I'd just left. In just a few steps I was standing over the sleeper sofa that had been pulled out. The glow of a nightlight showed Vega on her side, one arm draped over Tony, who was sprawled on his back, belly rising and falling with the profundity of a child's sleep. The frame creaked as I sat on the edge and set my cane on the nightstand.

"Ricki," I whispered near her ear.

She started, then rolled her head toward me. A comma furrowed the skin between her sleepy eyes. The borrowed police uniform I was wearing probably had something to do with her show of puzzlement.

"I'm back," I said. "It's done."

Her eyes cleared in a flash. In the next moment, she was wrapping her arms around me, pulling herself against me. We remained in the other's embrace for several minutes, her warm, solid body pressed to mine.

At last Tony snorted and stirred.

"Mr. Croft?" he croaked. "What's going on?"

"I'm getting you and your mom out of here, buddy," I said. "We're going home."

VEGA CLOSED THE DOOR TO TONY'S BEDROOM—HE'D FALLEN BACK asleep on the ride to their place—and joined me at the dining room table. I'd showered and was sipping from a steaming mug of coffee, one of several luxuries I'd missed while in the time catch.

"I made extra," I said.

"Thanks, I'm good." Vega stood behind me and began kneading out the knots in my shoulders.

I winced, but it was good medicine. Pain soon yielded to pleasure. On the ride here, I'd told Vega what had happened. From the version of 1776 New York we'd entered, to the tracking of Strangers two and three, to my grandfather's assistance, and finally to Arnaud being the fourth and final Stranger.

"So what's your plan for him?" she asked, a small edge in her voice.

"If not for my dream, I would have destroyed him tonight. But if I believe Arianna really visited me, I also have to believe she and the others are trapped in the Harkless Rift and that Arnaud is somehow the key to their release."

Her hands paused. "And you're sure it wasn't—"

"Just a dream?" I finished. "Earlier in the same dream Blade told me Arnaud had a bond-negating scepter, and that turned out to be true. I feel like I have to trust what came after," I said, remembering the way Blade's face had morphed into Arianna's. "Now that I have Arnaud, I'm hoping she'll contact me again, tell me what to do."

Vega's fingers resumed their work, climbing the back of my neck now, but I could feel their tension.

"Listen," I said, "Arnaud isn't going anywhere. Those are the most powerful wards I've ever built. They're designed to take whatever someone like Arnaud throws at them and hit him back fourfold. There are also sigils severing his connection to the demonic realm. Not even his master knows where he is. Denied that connection, Arnaud will weaken until he can't sustain his form up here. For all intents and purposes, he'll eventually die. So no matter how you slice it, he's no longer a threat."

"And you can guarantee that?"

"I'm tapped into the wards," I said. "He tested them after I left, and he's still recovering. So, yeah. Plus I've got four members of the Sup Squad watching his cell and two more guarding the floor."

Vega sighed and clapped my shoulders twice. "I think I'll take you up on that coffee."

She disappeared into the kitchen. A moment later, I heard a mug being poured. She returned and sat opposite me. Her hair was down and she tucked away a strand that had fallen in front of her pensive eyes.

"I know that look," I said. "What's up?"

"I did a lot of thinking while you were away."

"Uh-oh."

"No, it's nothing bad. I decided that you were right. At this point, you deserve to know about Tony's father. I was wrong to try to keep those parts of my life separate—you on one side, him on the other. Especially now."

When she glanced up from her coffee, I nodded for her to continue.

"I met Ramon before I became a detective. I was working in the Organized Crime Control Bureau, and he was a drug informant. Yeah," she said when I raised my eyebrows. "Ramon had grown up in a cartel family in El Barrio. From a young age, that was all he'd known, but he wanted out. With his knowledge of the business, he was a major asset to the Bureau. In exchange for ongoing intel, he got indemnity for himself and some of his family. I'm not going to get into how we ended up in a relationship, other than to say it was a bad idea with someone who was actually a really good person."

That must have been what Vega's brothers meant about her getting involved with a felon.

"We kept the relationship under wraps, of course, for both our sakes. But then I got pregnant with Tony. Given the circumstances, we agreed the baby would stay with me and that Ramon would stay away until the cases wrapped up and he was no longer in danger. We didn't even put his name on the birth certificate.

"Then one day, when Tony was two, I learned Ramon visited him at his daycare. I stupidly let that go. I even arranged it so Ramon could visit him once a month under the guise of being Tony's uncle. I didn't think it was fair keeping him from his son, and I could see how much Tony loved spending time with him. As long as we were discreet, you know. But a few months later, he took Tony out of the daycare so he could introduce him to his sister and her twins. And that's when I fucking lost it." Vega shook her head, eyes dropping back to her coffee. "I had him arrested for felony child endangerment. Ten years."

So that explained it.

"Wow," I said.

"The Bureau learned through other channels that Ramon had been drawing suspicion from cartel members. After his arrest, we made sure word spread that he was refusing to turn state's evidence, which by that point was true. He'd already given us everything we needed. The suspicions went away. So in a weird way, his arrest and incarceration were the best outcome for everyone. But he and I were over. Done. I didn't want to deny Tony his father, though. So, the monthly calls."

Guilt seemed to weigh on her dark brown eyes.

I reached across the table and clasped her hand. "You did the right thing."

She squeezed my hand back. "If I get weird when you bring up our future, it's only because I remember how I reacted to

Tony being exposed like that. My maternal instincts kicked in big time. So, it's not you I'm worried about. It's me, I guess."

"I'll never endanger your child," I said. "Or ours."

She nodded. "The way you handled Arnaud's return ... The wards and enchantments, the safe house..." She nodded again, though more to herself this time it seemed. "I knew we were vulnerable, but at the same time, I felt protected. And you got us home."

She leaned across the table and touched her lips to mine. Another luxury I'd missed in the time catch.

When she sat back, her brow furrowed. "Why do you keep doing that?"

"Doing what?" But even as I asked, I caught myself checking the sigil on my right hand. "Oh. The rest of the Upholders should have returned by now, but I haven't been able to pick them up through the bond."

"Maybe because Jordan released you?" Vega suggested.

"Yeah, maybe." But my mind was already considering the worst case. If I had to go looking for them, could I count on Caroline's help again?

Vega pushed herself up, came around the table, and took my right hand in both of hers. "And I know *that* look."

"You do?"

She pulled me to my feet. "Before you take on anything else, you're coming to bed, *my* bed, and I'm going to strip off that uniform, and we're going to make love, and then you're going to sleep deeply in my arms and not get up until we can see actual sunlight through the window. Got it?"

Talk about an offer I couldn't refuse.

With my hand pressed to her belly, I stooped down and kissed her. "I really missed you guys."

Vega's cheeks dimpled. "We missed you too."

As she led me to her room, I thought about what Grandpa had told Arnaud.

Our sentimental bonds make us stronger, not weaker.

I needed to remember that.

THE END

But the Prof Croft series continues. Keep reading to learn more...

NIGHT RUNE

PROF CROFT BOOK 8

Where to turn when all roads lead to ruin?

Last night I barely escaped 1776 New York City – now I have to go back.

My teammates are trapped in a time catch. Worse, the demon master Malphas is building a gateway there, one that could trigger a full-blown apocalypse.

But returning will require new allies: a crabby goblin, a fae princess and former lover, and the demon-vampire Arnaud. Yeah, that guy. And we're no longer facing one time catch, but several. All ruptured and on the verge of collapse.

Now a simple rescue has turned into a death-defying journey, one that's pushing my spell casting and stamina to their limits.

But as hellfire lashes up and day dims to eternal night, I'm facing an even greater test...

Choosing between my faith in magic and my love for Vega.

AVAILABLE NOW!

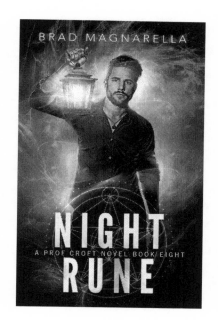

Night Rune
(Prof Croft, Book 8)

AUTHOR'S NOTES

Our sentimental bonds make us stronger, not weaker.

Shortly before sitting down to plot *Druid Bond*, I reformatted the Prof Croft prequel *Book of Souls*, which involved some rereading. It was fun seeing hints of what Everson's grandfather had been up to in those earlier years through a younger Everson's eyes.

It also got me thinking. What if I could somehow get them back together, with Everson now understanding all the sacrifices his grandfather had made up to, and including, his death?

And so, the time catch.

The reunion is imperfect, of course, given that we're dealing with an echo of the actual man, but as I wrote those scenes, I got the sense Everson was okay with that. The important thing was him feeling what he needed to feel and saying what he'd wanted to say for *some version* of his grandfather to hear. It ended up being crucial to the plot, but I was also glad Everson got that opportunity. Too many don't.

The particular period for the time catch came to me while reading Edward Rutherfurd's epic work of historical fiction *New York: The Novel*. He devotes almost two-hundred pages to the revolutionary years, and they're fascinating.

I went on to read *1776* by David McCullough, *The Battle for New York* by Barnet Schecter, and I binge-watched the PBS miniseries *Liberty! The American Revolution* as well as the HBO series *John Adams*. I also found some great survey maps of New York for that period, both in books and online. Basically, I geeked out.

For historical research of another kind, I found a great website called *The Right Rhymes*, a dictionary of hip-hop, that helped me with some of Gorgantha's phrasing. I'm still disappointed I wasn't able to slip in "chin check," meaning a punch in the face. But I did find a place for "assed-out," so there's that.

Some of you are no doubt wondering if Everson will have to return to the time catch, what's going on with the Order, and what the deal is with Caroline. Because I write the *Prof Croft* series in quadrilogies, all the big questions will be answered and all the major threads tied up in the next book, I promise!

For now, let's just enjoy Arnaud in a warded cell, Vega and Tony back home, and Tabitha in her new role as mayor. Oh wait, I edited out that last one. *snicker*

I have several people to thank for helping deliver *Druid Bond* into the world. They are the talented team at damonza.com for designing another stellar cover; beta readers Beverly Collie, Mark Denman, and Bob Singer for their invaluable comments and feedback; an awesome and growing team of advanced readers for doing the same, albeit later in the process; proofreaders Sharlene Magnarella and Donna Rich for final proofing; and Beck's Roasting House in Las Cruces, New Mexico for keeping me caffeinated, and generally tolerating my presence, while I banged this one out.

I also want to thank James Patrick Cronin, who brings all the books in the Croftverse to life through his gifted narration on the audio editions. Those books, including samples, can be found on my Audible.com author page.

Finally, thank you, fearless reader, for taking another ride with the Prof.

Until the next one...

Best Wishes,
Brad Magnarella

P.S. Be sure to check out my website to learn more about the Croftverse, download a pair of free prequels, and find out what's coming! That's all at bradmagnarella.com

CROFTVERSE CATALOGUE

PROF CROFT PREQUELS

Book of Souls

Siren Call

MAIN SERIES

Demon Moon

Blood Deal

Purge City

Death Mage

Black Luck

Power Game

Druid Bond

Night Rune

Shadow Duel

Shadow Deep

Godly Wars

Angel Doom

SPIN-OFFS

Croft & Tabby

Croft & Wesson

BLUE WOLF

Blue Curse

Blue Shadow

Blue Howl

Blue Venom

Blue Blood

Blue Storm

SPIN-OFF

Legion Files

———————

For the entire chronology go to bradmagnarella.com

ABOUT THE AUTHOR

Brad Magnarella writes urban fantasy for the same reason most read it...

To explore worlds where magic crackles from fingertips, vampires and shifters walk city streets, cats talk (some excessively), and good prevails against all odds. It's shamelessly fun.

His two main series, Prof Croft and Blue Wolf, make up the growing Croftverse, with over a quarter-million books sold to date and an Independent Audiobook Award nomination.

Hopelessly nomadic, Brad can be found in a rented room overseas or hiking America's backcountry.

Or just go to www.bradmagnarella.com

Made in United States
Orlando, FL
03 March 2023

30638645R00207